AWAKENING OF THE SHADOWED

Empire of Éire Series

Miranda Crowley

AWAKENING OF THE SHADOWED. Copyright © 2025 by Miranda Crowley

Text by Miranda Crowley.

Cover art and design by Matisse Jeffery.

ISBNs: 9798998844706 (hardback); 9798998844713 (paperback); 9798998844720 (ebook)

To Mom,

For being the first supporter of this idea before it ever became a book.
This novel wouldn't exist without you.

ABOUT THE BOOK

This book contains graphic language and dark elements that may be triggering to some. It includes elements regarding: violence, death, blood and gore, torture (implied, off page), abduction/trafficking of minors (implied, off page), and childhood trauma including abuse (implied, off page, and non-sexual). Readers please take note of these sensitive topics.

FIVE REALMS OF ÉIRE

Realm of Ossory (Oss-oh-ree) - Home to Ossorians (Oss-oh-ree-ans). Ossorians are born with shifting magic.

Realm of Draíocht (DREE-oct) - Home to Draíothes (DREE-o-shees). Draíothes are born with arcane magic, specializing in spells and rituals.

Realm of Saol (Sail) - Home to Saolians (Sail-e-ans). Saolians are born with cosmic magic, allowing them to draw celestial magic from the world, and specializing in the manipulation of different cosmic elements.

Realm of Sidhe (Shee) - Home to Sidhens (She-ens). Sidhens are born with elemental magic.

Realm of Oícha (E-ha) - Home to Oíchans (E-hans). Oíchans are born with psionic magic, allowing them to manipulate the mind.

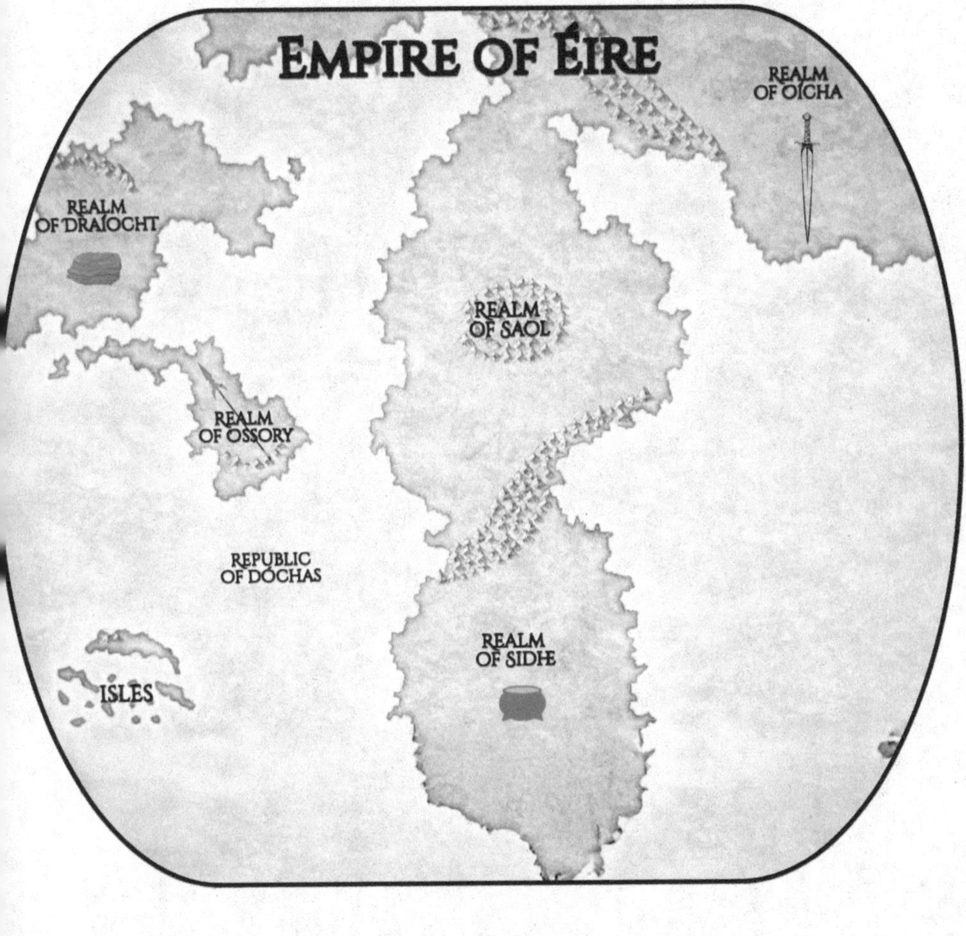

EMPIRE OF ÉIRE

REALM
OF OÍCHA

REALM
OF DRAÍOCHT

REALM
OF SAOL

REALM
OF OSSORY

REPUBLIC
OF DÓCHAS

REALM
OF SIDHE

ISLES

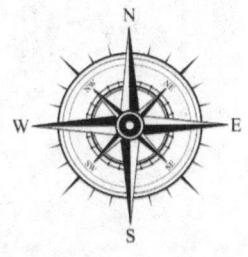

AWAKENING OF THE SHADOWED

EMPIRE OF ÉIRE SERIES
BOOK ONE

MIRANDA CROWLEY

PROLOGUE

"Everyone always says to follow your dreams, but what if all you ever have is nightmares?"

IT ALL STARTED THAT NIGHT.

A piercing scream ripped through the air.

Brynnlin ran to the corner of the room, crouching down to hide behind her dresser as another scream echoed around her. She tried to listen for more but couldn't hear anything past the pounding of her heart. The beating roared through her ears, stifling all other sounds.

Tightness expanded through her chest. A quick exhale of breath released the building pressure. She needed to breathe. Remember to breathe just like her mother said.

Inhale.

1, 2, 3, exhale.

Inhale.

1, 2, 3, exhale.

Inhale.

1, 2,

Her bedroom door slammed against the wall. She slapped her hands over her mouth to muffle her shriek and burrowed further into the corner.

"Brynnlin."

A small cry of relief escaped her at her father's panicked whisper. She scrambled out of her hiding spot and threw herself at him.

"Shh." Her father ran a hand over her hair and hugged her to him. "We have to go. We're under attack."

She jerked back at those words.

"Under attack? What do you mean? Where's Mom?" She couldn't ask the questions fast enough.

Her father ignored her, grabbing the closest pair of shoes from the floor and a nearby jacket that he tossed towards her.

"Brynnlin, please just hurry, we don't have time." He barely let her tug on the shoes before he caught her hand and rushed out of the room, dragging her along.

The hallways were dark as they ran. Whatever was happening had affected the power supply. Her skin warmed as the magic in her veins flared, helping her eyes adjust to the lack of light. That didn't stop the pit from forming in her stomach as they hurried through the shadows.

They turned right.

Left.

Left again.

Her father led them through the maze of hallways, heading for the stairs that would lead to the back lawn. He kept looking down and back over his shoulder as if to make sure she was still behind him, occasionally squeezing her hand in what was probably meant to be a reassuring gesture.

It wasn't.

Before they reached the top of the stairs, she risked a glance out of the large bay windows that overlooked the front lawn.

And froze.

Her knees scraped the wood as she stumbled to the ground from the force of her father still trying to pull her. But she couldn't tear her gaze away. Every muscle was tight, unwilling to move as she stared at what loomed outside. Fear clawed at her chest, so intense it threatened to crush her.

Dense fog circled the property. So startling black it turned the surroundings into a never-ending void. Inky, finger-like wisps floated along the ground pulling it forward, closing in on the estate. The closer it got, the more it seemed to grow. It built higher and higher like a wave ready to crash.

It was everywhere with no escape from it. She couldn't see the rest of the land or even the rolling hills beyond the gate. Only this wall of dark haze that was inching closer to the estate as if it meant to swallow everything in its path.

"What is..." she breathed out, unable to finish the question or try to figure out what to call it.

Her palms were clammy, and her breathing kept coming in uneven gasps, as if just looking at *that thing* was looking at death. And it had her in its grasp, its icy fingers held her in place not allowing for any movement.

Her body jerked away from the window, and Brynnlin found herself staring into arctic blue eyes more intense than she'd ever seen before. Her father cupped her cheeks in his hands, refusing to let her look back outside.

"Listen to me very carefully. We don't know what it is, but our magic is not working against it. We can't stop this. Your mother is trying to get the staff out through the tunnels, and we need to meet her at the entrance. We need to get up and keep moving." He used his thumb to swipe a stray tear that had leaked.

She struggled to understand what he was saying.

What did he mean their magic was useless against this?

That shouldn't be possible.

Her stomach turned, nausea overtaking her at just the thought.

Before she could voice her panic, her father pulled her to her feet, forcing her forward. Her legs struggled to hold her weight, but again they were running, aiming down the stairs and out the back door.

The entrance to the tunnels was hidden beneath the fountain in the garden. They only had to make it there. The tunnels led outside the gates and beneath the surrounding town to the forest edge and to safety.

They weaved through the shrubbery, and Brynnlin urged her feet to move faster even as bushes snagged against her. She ignored the stings of pain. Up ahead, the fountain stood tall. The gray stone was sleek from the water droplets still remaining from the already drained pool. At the base, the hatch sat open with the ladder leading below.

Her father reached for the first rung only to leap back, his steps faltering at the speed of reversing his momentum.

Dread curled around her.

Dark mist swirled, crawling up the ladder.

It blocked the one way they had to escape.

Her father paled and dropped to his knees, staring aimlessly at the empty hole.

As pain clouded his eyes, realization hit.

"NO." Brynnlin let out an anguished scream and darted forward. Her father threw out his arm to stop her. He yanked her away from the fountain and pulled her trembling body into his embrace. Tears streamed down her face as she looked helplessly at the opening.

Her mother had been down there. Was still down there. She fought to rip out of her father's hold and beat against his arms.

"Mom," she cried. "We have to help Mom," her voice cracked.

Her words seemed to snap her father out of whatever daze he'd been in. His grip on her tightened, and he turned her to face him.

"We can't save—"

"No," she interrupted and jerked her head away. "We're not leaving her."

Anger swelled in her chest.

How could he even suggest such a thing?

"Brynnlin, you're not listening," he shook her, and she stared at him with wide eyes. "Whatever that thing is, it kills. There's no saving. And I'm not losing you, too," his voice was harder and laced with pain. "We'll try and make it to the portal, it's the only way to get out of here."

Determination settled in his eyes, and his jaw was clenched tight to compose himself.

Brynnlin knew there was no arguing and numbly nodded her head. She tried to control her shuddered breathing, and used the back of her hand to clear her blurry vision as they changed direction to the far side of the garden. Her own chest crumbled into a million pieces, her mother's face flashing through her mind. Her tears fell harder. She would never see her smile or hear her soothing voice again.

How did it come to this?

Why was this happening?

It wasn't fair.

Only last night everything was—

"Brynnlin, hurry," her father urged, huffing and tightening his hold on her hand.

She sprinted to keep up with him as he led the way to the portal. The hidden escape route was a well-kept secret and was a rare commodity. Few people existed that were gifted with the ability of spatial manipulation to create portals. Even less were powerful enough to construct a portal that stayed open continuously. She had no idea how her father managed to have one opened on their land and had no idea where it went. But if this was their only chance to get out of this alive, she wasn't going to protest.

Her father picked up his pace and kept running.

Brynnlin tried not to fall behind and watched in horror as the dark cloud surrounded them and was moving in.

A few more yards.

She could see the abandoned and overgrown tool shed that hid the portal.

A few more feet.

That was all that was needed to get to the gateway that would take them to freedom.

Her father threw open the old door, cracking it against the wall.

The portal flared, its brightness a beacon in the dark.

The fog was closing in faster, and her father was just stepping into the luminous vortex when a dense coil snaked out and wrapped around her ankle. It tripped her to the ground and out of her father's grip.

Terror consumed her as a hooded figure stepped out of the darkness, gliding towards them.

Yet it wasn't the hooded figure that had her screaming as the coil around her leg dragged her towards the stranger...

It was the creature following from behind.

Black mist swirled around protruding bones. Massive wings emerged from its back. And glowing eyes bore into her from a horned skull.

Brynnlin's next scream caught in her throat as the creature spread its arms wide, and the fog moved with it.

Oh gods.

A demon was controlling it.

That's why their magic wasn't working.

A demon had been summoned from the Three Hells.

Brynnlin kicked out and clawed at the earth to no avail as the coil wrapped tighter around her leg and dragged her closer.

The hood hid the stranger's face. She could only make out an angular jaw and lips that curled into a sneer at her pathetic attempts to get away.

"Now Miss Brynnlin, you didn't think you were leaving did you?" A masculine voice echoed from under the hood, and he laughed coldly, pulling her off the ground.

Shivers raced down her spine at his unnerving voice while the coil released her ankle, withering away back into the fog. Not that it mattered, she was now in the hands of something much, much worse.

"Let go of me," Brynnlin shrieked.

Every muscle strained as she fought his hold.

At the same time her father's bellow echoed around them.

"GET YOUR HANDS OFF MY DAUGHTER."

Her father launched forward, summoning orbs of magic and attacked with a frenzy at the hooded figure.

Brynnlin used the distraction and managed to yank her arm out of the man's hold, stumbling to the side. She crawled across the ground, anything to put distance between the man and the demon lurking behind him.

As a governor within their realm, her father was a strong fighter and an even more powerful wielder. But with a flick of the stranger's wrist, the attacks were blocked, and her father was held in place unmoving.

Alarm crossed her father's face, and panic seized her at the realization of what they were dealing with.

This man was no amateur. His magic was powerful.

Much more powerful than her father.

Her stomach tightened. And her heart pounded as a sickening feeling enveloped her.

They weren't getting out of this.

"Brynnlin, get through that portal now," her father choked out, struggling to get free from the man's hold.

"NO. I'm not leaving you, I can help." She stood and tried to remember everything she had discovered about her abilities and the powerful magic that slumbered within her. She knew she wasn't supposed to, but she couldn't do nothing.

The man applied pressure on her father and forced him to the ground. A look of agony crossed her father's face as he stared into her eyes.

"I love you. More than you know. Be strong, I know you have it in you."

The last word trailed off, drowned out by the air around her coming to life. Her hair lifted and whipped in every direction. Wind picked up tunneling around her. She tried to move but was blocked in.

The stranger pivoted towards her, his hood fell back, and his cold mask broke for the first time into a look of uncertainty. A gasp escaped her, followed closely by rage, when she got her first unobstructed view of the man's face.

Or more importantly the magic brand marking his brow.

He was part of the uprising that had been rebelling against the Empire's rule. They had already staged attacks across the realms.

Now her family's estate?

This was how they were going to die? At the hands of a crazed heretic?

8

The man released her father and lunged at her. His hand stretched out to her, and she flinched back.

At the same time, the world tilted, her vision blurring and her body twisting. With a forceful and final gust, the wind shoved her through the portal.

The last thing she saw was the fog leaping forward and darkness devouring the rest of the land.

She screamed.

In protest.

Fear.

Both.

And that was when the pain hit.

Her back arched, and a burning fire coursed through her veins as she moved through the portal. She clawed at her skin trying to ease the sensation. It faded, and a coldness started to sweep through her, offering her a reprieve. She didn't have time to feel relief. Whatever had been keeping her upright disappeared. She was falling, plummeting towards whatever ground lay beneath her.

Her body landed on hard concrete. Pain radiated through every limb. Black spots danced in her vision. She tried to focus on her surroundings, but her head was still spinning. When she could finally see straight, she found herself laying in a dirty alleyway between two old buildings.

She jumped up, ignoring the wave of dizziness and turned to rush back through the portal. All she met was the dark, solid wall of the building.

Sharp, static electricity fizzled and popped through the air.

It was too late.

The portal was gone.

"NO. NO." She pounded against the wall over and over again. It wasn't working.

Why wasn't it working?

Make it come back.

"Dad no," she let out a harsh sob.

She scratched and tore at the wall. After her hands were a bloody mess, she resorted to beating it with her fist. Nothing worked. She never stopped, staying there for hours until her body finally collapsed in an exhausted heap to the cold ground.

CHAPTER 1

"Retribution was coming, and they would all get their due."

11 Years Later...

Damn that one was close.

Brynnlin dodged left, barely missing the fist flying at her jaw. She smirked at her opponent, and she danced back out of his range. He was better than most, she'd give him that.

Moving around the ring, she sized up the man across from her. He heavily outweighed her, and the intricate tribal tattoos running down both his arms bulged with each movement. His height, easily over six feet, added to his leverage. At only a few inches above five feet, she was at a disadvantage.

He charged at her again and went for another jab. The air whistled past her as she ducked back. He followed after her, swinging out his leg, trying to swipe out her feet from under her. She side-stepped and bounced to the other side of the ring away from his reach.

Nice try.

It was going to take a lot more than that.

His size might be his advantage. Speed was hers.

She watched him closely and focused on her next move, drowning out the shouting of the spectators.

He shifted his stance, exposing his side.

Brynnlin saw her opening and attacked low and fast, striking him with a two-hit combination to his abdomen and rib cage before retreating again. She circled around him and gleamed when rage entered his eyes. He was getting tired of her games.

She went in again and got a quick hit to his kidney. He spun, faster than she anticipated, and caught her by the arm. His vice-like grip halted her escape. Using his new hold on her, he lifted and slammed her to the ground. The side of her face and upper body hit the mat hard.

Brynnlin clenched her jaw as she found herself on the blood-stained floor.

Shit, that actually hurt.

She pushed to her feet before he could take advantage of her staying down. She rolled her shoulder back to shake out the stab of pain and could taste the blood that had gathered in her mouth.

"Need a timeout, little Bana-phrionnsa? That looked like it hurt," her opponent taunted and took on a relaxed stance.

Little Princess.

She fought to hide her irritation. Not at the taunt, but at his audacity to let his guard down and dismissing her as a threat. She wouldn't let his offensive gesture slide.

"Hm, Bana-phrionnsa?" She cocked her head to the side, as if considering the title. "I'd have to say that one's a first, but maybe if you're a good boy I'll let you kneel at my feet." The sneer she shot him was all teeth.

A few people in the crowd snickered.

His face flushed red.

In anger or embarrassment, she wasn't sure.

"Bitch," he spat, and his eyes flashed a glowing yellow. The electrical charge in the air heightened around them as magic started to flow off of him. A tremor racked through his body, and he lunged at her with newly extended claws.

She stifled a sigh and rolled her eyes. He was from the Realm of Ossory. She should've guessed by his size alone that he was Ossorian. Ossorians possessed shifting magic, and they all had an animal or beast form. The Ossorian shifters also always seemed to have a little issue with control. No wonder what she said sent him over the edge.

Use of magic in the ring was against the rules. It was never enforced. Magic use only made the fights more interesting.

Too bad she couldn't do the same.

As far as the world knew, she was a teip.

An outcast. A dud. A child born without magic.

An escalating occurrence since *Lugh's Spear,* an ancient, magical relic, was stolen from Ossory nearly two decades ago. That relic, along with three others, and the *Crann Bethadh,* the tree that fed life to their entire world, nourished the land with magic. Yet with the missing relic, magic had started to weaken over the years. A sickness was spreading through the land where children were born less and less powerful, few having no magic at all.

As one of the few, at least as far as everyone was concerned, it made fights like these much more inconvenient.

The threat of claws slicing through her skin had Brynnlin moving faster, and she waited a breath longer to make her move.

Now.

With the Ossorian's hand still outstretched, she snatched his wrist and pivoted to use his own momentum to flip him over her shoulder to the ground. She wasted no time in rolling over, locking his arm between her legs, and twisting to dislocate his shoulder.

A yelp of pain echoed through the ring.

He lurched upwards, a desperate attempt to escape her hold. A fatal mistake made, exposing his back. In seconds, Brynnlin abandoned his limp arm and was upon this new target. Repositioning her weight, her legs locked around his waist while her arm circled his neck, latching into a choke-hold. She threw her weight into squeezing tight, cutting off his air supply.

A strangled sound left his lips, even as he managed to crawl to his knees. With a surprising show of strength, the Ossorian pushed to his feet and heaved forward, trying to throw her off. She released a pained hiss when his talons dug across her forearm as he urgently fought to dislodge her. Her tight shirt offered little protection against the razor sharp claw. The cut stung like a bitch, and warm blood seeped down her sleeve.

Grinding her teeth, she dug her arm harder into his trachea. His struggles started to cease, and his body swayed. Muscles going limp, his body fell towards the floor.

Brynnlin jumped off his back, landing swiftly, just as the heap of flesh landed on the mat.

The crowd let out a violent cheer.

Brushing herself off, Brynnlin didn't spare a glance at her unmoving opponent. She climbed through the ropes, the pain in her arm barely registering, and jumped down from the ring.

People scrambled into the ring to remove her latest challenger as they prepared for the next fight. She pushed through the crowd, and people started to part for her as she made her way to the bar. A few eager patrons tried to reach out and get her attention. A well-placed glare had them backing away.

An empty stool stood near the corner that she slid into and waited for the bartender to bring her a drink. One of the guys started towards her. Before he could take her order, a glass of water was pushed in front of her.

Leila walked up and leaned against the countertop.

Leila had been a bartender for as long as Brynnlin had been coming down here, and it was her boss that owned the club above and ran the underground fights.

Like Brynnlin, Leila had been forced into this world and was probably one of the few reasons Brynnlin had survived this long. Leila had offered her kindness over the years, a rare commodity, and Brynnlin would always appreciate that small act. Yet that kindness was nowhere to be seen as Leila glared at the other bartender.

"No one serves the kid but me."

Brynnlin refrained from rolling her eyes. She hated being called that but knew it was pointless. She had barely been into her teen years when the boss first brought her down here, and the nickname stuck. There was no getting rid of it now.

"Are you ever going to stop calling me that?" She'd stopped being a kid a long time ago, even before she reached the age of maturity.

She took a sip of the water and eyed Leila over the ridge of the glass, waiting for a response.

Leila only smirked in return. "No. Now drink up, the boss wants you in tip top shape tonight, though you already did take a nasty hit."

Leila cringed as she reached out and tilted Brynnlin's chin up to see the scrapes on her face.

Brynnlin pulled away, shaking her head. "No more fights tonight, I only agreed to do the one."

"He'll be disappointed."

She didn't care. "I'm a free agent now. In case he forgot."

Zamir didn't own her.

Not anymore.

Leila frowned and shook her head. "You'd think with that freedom, you'd be smart enough to stop coming down here."

Brynnlin held Leila's disapproving stare. She had her reasons for being down here, and it was nobody's business but her own.

After a long moment, Leila sighed. "You know a rumor surfaced that you were done fighting. Yet from the looks of tonight, I can see that it was false."

Brynnlin straightened in the stool. That was the last thing she needed going around.

"They wish I was done, where'd you hear it?"

"Around," Leila answered vaguely, "I really wanted it to be true."

"Finally sick of me after all these years?"

"Worried," a rare seriousness entered Leila's golden eyes. "You're one of our top contenders. I've been watching you down here since you started. I know you refuse to kill your opponents, but these new guys coming up don't think like that. They'll do anything to not lose, and I've never seen you turn down a challenge. I'm afraid that arrogance of yours is going to get you into a fight that you can't win."

Brynnlin glared, "I don't lose."

"There's a first for everything," Leila frowned at her.

Her features tightened. "Why are you telling me this now?"

"I just want you to be careful and aware." Leila leaned closer, dropping to a whisper, "Word is the boss will let anyone fight you that's willing to pay for the privilege. I like you B, and I don't want to see you get hurt."

Brynnlin stayed quiet as she absorbed what Leila was telling her. None of this was anything she didn't already know. She was well aware how things worked down here. Her safety meant nothing, only money mattered. That was part of the

reason she worked so hard to be unbeatable. But she appreciated Leila's concern.

"Consider your warning heard. I'll take care of myself, don't
worry." She offered Leila a small smile.

Thankfully, Leila let the matter drop.

"You sticking around tonight?"

Brynnlin glanced at the crowd and the current fight. It was
rowdy tonight, and she wasn't feeling very sociable.

Plus she'd already done what she needed to do.

She'd won.

And now...

Three more fights left.

*She was only three more fights away for all of this to finally start
paying off.*

"No, I want to head out. Think you could grab my bag and
money from the back for me?" She batted her eyelashes
teasingly.

With a dramatic eye roll, Leila agreed, "Fine. I'll be right
back."

"You're the best," Brynnlin called out to her retreating form.

She sat in silence for a few moments, enjoying the time to
herself. She didn't hear but rather felt someone behind her in
the shadows against the wall.

"Lurking around and eavesdropping in a place like this will
only get you your ass kicked, or worse if you hear something
you aren't supposed to," she informed them tersely. She
continued to face forward, not bothering to turn around and
kept taking sips from her drink.

The person behind her released a soft chuckle.

"Oh little Ciarán, is that a threat?"

The honeyed voice was deep. Masculine.

She stiffened at the condescending use of her fighting alias and ignored the way his words seemed to wrap around her like velvet.

She shoved down her irritation. She didn't need to draw more attention to herself by giving him a reaction.

"Just some friendly advice. I don't bother with threats," she retorted with a bite.

"How refreshing," dark amusement laced his tone. "Are you often friendly?"

Hah. That idea was laughable. "No."

"Well then it must be my lucky night," he drawled out.

She opened her mouth to make a snarky reply when Leila coming back caught her attention. At Leila's approach, the sound of clothing brushing the wall and almost inaudible footsteps had Brynnlin spinning around.

The wall sat empty. The man gone.

The deadly ease in which he departed unnerved her.

She twisted, searching through the crowd for anyone walking away from them.

There was nothing.

Almost everyone's attention was focused on the ring.

"What are you looking for?" Leila gave her a strange look as she slid the bag and envelope over.

"Nothing."

She swiped her stuff from the bar-top, yet couldn't help giving the room one last scan. Her gaze stopped on a dark-haired man weaving through the crowd. His steps were determined, and he was staring at her.

She faltered for a second.

She'd never seen him before and didn't like being the target of his attention. His features were sharp, and more than one woman gave him an appreciative glance as he passed.

But his icy-blue eyes were focused on her, and her eyes narrowed in return.

He continued up to the bar and stopped in front of her. He didn't bother to spare Leila a glance and took a moment to give her a slow once over.

Brynnlin raised a single eyebrow.

Who the Hells did this guy think he was?

When he finally spoke his voice was low and gruff.

"I have a proposal that will be very beneficial to both of us. Is there somewhere we can go to talk?"

Brynnlin nearly snorted at his arrogant tone. "Is that supposed to be a pickup line?"

The man smirked. "Wrong type of proposal. Consider this an arrangement of the business variety."

Brynnlin studied him for a minute. Something was off. His shirt was simple, but the material was too nice. His pants were too tailored. His shoes too clean. He was also being too friendly for this place. One didn't talk business out in the open.

Not here.

He wasn't a local.

And she had no intention of getting involved in whatever mess landed him on the isles.

"Sorry to disappoint. I don't take part in business here."

The man's jaw clenched, clearly unhappy with her response. "I assure you, I can make it of your interest, if—"

"Not interested. I assure you." She gave him a syrupy-sweet smile. "Now go back to your seat like a good patron and enjoy the fights."

The man ran a hand through his raven black hair and glared at her.

Brynnlin notched her chin up and met his glare.

If he thought he could intimidate her, he was in for a rude awakening.

"If you'd just listen—"

"Sir," Lelia cut in, "if you wish to continue visiting this establishment, I strongly suggest you return to your table."

Leila looked over Brynnlin's shoulder and nodded at someone. Brynnlin didn't need to turn around to know one of the bouncers had been summoned.

The man noticed, too.

"That won't be necessary. Message received." The words sounded forced, but he took a step back.

Leila smiled. "Good."

Brynnlin's shoulders relaxed. She of course could handle things herself, but it was so much nicer when things were kept clean and tidy.

She inclined her head to Leila.

A silent thanks.

She didn't wait to see how this turned out. With her bag over her shoulder, she slipped away into the throng of people.

She would go out the back.

Brynnlin headed towards the hall that held the private rooms, nodding to the bouncer guarding the secure area. She made her way down the corridor and up the stairs to the street. She made sure her hood was pulled up over her head before stepping out on the sidewalk. Pushing the man and the strange encounter out of her head, she headed home.

Home.

That place wasn't her real home. Not really.

She didn't have that anymore.

HE STOOD in the shadows watching Ryker approach the girl. She had been such a pleasant little surprise to this visit. She hadn't been the prey.

Not originally.

But he was never one to pass up opportunities.

He watched with delight as Ryker talked to the girl. Ryker must feel safe here, the simple fool. Why else would he meet so openly with his little acolyte?

Then again they were in the uprising's territory.

Wait no...that's not what they called themselves.

The Creed of Resurgence.

That's what it was.

Either way, this was still turning out to be too easy.

She caught his attention when she was in the ring. And once he saw the brand on her neck, he had hoped to learn information about her. But he couldn't risk detection when her bartender friend came back.

He'd never thought he'd be lucky enough to run into Ryker's source so soon. Or that she would be so entertaining. This little trip was turning out to be well worth it.

Fate must be on his side tonight.

He couldn't contain his smirk.

Retribution was coming, and they would all get their due.

But not yet...

It wasn't time.

Ryker kept the conversation with the girl short and soon returned to his companion.

And with that he sat back and got comfortable. Doing what he did best, he waited and plotted.

———

RYKER SAT with Zale in the back corner of the underground club, waiting to see their contact. His body remained rigid. He scanned the crowd looking for any threats. Most people ignored them, too mesmerized by the fight taking place in the ring to pay them any attention.

"She's late."

"This place is packed. She's probably busy," Zale responded and sipped from his water.

"It's been almost an hour. I don't like this. And I hate this fucking island, it makes my skin itch just being here." He clenched his jaw and fisted his hand on the table.

"Damn it Ryker, you need to chill. I know you're on edge being here, but we want to at least try to blend in. So get a drink and watch the fight, she'll get to us when she can." Zale shot him a hard look and made a point to go back to watching the ring.

"Why are we even here? The last two times she's had no new information," he complained.

"Look, she reached out to Maddox saying she had something. He sent us to get it, you know it's important," Zale continued, "so, shut up."

"Damn, did you just see that hit?" Zale's eyes widened as he watched.

Ryker looked up, and they both flinched as the blonde was lifted and thrown to the floor. He would've bet money that would've ended the fight. He would've been wrong. The little thing got right back up and taunted her opponent.

Fucking taunted him.

He watched in surprise at how quickly she subdued him and ended the match before getting up to exit the ring.

"That's hot. Think she'd be interested in a new sparring partner?" Zale made that comment.

Ryker noticed his friend's eyes were locked on the blonde and were filled with appreciation.

He laughed. "I think she'd kick your ass."

Zale smirked at him. "I'd let her."

His eyes followed her as she sat at the bar. Even with the dim lighting and smoke filled air they could see her clearly from their spot. Some hair had fallen out of her long ponytail and perfectly framed her heart-shaped face. Her cheeks were rosy from the fight, and her green eyes lit up as she talked with the bartender. He could understand Zale's attraction to her, she was quite stunning.

She flipped the end of her ponytail off her shoulder exposing the pale curve of her neck along with the magical brand marking her skin. The dark ink swirled across her collar bone, and Ryker's muscles tensed.

Damn. What a waste.

Of course she was an acolyte.

He shouldn't be too surprised given their current location. They were deep in the Creed of Resurgence's territory, and this place was crawling with supporters of the anti-magical group rebelling against the realms that made up the Empire's rule.

He would never understand how these people thought destroying magic was the answer to a brighter future.

Yet here they were.

Right in front of him.

It made him sick, just thinking about it.

How many innocent lives were lost because of them?

How much land destroyed for their so-called "cause"?

They were determined to bring about a rebirth of the world. If they ever succeeded, they would only bring down civilization with it.

"Ryker," Zale's voice pulled him back, and the sound of the crowd came roaring back.

"What?"

Zale jerked his head to the side, and Ryker followed the gesture, scanning the crowd.

Relief flowed through him when he spotted their informant making her way toward them. Davina carried a tray of drinks and dropped a few off before making her way to their table.

"Sorry for the wait," she sounded out of breath.

"Run into any trouble?" Ryker kept his voice low. It was doubtful anyone could hear them over the fighting and the cheering, but he wasn't taking any chances.

"No trouble. I just couldn't get away."

"Well we're all here now," Zale eyed her carefully. "You reached out to Maddox, and we came as quickly as we could. What did you get?"

Davina cast a quick glance around, then said softly, "I finally have the name of the Draíothe that summoned the demon for the group of acolytes you captured last month."

Ryker straightened in his chair, and he noticed Zale perk up, too.

This was big.

They'd been waiting for this name for weeks.

Those acolytes had broken into their realm and had been out destroying some of the fields. Their sentries were able to apprehend the acolytes, but they had a low-class demon with them, who managed to escape.

After some small interrogation, the group admitted where they met the Draíothe who summoned it for them, but they didn't have a name, only a description.

Davina's job had been to find him, and it looked like her time here was paying off.

"What's the name?"

"August Penn."

"Are you sure that's his real name?" Zale questioned.

Davina frowned. "It doesn't matter, I saw him myself, and he matches the description."

Ryker leaned forward and narrowed his eyes at Davina. There was more to this, she should be more excited, not frowning and chewing on her lip.

"What aren't you telling us?"

Davina's shoulders sagged. "August Penn is dead. He was found outside this club two nights ago. I found out he was a Draíothe that did summonings because the other waitresses were gossiping about it. They think that's why he's dead, others say it was a robbery, or that he owed money. I don't know for sure, it's all speculation."

"Damn it." Ryker dropped his head forward and closed his eyes to take a calming breath. They were going to use the Draíothe to track down the demon running loose in their territory right now. If he could summon it, surely he could find it. None of that was going to work when he was dead.

What the Hells were they going to do?

"That is an unfortunate setback. We need to figure something else out and quickly." Zale also wasn't hiding his disappointment at the news, and his brow was drawn together in concentration.

"There might be an alternative," Davina murmured under her breath.

"Well spit it out, Davina," Ryker's patience was running thin.

"There's whispers of another Draíothe in the area. Word on the street is that she's powerful. She keeps to herself, and others leave her alone. So I don't have any information about her."

"Names, Davina," he urged, "we'll figure it out, but we need a name or at least an address."

"Selene Aspen," Davina whispered, and slid a scrap of paper onto the table.

Selene's Specialties was scrawled across the top with an address.

"She runs a bookstore a few blocks from here, that's all I know."

Ryker grabbed the paper and stuffed it into his pocket. "Good work, Davina."

Davina nodded. "There's one more thing..."

Ryker barely contained his sigh. "Yes?"

"See the blonde by the bar?"

Ryker didn't need to look over there. "The one who just fought?"

"Yeah, her. Supposedly, she's close to Selene. If you want to get to Selene, you might want to start with her."

Ryker nodded, his mind already working through a game plan.

"Thank you Davina, you did your job well," Zale praised her. "We're going to keep you here for a little longer, in case this falls through. But remember if anything happens, get out. It's not worth the risk."

"I don't think anyone is suspicious, but don't worry, I'll be smart. Now good luck to you both, I have to get back."

Davina grabbed her tray and was back to serving customers as if nothing had happened at all.

"She's good," Ryker admitted.

"She is, but this does put a dilemma on things." Zale's calm features were unusually strained. "At least with the other Draíothe we had leverage. We know nothing about this Selene."

"Maybe we won't need it. For the right price people will do a lot of things. We can try diplomacy first," Ryker suggested, "and see if her friend will set up a meet?"

Zale raised an eyebrow. "You really think that'll work?"

Ryker scoffed. "This girl is fighting for money. How hard can it be to convince her to set up a meeting with her friend? She won't even have to know what it's about."

Zale hesitated. "It's worth a shot. But take it slow, we don't want to scare off Aspen before we even get to her door."

Ryker smirked. "Relax, I got this."

He pushed away from the table and headed for the bar, the

blonde in his sights. It didn't take long for her to notice him, yet the look she shot him wasn't what one would consider welcoming. He tensed at the suspicion already dancing across her features.

This might be more difficult than he expected.

He crossed the rest of the way to her and leaned against the bar. He took a quick moment to study her, and he didn't focus too long on her marking. If he thought about her being an acolyte he'd never get through this. All that mattered was getting that meeting. He'd offer her a good deal, and she'd set up a meeting with her friend.

Simple.

Easy.

"I have a proposal that will be very beneficial to both of us." He kept his voice low and amiable. "Is there somewhere we can go to talk?"

Amusement flashed in those pale green eyes.

"Is that supposed to be a pickup line?" Her voice was soft, so at odds with the fighter he just watched. Then again, no one in their right mind would look at her and think of an underground fighter. He supposed that probably worked in her favor.

He smirked and attempted to be charming. "Wrong type of proposal. Consider this an arrangement of the business variety."

She was quiet for a minute before her expression turned guarded.

"Sorry to disappoint. I don't take part in business here."

He took a moment to process her words, and his jaw tightened at her quick rejection.

He needed a new approach. "I assure you, I can make it of your interest, if—"

"Not interested. I assure you." She shot him a condescending smile. "Now go back to your seat like a good patron and enjoy the fights."

He ran a hand through his hair, and narrowed his eyes at her patronizing words.

How could she turn him down so quickly?

For the love of the gods she hadn't even heard his request yet.

"If you'd just listen—"

"Sir," the bartender cut in, and he looked at her, noticing her for the first time. She continued in a frosty tone, "If you wish to continue visiting this establishment, I strongly suggest you return to your table."

Ryker's head jerked back.

Return to his table?

All he was trying to do was talk to the blonde.

The bartender nodded her head to someone, and he turned to see a bouncer heading this way.

Shit.

That took a downward turn fast.

He took a step back. "That won't be necessary. Message received."

The blonde smiled at the bartender and bounced off, and Ryker could only watch.

How did that go so poorly?

He looked back to the bartender who was staring at him with pursed lips.

"Is there a problem?"

"As long as you don't start one. Our contenders are valuable and are to be left alone. Her especially."

"What makes her so special?"

He was pushing his luck, if the look she shot him was any indicator.

"Many things. Now unless you're here to order something, I have other customers."

Ryker gave her a tight-lipped smile. "Best get to it then."

With that, he turned and headed back to Zale. They weren't getting to the blonde. Not here. Not with her friend behind the bar.

Zale chuckled as soon as he sat down again. "I thought you had it under control?"

Ryker flipped him off. "She wasn't as receptive as I expected."

"Are we going to have problems with Selene because of this?"

Ryker grimaced. "I didn't even get that far."

"Then everything is fine," Zale assured him. "We don't even need the girl, we'll go straight to the shop."

Ryker nodded. "Let's hope we'll have better luck there."

"We'll find out soon enough. Now let's sit through one more match then we can leave. Maddox will be anxious to have this information."

Ryker didn't argue, and soon enough they were exiting the club.

They were halfway down the street before he dared to ask, "What's our plan of action if we can't convince this shopkeeper to help us?"

Zale's shoulders tensed, and he rubbed the back of his neck. "It'll be fine, and I'm confident we'll get her cooperation."

Ryker wasn't sharing Zale's confidence, but he kept that to himself.

"What about the other Draíothe? Think his death was a coincidence?"

"Hard to tell. Too much happens around here, and he could have been involved in any number of things."

Zale's answer was vague, not like Ryker expected anything

else. There was little chance of them ever discovering the true motive, or who was behind it. He let the matter drop, and they continued walking down the sidewalk in silence.

Ryker grimaced as he eyed the dirty streets, and the smell of garbage bombarded him. Dirt and grime covered every surface, and the buildings were stacked on top of each other, making it impossible to distinguish the separate structures.

Gods, just looking at it made his chest tight, how did people live like this?

He didn't understand, and he couldn't wait to return home.

When they were finally far enough from the club, they turned into an empty alleyway. Double checking that no one was around, Ryker nodded to Zale.

"Ready when you are."

Zale knelt down and touched a hand to the cement.

The ground at their feet jolted as magic flowed from Zale.

Sparks of light flashed and swirled into a vortex as the portal home opened. The shimmering pale blue doorway was a welcome sight.

Ryker took one last glance at the empty street.

They'd be back in Kärsiä soon. And it wouldn't be long before they could put this city behind them, at least that was his hope, as he stepped through the portal.

IT WAS STILL DARK when they returned. The trees masked their arrival as they passed back onto palace grounds, and the portal closed behind them.

Ryker rolled back his shoulders and took a deep breath filling his lungs before letting out a long exhale. There was a sharp bite to the air, a hint at the colder months to come. But it relaxed him. He was able to release the tension that had built since leaving their land.

They started towards the palace, and up ahead he could make out the lights shining in the night.

"Think they waited up for us?"

Zale shrugged. "Probably, Maddox was pretty uptight about this meeting."

They reached the tree's edge and walked along the path that would lead them to the gate of the palace garden. The sentries patrolling throughout the property lowered their heads as Ryker and Zale passed.

Maddox was pacing in the foyer as they walked in. His dirty blonde hair reflected off the light, and relief flashed in his eyes as they made their way towards him.

"Took you long enough, I was starting to think you two got lost out there."

"And if we did? Would you go leave breadcrumbs to lead us back home?"

"That would be a waste of good bread," Maddox scoffed, but his eyes lit up with amusement.

"Davina had good information, but it puts us in a delicate situation," Ryker interrupted their banter.

Maddox's features tightened, and he rubbed the back of his neck, "Okay, let's hear it."

They made their way into the dining hall, and Maddox took a seat at the table, while he and Zale took one at each side.

Ryker grabbed an apple from one of the bowls before continuing. "Is Kodak back yet? Should we wait?"

"No, he's still in Ossory. He'll be back tomorrow," Maddox answered.

Ryker gave Maddox the rundown of what Davina told them. "Unless August Penn can track this demon from the grave, he'll be no use to us."

"Apparently, this Selene is another Draíothe in the area," Zale added and slid the paper to him.

Maddox was quiet as he scanned the paper with the address. "Well this isn't quite what I hoped for. Maybe we should wait to see if Davina can find out more about this woman. I don't want to send you into a blind situation."

Ryker hesitated. "Can we afford to wait?"

Gods only knew what kind of damage the demon was doing as it ran loose through the realm. And they hadn't been able to track it down on their own. Neither had anyone else they reached out to. They already went to the Realm of Draíocht to see if other Draíothes could find the demon, but almost all had given the same answer. They didn't have the knowledge of demons. Nor would they attempt the demonic magic necessary to summon it back. Demonic magic was forbidden and went against the very laws of nature. According to them, any Draíothe that supported the Creed was both a betrayer to Draíocht and to their goddess.

Without any help, they were now running out of options.

Maddox stiffened. "I shouldn't have to tell you of all people that acolytes, especially a Draíothe, are untrustworthy and unpredictable. So yes, Ryker, I'm taking a moment to consider the risks."

Ryker bristled in his chair at Maddox's reprimand, the words hitting their mark. And Maddox was right, he didn't need the reminder of the damage a Draíothe was capable of. He might not have experienced it firsthand like Maddox had, but he'd lost people because of it.

And he would never forget it.

But right now, it wasn't about their feelings, they had a realm to protect.

"Maddox, we might not have much of a choice," Zale added diplomatically, "time is not on our side."

Maddox seemed to consider all of this. "Fine, we'll take a chance with the shopkeeper. But I'm going with you both, I refuse to send you into an unknown situation alone. Verenna can keep an eye on things until Kodak returns."

Ryker couldn't contain his surprise and blurted, "You're coming with?"

Maddox glared at him. "As much as you manage to get on my nerves, I'd still prefer not to send you into an early grave, so yes I'm going."

Ryker didn't bother hiding his smirk. "I had no idea you cared so much. Can we see this sentimental side of you more often?"

Maddox rolled his eyes. "I'm going to make some preparations before I change my mind. Be ready to leave at first light."

Maddox turned, and the door clicked shut behind him.

"Guess we're heading out again," Zale said under his breath as he too left the room.

Ryker sat back and sighed. He knew it was important, but he'd just gotten back. Now he had to leave again?

And of all places, they had to go back to that Hells burning island. He prayed this trip would be more successful than the last.

CHAPTER 2

"But hope and determination were dangerous and powerful things."

BRYNNLIN MADE her way up to the apartment on the third floor and crept through the front door. The hour was late, and she was careful not to make a sound. Her efforts proved unnecessary as she turned and saw light streaming from the kitchen and the lamps in the living room.

Sprawled out on the couch was Selene, pouring over a bunch of books that surrounded her and covered the coffee table. Selene's head shot up at the click of the door, her auburn hair falling out of its bun at the abrupt movement.

"Oh, you're finally home. I've been waiting forever. You'll never guess—no never believe—what I found. You have to—need to—look at this." Selene tumbled through her words and picked up an open book with a marked page. "Wait, not this." She discarded it to reach for another one. "Here, this one." She held up the book victoriously.

Brynnlin stared at her friend with wide eyes and cautiously walked the rest of the way into the room, tossing

34

her bag on the nearest chair. She took in the mess of the living room and the scattered notes across the floor. Selene was always so calm and organized, seeing her flustered was alarming.

"What is going on? Have you not slept since I left?" She perched on the edge of the seat, eyeing her friend with concern.

"I can sleep later, this is impor—oh my goddess, what happened to your face?" Selene finished with a raised voice, finally focusing on Brynnlin.

Brynnlin grimaced. She'd forgotten about how that probably looked right now. It was barely tender, but she knew there was some swelling and a nasty bruise already forming along her jaw and upper cheek.

"Eh, off night, an Ossorian got in a lucky hit."

Selene frowned. "I hope you made them pay for it."

She gasped, faking offense. "Of course I did. What kind of question is that?"

Selene's lips twitched in amusement. "Let me go make a healing tonic for you, it'll be better in a few hours."

She got up, pushing away the books, and heading for one of the bedrooms.

"No, it's fine. Really," Brynnlin called out.

Selene ignored her and was already down the hall and in the other room. She came back out with a couple supplies, and Brynnlin slumped into the chair as she watched Selene mix a tonic.

"I said I'd be fine," she grumbled.

"I heard you, but why suffer? This will take away the pain."

"It tastes so gross though."

"Don't be such a baby." Selene finished mixing the tonic, and pushed the cup towards her. "Drink."

Brynnlin downed the drink in one gulp, and bitterness assaulted her senses. She let out a harsh cough.

"Gah, so bad," she whined. The herbal aftertaste lingered on her tongue.

Selene raised one of her perfectly sculpted eyebrows. "Are you done being dramatic?"

"I'm never dramatic," she said, trying to keep a straight face, until she gave up and started laughing.

"Yeah right," Selene snickered. "Now before you distracted me with your beat-up face, I was trying to say I found something important."

Selene didn't look flustered anymore. There was a sense of eagerness to her voice as if she couldn't contain the news any longer. She bounced back to the couch, grabbing the book from earlier, and hugged it to her chest.

"I did it. I found it. It arrived at the shop only hours ago."

Brynnlin studied the worn and aged cover. She struggled to make out the ancient lettering of the title. When she did, time itself seemed to stop.

Leabhar na Scrios.

The Book of Destruction.

A silent moment passed.

Then another.

Brynnlin could only stare in disbelief.

As time came roaring back, her heart started pounding in her chest at the realization of what this meant.

They'd been looking for this grimoire for years. Years without any luck. Years of dead ends, to the point that they'd practically given up. It wasn't until recently that they managed to get a new lead, but even with that, Brynnlin thought it fell through.

Yet Selene had found it.

She was standing there clutching the book like a lifeline.

"You did it," the words came out in a whisper, as if Brynnlin said them too loudly the book would disappear. "You actually found it."

Selene's smile turned soft, and she sat back down on the edge of the couch. "We did it."

"How? Where?" Brynnlin struggled to wrap her head around what was right in front of her. "I thought Penn gave us bad information."

It had been pure luck that August Penn had showed up at the club a few weeks ago and had gotten on Brynnlin's radar. The Draíothes that worked for the Creed were scarce on the outer islands of the Creed's territory. Brynnlin should know, she'd been trying to locate and identify the Draíothe acolytes for years.

The Creed kept their Draíothe acolytes close, as they were the only ones with magic capable of summoning the demons. So when August Penn sauntered into the club to do business with Zamir and Brynnlin discovered what he was, she wasn't letting that opportunity slip past her.

With Selene's help, the plan had been to question him and obtain the locations of the other clubs the Draíothes frequented on the inner islands. That plan quickly changed after she overheard him bragging about a demon he summoned for a group of acolytes that ransacked some small towns in Sidhe.

After discovering that...she might have let things get a little messy.

Brynnlin went after more than just information about the clubs. She extracted every little detail that asshole could tell her about summoning that demon, which unfortunately was not much. And his knowledge of the grimoire they used for the summonings was painfully limited. But when all was said and done, she'd made sure he wouldn't be hurting anyone else.

It was a risk she probably shouldn't have taken, but she didn't regret it.

Not at all.

Selene's smile dimmed slightly. "His information about the grimoire's location was incorrect, but I've been trying to find this book for years. So it was enough to finally point me in the right direction to track down where it was. Or more importantly who had it."

Brynnlin's chest tightened at the implication of Selene's words. "Who had it? And how did you get it from them?"

Selene looked down and mumbled, "As far as they're concerned, I'm borrowing it for the foreseeable future."

Despite the situation, Brynnlin threw her head back and laughed. "It's called stealing, Selene. Not borrowing. You stole it."

Selene's head whipped back up. "I did no such thing."

"Really?" Brynnlin drawled. "Then how'd you get it?"

Selene held her head high, and her tone was full of indignation. "A well-paid group of individuals retrieved it for me."

Oh this was getting better and better. "So you paid to have it stolen."

"Retrieved," Selene insisted, "stealing has such a negative connotation to it."

Brynnlin was still laughing. "I think the previous owner would disagree. Which you never said who it was anyway?"

Selene chewed on her lower lip. "I'd prefer not to disclose that information. On the off chance this goes poorly, the less you know the better."

A wave of anxiety rushed through Brynnlin, erasing all of her humor. Selene's reluctance to give more details was not a good sign.

"Who, Selene?"

Selene ignored her. "It doesn't matter. What does matter is

this book. This is still a huge accomplishment, but this grimoire isn't exactly what we expected. The Creed is much smarter than I ever gave them credit for...unfortunately."

Brynnlin frowned. "What does that mean? Is it not the right book?"

Selene shook her head. "No it is. I translated it, and it's legitimate, but this isn't the whole book. Everything I learned over the years and the legends about the grimoire indicated something very powerful and expansive. If I had to guess, this is maybe a quarter of that. Everything in it is real, but key information is missing. It looks like the Creed separated the grimoire into pieces."

Brynnlin closed her eyes. Of course they didn't find the whole book, that would've been too easy.

"Hey..." Selene's prodding had Brynnlin opening her eyes again. "I know this isn't quite what we hoped, but Brynn you have to understand this is still huge," Selene's voice was adamant. "This is still information we can use that we didn't have. It's going to put us closer than we've ever been before."

There was something in Selene's words that had Brynnlin eyeing her carefully.

"You found something in those pages didn't you? That's why you're so excited."

Selene's eyes glinted with delight. "I found more than just something."

There was no stopping the spark of hope that flared in Brynnlin's chest. They'd been at this for far too long, and after so many disappointments and dead ends, they needed something to go in their favor.

"What'd you find?" Brynnlin moved to the couch, needing to see what Selene uncovered.

"Look here." Selene opened the book and started flipping through the pages. Brynnlin tried to follow along, but it was written in the Theban language. Selene had taught her how to read quite a bit of it, but there was still a lot she didn't know. She gave up trying to translate it and waited for Selene to explain.

"There's a lot of information about the types of demons and where the different classes are located in the Three Hells, which of course is invaluable knowledge." Selene started talking as she was scanning through the different pages. "But that's not quite what I was looking for. I was hoping this grimoire contained the rituals they used to summon the demons because if we knew how they summoned them maybe, just maybe, we could learn how to prevent them."

Brynnlin released a sharp breath, and her gaze shot to Selene. "Are you saying you found the rituals?"

Selene offered her a tight-lipped smile. "Not quite. But I did find this."

Selene stopped on a page and pointed to a column halfway down. "This part of the grimoire doesn't outline the rituals that need to be performed to do the summonings. But next to the information about the demons, it outlines the items required for each summoning. That's how they are able to summon these different demons. Each species has different items required for each ritual. And for these higher class demons, the items are rare, and a Draíothe needs to be powerful enough or they won't survive."

Brynnlin was quiet as she absorbed what Selene was saying. It made sense that the rituals would be more difficult to perform for higher class demons. It also explained why the Creed summoned mid-to-lower class demons. Maybe they didn't have many Draíothes strong enough to handle the more powerful demons. Which definitely worked in their favor.

"Selene, this is great, it really is." Brynnlin tried not to show her skepticism. "But does this really help us that much?"

Selene shot her a disapproving look. "Have a little faith. It's insulting that you doubt me so easily."

Selene skipped forward in the grimoire and opened up a bookmarked page. On the page was a roughly illustrated island surrounded by crashing waves. The black and white image of the rocky mass was weathered by age. A short description was printed beneath the picture in another language she didn't understand.

"The Island of Donn," Selene explained. "Where the souls of the dead gather before entering the underworld. And if this translation is to be believed, it's rumored blood-red shores are needed for almost all of the rituals."

Brynnlin's mind raced as she tried to comprehend what that meant. "I don't understand. The island of the dead? Like the god Donn?"

"Exactly," Selene agreed. "I don't know how they're managing to get this soil, but somehow they are. This is rare and not easy to come by. I can guarantee the Creed is going to a collector to obtain this, and there are very few in the entire world that are capable of obtaining this." Selene shot her a sly smile. "With this information, I'm convinced I can track down their supplier."

Brynnlin's breath caught in her throat, and she stared at Selene with wide eyes. "Selene, if you find the supplier it would lead us straight to the top Draíothes and the Creed members running everything."

"I know."

Brynnlin's heart pounded, a surge of adrenaline rushed through her veins, as her mind worked a mile a minute. She was too afraid to say it aloud, but this might actually work.

She sat forward and grasped Selene's hands, "Selene, this is actually huge."

"I know," Selene said again. "And it won't be easy," she

warned, "but I have a good feeling about this. And I know you're close to being invited to the club on the inner island, which I think you should keep doing. In case that doesn't get you in, we now have this, which should lead us straight to the top."

Brynnlin slumped back onto the couch and stared at the ceiling. A feeling of euphoria swirled around her. They were getting somewhere. It had been so long since she had hope that they were actually gaining ground. And for the first time in a long time, she thought about that promise she made to that scared little girl years ago.

They were going to pay for what they did. No matter how long it took, vengeance would be hers.

"Where do we start with tracking down this collector?" Brynnlin found herself asking, eager to get started.

"I was planning on going to the shop in the morning. I have some texts I need to go through regarding the origins of the island."

"Perfect," Brynnlin pushed off the couch. "I'll join you at the shop."

"Brynn..."

Brynnlin had every intention of leaving the room, Selene's hesitation had her turning back around. The worry she saw in Selene's gaze had her frowning.

"What's wrong?"

Selene chewed on her lip, before motioning her to sit back down.

Brynnlin slowly returned to her seat with a raised eyebrow. "Selene?"

"There's one more thing I need to show you."

Brynnlin's muscles tightened at the sympathy now swimming in Selene's gaze.

"What?" She didn't mean for that single word to sound so harsh, but Selene was making her nervous.

Selene broke her gaze and started playing with the edge of the book. "I wanted to share the good news with you first, before I showed you this, but you deserve to see it."

Before Brynnlin could demand Selene to stop talking in circles, Selene opened the book to another tabbed page and pushed the book towards her.

Brynnlin glanced at the page. And despite her best efforts, her breathing hitched at the image depicted before her. Her chest tightened, and fear that she had long ago suppressed threatened to claw its way forward.

The inked creature staring back at her was one of nightmares.

Hers specifically.

She struggled to tear her gaze away from the demon that haunted her eleven years ago.

"What is this?" Brynnlin snapped at Selene.

Selene was slow to answer. "I came across it as I was studying the grimoire. Based on the description you once gave me, I made the connection."

Brynnlin shoved the book away. "This changes nothing, we already knew a Draíothe summoned that demon. Trust me, I don't need the reminder."

"Brynn, I didn't show you this to change anything, but you need to be aware of what we might be dealing with." There was a note of desperation in Selene's voice. "This demon is one of tremendous power. You and your family never stood a chance against it. It's one of the highest classes I've come across so far, and whoever summoned this demon had to be extremely powerful in his own right. I know this won't stop you, but you need to be careful because, if we find him, we need to be prepared."

The pain of the past shoved its way to the surface, and the memories of the night and that feeling of helplessness bombarded her.

Never again.

Never again would she feel that.

She fought tooth and nail to get to where she was at, to survive what life had thrown at her. She would not give up the one thing that got her through it all.

They would all pay.

"Like I said Selene, this changes nothing. That man will pay for what he did, and I know you feel it too, we're getting closer."

Selene met her hard stare. "I know this hasn't been easy, but I didn't save you all those years ago only for you to throw it all away for vengeance. You know I'm in this with you one hundred percent, but we need to be careful Brynn. We need to be smarter than them."

Some of Brynnlin's ire slipped away at Selene's reminder. She wouldn't be where she was without Selene. And it wasn't just herself at risk, Selene was risking everything, too.

If it weren't for Selene, Brynnlin would still be prisoner to that cage and never-ending debt. She wouldn't throw the opportunity Selene gave her away.

Brynnlin released a slow breath. "We'll go at this the right way. I promise."

Selene's shoulders sagged in relief. "Good. Now we should both get some rest. It's late, we can start fresh in the morning."

Brynnlin conceded, "Alright."

Pushing off the couch, she made her way down the hall. Halfway to her room she stopped, turned around, and went back to Selene.

She pulled Selene into a tight hug. "I don't tell you this enough. But thank you. For everything. I wouldn't be here without you."

Selene hugged her back just as fiercely. "Yes, you would. You're a survivor. And we're gonna figure this out."

Brynnlin didn't let go and clenched her eyes shut as they pooled with tears that she refused to let fall. She owed Selene everything. She didn't know what she did to deserve Selene's friendship, but she would forever thank the gods for the fateful day that their paths crossed.

Selene pulled back, and Brynnlin couldn't help but smile at the playful glare Selene was shooting at her.

"Don't you dare start getting emotional on me Brynn, you know how I feel about tears. If you start crying there's no stopping my own, so stop it now."

Brynnlin wiped at her watery eyes, "So bossy."

Selene shooed her away. "Always, now go to bed, I'm too tired for this."

Brynnlin let out a soft laugh and went to her room. She tossed her dirty clothes in the hamper and grabbed a sleep shirt. She made sure the lamp on the nightstand was turned on before collapsing into bed. The lamp provided a nice warm glow around the room, and she stared at the ceiling as she went over everything.

Over the years it had been so easy to want to give up. Her family was dead. Her home destroyed. There was nothing to go back to, so why bother? She was forced into a painful and cruel world, and she questioned if it was still worth fighting for. So many times she had been ready to close the door on the past and give up.

But hope and determination were dangerous and powerful things. And they both had a tight hold on her. Her parents died so she could live, the least she could do was avenge their murderer. And no matter how many obstacles she faced, she would find him eventually.

That declaration was like a knife digging deeper into an

open wound that she was trying so desperately to heal. And yet she still couldn't resist the temptation.

She would find him and the other Draíothe acolytes that worked for the Creed.

They were finally on the right track.

And this time was different.

It had to be.

That was her last thought before sleep claimed her.

FEAR FLOODED through Brynnlin's body. She jerked upright, her hands pulling against the restraints that were no longer there. Her fingers brushed the silk covers, the softness reminding her where she was. Slowly recognition settled into her sleep-addled brain. She forced her eyes open, taking in the dimly lit room and seeing the familiar walls.

A heavy pressure weighed down on her chest. She took a deep breath and tried to practice her breathing exercises to calm her racing heart.

Inhale, 1, 2, 3, exhale.

Always the same mantra.

Repeat.

Repeat.

Repeat.

Once she felt like her heart wasn't going to beat out of her chest, she pushed her sweaty hair away from her face and glanced at the glowing numbers of the clock.

Six fourteen.

She groaned and rolled back over. She'd only gotten about four hours of sleep. And it was obvious she wasn't getting anymore.

Damn nightmares.

It had been a while since she had one that bad. She used to have them all the time, but they slowly dissipated through the years.

Until now, apparently.

It had to be the conversation from last night, reopening old wounds better left forgotten.

Remnants of fear still clung to her, and the room felt small. Frustrated, she shoved off the bed and changed into a long sleeve and leggings, before grabbing her running shoes.

She needed air.

She wrote out a quick note for Selene that she would meet her at the shop and walked out the door. It was dark outside, the sun still hiding under the horizon. Yet the streets were already filling up with people rushing to get their day started.

Brynnlin ignored the people around her and did a few quick stretches before starting down the sidewalk at an easy jog. She breathed in the cold air. With the recent rain, there was a freshness to it that distracted from the usual polluted taste.

She headed in the direction of Selene's shop. There was a coffee shop on the way that she could stop at before continuing on. She crossed over to the other side of the street with less foot traffic and continued to jog block after block. She used the time to clear her mind. She focused on drowning out the extra noises and only listened to the sound of her shoes on the pavement.

Brynnlin was feeling lighter by the time she reached the small shop on the corner. Her nightmares practically forgotten as she joined the line. The aroma of freshly brewed coffee and baked treats surrounded her. The line moved quickly, and it wasn't long before Brynnlin was back on the street with two orders in hand. She opted for their regulars, it would be a pleasant surprise for Selene, once she joined her at the bookstore.

The crowd on the streets started to thin out the further Brynnlin ventured downtown. It wasn't until she was around the corner from Selene's shop that her skin started to prickle with unease.

Her steps slowed. She cast a subtle glance around. Nothing was out of the ordinary. A few people walked along the opposite side of the street, and all the storefronts she passed were still closed this early in the morning.

She tried to ignore it, to shake off the forbidding sense now cloaking her. But she was never one to ignore her instincts. She wasn't imagining it. Someone was watching her. She could feel their eyes on her.

She ground her teeth together, any serenity she gained from her run completely evaporated at this unwelcome intrusion. She hadn't been followed from the apartment, she knew that for a fact. And someone couldn't have been waiting for her. This run had been unplanned. Which meant whoever the Hells this was had happened upon her by chance.

She picked up her pace, debating her options. She could still try and go to the shop, but she didn't want to lead whoever this was straight to her destination.

She could try to lose them...

The faintest of footsteps behind her had Brynnlin abandoning that idea. Out of the corner of her eye, she caught the slightest movement of a figure further behind her. Their reflection glinted off one of the shop windows.

Making a quick second decision, Brynnlin sped up and ducked into one of the alleyways between the shop buildings. She ditched the drinks and grabbed the small knife she kept in her pant's pocket. She slipped behind a dumpster letting it shield her from view. Footsteps hurried towards her. They were heavy as whoever it was rushed to keep up.

She palmed the knife in her hand, preparing herself as the person rounded the corner.

As soon as a figure stepped in front of her, she pushed off the wall and shoved them against the opposite building, holding the knife to their throat. Her eyes widened as she stared at familiar black hair and icy blue eyes.

It was the man from the club.

Was he stalking her?

"You were at the fight last night. Who are you? And why are you following me?" she hissed softly.

She had to angle her head up to look at him. His muscular body tensed under her, and his jaw clenched as he glared down at her. Ever so slowly, he lifted his hands up in a placating manner.

She didn't drop her hold.

"I won't ask again. Who the fuck are you?" She applied more pressure, letting the knife draw a drop of blood.

"It doesn't matter who I am," his lips twitched upwards into a smirk. "What does matter is that you just attacked a Commanding General of one of the realms. Consider yourself under arrest," his tone was callous as he spit those words at her.

She raised her eyebrows and pushed him harder against the wall.

He was in for a rude awakening.

"Try again, General. I believe Kärsiä is a little out of your jurisdiction. So tell me why you've been following me, or I will slice your throat right here, right now." She held his stare and didn't release the pressure of the knife. She wouldn't hesitate. She knew that was clear in her gaze.

He remained utterly still as he considered her. Only his eyes darted around as if looking for an escape. He focused a millisecond too long on something above her, before returning to glare at her.

It was a small move.

But she caught it.

Her eyes narrowed. He wasn't alone. That was why he wasn't fighting her. She moved, ready to cut his throat.

His hand shot up and grabbed her wrist.

Shit, he was fast.

He twisted, and pain shot through her arm. She was forced to drop the knife before he broke the bone.

Her other fist jabbed at his throat. Her knuckles slammed into the soft weak spot. He choked and bent over gasping for air. She used his distraction to rip out of his hold. She dove to the side just as another man dropped down into the alleyway.

He must have been on the roof, it was the only explanation for why she didn't notice him sooner.

The newcomer was about the same height and build as the other one. His brown hair hung in waves that reached his shoulders, and his amber eyes were full of contempt as he regarded her. Dark ink peeked out of his shirt and ran up his neck, the detailed swirls coming to life every time he moved. He carried himself with confidence and lethally sauntered towards her.

From his stance there was no doubt in her mind that he had some type of formal training—especially if his friend hadn't been lying about his position. For every step he took towards her, she retreated one, buying herself time and looking for any sign of weakness.

This wasn't going to be an easy win.

He stopped advancing and crossed his arms over his broad chest.

"Come on now, let's do this the easy way. No one has to get hurt." He eyed his companion, who was standing tall and breathing normally again. "At least not more than what's already been done."

His voice was smooth and deep. There was a hint of an accent, but she couldn't place the region, she'd been gone too long. When she remained quiet, his lips curved up into a charming smile.

Brynnlin saw straight through the facade. Did he really think she would fall for that? He might be trying to appear relaxed and easy-going, but his partner wasn't bothering to hide his fury. If looks could kill, she'd be dead on the spot.

What was with all this hate towards her, anyway? She couldn't possibly have done anything to draw the attention of one of the royal houses.

"The easy way?" she questioned, as if considering it. "And what would that be?" She hoped to keep him talking and distracted. Her knife was on the ground behind them, but there had to be something else in this alley that would give her an advantage.

He seemed pleased with her response. "The easy way is you coming with us without a fight, and answering our questions. Once you tell us what we need to know, you're free to leave. We just want to talk. No violence necessary."

Gods, they really did take her for an idiot. He really thought she would willingly go with them.

Something glinted off the ground, catching her attention. Broken glass laid shattered underneath a window. Not ideal. But it would have to work.

"You know, I don't take too kindly to being stalked and threatened," she said in a casual manner, while making the slightest adjustment to her stance. "So I hate to disappoint, but I'm going to have to pass on your offer."

She saw the moment her words registered, but it was too late. She had already lunged to the ground, grabbing a long shard of glass, and throwing it at the man before her.

He moved fast enough for it to miss his heart, but it

embedded itself deep into his shoulder. He staggered back with a pained grunt.

She used the diversion to knock over one of the dumpsters and kicked it into their path, before taking off for the other end of the alleyway.

"Burning Hells. Ryker, don't let her get away."

She was almost to the other street when she was tackled from behind. Her head smacked into the concrete. For a few precious seconds, her vision dimmed.

She struggled as Ryker tried to restrain her. He rolled over, wrapping one arm around her neck, and silencing her with his other hand.

She bit down on his hand. Hard.

Drops of liquid landed on her tongue. The taste overwhelmingly metallic. She'd drawn blood.

"You fucking cannibal," he growled out behind clenched teeth. He jerked his hand back, causing his hold around her neck to loosen.

His mistake.

She slammed her head back and heard the satisfying crunch of his nose. His arms dropped from around her. She threw her elbow into his rib cage and crawled to her knees, ready to take off again.

Before she could make her escape, a heavy hand gripped into the back of her neck, ripping through her hair. She was lifted, and her head started spinning from the pain. Casting her eyes to the side, she found herself staring into a furious gaze.

He was holding her with his good arm, the other one was wet with dripping blood.

"You just had to make this difficult didn't you."

He almost sounded disappointed in her.

She squirmed, kicking out at his legs, when a loud voice echoed through the alleyway making them both freeze.

"Zale. Ryker. What in the actual Three Hells is going on?"

The bellow was followed by footsteps running towards them.

Son of a bitch. How many of them were there?

She twisted her head to get a good look at who had just joined them. Her heart clenched, and her knees buckled from under her.

"Shit," the man gritted out as her weight collapsed into him. His hold on her the only thing keeping her upright.

She ignored him, and her head buzzed as it tried to comprehend what she was seeing. The man that ran into the alley was slightly taller, and his build a little more muscular. A tattoo running down one of his arms was clear to see. The black spirals were stark against his sun-kissed skin. The elemental markings and their meaning would be unrecognizable to anyone else. Not to her, though. His dark blonde hair was swept back from his face and desperately needed a trim.

It may have been years, but he hadn't changed at all.

She would also recognize those violet-blue eyes anywhere.

"Maddie, is that really you?" Brynnlin barely breathed at the sight of her cousin.

CHAPTER 3

"She hadn't given him enough credit for the threat he was."

EVERYONE HEARD Brynnlin's whispered question, and Maddox's steps faltered. He froze a few feet away from them.

"Wh—what did you just call me?" The slight tremble in his voice vibrated through the air. The gruff tone sounded foreign after all these years, yet so familiar at the same time.

It was him. It was really him.

"Oh my gods. Maddie. It's you. You're alive." Saying those words out loud broke the dam that was holding her together.

Brynnlin clamped a hand over her mouth to stifle her cries, but there was no stopping the tears falling down her face. She shoved away from the man holding her, only his grip tightened, halting her efforts.

Maddox's eyes widened and emotion flashed through his features. Confusion was the most prominent, yet it was the lack of recognition that tore at her heart.

He didn't recognize her.

"Maddox, it's me. Brynn." Her voice cracked.

54

Maddox's next words were barely audible. "It's not possible."

He didn't sound very convinced. She watched the turmoil in his eyes, hope fighting with disbelief.

Hope finally won out.

His voice was hoarse, "Brynnlin?"

She shoved away again, and this time the man didn't fight her. She flung herself at Maddox, wrapping her arms around him. He was stiff at first. After a shuddered breath, he pulled her up into a bone-crushing hug. He was squeezing the breath right out of her. She didn't care. She inhaled deeply, breathing in his pinewood scent.

Gods, it was really him.

He was here.

Alive.

She tightened her hold, clinging to him.

"Brynnlin. How are you alive?" Maddox's voice was muffled against her hair.

"I could ask you the same," she said into his shoulder. Tears were still running down her face, and when she leaned back to look at him, his own eyes were misty. He had always been more like a brother to her than a cousin. Having him back was like finding missing pieces to her shattered soul.

Maddox set her back down with ease without fully releasing her. He pushed some hair out of her face, cupping her cheek for a moment, before his hands rested on her shoulders.

His features were still dazed.

"You're really here," he said in wonder, as if it was hard to believe what was right in front of him.

She completely understood the feeling.

The harsh sound of a throat clearing pierced through the air, interrupting their little reunion.

Maddox broke eye contact with her and looked up. The

emotions he'd so easily displayed with her vanished. His features tightened, turning serious, as he regarded the two men behind her.

"Maddox, what in the Hells are you doing?"

She turned, finding the one that tackled her glaring at the two of them.

Maddox's lips thinned into a flat line. "Take it easy, Ryker."

Ryker looked pissed and shot her a look of disdain. His nose was back in place, but he was still smeared with blood. She took great satisfaction in his discomfort. After all, he probably gave her a concussion, her head was killing her.

She glared back.

Maddox caught Ryker's scowl and angled himself in front of her. The action was sweet, though completely unnecessary.

"She's not a threat," Maddox told them.

Brynnlin stiffened, and her glare shot to Maddox.

Well...to his back.

What was that supposed to mean?

"Oh, she's not a threat?" Ryker's chuckle was dark and lacked humor. "Is that how you're going to describe the acolyte that not only resisted arrest but assaulted us?"

Maddox held Ryker's hard stare. "I'm sure it's all a misunderstanding."

The other man, Zale, stepped in and pulled Ryker back a few steps.

"Let's take a breath man." Zale was calm and controlled, despite being a mess. He was covered in blood, but it had at least stopped flowing down his arm, and his wound was starting to clot. She should probably feel guilty about stabbing him.

She didn't.

Zale stared at her, regarding her carefully.

She stared back, refusing to flinch under his intense gaze.

After a moment, he turned to Ryker.

"Didn't you hear Maddox? It's her. Brynnlin."

Her head jerked back in surprise at hearing her name and at the fact that they seemed to recognize it. Yet that was nothing compared to Ryker's reaction.

"You're shitting me, right?" Ryker burst out, eyeing all three of them. He did not look pleased at this new development.

"No, I'm not, Ryker." Maddox's voice was soft, and there was an edge of warning. "And I don't need enthusiasm from you, but maybe try not to sound so disgusted that I just reunited with my cousin."

Despite herself, Brynnlin winced. Ryker really did seem revolted if his appalled expression was anything to go by. And if she hadn't been sure how they knew her before, she had her answer now. They definitely knew about her relation to Maddox.

Ryker either missed Maddox's warning or didn't care, because he kept going.

"Maybe this would be a little more heartfelt, if your 'said cousin' hadn't tried to kill," Ryker emphasized the word, "me and Zale."

Brynnlin stepped forward, ready to go off on Ryker. No way would she just stand here and let him throw accusations at her.

She pointed a threatening finger in his direction. "Maybe if you didn't stalk and threaten me, I wouldn't have felt the need to defend myself."

"Don't flatter yourself," Ryker sneered, "I was not stalking you."

She raised an eyebrow. "Do you not know the definition of stalking?"

"I swear to the gods—"

"Enough," Maddox growled, cutting them both off. "Ryker, tone it down. And Brynnlin—"

"Excuse me?" Brynnlin twisted and shot Maddox an affronted look. "What did I do?"

Did he forget they were the ones that attacked her?

"You're antagonizing him."

She scoffed. It wasn't her fault Ryker didn't like hearing the truth.

"Okay, let's just take a moment," Zale intervened and stepped in the middle. He scanned the alley and the entrance to the street. "We don't need to attract attention, not here. So how about we bring it down a few notches. And Maddox, I know you just found your cousin and that's great, but don't forget we came out here to do a job. Try and keep that in mind."

Maddox nodded even though his muscles remained tense. "I know why we're out here."

Brynnlin narrowed her eyes at Zale's words. "What job?"

They ignored her, and Zale shared an uncomfortable look with Maddox.

Ryker didn't seem to share their concern.

"Really, Maddox?" Ryker scoffed, and crossed his arms over his chest. "After all this, you're going to hesitate? Cousin or not, she's an acolyte with ties to a known Draíothe in the area. And if that isn't enough, she was taking part in illegal activity last night at that club. And to top it all off, she attacked us. We were lucky enough to run into her like this, don't throw it away. We have every right to arrest her."

Maddox whirled on Ryker, his temper peaking through his usual calm composure, and snarled. "Gods damn it, Ryker, don't be dense. We're not arresting her. I know what you told me, but there's an explanation for this."

Brynnlin's mind reeled, and she stepped back. Her gaze pinged between the three men around her.

Arrest her?

Acolyte? Draíothe?

"Maddox, what's going on," she demanded.

Maddox ran a hand through his hair, pushing some of the loose strands back. "Nothing. This is just a misunderstanding."

"About what?" She wasn't letting this go, and when Maddox reached for her hand she took another step back, avoiding his reach.

This wasn't nothing.

Ryker wanted to arrest her.

At the same time, Ryker echoed her frustration.

"A misunderstanding?" he spat out. "Don't be blind to what's right in front of you, Maddox."

"Ryker." This time Zale shot him a hard look. "This is not the time or place. Give him a minute."

Brynnlin risked another subtle step back. She didn't know where this conversation was going, but she doubted it was in her favor. Cousin or not, she had no intention of getting caught up in whatever was going on.

Maddox eyed Ryker with warning, and his voice turned to steel. "I don't want to hear another word from you, Ryker, while I take a moment to get to the bottom of this. And Brynnlin..." Maddox angled himself towards her. "Stop backing away. I didn't just find you for you to run off."

Brynnlin rolled her shoulders back to shake off some of the tension. "I wouldn't say you found me in this situation, and I have no intention of going anywhere as long as you drop this ridiculous arrest talk."

"We're not arresting you, but Brynnlin..." Maddox ran a hand through his hair and there was a desperate edge to his tone, "you have to know this looks bad. I can't begin to imagine what's happened to you that led you to this point, but to be an acolyte? To be living on these fucking isles after all this time?"

Brynnlin's stomach dropped at the hint of betrayal that flashed across Maddox's features.

He really thought that little of her?

She fought hard to keep her composure.

"You don't know what you're talking about," she said carefully.

"Don't I?" Maddox threw his hands up. "Don't lie to me. I can see that damn brand crawling up your neck. I just don't understand. After what they did to our family?"

Ice flooded through Brynnlin's veins, and for a brief moment she struggled to stay standing at his insinuation.

"Don't you dare throw that at me, and think very carefully about your next words, Maddox." Inside she was fuming, and her words came out raw, "You have absolutely no idea what I've been through, and what I've had to do to survive. And everything I've ever done has only ever been for our family."

Maddox flinched slightly at her words. Some of her anger faded as his gaze filled with remorse.

"Brynnlin, I didn't mean it like that, it's just...fuck..." he took a step forward, before stopping again. He cupped the back of his neck and looked around the alley. "This is all just a mess... finding you like this...why we're here now..."

She crossed her arms, and her words were still a little defensive. "There's a lot you don't know, Maddox. A lot that has happened over the years. But we can't talk about it. Not out here."

"Then let's go somewhere we can talk." Maddox moved again, but Ryker's hand shot out, stopping him.

"Maddox, do I have to ask again? What do you think you're doing?" Ryker growled

Maddox glared back at him. "I thought my actions were quite clear. And it would be wise to remember who answers to who here."

Ryker released Maddox, but that didn't stop him from continuing. "Maddox, I'm not going to try to understand the emotions you might be feeling right now. There are obviously some things that need to get sorted out, and Hells, maybe there are some explanations. But we need to remember our priorities. What about the bookstore?"

Brynnlin stiffened. She had no rational explanation for the flicker of fear that raced through her at Ryker's mention of a bookstore. She was fairly confident they weren't talking about Selene's place, but they were too close to the shop for it to not cross her mind. She had to bite her tongue to prevent her from demanding clarification and waited for Maddox's reaction.

"It's not going anywhere, a little longer isn't going to change anything," was Maddox's only response.

Ryker started to open his mouth, when Zale interrupted. "All due respect, Maddox, none of us want to risk being here longer than necessary. Why don't Ryker and I go take care of the situation," Zale cast her a quick glance, "and you can sort this out."

Maddox was already shaking his head. "Like I said earlier, I'm not sending you guys into a blind situation."

Ryker scoffed and rolled his eyes. "If you're so concerned, just have your dear little cousin take us now. We're around the corner, and she knows the godsdamn owner."

Brynnlin's stomach turned to lead as Ryker's words registered.

They were talking about Selene.

How in the Hells was Selene on their radar?

She eyed Ryker with apprehension. She hadn't given him enough credit for the threat he was. He knew an alarming amount.

Ryker caught her expression and chuckled. He knew he caught her off guard.

"Weren't expecting that were you? We know all about your relationship to Selene Aspen, so don't bother denying it."

Her eyes only narrowed. She seriously doubted that, but he knew enough. Her connection to Selene wasn't a secret. It wasn't common knowledge either. And she had no intention of denying it. If she had any chance of protecting Selene, she needed to figure out what they wanted with her.

She crossed her arms and shrugged. "I know lots of people, what's it to you?"

Ryker smirked back at her, before his gaze cut to the side.

"How much more do you need, Maddox?" Ryker drawled out, "Is it still not enough? She openly admitted her association with Aspen. The least you could do is make use of it."

Brynnlin frowned, and her stare shot to Maddox, who's expression turned grim.

He straightened his shoulders and studied her intently.

Brynnlin took a slow breath and steeled herself. She knew that look. Standing in front of her now, he was Lord Chancellor, the second in command for Rí Kodak, the ruler of Sidhe. Being her cousin came second to his role and duty to his realm.

She didn't hold it against him, but she had loyalties, too.

She gave him a slow shake of her head. "Maddox, I don't want to disappoint you, but whatever you're about to ask, I can't help you."

"I wouldn't ask you to be involved, but this situation is bigger than both of us. People's lives are at risk, Brynnlin."

She frowned at the intensity in his statement.

"Who's at risk? And how is Selene connected to this?"

"Innocents, Brynnlin," Maddox's voice sounded pained, "good, innocent people are in danger. And if you really are close to Selene Aspen, we need to meet with her. I can tell from that look on your face that you're worried, but it's not what you think."

Before Brynnlin could question what he meant, Maddox kept talking.

"We don't mean Selene any harm. Quite the opposite. We're going to her for help."

Shock radiated through Brynnlin at his words. Of all the things she possibly expected him to say, it certainly wasn't that.

"Help?" She couldn't stop herself from questioning it, the whole idea was totally absurd. "You're going to Selene for help? What could she possibly help you with?"

Maddox blew out a rough breath and stepped closer to her. His voice dropped to a whisper, "You said earlier it was best not to talk out here, I'm inclined to believe you. Let's go somewhere, and I'll explain everything."

She hesitated and looked around the alleyway. He was right, they really shouldn't be talking so openly. Yet she wasn't quite sure where they should go. She needed to talk to Maddox, but didn't exactly welcome the idea of Ryker and Zale coming along.

Maddox must have seen the indecision in her eyes because he tried again. "I get that Selene is probably your friend, but I need you to trust me."

She couldn't help flinching at that word.

Trust.

That wasn't something she had much of anymore. But as she looked up at Maddox, she found herself nodding her head.

She would take this chance. For him.

"Okay," she said softly. "We can go to the shop. Selene's not there yet, but we can talk. It's secure."

Maddox reached out and squeezed her hand.

"Lead the way." Maddox motioned for her to go first, before following a step behind her.

CHAPTER 4

"And for the first time in a long time, she prayed to the gods."

BRYNNLIN GLANCED to the side for what seemed like the thousandth time.

Maddox's curious gaze met her own, the same as it had every other time she looked over at him.

He was really there, walking beside her. She kept waiting for him to disappear and for reality to seep back in, yet here they were still continuing towards the shop.

Was she in shock? Was that what this was? Or maybe a delusion, courtesy of her concussion? Perhaps, she was knocked unconscious when Ryker tackled her to the ground?

All of those seemed more likely than the probability that what was happening was actually real.

Now that she had more time to process this, the idea of Maddox being here really did seem too good to be true.

Fate wasn't something that favored her.

So, what was the catch to this situation?

Maddox cleared his throat and arched a brow. "Everything alright?"

Oh gods.

She was still staring at him.

She tried to hide her grimace and forced a smile before focusing forward again. "Of course."

She wasn't sure if Maddox believed her, thankfully he didn't push the subject, for which she was grateful. She didn't know how to explain everything racing through her head. If she had any chance of getting through this next conversation, she had to get it together.

With a calming breath, she forced herself to focus on the walk to the shop. Once they were there, they could unload everything. She was still hesitant about bringing them all here, but she was limited on options. They continued the rest of the way in silence. Before she knew it, they were standing at Selene's door.

"This is it?" The question came from Maddox.

"Yeah." Her answer was quiet as she unlocked the door to the small shop squished between other businesses.

It might not look like much, but this shop was her solace, and she loved it almost as much as Selene did. The latch unlocked with a small click, and Brynnlin tried not to falter as she let the three men behind her pass the barrier.

RYKER NOTICED the tension in Brynnlin's shoulders as she pushed open the door to the bookstore. Sure enough, *Selene's Specialties* was scrawled across the small window. He was more than a little surprised she actually took them here. The others entered the shop, and he was quick to follow before Brynnlin could change her mind. She closed the door behind him, locked the door again, and flipped a switch on the wall.

Overhead lights flickered on, bringing the shop to life.

Shelves of books lined the space, and small signs hung from the ceilings, categorizing each section. The smell of leather and vanilla lingered in the air, along with an underlying trace of clover—the only evidence that revealed a Draíothe's magic was practiced somewhere within these premises. Against the walls, glass cases displayed a variety of odd items.

Ryker took a step closer to one of them, eyeing the contents. The small oddities ranged from jewelry, to figurines, to glass vials filled with who knew what. He leaned closer, studying a wooden plaque with intricate tribal carvings.

"There's a small bathroom down the hall in the back, you should make use of it."

He looked up to see Brynnlin directing her statement to him and Zale.

He nearly rolled his eyes.

Their current state was entirely her doing. Either she felt guilty, or she was trying to get them out of the room, so she could speak to Maddox.

He would put his money on the latter.

He was ready to decline when Zale nodded his head and started across the shop. Ryker decided to join him. Brynnlin wasn't the only one who wanted a private word.

In the hall, the bathroom door was clearly marked, while another door labeled office sat further back. Zale shut the door behind them and went to the sink. Ryker joined him and grimaced at his reflection. His nose was stained red, as was his chin and neck. He ripped some paper towels from the holder and started scrubbing.

Damn that fucking girl.

She couldn't just cooperate, she had to make shit difficult.

And his face had paid the price.

He glowered at the mirror.

Zale wasn't in much better shape. He ripped off his shirt and was cleaning the wound near his shoulder. Ryker shook his head. A few more inches to the side and that would have pierced Zale in the heart.

"What the fuck is Maddox thinking?" he growled, gripping the edge of the counter.

Zale side-eyed him. "Probably rejoicing in the fact that his cousin is actually alive after all this time."

"That's not what I meant, and you know it. She's erratic and violent, and Maddox ignored all of that. She could've killed us."

Zale rolled his eyes, and Ryker gritted his teeth.

How was he the only one seeing this?

"Ryker, he's not ignoring it. He's in a tough situation, and you know Maddox, he'll do what's right. He always does."

"She still attacked us."

Zale shrugged. "As far as she knew, two strange men followed her, and she reacted. Look at us, we have nothing more than flesh wounds."

"Not from her lack of trying," Ryker grumbled.

Zale ignored him. "Just let Maddox handle this, he doesn't need you making it worse."

Ryker crossed his arms and glared at Zale. "How could I make it worse? We wouldn't even be here right now if I hadn't pushed him."

"Everything would've gotten sorted out, and we would've ended up here eventually."

He snorted. "Yeah, because she was so willing to help last night, and then Maddox practically had to force her to take us here. Both of those are great examples of her compassionate character."

Zale's lips twitched. "I'm trying to stay neutral."

"Don't pull that neutral shit with me. You know as well as I do that this isn't adding up. She's hiding something."

Ryker didn't bother to hide his frustration, Maddox might be blind to it, but Zale had to see the truth.

Zale shot him an exasperated look. "She's on the isles. Of course she is."

"And that's not concerning to you?"

"What's concerning to me is a demon running loose through our realm." Zale pulled his shirt back on. "Whatever secrets Brynnlin has are irrelevant right now. All that matters is that she can get us to Selene Aspen."

That was a 'big if' on whether or not that was actually going to happen, yet Ryker kept that to himself.

He pointed to the door. "Let's just go get this over with then."

Back in the hall, muffled voices drifted from the main room. Zale started in that direction, but Ryker stopped him, and nodded his head towards the other end of the hall.

"What are you doing?" Zale hissed.

Ryker rolled his eyes as he headed for the office. "Relax, I'm just going to take a look around."

"Are you out of your mind?"

Ryker shrugged, "It's only a problem if we get caught." He paused and listened to Brynnlin and Maddox still talking, "They seem rather occupied at the moment."

Zale shook his head. "You're an idiot."

"And yet, you're still here."

"Just be quick." Zale shoved him forward, and Ryker couldn't stop his smirk.

He moved slowly towards the office door. He didn't know if there would actually be anything useful, but it was worth a shot. The door was slightly cracked open, and using his foot, he pushed it open further.

68

The rest of the office came into view, and his shoulders slumped.

Ryker ran a hand through his hair as he stared at the wreckage of the overturned office. "Well, shit."

"So, you really do know Selene Aspen?" Maddox asked a second after Zale and Ryker disappeared down the hall.

Brynnlin rolled her eyes at the question. "I thought that was obvious. And is that really the question you're asking me right now?"

She crossed her arms over her chest as Maddox wandered past one of the shelves and examined the book titles. There were so many things they had to say to each other, and he was browsing through books.

He looked over at her, his eyebrows rising. "Is there somewhere else you'd like to start?"

She almost laughed at the question. She didn't know where to start, but she asked the obvious. "How about the help you think you'll get from Selene?"

Maddox's lips thinned, but he nodded his head. "Alright, there's a demon loose in Sidhe. We're hoping she can track it down for us."

Brynnlin stilled as Maddox's words registered. She wasn't surprised about the demon, she knew what August Penn had done. But why did they think Selene could track it for them?

She asked as much. "What makes you think Selene can track it?"

Maddox was silent for a long moment.

She waited to see if he would give her an answer.

Finally, he said, "We went to other Draíothes on the mainland, but even the powerful ones couldn't track it. They didn't know enough about the demons or wouldn't mess with demonic magic. It was a wasted effort. So we decided to go to the source. And yet in a convenient play of fate, the Draíothe who summoned it is dead."

It took every ounce of Brynnlin's control not to react to Maddox's statement.

So, they knew about Penn's involvement, and his treachery against them. But did they know the details of his death?

Considering Maddox wasn't staring at her with accusation, she would assume not.

She studied him, before carefully asking, "How did that lead you to Selene?"

"We were informed that she was another Draíothe in the area, and that she was powerful. Considering her current residence on the isles, it was a safe assumption she had some knowledge of demons."

"Just because she's on the isles doesn't mean she automatically knows about demons. She's not an acolyte or part of the Creed," Brynnlin cut in, immediately jumping to Selene's defense.

After everything Selene's done, she didn't deserve to be categorized into that.

Maddox seemed taken aback by the vehemence in her tone. "Well that's reassuring to hear, can the same be said about you not being in the Creed?"

She snorted at his blatant question. "I told you, it wasn't what you thought it was."

Maddox perched on one of the stools by the counter and held out his arms. "I'm all ears."

Brynnlin debated for a moment before answering, "The short version for now—I wasn't brought to these gods forsaken isles by choice, but for the time being I have certain business here. Both for protection and to gain trust, Selene gave me this sigil," she gestured to the mark that peeked through her shirt. "It's almost an exact replica of the Creed's brand, but it's not real."

She didn't miss the tension easing from Maddox's shoulders at her answer.

"What business requires you to have a sigil?"

She grimaced. "That's a loaded question with a complicated answer."

"I can handle complicated."

Despite herself, Brynnlin smiled. He didn't even know the beginning of complicated.

"Look it's—"

"Maddox, Brynnlin," Ryker's raised voice echoed from down the hall. "You two might want to come see this."

Brynnlin frowned, and she jogged past Maddox and into the far hall.

She spotted Ryker and Zale standing in front of the office.

"What in the Hells do you two think you're doing back here?" She glared at them and shoved them out of the way, "This area is private..."

Her sentence trailed off as she got a good look at the room in front of her.

Drawers were pulled open. The filing cabinet was knocked over. Glass and papers covered the floor.

But what had Brynnlin's blood run cold were the words carved into the wall.

Return what you stole.

"What the fuck?" Maddox's words barely registered.

She couldn't stop staring at the wall and at the implication of one single sentence.

It wasn't very difficult to decipher the meaning. And she

might not know who was behind this, but she sure as Hells knew what they were after.

Shit.

Shit.

This was not good.

How did they get into the office?

How did they get through the wards Selene had in place?

And none of the alarms were triggered.

Selene had said she just got the book hours ago. Yet they were already this close.

If they didn't find it here, did that mean they would go to the apartment...

Her stomach turned as horror consumed her.

Gods.

The apartment.

Selene.

"Brynnlin," Maddox grasped her shoulder and the sound of his voice pulled her out of her panic. "What the Hells is going on?"

Brynnlin forced breath into her lungs.

Act now.

Freak out later.

"I need to grab something, and then we need to leave now." She ran into the office and grabbed one of the bags that was thrown on the floor. Rushing to the desk, she shoved some papers into it, before grabbing a few small books and shoving them into the bag as well.

She didn't have time to grab more.

Couldn't risk it.

She cursed Selene for refusing to have any communications between the shop and the apartment.

She couldn't even warn her.

She had to get back now.

She turned back to the three men staring at her with varying looks of concern and suspicion.

"Come with me or don't, but it's not safe here." That was the only explanation she bothered to give them before sprinting past them.

She needed to get to the apartment.

And for the first time in a long time, she prayed to the gods.

Please don't let her be too late.

CHAPTER 5

"She'd already accepted her fate and knew what she was getting involved with."

BRYNNLIN PUSHED herself to move faster. She ignored the shouts and curses directed at her as she shoved past people on the street. She didn't care about them or how she might look right now.

All that mattered was getting to the apartment.

She thought she heard Maddox's voice calling for her, but she wasn't stopping to find out. She didn't even slow down.

She just had to make it.

That was the only thought she allowed herself.

Any other alternative...

She couldn't stomach it.

If Selene wasn't okay...

No.

She violently shook her head to clear that notion before that image could take root.

She wouldn't allow it.

She wasn't losing anyone else.

Not today.

The few miles that normally seemed like a short distance suddenly felt endless. Even when the corner of her building finally came into view, the tension still didn't ease. The door bounced off the wall as Brynnlin threw it open. She raced through the lobby to the stairwell. She bounded up the stairs, not slowing, even after she reached the third floor. She burst through their door, and her gaze swung around widely, needing to find Selene.

When she didn't see her, panic started to creep in.

No. No. No.

Brynnlin aimed for the hall. "Sele—"

"Shit!" Selene's shriek registered a second too late, and Brynnlin barreled right into her.

Selene's hand shot out to the wall to steady herself. "Goddess! Brynn, you scared the Three Hells out of me."

Brynnlin didn't respond.

She couldn't.

Words evaded her as relief washed over. Her shoulders sagged, and her muscles fell weak with the adrenaline starting to sweep away.

Selene was okay.

More than okay, as Selene stood across from her clutching a hand to her chest and glaring at her. Without thinking, Brynnlin threw her arms around Selene.

"You're okay." She hadn't realized she said the words aloud until Selene responded.

"What? Of course I'm okay—"

The door to the apartment burst open again, cutting off Selene.

They both spun around to see three men pushing their way into the living room. Brynnlin cringed.

Maddox did follow her after all.

But surprisingly, he wasn't the biggest concern at the moment.

"What in the Hells?" The low growl came from Selene.

Out of the corner of her eye, Brynnlin caught Selene raising a hand.

Shit.

Brynnlin threw herself between the two.

"Wait. No. Stop." Brynnlin's words stammered as she put up her hands, trying to prevent any escalation.

Her two worlds were colliding. Past and present were about to clash, and too many emotions were racing through her.

"Just wait." Brynnlin tried again, her gaze swinging between the two.

Maddox was walking towards her with a fierce frown. That was nothing compared to the deadly glare Selene was shooting at the trio.

"Brynn, get behind me now," Selene ordered.

"It's not like that."

Selene scoffed. "You come running in here terrified and all torn up. I don't think so. I promise you're okay now. Whatever they did, they'll pay."

Brynnlin's heart hammered in her chest as she realized how bad this actually looked. It would take a lot of convincing to calm down Selene.

"Are you threatening us?" The low voice came from behind her.

Brynnlin let her shoulders drop, and her eyes fell shut as Ryker's words surrounded them.

That definitely wasn't going to calm anyone down.

Selene's glare turned into a cold smile.

"Ryker, shut up." Maddox snapped, before Selene could

respond. "Brynnlin, would you care to explain what is going on, and why you took off like that?"

The reminder of what started all of this had Brynnlin stiffening.

"That's not your concern." Her words came out harsh, but she didn't care. She didn't want him anywhere near this. There was already too much at risk.

"The fuck it isn't. You're my concern."

Selene's focus whipped towards Maddox at his statement, and her eyes narrowed. "Burning Hells, she is. Who do you think you are?"

Maddox side-eyed Selene. "I would ask the same, but you must be the esteemed Selene Aspen."

"That didn't answer my question," Selene shot back.

Brynnlin chewed on her lip at their exchange. In all of her wildest dreams of seeing her family again, it definitely wasn't like this.

"Selene, this is Maddox."

"Maddox," Selene said the name slowly, before her eyes widened. "The cousin?"

Brynnlin could only nod her head.

"What? How is that possible?" Selene's stance seemed to relax the slightest as shock swept over her.

Brynnlin moved closer to Selene and lowered her voice. "I know it's a lot to take in, and I'll explain, but we have a bigger issue on our hands."

"What are you talking about? What issue?"

Brynnlin glanced at the three men flanking the hall. She didn't relish the idea of elaborating in front of them. Yet she sincerely doubted they would leave to give her some privacy.

With a quick exhale, she turned back to her friend.

"The bookstore was broken into," her words were soft, meant only for Selene, but she knew everyone could hear her.

"What?" Selene's features fell, and Brynnlin could see a flash of hurt in her eyes.

She grimaced and hated what she had to say next. "Your office was trashed. They know what you have...they..." she swallowed to ease the dryness in her throat, "I thought they came here."

She had been around Selene long enough to read her expressions. She could tell when fear replaced the sadness. And that fear was more worrisome than anything else.

Selene stared back at her in quiet horror.

"Who's they? What did you take?" Maddox's raised voice was thick with tension and broke the silence.

Brynnlin broke eye contact with Selene to look over at him.

"I told you, that's not your concern."

"And I told you, that was bullshit."

"This isn't up for debate." She forced herself to remain stoic. If Maddox had any idea she was trying to protect him, he would never let the matter drop. He'd probably try even harder to get involved.

Maddox's frown intensified. "I don't recall asking your permission. Now, are you ready to tell me what's going on?"

"No."

"Fine." He leaned against the wall and crossed his arms. "I've got all day, I can wait."

She glared at him. "Gods, have you always been this difficult."

"Must be a family trait."

"You only came here for one reason," she snapped and pointed at Selene. "That reason is right there. But she can't help you. I'm sorry, but you're going to have to figure out your demon problem another way."

"You think I give a shit about the demon right now. Who are you running from?"

Brynnlin ignored his question. Ignored him.

She focused on Selene. "We can't stay here, you should pack. It's only a matter of time until they find the apartment."

Selene looked conflicted. "I have precautions in place, they shouldn't be able to find the apartment but..." Selene shook her head, "You're right, we shouldn't push our luck. We can stay elsewhere for the time being. I'll grab the essentials."

Brynnlin tried to walk further down the hall, but Maddox jerked away from the wall and blocked her path.

"It's time for you to go home now," she said before he could say anything.

Maddox's mouth twitched upwards, catching her off guard. "I didn't just find you to lose you all over again. If you think I would ever go home without you, you don't remember me very well."

"That's not my home anymore, Maddox."

"And this is?" he hissed softly. "You don't belong here Brynnlin, you never did. And I don't know what brought you here, but unlike some, you have a life and a family back on the mainland. Whatever you're running from, we can protect you. Or does that mean nothing to you?"

She flinched at his words, but met his hard stare. "Less than an hour ago, as far as I was aware, I didn't have anything for me on the mainland. And I'm so incredibly happy you're alive, I really am. But I can't abandon everything here, there's too much at stake."

"What could possibly be more important than your family?" Maddox growled.

He had no idea.

Everything she's done...

"This is for my family."

"Is it? Because I'm standing right here, Brynnlin."

She did her best to ignore the hurt in his tone. "This isn't about you."

"Then what could it possibly be about?"

"Three Hells Maddox, do you ever stop?" She couldn't stop herself from yelling.

"No," he yelled back, "not when you—"

"You don't get it," she cut him off.

"You don't think I would understand? If you'd just—"

"They need to pay."

The room fell silent. Brynnlin closed her eyes as she realized what she said.

"Brynn." Selene's warning was unnecessary.

She revealed too much. She never meant to say that.

Maddox sucked in a slow breath and asked softly, "Who needs to pay?"

"Move."

"Who needs to pay?" he asked again.

"I said move."

"Is it the people after you? Do they need to pay?" His questions didn't stop, and her patience was thinning. "Is that why you stole from them?" he tried again. "Or does it have to do with the club?"

"Maddox, for the love of the gods, enough!" Her bellow stunned him into silence. "Can't you see I'm trying to protect you!"

The coldness in his expression melted away, and he reached for her. "Brynnlin."

"Don't." She jerked away. "Just go home. I need you to go home."

"I can't do that. Not unless you're coming with me."

Brynnlin looked up at him and didn't bother to hide her emotions. She let him see it all. The fear. The exhaustion. The determination.

"I can't leave, I've come too far to throw it all away now. I know you don't understand—"

"Then tell me."

"I can't."

"Brynnlin."

To Hells with it.

"Maddox, who do you think needs to pay?" she finally cried out. "They took everything from me. He killed everyone. And if I leave now, all of it will be for nothing."

Maddox's face paled as understanding clicked. "That's what this is about. You know who's responsible for that night?" His question was whispered.

"Not specifically," she admitted, "but, we think we know how to find him."

For the first time, Maddox was quiet for a few moments. Brynnlin reflected on her outburst. She shouldn't have said anything. There was no way Maddox was going to let this go. And while part of her admits that she wanted Maddox to know the truth to why she was resisting, she still should have held out. Before she could react, Maddox's arms were around her, enveloping her into a hug.

"I'm so sorry." His quiet words caught her by surprise.

"What?"

"All this time, I've been living my life, mourning their deaths, mourning yours. And you've been living through the Hells, fighting for them."

She pulled away and the pain in his eyes gutted at her. "Maddox, please don't be sorry. You couldn't have known. And yes, I'm fighting for them. But I'm fighting for myself, too."

She didn't want him taking any of the guilt. She also didn't want him knowing she needed this to keep her going. Some things were just too dark to share.

"Why wouldn't you want to tell me this?" He shook his

head. "You don't want me involved." He answered his own question.

"No, I don't." She was honest with him.

"That's not your decision to make," his tone turned hard, "consider me completely involved."

She glared at him. "That's not how this works."

"Oh, but it is. If you're involved, I'm involved. I would never abandon you while you're obviously in trouble. And you're not just avenging your family, it's my family, too."

She shook her head. It didn't matter that if roles were reversed, she would do the same thing. She wasn't dragging him into this. She refused to bring danger right to his door. She'd already accepted her fate and knew what she was getting involved with.

But he didn't.

He deserved better.

"For the last time, go home, Maddox." She shoved past him, but he grabbed her arm and spun her back around.

"Stop trying to push me away. I'm not going anywhere without you. So, if we need to leave, fine, grab your shit and we'll all leave."

She took in the blue eyes that stared at her and at the sharp features of his face. A face she never thought she'd see again, and her composure cracked. "Why can't you see that I'd never forgive myself if something happened to you?"

His eyes softened. "Why can't you see that I'd never forgive myself if I let you disappear again? Especially knowing that I can help you."

"Maddox..."

"No," he interrupted her, "no more excuses. We all have someone to fight for in this, someone who deserves retribution. We may not have found who was responsible, but that doesn't mean we didn't look. You just happened to be more tenacious."

"You say that like it's an insult."

He offered her a small chuckle. "Never. It's one of your strongest qualities."

Brynnlin was quiet as she absorbed all of this. Could this really be the way to move forward? Could she accept his help? She had no doubt their resources would be invaluable.

"You have to know how dangerous this is, the people we've been dealing with..."

"Brynnlin, stop trying to change my mind. I know what dealing with the Creed entails."

She looked past Maddox, at Selene who had remained quiet during all of this. "What about Selene?"

"What about her?" Maddox turned around and stared at Selene while he answered Brynnlin's question. "She would come with us, of course. Didn't you guys say you couldn't stay here anymore?"

"Nothing is offered that freely," Selene cut in. "What would that cost me?"

"I won't lie, we were hoping you'd be able to assist us with a situation we have. However, our offer remains even if you decline."

Selene chewed on her lip. "What situation? I'm already helping Brynn find the other Draíothe."

"It's what led us here in the first place, we have a demon we need tracked down. We were hoping you might be our solution."

Selene's eyes narrowed. "And if I can't?"

Maddox shrugged. "Are you willing to try?"

Selene didn't answer right away. "And if I can?"

"We'd be extremely grateful," Maddox admitted. "And we can offer you a large reward for your services."

Selene scoffed. "I don't need nor want your money."

"But you want something?"

Selene shifted her weight. "Would you be able to offer me protection instead?"

Maddox stilled. "I thought that would go without saying, but if you need to hear it...absolutely."

Selene's relief was clear to see, while Brynnlin's stomach sank at their exchange. She eyed Selene with annoyance. There was only one reason Selene would actively seek protection for something, and it was from whoever she stole that damn book from.

Which she still hadn't shared.

They were going to be having words over that later.

Maddox turned back to Brynnlin. "I think that settles everything."

She hesitated.

Was this really happening?

Was she really going to leave with them?

Did she have any other choice?

"I need a minute," she said and started for her room. This time Maddox didn't stop her. She grabbed Selene's hand and pulled her along. Once enclosed in the room, she collapsed on the bed as her mind raced in circles.

"So, that was a lot," Selene sat next to her.

Brynnlin snorted. "That's an understatement."

"Are you alright?"

Brynnlin shook her head. "I don't even know how to answer that right now."

"You're right, that was a stupid question."

"Are we really leaving?" She couldn't be the only one that felt like they were jumping head first off a cliff.

Selene considered the question. "What other options are there? You said it yourself, we can't stay here."

"I know. But what about everything we've worked towards?"

"It sounded like Maddox is ready to pick up where you're at without hesitation. And I'm sure their resources are vast."

She didn't want to admit that Selene was probably right about that.

"What about the club? If I just disappear, Zamir won't be happy. And if I don't keep fighting, I won't get an invite to the inner island."

"Well the fights might not be necessary, not if we find another way to get to the Draíothe. And you just passed into the qualifiers which don't start until next month, that gives us a little bit of time. We can see where we're at then."

"That might work," Brynnlin admitted, "but what about the whole thing with the demon? I know Maddox probably caught you off guard with that. Is that something you'd even be able to do?"

"I don't know," Selene answered honestly. "I might be able to, and if they can identify the type of demon it'd be more helpful. Now stop with the questions, you're just making excuses at this point. This is our best and safest option."

Brynnlin groaned. "Stop making so much sense."

"What's this really about?"

Brynnlin sighed and whispered. "What if I'm not ready to go back?"

Selene nodded in understanding and sympathy danced in her eyes. She grabbed her hand and gave it an encouraging squeeze. "You always knew you'd go back one day. And you're not alone. Whatever's waiting for you over there, we'll handle it. Together. And you said it yourself last night, we're finally starting to get somewhere. This is how we keep moving forward."

Brynnlin only wished it would be that simple.

CHAPTER 6

"The darkness was back, and it wasn't letting go."

MADDOX WATCHED Brynnlin walk down the hall, and he fought his instinct to follow her. She made it clear she needed a moment.

This was a lot for her.

Hells, this was a lot for all of them.

"Maddox."

Ryker's voice pulled his attention away from the closed door.

"A word?" Ryker inclined his head in the opposite direction of the rooms.

Maddox frowned and looked back to the door, but he followed Ryker towards the entrance of the apartment. Around the corner, Ryker turned, and Maddox barely held in a sigh at Ryker's expression.

This was going to be a fun conversation.

Ryker didn't waste a moment, crossing his arms and jumping to his concern. "Is this a smart course of action?"

"Are you questioning something specific?"

"Maddox, I'm being serious," Ryker's tone was full of warning. "Shouldn't we consider the repercussions of bringing them back with us?"

Maddox's temper flared.

"She's my cousin, Ryker," he bit out, "do you expect me to leave her here?" Even saying those words made his stomach sick.

"I just think—"

"And for arguments sake," he didn't let Ryker finish, "we'll set aside that she's family. Selene is willing to try and track down that demon only because of Brynnlin. Were you planning on eradicating that issue for us instead?"

Ryker ran a hand through his hair and glared. "She's a Draíothe living on the isles, that we know nothing about. And we're going to lead her right back to the palace? Maddox, be smart."

"What other options do we have?" Maddox hissed back. "We're running out of time. And Brynnlin obviously trusts her, and I trust her judgment."

"How can you say that though? She was what, thirteen, the last time you saw her? How can you trust her judgment?" Ryker's agitation was clear in his tone.

Maddox took a steadying breath as he stared at Ryker before him. Ryker didn't get it, didn't understand everything he was feeling right now.

"It doesn't matter how long it's been, I trust her," his voice turned hard. He was aware there were still things he didn't know. He had no idea what's been going on this past decade. He had his doubts earlier, but he saw the emotion Brynnlin tried so hard to hide. The pain.

She never stopped fighting for their family. Anything else that happened over the years, didn't matter, not to him.

He trusted her.

Ryker didn't seem as convinced and continued to argue. "You know she's still keeping things from you. Burning Hells, someone is after them, and you're going to bring that right to our doorstep?"

"Do you expect me to turn my back on her?"

"Of course not," Ryker growled, "I'm only reminding you that we have an entire realm to think of."

"Yes, we do. A realm that is being traumatized by a demon on the loose. And a realm that has suffered continuous attacks from the Creed. The same Creed, that Brynnlin," he emphasized her name, "you know that girl in the other room that you don't want to trust, has managed to infiltrate." He stretched the truth on that one a little—he wasn't completely sure of her association with them, but he was able to piece together that she was working against them. "And she's also managed to possibly track down the Draíothe who was responsible for that horrific night. Something we never even got close to discovering. Don't even try to tell me that doesn't mean anything to you."

"You know it does," Ryker snapped. "And I fully plan on assisting with that in any way I can. But that doesn't mean that I have to blindly go along with bringing two strangers straight back to our capital. I was there in that alleyway, I saw her in that ring, maybe she's not with the Creed, but that doesn't make her innocent."

With every word Ryker threw at him, Maddox's frustration only grew. This conversation was over.

"We're done here. I don't need you to trust Brynnlin, but you will not disrespect her. We have no idea what she's been through. What she had to do to survive. Do you think it was easy? Cause I sure as fuck don't. So what if her hands are dirty, ours sure as shit aren't clean either." Maddox shook his head,

Ryker was like a brother to him, but Brynnlin was family, too. "They're coming back with us. That's a godsdamn order."

Ryker's jaw clenched, yet he backed off. "Okay Maddox, have it your way. But just so you know, it's not just me, Kodak will need an explanation for this."

"And he'll get one."

Of all things, convincing Kodak of his decision was not one of his worries. Unlike his biggest concern at the moment, getting Brynnlin to go with them. She was still hiding in the other room. He stalked back down the hall and knocked on the door.

"Brynnlin, start packing if you haven't. The less time we spend here the better."

Silence radiated from the other side.

"Brynnlin." He knocked again.

"I heard you." Her muffled voice answered back.

Tension eased from his chest. She might not like it, but at least she seemed to be going along with it. Another minute passed, and Selene slipped out of the room. She seemed surprised to see him still standing there.

"She, well," Selene chewed on her bottom lip, and her hazel eyes bounced between him and the door, "she's grabbing her things."

"Is she alright?"

"Would you be?"

No, probably not.

"But she will be," Selene added on, "once the shock of today fades, you'll see."

Maddox offered a small smile. He knew Brynnlin would be fine, but it was obvious how much Selene cared about her. When they first entered the apartment Selene had been ready to defend Brynnlin in an instant, and now her concern was evident.

"She's lucky to have you," Maddox meant every word. "I don't know the history of your friendship, but thank you for being there for her."

Selene reared back, and her eyes narrowed before softening a second later. "We're there for each other. Now if you'll excuse me, I also need to grab a few things if you're so adamant about leaving."

"I am."

Selene raised an eyebrow and pointed to the door across from Brynnlin's.

The door he was blocking.

Maddox stepped aside. "Twenty minutes. Then we leave."

Selene's laugh filled the hallway. "You want us to pack up our lives. We'll take as long as we need."

The closing of the door didn't allow him to respond, but Maddox chuckled to himself. They would both fit in just fine at the palace.

It turned out his deadline was unnecessary.

They were ready in fifteen.

BRYNNLIN CHECKED HER BAG AGAIN. She couldn't help but feel like she was missing something.

She had heard Maddox tell Selene twenty minutes.

It had already been ten.

She looked around the still very full room. There was so much she was leaving behind. She didn't need it, she knew she had everything that mattered, but that didn't stop the ache in her chest. She stared at the meager belongings she had managed to accumulate over the years. It might not be much to some, yet she had still managed to build a life for herself despite her circumstances.

She hated that she was being forced to leave it all behind. It didn't matter if it had been a good or bad life. She was having to run.

Again.

At least this time she wasn't alone. She grabbed the strap of her packed bag before dropping it.

Maybe there was another way.

They could manage...

She shook her head. She was stalling. She needed to go.

Now.

She took a deep breath and released it slowly. She could do this. She was ready.

Sort of.

She slung her bag over her shoulder and marched out before any more doubt could cloud over her. In the living room, Maddox was pacing across the small room. Zale was sprawled out on the couch, and Ryker was leaning against the wall, brooding.

They all looked up at her entrance.

Maddox stopped pacing and relief flashed in his eyes. "Ready?"

"As I'll ever be."

Out of the corner of her eye, she caught Ryker's jaw clench at her response.

She frowned at him.

He ignored her.

She didn't push the issue, he'd been permanently pissed off since she met the man, this was probably his usual state.

"You were pretty insistent about getting out of here, I assume you all have a way for us to get to Sidhe?"

Brynnlin waited for one of them to answer. It was no small distance between the isles and the mainland. She figured they had some form of transportation to get back.

Maddox gestured to the couch. "He's right there."

She raised an eyebrow in question.

Zale smirked at her obvious reluctance. "Relax, I can get us out of here."

Brynnlin tried to guess which magic he possessed that would allow him to get them to Sidhe. To be able to travel that great of a distance...

"You're from Saol," she blurted out and couldn't keep the surprise out of her voice. She had assumed he was Sidhen and was an elemental wielder like the others.

To be from Saol though...

The citizens of Saol were well known for their powerful abilities. With Saol being where the *Crann Bethadh*at was planted, their magic was drawn from the very tree itself. Unlike other realms, whose magic was drawn from relics. By pulling energy straight from the tree, a Saolian's cosmic magic was vast. Some of their capabilities ranged from warping matter, manipulating spatial energy, and she heard a few could even glimpse visions of the future.

"I was born there, yes," Zale confirmed, though the look in his eyes told her to drop it.

Yet it wasn't the fact that he was from Saol that surprised her. It was the fact that he was obviously involved with Kodak. It was rare to find common citizens living within a different realm than they were born. For someone of the higher class, and with powerful magic, to be working for a different ruler...

That was almost unheard of.

She might have been away for a while, but her father had been a governor. She knew the stigmas of the upper class.

What would drive Zale to make a decision like that?

But it was clear Zale wasn't going to expand, and she of all people understood not wanting to dive into the past.

Instead, she asked, "Will it be a difficult trip?"

Zale's shoulders relaxed. "Not at all."

"That's a relief."

Selene's entrance into the living room saved her from having to say more. Brynnlin turned towards her, and Selene was all packed up as well.

Maddox cleared his throat. "Now that we're all ready, let's go home."

Even though Brynnlin knew this was coming, her heart still stuttered at the words. Silently, Maddox approached her and took the bag she was carrying. He gestured towards the door.

This was really it.

Zale stepped up, also going to grab a bag from Selene.

With a smirk she handed over one. "You can take this one."

Zale rolled his eyes, but as he lifted the bag he frowned, "Damn woman, what's in this thing? Rocks?"

"Close," Selene grinned, "grimoires. A lot of them."

Zale grumbled and hefted the bag over his shoulder. "Let's go before they decide to pack the whole apartment."

It was Brynnlin's turn to roll her eyes at his dramatics, and they all shuffled out the door. She threw one longing glance back at the apartment. How many nights had she curled up on the couch with Selene at her side? How many times did these walls protect her from the outside world? And more importantly when would she ever see it again?

Deep down she knew the answer would be a while. And yet ever so slowly, she still shut the door, accepting her fate.

Out in the hall, Ryker started leading them to the stairwell that would take them to the roof. He talked softly to Zale, while she stayed a few paces behind with Selene and Maddox.

Maddox looked down at her, "Are you ready?"

"Yes," she said with much more confidence than she actually felt.

"Good, it's where you belong."

Brynnlin didn't argue. She didn't necessarily know if she agreed, either.

Luckily, Maddox didn't seem like he expected a response.

It was a short trip to the roof of the building. They circled around Zale. He kneeled down and touched a hand to the ground. Brynnlin watched in fascination as magic flowed off of him. Static electricity surrounded them, disrupting the still air, and with a flash of light, a portal opened before them.

Zale stood and turned his attention to her and Selene, "You'll walk straight through, you might feel disoriented, but it will pass after a few minutes. It's normal, don't be alarmed."

Selene nodded her head and stepped forward.

Ryker's hand shot out, stopping her from going further. "Wait."

"Ryker." Maddox warned.

Ryker rolled his eyes and pointed to Brynnlin, "She needs to get rid of that thing before we show up there. We're already going to have enough questions as is, she can't be there with that brand. Hide it or some shit."

Brynnlin's head reeled back before she remembered Ryker had been in the bathroom when she explained to Maddox that the mark across her neck wasn't a real Creed brand.

She said as much.

Ryker only shrugged. "Wonderful, then it'll be easy to remove. You won't need it at the palace."

She hesitated, her gaze shooting to Selene.

Selene stared back at her with wide eyes. "He's right, it'll draw too much attention."

Her chest started to feel tight. "Can you change it to some-thing else?"

Ryker's brow furrowed at her question. "Can Selene not remove it?"

Brynnlin didn't acknowledge him and continued to stare at Selene.

Selene offered a tight-lipped smile. "It'll be okay, you don't need it anymore."

Her heart hammered in her chest, and she shook her head. "Selene, that's not a good idea."

Selene grabbed her hand and pulled her to the side.

"If you keep arguing, they're going to know something is up," Selene whispered and frowned. "You'll be okay without it. I trust you. Now you need to trust yourself."

Brynnlin's mind raced as she tried to think of an alternative. The sigil Selene gave her as a cover might not look like much, but to her it was everything. She knew she couldn't have it there, but she couldn't get rid of it.

"What if you get rid of this one, but once we're at the palace you replace it with something else? Where people can't see it?" she added.

Selene seemed to think it over.

"I can do that," she agreed, "I'll need some prep time, but yes, that should work."

"Okay," Brynnlin relaxed.

"I still need to remove this one though," Selene cautioned her.

Brynnlin forced herself to nod. There was no way around it. "That's okay, I can make it a few hours."

Selene studied her before taking a deep breath. Selene put a hand over the mark she gave Brynnlin a few years ago. Brynnlin squared her shoulders and stayed quiet as Selene began murmuring something incomprehensible. Brynnlin's stomach dipped when a tingling sensation flowed through her.

But she stayed still. She could do this.

Her confidence faded when her skin started to prickle with

small stabs of pain. That was all it took before the real agony began.

A searing heat filled her body from the inside. She tried to gasp for breath, but everything burned. She clutched for Selene as she fell to her knees, her muscles giving out. Her mouth was open though no sound was coming out. She barely registered Maddox yelling something before she felt hands grab her shoulders. She couldn't focus on him.

The fire inside her was expanding, coursing through every vein. She couldn't think past the pain. Shadows danced across her eyes, blurring her vision. She tried to fight the pain, but it was too much.

After a moment that raging fire started to fade, a cold numbness taking its place. She didn't know which was worse.

Her eyes closed for a moment, succumbing to the darkness trying to welcome her. She forced her eyes back open, fighting the heaviness. Maddox was above her, his mouth was moving, but there were no words.

She wanted to answer him. To tell him everything was okay.

But this was what she'd been afraid of.

The darkness was back, and it wasn't letting go.

Not this time.

She lost the battle with her eyelids, and slowly, everything faded to black.

CHAPTER 7

"She needs you."

MADDOX WATCHED in horror as Brynnlin dropped to her knees before them. He rushed to her side, his hands going to her shoulders to support her.

"Brynnlin," he couldn't help that her name came out harsh, she was scaring the shit out of him.

One minute, Selene was supposed to be removing the brand. The next, Brynnlin was falling to the ground. She lifted her head to look at him, but her gaze was unfocused. Pain clouded her eyes, and she shuddered against him. Her lips started to move, yet silence surrounded them.

"Brynnlin," he shook her shoulders.

Her eyes fell shut, and his stomach dropped as she collapsed against him.

"Brynnlin," he tried again.

No response.

His heart hammered in his chest. He just found her, he couldn't lose her. His fingers went to her throat and relief flooded through him when he felt her pulse. But her skin was burning up.

"What did you do?" he snarled at Selene.

Selene didn't answer. Didn't even look at him.

Her gaze was focused on Brynnlin, and her eyes welled with unshed tears. In an instant, Ryker was behind Selene. His arm locked around her, and his knife went to her throat.

"Just say the word, Maddox."

"No," Maddox rushed out. They had no hope of finding out what happened if Selene was dead. "She's the only one that knows what the Hells she just did."

Selene didn't fight against Ryker, Maddox started to question if she was even aware of her situation. She still hadn't looked away from Brynnlin.

Maddox forced himself to be rational.

This wasn't adding up.

He might have just met her, but he saw how Selene was with Brynnlin. She wouldn't hurt her. Not like this.

"Selene," he said her name slower and tried to remain calm, "I need you to tell me what just happened."

"I don't know," Selene finally answered, and Maddox had to strain to hear the whispered words.

Selene started to shake her head frantically. "It's wasn't supposed to hurt her," she rambled, "we were only removing the mark, she was—"

"Selene," Maddox barked. "I need you to focus. We're going to get her to a healer, and you're going to tell them anything and everything about that mark. Am I clear?"

Maddox didn't wait for a response. He scooped Brynnlin off the ground and cradled her to his chest.

"We're going to get you help," he promised under his breath.

"Through the portal. All of you, now," he ordered the others.

Zale's portal delivered them straight into the foyer of the palace.

"Zale, find Vee. Have her meet me upstairs," he snapped over his shoulder, rushing up the stairs. "Ryker, find Kodak, he needs to know what's going on. Selene, you're with me."

He looked down at Brynnlin again. He could feel her breathing, she was just unconscious. Upstairs, he barged into one of the bedrooms.

"Fuck," the snarl burst out of him as he carefully laid Brynnlin onto the bed.

In the matter of minutes it took them to get her here, streaks of ebony webbed their way up Brynnlin's arms, starting at her fingertips. She was pale, and even her hair appeared lighter and was whitening before their eyes.

What in the Three Hells was happening to her?

He ran a hand through his hair, and his stomach knotted when Selene rushed to Brynnlin's side. Tears streamed down her face as she quietly begged Brynnlin to be okay.

"Verenna is a healer and a very skilled one at that, she'll help Brynnlin." He didn't know if he said the words to comfort her or himself. Anything else he was about to say was interrupted by Zale rushing through the door.

"Vee's right behind me," Zale panted.

Thank the gods.

Verenna hurried in and stopped dead in her tracks. Her gaze shot to the bed, to Maddox, back to the bed.

"What is this?"

Maddox moved around the bed, towards his sister. "I have a lot to explain, I know, but she needs your help."

Verenna lifted a finger and pointed it at the bed. Her hand was shaking.

"Who is that?" she demanded. "I know who Zale said it was, but tell me right now that's not who I think it is." Her violet eyes filled with pain and fear. "Tell me he was lying. That you didn't bring Brynnlin back here after all this time, only for her to be dying in front me." The last word ended in a broken whisper.

Maddox hated that he couldn't tell her differently. "She needs you."

"Maddox…"

"You're the only one that can help her."

Verenna stared at him, silently. He saw the moment determination replaced her fear.

"All of you, out. I need room to work," Verenna ordered and went straight to the bed. She was focused on Brynnlin now, and Maddox knew they would only be in her way.

If anyone could fix this, it was Verenna.

They all moved towards the door.

"Not you," Verenna's sharp tone had Maddox turning around. She was looking at Selene.

Selene stopped and nodded solemnly.

Verenna glanced over her shoulder at Maddox and narrowed her eyes. "Out. I'll get you when I have an update."

Grudgingly, Maddox listened and continued to the door. Over the years, he learned it was best not to argue with her. And this wasn't a battle worth having. Verenna could handle this. She was just demanding an explanation from Selene as he shut the door.

MADDOX RESTED his head against the closed door and took a few deep breaths.

This was going to be alright. Everything was going to be

alright. Maybe if he thought it enough, he would actually believe it.

A soft beeping interrupted the quietnesses out in the hall. Maddox glanced down at his orenda band on his wrist to see the golden beads lighting up. With a sigh, he pressed one of the beads to silence it.

Ryker's voice filled the hallway. "Kodak would like to see you in his office."

Maddox gritted his teeth. "Did you fill him in?"

"I'll let you do the honors."

Ryker's voice cut off, and Maddox started down the hall. It was time to get this out of the way.

Back downstairs, he followed the well-known path to the office. Kodak's door was partially open, and he knocked once before walking in. Sunlight streamed through the windows, lighting up the large room. Kodak sat behind his desk reading through some papers. He looked up at their entrance.

"Maddox," Kodak dragged out his name. "So glad you're back, take a seat." There was a sharp edge to his voice.

"Kodak," Maddox greeted as he cautiously sat down. "How was Ossory?"

Ryker was already seated on the couch at the other end of the room, and Zale joined him.

"Boring," Kodak bit out, "now would you like to tell me what in the burning Hells is going on?"

Maddox shifted in his seat, uncomfortable at being the center of Kodak's anger. It was unusual to see Kodak riled up.

"Kodak—"

"No." Kodak slammed his fist on the desk. "You wanted to send Zale and Ryker to the meeting with Davina. I didn't want both my Minister of Intelligence and Commanding General going—especially when I was going to be gone—but I agreed with you."

"It was extremely sensitive information," Maddox started to argue. Was that what Kodak was mad about? Who went to the meeting? They couldn't have the information Davina passed on getting out. They were keeping quiet about the lost demon.

"Again, I agreed with you, and we sent them. Yet imagine my surprise to come back home to find my Chancellor, Minister, and General all gone," Kodak finished on a yell. "We are dealing with a loose demon, and you left Verenna alone, and the realm completely vulnerable. That is not her responsibility, and you put our people further at risk. To top it all off, you return with two unknown women from the isles. What is going through your godsdamn mind right now?"

Maddox clenched his jaw to keep from arguing with Kodak. Going back and forth wouldn't help anyone.

He reasoned instead, "The information Davina passed on was about the Draíothe that did the summoning, she discovered his identity."

Kodak's eyebrows raised the slightest.

Maddox shook his head. "He was found dead. However, she had knowledge of another Draíothe in the area. One that might be powerful enough to track down the demon. I couldn't send them to meet her without any reinforcements. You know how dangerous that could be, of course I went with them. And yes, I left Vee here, but she is more than capable of handling things."

The hard glint in Kodak's eyes softened the slightest. "Fine. I admit that they should not have gone to meet a Draíothe associated with the Creed alone. But there could have been other alternatives. And what of the two women upstairs?"

Maddox ran a hand threw his hair. "One of them is Selene Aspen, the Draíothe. She's willing to try and track the demon for us..."

"Why would she agree to that?" Kodak interrupted.

"For starters, she would like protection as she has enemies

within the Creed—the exact nature is still uncertain. More importantly, she has a close connection to the other woman, which is Brynnlin."

Kodak froze, his eyes widening. "Brynnlin?"

"She's alive," a ghost of a smile graced Maddox's lips. "She survived that night and has been on the isles."

"Gods, that's a miracle. And damn it Maddox, you're not off the hook. But you probably said the one thing that just saved your ass," Kodak sighed, his visible anger sliding away. "She's alive? And well?"

"I don't know. Something happened before we passed through the portal. Vee's with her now."

Kodak frowned as Maddox filled him in on the details.

"You're certain this Selene didn't do something to her?"

Maddox's expression turned grim. "I'm certain, once you meet her, you'll see. She wouldn't harm Brynnlin."

Kodak nodded. "Then the best course of action is to let Verenna determine what's ailing her. We also need to discuss how we're going to move forward."

"What do you mean?"

"I don't want anyone knowing the real reason Selene Aspen is here. Think of something that will explain her presence. And on that same note, how are we going to explain Brynnlin returning? We never discovered who ordered the attack on her parents. If they think she died, bringing her back could put her on their radar, and she could be in danger." Kodak gave him a pointed look.

That was a dilemma, yes, but nothing they couldn't solve.

"I've already been thinking about that," Maddox assured, "I want Remi to set up a new background and documents for her. With a new identity, we should be able to keep her safe."

Remi was gifted in all things digital, he could have Brynnlin set up with an identity in no time at all.

"Good," Kodak went back to the work on his desk. "Take care of that, sooner rather than later. Also keep me updated on Brynnlin's status."

"Will do," Maddox pushed off the chair and headed for the door. Remi might as well get started as soon as possible. He was almost to the door when Kodak's voice stopped him.

"And Maddox..."

He turned around to see Kodak offer him a small smile. "No matter the circumstances, I'm happy you found Brynnlin."

CHAPTER 8

"All this time..."

BRYNNLIN SLOWLY OPENED HER EYES. Sunlight and a light breeze filtered through an open window, the streams of light bouncing off unfamiliar walls. She gasped in pain as she tried to sit up, and everything came rushing back.

Selene.

The mark.

Maddox.

The portal.

Passing out.

She pushed herself further up, and her muscles screamed in protest. She was weak and sore all over.

"You're finally awake." A voice said off to her right.

Her gaze shot to the speaker.

A woman was sitting in a chair at her bedside reading. Dark hair streaked with lavender hid her face. But when she looked up, violet eyes twinkled back. Brynnlin's mind was slow to comprehend what was right in front of her.

105

There was only one other person she knew with violet eyes like that.

Her heart hammered in her chest. She was terrified to hope.

"Verenna?" Brynnlin's voice came off scratchy, her throat dry.

Verenna had been fifteen the last time Brynnlin saw her. Maddox's little sister had been her closest friend growing up. Brynnlin had used to spend her spring and summer months with her aunt and uncle, while her parents traveled during the court season. That time together had only strengthened her and Verenna's bond. They had been inseparable, until fate had dealt its cruel hand.

"Hi Brynn."

"You're alive—"

Verenna jumped onto the bed and pulled her into a crushing hug. Anything else Brynnlin was going to say was completely forgotten.

Tears burned the back of her eyes, and she blinked rapidly to stop them from falling. She clung to Verenna, too afraid to talk in fear that this would all disappear, and she would wake up from this dream.

"I can't believe you're actually here. Maddox told me a little, but I don't know how you made it. You've been alive this whole time. I'd always dreamed that I'd see you again, but I never thought it would actually happen," Verenna kept babbling, some of her words incomprehensible through her crying.

Brynnlin could only nod her head. Her body started to shake as silent tears racked through her. Never in a million years did she think she would get both Maddox and Verenna back. Brynnlin pulled away an inch and stared at Verenna, though her features were a blur through the tears.

"You're alive. You're actually alive. But how?" She needed to know. "How? You? Maddox?"

Her tears fell harder.

"Hey, it's okay." Verenna rubbed her back in a soothing gesture. "Take a breath."

Brynnlin did as she said, her body shuddering as she forced air into her lungs. She wiped at her eyes, trying to clear her blurry vision.

"How did you guys get out that night?" she asked again. She couldn't let this go. Not after she spent the last eleven years thinking they were dead.

Verenna gave her a sad smile. "We weren't there."

"What?" Brynnlin frowned at her. "Yes, you were. You, Maddox, and your parents were visiting the house that night. You had the evening meal with us. They sent me to bed, but you were all still in the study and..."

"Brynn, shh, breath," Verenna continued rubbing her back. "Don't get upset, it's not good for you. After you went to bed, Maddox took me home, we weren't there."

Brynnlin's mind raced at this information.

All this time...

They hadn't even been there? They'd been okay.

"Your parents?" she dared to ask.

Verenna's eyes cast downward. "They stayed."

Brynnlin immediately felt guilty for asking and reached for her hand. "I'm so sorry."

She knew the words offered little comfort. She said them anyway.

"Me too."

A silent moment passed between them. Yet the longer they sat there, the more Brynnlin's heart started to break.

All this time...

They'd been alive.

She missed out on so much.

She didn't know if she wanted to rejoice in this turn of

events...or if she wanted to weep at their lost time. It was a little of both.

"We've missed out on so much," she admitted out loud.

"I know." Verenna looked back up, her eyes red-rimmed. "I want to be mad at you for never coming back. But if I thought my family was dead, I guess I wouldn't return either."

Brynnlin flinched at Verenna's statement. She was sure Verenna didn't say it to make her feel guilty. It was there nonetheless.

"If I had known you guys were here, I would've done things differently."

She probably would've even risked trying to get to Sidhe.

"Maddox told me you were on the isles to track down the man who killed your parents. Was it at least worth it?" Verenna probably didn't mean for the question to come off harsh, but there was an underlying bite to her words.

Brynnlin's head whipped up, and she frowned. "I never went to those isles by choice, Verenna."

Verenna's brow furrowed, and her cheeks flushed pink. "You didn't go there to find him?"

"Gods no," Brynnlin shook her head at the absurdity. "I started looking for him, among other things, after I already ended up there."

"How did you get there?"

Brynnlin knew that question would come around eventually. It didn't mean she was ready to answer it. She played with the edge of the blanket across her lap and debated her response.

She looked up and met Verenna's pressing gaze. "I promise one day, I'll tell you everything that happened. But not today. Not right now."

She knew Verenna wanted an explanation, but she wasn't

digging into the story of her past. It wasn't pretty. And everything else was too raw right now.

"But—"

"Vee," she warned, "the past is ugly, let's leave it there for a little while."

Verenna pursed her lips and looked like she wanted to argue.

"Fine," she eventually agreed.

"Thank you," Brynnlin sighed and pushed herself up to sit against the headboard. She immediately groaned as pain shot down her back.

Verenna sprang forward to help.

"You need to be careful," she chided and put a pillow behind Brynnlin's back for support. "Your body's been through an ordeal."

Brynnlin winced and tried to get comfortable. "What even happened?"

"You don't remember?"

"Some," she admitted. "I know Selene was removing a sigil for me, and it went to shit."

Verenna rolled her eyes. "Is it even worth lecturing you on what a stupid idea that sigil was?"

"Hey," Brynnlin frowned, "I'd like to inform you that the sigil worked for years and was necessary to my well-being."

"I'm not messing around, Brynn," Verenna turned serious, "that could've killed you. You were dying when you showed up. I was at your side for fourteen hours until you finally stabilized."

Brynnlin remained quiet. She hadn't known she'd been out for that long. She knew the sigil was a risk, but going without it seemed worse.

She swallowed carefully. "Did Selene tell you what it was?"

Verenna glared at her. "Yes, she told me what it was, and how you guys used it as an inhibitor on your magic." Verenna shook her head again. "Why in the Hells would you purposely block your own magic like that?"

Brynnlin held her head high. "I did it to survive."

She wasn't going to apologize for her decision.

Had it been a risk? Yes.

It also kept her alive.

"Well you almost didn't," Verenna snapped back. "Don't ever do some shit like that again. Blocking your magic isn't going to get rid of it, it'll only make it worse. It needs an outlet, and if you don't start giving it one, it's going to destroy you."

It was Brynnlin's turn to roll her eyes. "Don't pretend my magic is like everyone else's."

Verenna's gaze softened. "Magic is magic, even yours. It needs an outlet, or it'll consume you."

Brynnlin looked away and fidgeted with the blanket in her lap.

Consume her?

It was too late for that.

It was back.

She could feel it.

Her skin was warmer. She was on edge. The details of the room were more vivid. Even the darkened corners of the room shifted with her attention, as if the shadows had a mind of their own. It was like a part of her had been locked away, but now that door was sitting wide open. Restless energy flowed through her, settling within the deepest parts of her body. An endless well of power ready to be unleashed. She could sense the magic just under the surface ready for her summons.

She shoved it down. Control had never been her strong suit. And if she was ever going to live with this, it needed to be.

"It's important to me that you know why I used the sigil,"

Brynnlin said in a soft tone. "I didn't do it to be reckless. The older I got, the harder it was to control. And in the..." she paused, "...environment that I was in, if they found out I had magic they would've killed me. If they discovered what magic I had, they would have done worse. I needed to hide it, especially if I couldn't control an outburst."

Verenna grabbed her hand, "I wasn't trying to judge you, Brynn. You just scared me. I'm not going to try and figure out what happened, but I believe you when you said it wasn't pretty. Whatever you needed to do, it was the right call, because you're here now. But you can't do it again."

Brynnlin squeezed her hand in silent thanks. And then she forced herself to ask Verenna the question she'd been dreading. "I need to know if you told the others?"

"Told them what?"

"About why I was sick, the sigil blocking my magic?"

"No."

Brynnlin slumped in relief. Growing up, her parents had made it very clear that she would be in danger if people ever found out about her magic. She'd always kept it a secret. Or at least tried to. Verenna and Selene were the two living exceptions.

She studied Verenna. "Why didn't you tell them? Even after you thought I was dead, you still never said anything?"

Verenna shrugged one delicate shoulder and looked away. She played with the sheets on the bed before answering. "I promised you I'd take that secret to the grave. I fully intend on keeping that promise."

"Thank you."

"But you are going to tell them," Verenna said in a matter of fact tone. "You're an adult now, and you can trust them. They deserve to know. Especially Maddox."

"I will," she promised. "When the time is right."

"Good," Verenna said and pushed off the bed. "Now that you're fully stable, why don't I leave you to get some rest?"

"Wait," Brynnlin stopped her, "stay please. I don't want to rest. Stay and talk to me."

The last thing she wanted was to be alone.

Verenna studied her, seemed satisfied with whatever she saw, and nodded, crawling back onto the bed. "What do you want to talk about?"

"I don't know," Brynnlin sat up and pulled her knees into her chest. "What has your life been like? What'd you do after everything that happened that night?"

"For a while it was chaos," Verenna admitted and shadows danced in her eyes. "Maddox was a mess. I was a mess. We had to endure not one, not two, but five burial services. And while we were trying to mourn, Rí Atlas was pulling us in for interrogations."

"What?" Brynnlin snarled. "You're joking right?"

Verenna shook her head. "No. And I mean I get it, your father was a respected governor for him. A noble family was just killed, and we were the only surviving members. But it was rough. Luckily, Maddox and Kodak put a stop to it."

Brynnlin could only imagine. Maddox would never allow his little sister to suffer through that—and with Kodak at his back? Yeah, she didn't see that going well for Atlas.

"Surprisingly, things moved quickly after that," Verenna continued. "Atlas appointed some younger guy to govern your father's district after his death. And Maddox moved me in with him. Neither of us wanted to keep our parent's home after what happened, plus he was already living with Kodak. Kodak was more than happy to let Maddox bring me here." Verenna spread out her legs and got comfortable as she filled Brynnlin in.

"What about after that? I've missed so much of your life."

Verenna told her about moving to the palace, growing up with Maddox, and all about her training in the capital to become a healer. They ended up talking for hours and only stopped when a knock sounded on the door.

Verenna got up to answer. Brynnlin couldn't see who it was, but she heard someone tell Verenna the evening meal was ready. Verenna thanked them before closing the door again.

"Do you feel up to going downstairs to eat, or do you want food brought up?"

"No, I can go downstairs, I need to get out of this bed," she laughed. Too bad being unconscious didn't make her feel well-rested. She'd probably never be out for that long again. She pushed off the bed, her muscles aching with each stretch.

"Is the evening meal a big deal? What do I wear?" Her thoughts were a whirlwind as she tried to imagine a meal at a palace.

For the first time, it clicked that she was actually in a palace —that she was actually staying in one of the royal houses. She was under the same roof as one of the realms' rulers. It was almost too much. She'd been living on the isles—fighting for money. To go to this...

"Oh no, it's almost always just our little group. You can dress casually," Verenna rushed to reassure her. "A few months through the year, we might have court members here, but not right now. Same with the rest of Kodak's council, they all have their own homes. So it's actually pretty empty."

"Good to know." *That didn't seem too overwhelming.*

Brynnlin looked around for her bag, not seeing it anyway around the room. She needed to change, her clothes were sticking to her after sleeping in them from so long.

"Do you know what Maddox did with my bag?"

"It's in here," Verenna pointed towards a closed door that must be a closet. "But I'll grab you something of mine to change into," she walked towards the door. "Maddox made sure to have clothes bought for you. They should be here tomorrow, so you'll have your own soon."

With that, Verenna left, promising to be right back.

Brynnlin took the time alone to study the room. It was huge with the canopy bed arranged in the middle. Another door was propped open revealing an en-suite bathroom. Two dressers and a desk sat along another wall. But it was the double doors that drew her attention and had her wandering towards them.

She stepped out onto the balcony, and goosebumps prickled along her skin at the brush of cool breeze. Her breath caught at the sight in front of her.

The rest of the palace towered around her. The setting sun reflected off the creamy walls, casting the whole place in a dusky glow. Manicured gardens and a courtyard were encircled by a bronzed gate, and she could spot sentries at their posts. Outside the gate a woodland grove surrounded the property. The balcony she was on rose high above the ground, giving her the advantage to see even beyond the trees. A small town could be seen not too far out, the lights and buildings distinct against the rolling landscape.

She was enthralled by the scene, so much so that she never heard Verenna re-enter the bedroom. Not until Verenna was at her side.

"Incredible, isn't it?" Verenna asked, and Brynnlin could hear the smile in her voice. "When it gets dark and the night is clear, you can even make out some of the lights from the capital," Verenna pointed along the horizon, where the capital must be.

Brynnlin looked up at the sky and at the few stars starting to peek through. She sincerely hoped tonight was one of those nights. Her father's estate had been isolated, and she'd never really been allowed to go to any of the cities. To be able to see a capital's lights, even from the distance, would be surreal.

Verenna nudged her side, "The clothes are on the bed. Go ahead and change. I'll wait outside for you in the hall."

Brynnlin took one last sweep and went back to the bedroom. She stripped quickly and put on the new clothes. The maroon pants were silk and soft against her skin. They were a little loose, but cuffed at her ankles, hiding the extra length. The shirt was a fitted, black, long sleeve that was made out of the same material and just as soft. Even in its simplicity, the outfit was much more extravagant than the ragged shirt and cotton leggings she had just discarded. Verenna forgot shoes, so she searched the closet and found some leather flats. These would have to do.

Outside the door, she followed Verenna as they made their way down the hallway towards a set of stairs. Verenna stopped at one of the doors they passed.

"The evening meal is ready," she called out as she knocked.

Selene walked out. Her eyes immediately landed on Brynnlin, and a smile lit up her face. "You're up. How are you feeling?"

Brynnlin smiled back. "Better and hungry."

"Well, food awaits." Verenna said, leading them downstairs.

They passed a few staff members, all of whom stopped what they were doing to greet Verenna with smiles. Brynnlin tried not to gape as they continued on and descended the grand staircase into a huge foyer. Polished floors opened up into a throne room with high ceilings. Marble statues stood along the walls leading to the raised dais, where two silver thrones sat.

She stared in awe at the large room, and her jaw almost dropped at the artwork on the ceiling. Glorious depictions of the goddess Brigid spanned the entire length of the room.

"You coming?" Verenna interrupted and smirked as she stood waiting across the foyer that led to another hall.

Brynnlin silently nodded and hurried after her. After walking past several rooms, they turned to the dining hall. Verenna pushed through a set of double doors where a large table sat in the middle of the room. Yet Verenna kept walking through the empty room towards another door.

"We only use this for formal meals," Verenna offered in explanation.

Instead, she entered a room off the kitchen with a much more intimate setting. Inside, Maddox and Zale were seated at a small table. At the head of that table was a man she'd never seen before. There was no crown atop his head, but she knew exactly who he was.

So, this was the infamous Kodak Aichir.

One of the five rulers.

The Rí of Sidhe.

Even sitting, she could tell he was tall, like Maddox, with broad shoulders and a defined muscular build. His dress shirt was immaculately ironed and the sleeves were rolled up. His golden brown skin glistened under the dim lighting, and his long black hair was tied back away from his face.

When she stepped fully into the room, his gaze shot to her. His eyes were the most unique shade of hazel. Even from a distance, it appeared as if orange flecks danced in his eyes like fire.

"You must be Brynnlin," his voice was kind, and he offered her a warm smile. "It's a pleasure to finally meet you."

She immediately lowered her chin and bowed at the waist. She might have been gone for years, but she knew disrespecting a royal would be signing her death warrant. It didn't matter if she was Maddox's cousin or not.

"It's nice to meet you, too. Maddox used to talk so much

about you when I was younger, your...um," she stuttered, "um your highness." It sounded more like a question, and she cringed at the squeak in her voice.

Kodak chuckled softly, "There's no need for all of that, Kodak is fine. And please rise, the formality is unnecessary. Come join us for the meal."

Brynnlin straightened slowly and followed Verenna to the table. Verenna took one of the open seats on the right side, Brynnlin slid in next to her, and Selene followed suit.

Brynnlin nodded a greeting to the others.

"How are you feeling?" Maddox asked, studying her.

"I'm recovered," Brynnlin responded, keeping a neutral smile. She still felt exhausted and would never admit how hard it was just to get down the stairs. But she knew the feeling would fade. Food would be her first step to recovery.

The door was opened again, and Ryker walked in followed by a woman she didn't recognize. She must be Juniper. Verenna had filled her in on how the others made up the head of Kodak's council and had also told her about his wife, Juniper.

Ryker strode in wearing tactical pants with combat boots and some type of thinly armored vest. Juniper was dressed similarly, and they were both sweaty. They must have just come from training. She didn't recall seeing any barracks or training grounds from the balcony. They must be somewhere extending behind the palace.

A part of her was surprised that, as Ríona, Juniper took part in training. But it was a smart move. If Brynnlin was in her position, she would do the same.

Even after just training, she could see that Juniper was beautiful. Her honey brown hair was pulled into a ponytail and a few blonde pieces peaked through. Brynnlin was sitting, but she could still tell that Juniper was a good few inches taller than herself. Juniper's flawless skin was tan, and the training clothes outlined her athletic frame. Juniper smiled at Kodak, her blue eyes flashing in delight as she sat next to him.

"Nice of you to finally join us, we're starving," Zale grumbled at them.

"And yet it still doesn't inhibit your ability to complain," Ryker retorted as he crossed the room and took a seat next to Zale.

Ryker eyed Brynnlin from across the table, his lips forming a frown, but he stayed quiet. She bit her tongue to do the same. No need to start her first meal by throwing out an insult.

"Brynnlin, right?" The question came from Juniper, and Brynnlin turned to her.

"Um yes, your highness, but uh...you can call me Brynn, no one uses my full name," she stumbled through her answer, still not used to addressing royals.

Juniper smiled and continued on, "Well Brynn, it's nice to properly meet you and see you up and about. And please call me Juniper.

"It's nice to meet you, too," Brynnlin returned.

Before more could be said, two younger girls, probably in their teens, came out of the kitchen and started serving the food.

"Those are the cook's daughters, they sometimes help out around here," Verenna explained.

Brynnlin only nodded and focused on the plate that was set in front of her. Steam rose from the plate of meat and vegetables. The others talked quietly while she tried to eat politely. Gods, she was starving. Flavor danced along her tongue as she took a bite. She'd forgotten how fresh the food was here. She barely refrained from shoveling down the rest of her meal. Maybe she could bring more food up to her room. This was delicious, and she didn't have to cook it, another score.

"So Brynn, are you feeling better? Is there anything we can do to help you settle in?"

She looked up, caught off guard that someone addressed her. She had been lost in thought and hadn't realized she'd been brought into the conversation. She saw Juniper looking at her expectantly.

"Oh, I'm feeling much better, and I'm settling in just fine." Her cheeks warmed in embarrassment at being caught not paying attention, and she tried to recover. "The room you've so kindly let me stay in is wonderful."

"That's good to hear, it's yours for as long as you need. Maddox filled us in on everything going on and about your situation on the isles," Juniper's voice turned soft and sincere. "I'm sorry you had to endure that."

Brynnlin didn't know how to respond. She knew Juniper was only being kind. But it was uncomfortable that everyone knew about her life, even if they only knew the barest of details. She desperately wished to change the topic.

Luckily, Verenna came to her rescue.

"Yes, we're very lucky to have Brynn back despite everything. But let's not dwell on the past. Especially, when we have such an exciting future ahead of us."

"Exciting future?" Maddox stared at his sister in disbelief. "Not quite the word I would use when we have a demon on the loose and a Draíothe to hunt down."

Verenna's face immediately fell. "That's not what I meant. I was talking about after that all gets sorted out. I was just saying Brynn is back home, and that's exciting."

"Of course it is," Maddox said to appease her, "it's great that Brynn is home." Maddox looked at Brynnlin. "It really is."

Brynnlin offered a small smile. "Thanks, Maddox. But you're not wrong, circumstances are not in our favor. Speaking of which, what's our next move now that Selene and I are here?"

It was Kodak that answered.

"Zale has started to reach out to some contacts in regards to finding some collectors. Selene believes that will lead us in the right direction. While we wait for that, our primary order of business is finding that demon. Selene wanted to wait until you were awake, now that you're recovered there's no reason to postpone any longer."

CHAPTER 9

"Make sure not to find yourself alone with it, you especially wouldn't survive the encounter."

THE ATTENTION in the room turned to Selene as Kodak's words sank in.

It was time to track down a demon.

Brynnlin turned in her chair and offered Selene a nod of encouragement. They were putting a lot of faith and pressure on Selene being able to find this thing, but Brynnlin would help in any way she could.

Kodak cleared his throat. "One of my men was able to identify the demon from that book of yours. Are you truly going to be able to find it?"

Selene hesitated for a moment, seeming to collect herself, before finally saying, "That depends on what you mean by finding it. I'm willing to try and help locate it. But, as I'm sure you've discovered when you contacted other Draíothes, there's not a lot known about the demon race. Now I've spent years researching these things, so I know more than most. However, if you think I'll be able to summon it or send it back to the Hells, you're mistaken. I don't have the materials nor know the rituals."

Kodak paused, absorbing the information. "Locating it will be enough. If you can get us close to it, we can handle disposing of it."

Selene nodded. "Let's get started then." She pushed away from the table, "I'll be right back with the book, and you can point out which one your man identified."

"Do you need anything else?" Kodak asked.

"A map of your realm. I'd like you to show me where your men last spotted it."

"On it." Zale offered. "I'll be right back with one," he said as he left the room.

Selene hurried after him and was back within minutes, the grimoire held tightly against her chest. Brynnlin tried not to think too hard about how one small book turned their life upside down.

Zale wasn't far behind Selene, coming in with a large map in his hands. Brynnlin helped clear the table, allowing Zale to lay the map out, while Selene went to Kodak's side and started flipping through the pages.

"That one."

Everyone, Brynnlin included, pushed closer to the table to see which demon Kodak indicated.

"A pucá," Selene said under her breath.

The name didn't sound familiar to Brynnlin, and she stretched to see the image on the page. Even the roughly drawn creature wasn't recognizable.

Kodak frowned. "What do you know about it?"

"It could be a lot worse." Selene shrugged. "It's a shapeshifter, pretty low-level, but don't let that fool you.

They're known to be erratic. Violent. If it feels cornered, it will attack you."

Ryker scoffed. "Sounds familiar," his gaze met Brynnlin's across the table.

She cast him a withering glare. "Make sure not to find yourself alone with it, you especially wouldn't survive the encounter."

"Enough," Maddox huffed at them, "please continue, Selene."

Selene pursed her lips, but went on, "It lacks intelligence, it should be fairly simple to draw its attention."

"I wouldn't be so sure about that," Kodak disagreed. "The few times my men have gotten near it, they've lost it."

"Interesting, can you show me where they've been able to spot it?"

Kodak stood and rounded the table. "We're here," Kodak pointed to an area westward, indicating the palace. "But the demon seems to be keeping to this area," he circled up north. "It got close to some towns, however, it seems to be drawn to the fields. It attacked in several fields when it made its way northward."

Selene arched a brow. "What were in the fields?"

"Cattle."

"It was feeding," Selene mused.

"It killed a Hells of a lot of cattle just to feed."

Selene gave him a grim look. "Bloodlust, very common among demons, however, that will probably be the best way to get close to it."

"How's that?"

Selene ignored his question, lost in thought as she stared at the map. "How long ago was the last spotting?"

"Over a week ago, in this area," Kodak generalized a small

area on the map. "My men lost it when it disappeared in the woods up the hills. We haven't been able to find it since."

"That's where we start then," Selene strategized. "We'll survey a good spot and attempt to lure it to us, that'll be your chance to get close to it."

"And how exactly do you plan on luring it?" Ryker drawled, crossing his arms over his chest.

Selene eyed him over the table. "We're going to give it a meal."

"Risky," Maddox shook his head.

"Demons can sense blood for miles, according to my readings at least. Lay out a fresh kill, and it'll come right to you."

"That's brilliant," Brynnlin breathed, thinking it over. "Scout the area, find the best place to put the bait, and you'd create a perfect ambush."

Kodak was quiet for a long moment, his eyes scanning over the map. "I like the idea, I do. Although my concern is even if we do manage to draw it to us, I'm worried about it escaping once we engage."

Selene chewed on her lip. "I can prevent it from escaping," she offered quietly.

Kodak raised an eyebrow. "How so?"

"Once it comes to us, I can put up a ward around the area. It won't get away."

Brynnlin almost laughed at the way Kodak's eyes widened.

"You can really do that?" he asked.

Selene only nodded.

"Very impressive."

The compliment from Kodak sounded sincere, and when Selene's gaze met Brynnlin's, she winked. Brynnlin smirked. Her friend might try to sound modest, but her power was expansive.

"Ryker, pull up this section of the map," Kodak commanded, "I want to see it in full-scale."

Ryker nodded and pushed up his sleeve, revealing a thick, black corded band on his wrist. She tilted her head, her interest caught as the light glinted off the cuff-like bracelet. At closer inspection, it seemed like small, gold beads were interwoven through the material.

How fascinating.

She had noticed Maddox wearing one as well but hadn't thought too much of it. Now she wished she had. Ryker held his wrist over the map and pressed on one of the beads. Brynnlin's eyes widened as a series of holographic symbols projected in front of him. He swiped through the symbols quickly before he selected one. A scanner moved over the map, creating a three-dimensional duplicate that hovered above the original on the table.

Ryker moved it around, zoomed in, and focused on the area Kodak specified. Kodak continued to direct him, and Ryker moved the map around to Kodak's liking.

"There," Kodak stopped him, settling on a small clearing further up the hills. "That's ideal, isolated and easy to maneuver. Let's try and lure it to this area. Note the coordinates."

Ryker pressed one of the beads, and after a moment the holograms disappeared.

Her gaze shot to the bracelet again.

What was that thing?

Something that advanced never would have been allowed on the isles. But she wasn't on the isles any longer. And she was eager to get a hold of one. She swung her head to look at Maddox, and he must have seen the questions written all over her face because his lips twitched upwards.

"Later," he whispered.

She fought her smile and nodded her head, it was only a little too eagerly.

Kodak cleared his throat, drawing their attention. "I want this matter settled as quickly as possible. We leave tomorrow. I'll take you myself." Kodak glanced at the rest of the group, "Ryker, get some men to gather some of the herd, it'll be the perfect bait. Zale will bring us there, but I don't want you staying," he directed at Zale. "The less people at risk the better. Ryker, Maddox , and myself will take Selene with us—"

"Wait, I'm going, too. I'm not staying here," Brynnlin interrupted. They weren't leaving her behind.

Kodak stopped and frowned. "I don't think that's the best idea, Brynn. You're still recovering, and we don't know what we're about to encounter."

"I'll be fine—"

"He's politely telling you that you'll only be in the way," Ryker cut her off with an eye roll.

Her head whipped towards Ryker, and her eyes narrowed. "Excuse me?"

"Your experience fighting low-lives in some trashy club isn't going to help you with this."

"Because you know so much about taking down a demon?" she snapped back. If she remembered correctly, she was the only one here that survived one.

Ryker opened his mouth, but Selene started talking first.

"Brynn goes with me. Where I go, she goes." There was no room for argument.

Brynnlin shot her a grateful look.

Kodak studied them all and relented, "I don't feel like arguing about this, so all right. Just be careful and stay back. Is there anything else we need to know about the demon?"

Selene thought it over.

"Remember that it can change forms...oh and for the love

of the goddess, do not let it bite you. It's extremely poisonous, the venom will kill you."

"This keeps getting better and better," Maddox deadpanned.

Kodak appeared unamused. "The best we can do is be prepared, now everyone go get some rest. Tomorrow will be a big day."

Brynnlin left with Selene first, leaving the others at the table. Saying goodnight, they headed for the rooms they'd been in. The heaviness of what they were about to do started to settle in.

"Are you sure about tomorrow?" Brynnlin waited until they were away from the others.

"We have to try," Selene said as they reached her door.

"I understand that, but even a low-level demon is extremely dangerous. We can find another way." Brynnlin knew the others wanted to find this thing, but she didn't think they fully understood what they were getting involved with. She'd seen a demon up close, it wasn't something someone easily walked away from.

"If it's too much, we'll figure something else out."

"Alright, I'll see you in the morning then." Brynnlin went to her own room and collapsed onto the bed.

The room was chilled from the window being left open. She didn't have the energy to get up and close it. Plus, the cold air was refreshing. She expected sleep to evade her, especially with sleeping in a new place. To her surprise, she was out within minutes.

BRYNNLIN'S HEART sank as she watched the portal close after Zale's departure.

This was it.

This was actually happening.

"Let's move quickly and get in positions," Kodak ordered.

Maddox, Ryker, and Kodak had discussed strategies this morning for taking out the demon.

Brynnlin had been very vocal about her objections, as she listened to their plan. This thing wasn't going to go down easy, and they needed to be prepared. After several assurances that they were going in with the utmost of caution, she finally relented and sat back.

She was allowed to go under the promise that she keep her distance. Brynnlin had scoffed and refused to make such a promise, but did agree to stay out of the way. Selene was also under orders to let them take the lead, and her main focus was putting up the ward.

"You know this is going to get messy right?" Brynnlin arched a brow at Selene nearly an hour later, as they sat in their positions. They were hidden behind some boulders at the edge of the clearing.

Maddox, Ryker, and Kodak were spread out across from them, and the cattle had been quickly slaughtered in the middle of the field.

All they had to do now was wait.

"I know," Selene whispered back. "Before it seemed like a solid idea, but being out here now..." Selene shook her head, "...someone's going to get hurt."

"It's not too late," Brynnlin offered, "we can still leave, think of an alternative."

"They're not going to want to do that, they want this resolved."

Brynnlin blew out a rough breath. "But will it have the resolution they want?"

She didn't have a good feeling about this. Over the years

she'd learned to trust her gut. And the longer they sat there the worse it got.

Hours passed and still nothing. The clearing remained quiet, while the sun started its descent.

"I think we need to regroup," Brynnlin admitted.

"I think you're right," Selene stood, stretching her muscles.

Brynnlin followed. Together they started the climb over the boulders that'd been concealing them. Halfway over the rocks, a breeze fluttered through the field rustling the leaves around them. Brynnlin froze, every muscle going on alert, and the hair on her nape rose.

"Stop moving," Brynnlin ordered Selene in a whisper.

Her gaze scanned the clearing, searching for anything out of the ordinary. She couldn't explain it, but something was out there. She could sense it.

The field sat empty, and Brynnlin studied the tree line. The tall trees cast shadows, concealing the inner forest. She squinted, trying to see within. Her attention was pulled to a darkened area off to the right. She focused there. Her heart pounded the longer she stared at the veiled space.

The veil shifted.

"Get down," she hissed, praying Selene listened, and flattened herself against the rocks.

Not a moment later, a creature emerged from that shadowed area, halting at the edge of the field. Brynnlin let out a low curse as she stared at the pucá. It barely resembled the drawing in the book.

The four legged, wolf-like creature easily reached at least five feet in height. Its razor-sharp claws scraped against the earth as it inched closer to the bait, and saliva dripped from its fanged teeth. Teeth that appeared just as deadly as the two horns protruding from its skull.

In a flash of movement, the pucá was across the field digging into the cattle. It shredded it apart at a speed which made Brynnlin's stomach turn.

They were so unprepared to deal with this.

A warming heat swept through her veins, her own magic flaring on instinct, as it detected the threat in its presence. For once, she didn't bother to try and subdue it.

Next to her, Selene chanted under her breath.

"What are you doing?"

Selene ignored her, and before Brynnlin could demand an answer, a spiral of magic shot upwards. Sparks rained down on them as a ward formed, enclosing them in a dome.

The pucá's head shot up. Its snout bloodied, and its lips curled, snarling at the blast of magic it sensed.

Brynnlin turned an accusing glare to Selene. "Why would you do that?"

Selene frowned. "We don't want it getting away. Kodak wanted it trapped, remember?"

She shook her head at her friend and scoffed. "It's not the one that's trapped."

CHAPTER 10

"She wasn't going to make it in time."

"FUCKING HELLS." Maddox attempted to take in a calming breath. The pucá released a low growl of warning, its head swiveling side to side, detecting the ward Selene constructed. She had said she would keep it from escaping.

This was their chance.

After another snarl, the pucá went back to devouring its prey. Maddox met Kodak's stare from across the tree line, and Kodak gave him the slightest of nods.

With another slow breath, he shifted the wind. Dense fog started cascading into the clearing. He only needed to mask Ryker and Kodak so they could get close to it. If Ryker could subdue it, Kodak could handle the rest.

Selene had warned Kodak that his fire-wielding would be useless against a demon, but Kodak didn't need his magic for this. Kodak was going to behead the damn thing. And the obsidian sword attached to his back would do the job just fine.

Maddox pushed more fog into the field. He could see

through it with clarity. Ryker and Kodak were almost upon the demon, each approaching from opposite sides.

Ryker took a knee, both hands going to the ground.

Maddox tensed.

This was it.

RYKER KNELT TO THE GROUND. His body only several feet from the demon. He was surprised he'd been able to get this close.

The demon appeared to be unaware of their presence. It continued to devour the cattle, and the sound of bone crunching had him wincing. They needed to act fast, while it was still distracted.

Without hesitation, he dug his hands into the soil. Magic flowed off him, and he forced it into the ground.

Slabs of rock erupted from the earth.

He contorted and bent them to his will, enveloping them around the demon and slammed it down. He trapped the demon to the ground.

An ungodsly screech erupted from the creature.

"Kodak, now." Ryker shouted.

Kodak was already lunging forward, his sword drawn. The obsidian blade shimmered with the magic Selene infused into it. It was unbreakable now. Kodak closed in on the thrashing demon. Hands raised, Kodak swung down the sword...

And sliced through air.

Kodak stumbled forward, his gaze flying around.

Ryker's stomach plummeted.

Where did it go?

The rock cage crashed through the now empty space, to the ground. Not even a second ago, it had been right there.

Ryker spun, his eyes whipping around the clearing. The fog that had hid them, now hindering them.

Ryker stood to run to Kodak.

Two steps forward—

A burst of magic erupted in front of him.

He staggered backwards, his face inches from the snarling demon. It slammed its head into him, its horn slicing into his chest, and Ryker flew through the air. A pain like he never felt before erupted across his skin, and he crashed into the ground.

His body screamed in protest at the impact.

"Ryker!"

He lifted his head at Kodak's shout.

He watched in horror as Kodak charged the demon. The demon turned to the newest threat. A deadly claw swiped at Kodak, and he ducked down rolling to the side. Jumping up, Kodak plunged the blade into the demon's side.

The demon threw its head back and roared. It whipped its body around and barged itself into Kodak, knocking him back.

Lifting a broken boulder, Ryker hurled it at the creature, bringing its attention back to him.

The creature spun with unnatural speed and sprang at him.

Fuck.

THE GROUND RUMBLED beneath them and a moment later the fog dissipated from the clearing.

"No!" Brynnlin scrambled forward as she took in the scene before her.

It was safe to say their plan had gone to shit.

The pucá circled around Ryker, its muscles bulging, and it seemed bigger than before. While Kodak pushed himself off the ground a few feet away.

The ground continued to rattle, Ryker manifesting blockades of the earth over and over again. They were the only things keeping the creature back as it leapt forward trying to attack.

Even from her distance, Brynnlin could see Ryker was hurt. He struggled to stand, and a hand was pressed to his chest. Kodak ran to him, throwing his arm around him for support.

The pucá charged forward, crashing past the newest barrier, aiming straight for the duo. Ryker and Kodak dove to opposite sides, barely escaping the pucá's deadly bite.

The pucá twisted and lunged towards Ryker. Ryker spun dodging the swipe of its claw, and it wailed when Ryker embedded his dagger into its leg. But that wasn't enough to stop it, and the pucá slammed its leg into Ryker, knocking him to the ground.

Brynnlin's stomach dropped as Maddox rushed across the field towards Ryker. She slid down the rocks and started racing towards them.

She wasn't going to make it in time.

The pucá spotted Maddox. Its tail whipped towards him, spikes elongating from the fur that hadn't been there before.

"Maddox," Brynnlin could only scream in warning.

Maddox turned to see the tail swinging towards him. He dropped down barely avoiding being impaled. Yet the pucá didn't relent in its attack. Its tail slammed into the ground near Maddox repeatedly, and Maddox rolled to the side attempting to dodge each time.

Brynnlin watched in horror as the others continued to relentlessly fight back. Even as she ran forward, she knew deep down it wouldn't be enough.

She stopped.

Selene crashed into her so hard Brynnlin almost stumbled to the ground.

"Why'd you stop?" Selene gasped, pushing past her, "They need help."

"Selene," Brynnlin grabbed her friend's arm and forced her to look at her. "Get to the others and put a ward around yourself."

"What?"

"Do it now," she snarled.

Brynnlin took a few steps back and didn't let herself think.

They were all going to die if she didn't do something. She ignored every instinct telling herself this was a bad idea.

With a deep breath, she tore the lid off her magic, releasing it into the world. Shadows burst from her, shooting into the dusk and pouring through the entire clearing. They slithered through every inch, encasing it in darkness.

The entire area blacked out.

CHAPTER 11

"Fear made people react in unpredictable ways."

FEAR WAS A FUNNY THING.

It made people act irrationally.

Her parents had been afraid of her—well maybe not of her, but of her magic.

They'd wanted her to be afraid of it, too.

Since she was old enough to understand, she'd been warned that her magic was dangerous.

Too powerful to exist...

Unnatural in the world...

She'd been forbidden to use it. To protect herself. To protect others.

Despite everything, she never feared her power. The magic called to her. Soothed her.

Late at night, when she was young, and the house was asleep, she would summon it and found comfort in its endless depth.

She only feared that she couldn't control it. The older she got, the stronger it became.

And she did believe her parents.

If others witnessed her magic, the response would not be kind.

She feared that, too.

What would happen to her if the world knew?

And now here she stood...

Revealing it all...

Risking the world's discovery...

But she couldn't let them die. Not when she could stop it.

There'd already been too much death in her life.

THE PUCÁ'S attention whipped towards her.

It sensed the true threat here.

She could see it clearly as it abandoned the others and stalked to her. It bared its teeth, and its tail swished dangerously. She let it get closer. She wanted it away from the others.

Shadows swirled at its feet, all around it, but not touching it.

Not yet.

Not until she gave the command. They acted on her will— were a part of her.

The pucá sank back, ready to spring forward.

It twitched.

Shadows struck.

They wrapped and twisted themselves around the demon, holding it down. It fought hard, clawing at something it had no chance of escaping.

It was time to end this.

The shadows squeezed tighter, their vice grip unrelenting.

The pucá's body trembled and before she could blink, the wolf-like creature was gone. Fur floated to the ground out of her shadow's hold.

Shit.

Brynnlin spun, her gaze frantic. Movement to her right caught her eye.

She turned—

A lanky figure slammed into her, tackling her to the ground. In a flash, the demon slipped back into the wolf form, and snapping teeth lunged for her throat.

Shadowed hands curled around its neck, jerking its head back. But it wasn't enough to dislodge the demon above her. Its paw sliced at her, and Brynnlin rolled while reaching for the dagger at her thigh. She lunged upwards, driving the dagger into the demon's chest.

The pucá howled in pain and went for her again.

Her hold on its head loosened slightly, and its long horn slashed down her cheek. Warm blood trailed down her face.

"Burning Hells," Brynnlin bit out at the slice of fiery pain.

She fought harder to pull the pucá back with little success. Doubt started to cloud her as she eyed the still embedded dagger.

Why wasn't it weakening?

Did she miss its heart?

It's heart...

Brynnlin wanted to bang her head on the ground.

How could she have been so stupid to forget that?

With surprising ease, Brynnlin commanded her shadows to seep into the demon. A trick she'd learned to master not long after she arrived on the isles.

The shadows probed through the pucá, going straight for the inner cavity of its chest.

There.

Her shadows curled like fingers around two other beating hearts.

A demon had three hearts.

She hadn't missed. She'd just forgotten the number of targets. With a savage roar, Brynnlin yanked back, pulling the hearts right of the demon.

It collapsed on top of her.

Brynnlin shoved it off and stood on shaky legs. She wiped away the blood and sweat from her face. Her chest heaved as she stared down at the demon at her feet.

It was done.

The shadowy darkness in the clearing withered away, slipping back into Brynnlin, as if never existing. She found herself holding the two hearts in her own hands.

She crushed them to dust and watched the pucá shrivel away with them.

THE VOID of shadows lifted from the clearing. The dim sky returned. With the veil gone, Maddox could easily see Brynnlin standing over the demon right before it disintegrated at her feet.

His mind refused to accept what he was seeing.

When Selene had found him and dragged him over to Ryker and Kodak, he'd been livid to leave Brynnlin out there. When she put up that ward around them, he only got worse. Nothing he said made her budge.

This was why.

Over and over again, Brynnlin had warned them that they were in over their head.

She'd been right.

But what she did...

He didn't know the details. He did know it shouldn't have been possible.

She didn't have magic. She never did.

At least he thought...

The ward around them disappeared. Selene was up and running over to Brynnlin, throwing her arms around her. Selene had known what Brynnlin was going to do, there was no other explanation.

He was ready to go demand an answer, until Ryker groaned next to him. Maddox dropped to a knee to help him up.

"Are you going to be alright?" Maddox frowned at the blood across Ryker's chest. The pucá had slashed him good.

"I'll be fine, let's just get the fuck out of here."

Maddox's lips twitched. That was Ryker. Hurt and probably in a lot of pain, and all he did was glare at his injury and demand to go home.

"Maddox," Kodak's tone seemed off. Maddox looked up to see him frowning and staring at Brynnlin.

He hesitated. "Yes?"

Kodak turned his frown to him. "What is she?"

Maddox's chest tightened. "I don't know."

In all his years alive, he'd never come across anything even similar to what just happened.

Kodak glared. "I'm not asking as your friend, you told us she was born without magic, that is not—"

"I didn't know," he snapped. The pain in his chest amplified at that admission.

He hadn't known.

She lied to him.

"But you can sure as Hells count on me finding out." Maddox stood and stomped over to Brynnlin, his anger rising with each step.

She looked up at him and relief flashed through her eyes before wariness took its place.

She damn well should be wary.

"I want an explanation."

She raised an eyebrow. "That's a real shitty way of saying thank you for saving your life."

Maddox closed in on her. "Enough of the games, Brynnlin."

"I'm not playing games." She refused to retreat even a step. She never was easily intimidated, not by him, or anyone.

He scoffed. "You're not? So you just stick to lies then?"

She opened her mouth.

"Don't bother," Maddox snarled, his words full of pain and outrage. "I don't need to hear more lies. And it was all lies. You always had magic. Your parents didn't keep you so isolated because they were overprotective. It was to hide what you really are." He started yelling. "Wasn't it?"

"Maddox, tread very carefully," she whispered.

Her eyes were wide, and she was shaking her head, but he didn't care.

He'd always been there for her. Supported her.

And what did he get in return?

Her lying to him.

And he wasn't going to let this go.

"Why would you not tell me?" Maddox was still yelling. "I'm your family. How could you keep something like this from me?"

Brynnlin tried to talk, but he kept going.

"Does Verenna know?"

Her non-answer was enough.

He scoffed. They'd always been close.

"Of course she does." Maddox shook his head and stalked away from her. He spun around again. "Who else knows?" he demanded.

She bit her lip.

"Just Vee," she said softly, "and everyone here now."

"Why the secrecy from me? From us?"

She crossed her arms. "I did it to stay alive. You can be angry all you want, but I'm not going to apologize for that."

He paused. He hadn't been expecting that answer.

"Why?"

She kept quiet.

"Brynnlin," he growled, he was tired of this. "Answer me. Why? What are you?"

She surprised him again by rolling her eyes. "Great fucking question Maddox, wish I had the answer."

"What?"

She glared at him. "You heard me."

"How do you not know?" he threw back.

"If you have an answer, I'm all ears," it was her turn to yell. "I have theories, but that's all they are. I don't know. My parents didn't know. And as soon as I was old enough to understand, my parents made it clear there was only one way I would ever survive, and that was to keep this very unknown magic hidden. From everyone. I will not apologize for my decision."

He turned quiet. It didn't matter that her answer made sense. "I'm not everyone."

She flinched. "Maddox..."

"No. I can't do this right now." Maddox cursed under his breath and stomped away from them. It was time to call Zale. Ryker was right, they needed to get the fuck out of here.

———

BRYNNLIN STARED AFTER MADDOX, her mind numb.

Her body hurt. She was physically and mentally exhausted. And she knew he probably felt betrayed, but couldn't he see that everything she'd done had only ever been to survive?

Arms wrapped around her, and she let Selene pull her into a hug.

"He'll come around," Selene murmured, "just give him time."

Brynnlin wasn't so sure. She'd never seen Maddox that angry before, let alone at her. But she had to believe Selene was right.

"Is that really true? You don't know what you are?"

Brynnlin pulled away from Selene and turned cautiously to Kodak. He raised an eyebrow, waiting for a response, his features giving nothing else away.

"And if it is? Are you going to try and kill me?" She didn't think Kodak was the type, but she'd been wrong about people before. Fear made people react in unpredictable ways.

Ryker staggered forward. "Could he even if he wanted to?"

Her muscles tensed, and she cast Ryker a side glance. "No."

Ryker rolled his eyes. "Then you obviously have nothing to worry about."

That did little to comfort her.

"I would consider your next words very carefully, Ryker," she warned.

"Relax, I'm not the threat here, remember?"

Kodak glared at Ryker. "Please excuse Ryker's inability to read this situation. And since you don't know me very well, I'll do my best not to take offense to your question."

Brynnlin's shoulders sagged. "I meant no offense."

"I know." Kodak walked up to her and put a hand on her shoulder. "You carry a heavy weight. You don't know who to trust. Rest assured, the knowledge of your abilities will remain hidden. You are safe here and with us. We would never mean you harm."

She gave him a blank stare. He might say that now. But did he mean it?

"The sentiment is appreciated."

"You don't seem convinced."

"I'll always have a target on my back with this magic. Others won't want to see me have it. They'll either want it for themselves or want to kill me because they're afraid of it. Don't act like you aren't afraid of me. I can see it."

Kodak surprised her by smiling, "It would be stupid not to be wary of so much power. And yes, I'm a little disturbed by what I saw. Brynn, you single-handedly took down a demon. However, even with all that, it doesn't mean I'm afraid of you, or want to see you destroyed."

She gave him a doubtful look.

"Brynn, wary does not equate to fear."

She didn't quite believe him, but appreciated that he was trying to make her feel better.

Selene nudged her in the side and smiled. "I'm not afraid of you."

Brynnlin's lips twitched. "Thanks."

"Is this the part where I also say something to make you feel better?" Ryker rocked back on his heels, a smirk crossing his face, "If so, don't hold your breath."

"Ryker," Kodak growled.

"What? I was joking," Ryker frowned.

Kodak shook his head. "Enough, let's go home before you say something else stupid."

Maddox walked back towards the group. "Zale's been informed we're ready for him."

Brynnlin didn't even try to approach him. Now wasn't the time.

Thankfully, Zale showed up almost immediately. He took them all in with wide eyes. Between the blood and dirt covering them, Brynnlin knew they were a mess. She was leaning against Selene barely able to stay upright. Every part of her ached after using that much magic. She was a few steps away from literally collapsing and only sheer will held her up.

"Let's get you all home." Zale acted quickly and had them standing outside the palace doors.

Finally, they were back.

All she wanted to do was collapse into bed and forget this day ever happened.

CHAPTER 12

"I never wanted this."

BRYNNLIN PEELED her eyes open at her door squeaking open. She rubbed her eyes and tried to focus on whoever just walked in.

"Rise and shine."

Oh gods. Verenna.

She groaned and rolled back over, burying her face in the pillow. For once, she had actually been having a dreamless sleep. "Go away."

"It's the middle of the afternoon, don't you want to get up?"

"No."

She heard Verenna's footsteps cross the room, but she wasn't prepared for what Verenna was about to do. Verenna threw back the curtains, letting the light spill across the dark room.

"You bitch." Brynnlin grumbled and blinked rapidly to clear the sting in her eyes as they tried to readjust.

"I know." Verenna shot her a winning smile. "But I brought you food."

Brynnlin sat up against the headboard, crossing her knees in front of her. "Are you trying to bribe me with food?"

Verenna crawled onto the bed and sat across from her, setting a tray between them. "Maybe. Is it working?"

Brynnlin lifted the lid and saw a mound of pastries next to some sliced fruit. The smell of fresh bread wafted up to her and made her mouth water.

"Maybe."

She snatched a pastry. It was still warm and when she took a bite, it practically melted in her mouth. Verenna was slightly redeemed for her earlier actions. She said as much.

Verenna laughed and snacked on some of the fruit.

"So, I heard what happened yesterday," she said between bites.

Brynnlin tensed.

"Oh yeah?" She reached for a napkin, pretending nonchalance. "The demon is officially no longer a problem."

"I know, everyone is very relieved. But that's not what I meant."

"Oh," Brynnlin's response was much less enthusiastic than before.

"Oh? That's all I get?" Verenna teased. "Do you know the earful I got from Maddox last night?"

Brynnlin's mood immediately fell at the mention of Maddox. She hadn't seen him since they got back yesterday.

Verenna sobered. "I know what happened with that, too. Don't worry, I already told Maddox he's being an idiot."

Brynnlin shook her head. "He has a right to be mad."

"No, he has a right to be upset, not mad," Verenna countered. "He's hurt, and he doesn't want to admit it."

"I never meant to hurt him."

"I know and whether he admits it or not, he knows it, too. He has no idea what you've had to deal with growing up, and it might take some time, but his brain will eventually catch up."

"Do you think he'll forgive me?" she whispered.

"Of course he will," Verenna said immediately. "But he isn't innocent in this situation either, and you guys just need to talk it out."

"Yeah, I don't see that happening anytime soon."

Verenna pursed her lips. "It'll get sorted out, we're family. A small spat like this is nothing."

Brynnlin grabbed some more food and gave a small smile. "Thanks for the pep talk."

"Anytime." Verenna smiled back and helped herself to more fruit. "Now eat up and get dressed. Kodak wants to talk to everyone tonight, but until then, we're getting you out of this room."

"What? Why?"

Verenna hopped off the bed. "Because I let you have your rest, but now you need fresh air and to stretch your muscles."

Brynnlin scrunched her nose, not liking this plan. "Do I have to?"

"Yep. I'm the healer, no arguing." Verenna clapped her hands to get Brynnlin to hurry. "Let's go."

"Fine," Brynnlin agreed with extreme reluctance. It was easier just to go along with Verenna than argue, and maybe getting out of bed wasn't the worst idea. "But I'll meet you downstairs. I want to shower and change."

"Deal." Verenna smirked. "However, if you're not down in thirty minutes, I'm coming back and dragging you out."

Brynnlin knew the threat was a real one and couldn't help but smile as Verenna bounced out of the room. Verenna hadn't changed at all. She was still bossy, and demanding, and gods, Brynnlin had missed her.

RYKER'S HAND paused halfway to the door. Gods, this was a bad idea.

He dropped his hand and turned away from the door. He took one step, muttered a curse, and spun back around. He knocked softly before he could talk himself out of it. He rolled his shoulders back, trying to ease the tension, and waited.

And waited some more.

There was no answer.

He knocked harder. "Brynn, can we talk?"

The door still didn't budge. He blew out a rough breath.

Damn. He knew this was a stupid idea.

Was she even in her room? Maybe she was out?

Curiosity drove him to try the doorknob. It turned under his palm.

Unlocked.

The rational side of his brain told him to leave it, the other part only wanted to see if she was ignoring him. His bad idea continued, and he pushed the door open to peek his head in.

"Brynn?" He called out and looked around the room.

It was most definitely empty. Wherever she was, it wasn't here. He had every intention of backing out and leaving her room undisturbed. That was until a cool breeze blew into the room, fluttering the curtains.

Interesting.

The balcony doors were cracked open. If she was on the balcony, he doubted she heard him knocking.

At least that was what he told himself.

He stepped further into the room, carefully shutting the door behind him. Every part of him felt like he was crossing some line, but he really did need to talk to her. Shaking off his concern, he strode across the space, going straight for the balcony.

"Brynn can we—"

He stopped short, his eyes scanning the area.

Well, shit.

She wasn't out here either.

His unease returned, now he really was crossing the line by being in her empty room. He needed to get the Hells out. He shut the balcony doors and beelined it for the exit. He was halfway across the room when the bathroom door opened.

Ryker skidded to a halt and swallowed sharply.

Steam billowed out of the bathroom. Brynnlin walked out with her hair piled on top of her head, and only a small towel wrapped tightly around her. Her skin glistened from the shower she'd obviously just taken, and water droplets clung to tendrils of her hair.

She stopped abruptly, her eyes widening as she spotted him.

"Ryker," she said his name slowly, suspiciously. "Not quite the person I expected to find waiting for me. Care to explain why you're in my room?"

Gods, his luck could not be worse.

The towel didn't cover much, and he forced himself to focus on her face as she spoke. The last thing he needed to do was make her even more uncomfortable.

"Um." He opened his mouth then closed it.

"I..." he trailed off. *'I walked into your room like a creep and now it looks ten times worse because you just got out of the shower.'*

He closed his eyes for a moment, trying to find some type of reasonable explanation.

There wasn't one.

He pointed at the door like an idiot. "I tried knocking, but you didn't answer."

She raised an eyebrow. "So, you decided to let yourself in? Do you often barge in uninvited, or am I just lucky?"

He rubbed the back of his neck and looked to the ceiling. "No, it wasn't like that."

"Sure it wasn't." She rolled her eyes at him. "By the way, you're blushing like a schoolgirl."

He narrowed his gaze at her. "I assure you, I'm not."

She didn't look like she believed him, which only added to his irritation. How was he the one standing here acting uncomfortable? She was the one in the godsdamn towel.

"Whatever you say." She shrugged and started to move across the room. "It's just skin. I'm sure you've seen your fair share of it."

"Of course I have," he bit back, no longer concerned about her state of undress. "I was trying to be respectful."

But Hells, if she wasn't going to worry about it, why should he?

That made her chuckle.

"Respect definitely hasn't been your concern since meeting me." She walked past him, going to the dresser.

"What the Hells does that mean?" he snapped and turned, crossing his arms. "Since meeting you—"

The rest of his words floated away as if they never existed.

With Brynnlin rifling through the drawers, her back was to him, and what he saw had his blood running cold.

An ellén trechend was tattooed on her back. The large creature was displayed in shades of black and gray, and its scaled wings extended across each shoulder blade. Two of its heads curled up the sides of her spine, reaching towards her neck, and the third head was thrown back in a roar. He could only see the upper half of the tattoo and assumed the other half of the body continued down her back, hidden by her towel. The artwork was absolutely exquisite, and whatever artist did the work was extraordinarily gifted. But the impressive tattoo wasn't what had his stomach knotting.

It was what the tattoo attempted to cover.

Thin, raised scars covered the expanse of her exposed skin. The jagged, white lines were old and should have healed. The fact that they hadn't, told him everything he needed to know.

These were inflicted with intent.

The tattoo did its job well, but standing this close to her, he could see that the inky veil didn't hide everything. And the clarity of why she chose the sacred, ancient beast as her tattoo hit him hard. Back when the gods and goddesses used to walk this land, ellén trechends were the guardians of the empire. They were the wall that stood between the land and the entrance to the Three Hells, preventing demons and lost souls from escaping. But after a war of the gods broke out, nearly destroying the land, the gods and goddesses disappeared into the celestial plane of Albios, leaving this land behind for the lower races to rebuild. Ellén trechends faded away with the gods, and in their place a barrier was created, locking away the Three Hells in another plane. And while an ellén trechend hadn't been seen in millennia, their embodiment of strength and protection was well-known. For Brynnlin to have used one as a tattoo to hide whatever happened to her...

He must have been quiet for too long.

Brynnlin glanced at him over her shoulder. She frowned at him when she saw his attention on her back.

He wanted to ask what happened. He didn't dare.

She barely tolerated him as is, pushing into her past would only make it worse. Though that didn't stop the sickening feeling that developed the more he thought about it.

What had she endured to end up with that? Who knew what other scars she hid? Both visible and internal?

He'd always judged her for being on those islands, for fighting in that club...

But he'd never really thought about what her life was actually like there.

Gods, he'd never been so wrong about someone.

"Don't like what you see?" Brynnlin's smile was cruel, and her words were taunting.

He saw past the defense mechanism, the vulnerability in her eyes was only too clear.

"Brynn, I'm..." He was what? Sorry? That seemed entirely too inadequate.

"Not everybody has a pretty past, Ryker. Mine even less so. Now unless you came in here to gawk, I don't believe you ever answered my original question."

It was a cowardly move, but he was more than happy to let her change the subject.

"I wanted to talk to you."

She pulled some clothes out of the drawer and when she faced him, she stared at him.

He stared back. "What?"

She waved the clothes. "If you're not going to get out, then at least turn around. I think you've seen more than enough today."

"Right." He couldn't spin around fast enough and stared hard at the wall.

He ignored the sound of clothes rustling and again went over what a bad idea it had been to come up here in the first place. Though, it could have been worse. She could have kicked his ass when she first saw him, and she didn't. He would count that as a win.

After another several moments, Brynnlin spoke, "You can turn back around."

He did and let out a sigh of relief when he found her fully clothed and sitting on the edge of the bed.

Her arms were crossed. "What was so important that it couldn't wait?"

"It's about yesterday."

She immediately tensed up. "Ryker, ignore it. Pretend it didn't happen. I don't care. Whatever you need to do, but don't talk about it."

"I can't do that," he admitted. "I know we haven't gotten off on the right foot, but you saved our lives yesterday. Saved my life. And I didn't even have the decency to thank you. All I did was make some stupid-ass joke. A poor one at that, and I'm sorry."

"Oh."

He could tell she was surprised by his words and that made him feel even worse. Had he really been that much of an asshole?

He kept going. "You deserve a real thank you and a decent apology. We've had a rocky start, but that doesn't mean—"

Brynnlin's door burst open, startling them both.

"Brynnlin, I told you what would happen if you didn't come down—oh—" Verenna waltzed into the room, but stopped short at seeing them. "Am I interrupting something?" She pasted on an innocent smile.

He rolled his eyes. "No, I was just leaving."

He stalked to the door, ready to put this miserable attempt at an apology behind him.

"Ryker, wait."

He paused and glanced back at Brynnlin.

"Thank you, for what you said."

He gave her a terse nod, not feeling comfortable enough to say anything else. He hadn't even gotten to the decent apology part, or to what he wanted to really say. Yet she was thanking him. She really thought so little of him, and he had no one to blame but himself.

He left without another word.

BRYNNLIN STARED at the open door, trying to make sense of what just happened.

"What was all that about?" Verenna glanced between her and the door.

Brynnlin only shook her head. "Honestly, I'm not sure. He was trying to say thank you about yesterday."

She was still a little thrown off by the whole thing.

"Really?" Verenna's eyes widened. "Well, that was sweet."

Brynnlin nodded in agreement. It was a sweet gesture. She appreciated his attempt to make amends, though his timing could've been better. She wished that he hadn't seen her scars. That he hadn't seen the glimpse of her past she tried so hard to bury.

The scars stopped bothering her a long time ago, she'd come to view them as a reminder that she was a survivor. A show of her strength. And she turned them into something beautiful. But she didn't want to share that past with anyone, and she could have gone without seeing the disgust on his face when he saw her back. She didn't consider herself a vain person, yet she had her pride after all. She needed to be more vigilant about locking her doors. She didn't want a repeat performance with him or anyone else.

"What's on the agenda?" she asked Verenna, trying to distract her. She really didn't want to get into the details of the Ryker-fiasco that just happened.

"A walk through the garden. Some sun will do you some good."

Brynnlin wasn't sure if she should be insulted or not. A few minutes later, that's where they ended up. They strolled through the gardens, talking about nothing in particular, and it was lovely.

When they came to the end of the garden, passing the last of the manicured hedges, Verenna kept walking. Curiosity had Brynnlin following.

"Where are we going?"

"Don't you want to see more of the grounds?"

Brynnlin perked up. "Absolutely."

Verenna cast her a coy smile and led her along a path she hadn't seen earlier. The new path cut through a small patch of trees that stood like a barricade along the back of the garden. Past the trees, a large grass field opened up in front of them. Lines of buildings were spread out in the distance. Throughout the field, dozens of men and women decked out in black attire were running through drills.

"Welcome to the royal auxiliary training grounds."

Brynnlin nodded in approval and let out a low whistle. "Impressive."

Verenna hooked her arm through Brynnlin's and dragged her along. "Come on."

The closer they got, Brynnlin could make out chalked circles where pairs were practicing with a variety of weapons. Across the way, archery targets were lined up, and there was even a track for running.

Their arrival attracted attention, and heads turned as they passed. Verenna received a series of warm welcomes. Much like with the palace staff, others greeted her with a smile, which she returned. Some of those smiles extended to Brynnlin, most didn't. Brynnlin tried to ignore the stares. They must not get many visitors, it was only curiosity. At least, that's what she told herself.

"Is there a particular reason we're here?" Brynnlin asked under her breath.

"That's the reason." Verenna nodded her head to one of the chalked circles.

People were gathered around the edge, watching whoever was in the middle, blocking her view. Verenna pulled her along, pushing through people and stopped along the line.

Brynnlin's stomach dropped.

Maddox stood in the ring, fighting against some other man. Though fighting was a generous term. She'd seen fighting, partook in fighting, this was practicing. Intense practicing. But still practicing.

She glared at Verenna. "Really?"

Verenna's lips thinned. "I'm not going to let you guys ignore each other. There's too much on the line right now. So talk it out, beat it out, I don't know, just do something."

Brynnlin crossed her arms, and her eyes wandered back to the ring.

The two were fighting with bo staffs. The slamming of the wood echoed through the circle every time they made contact. It was a constant series of attacks being deflected.

Maddox made a wide arc, his staff moving at a speed faster than she thought possible. The staff let off a slight golden hue, barely visible in the sunlight. The reason behind the enhanced speed clicked.

The staffs were amplifiers to the user's magic. She couldn't help being intrigued. She'd heard of such technology, but never thought she would have the opportunity to see it.

Maddox's attack closed in, and she was sure his opponent wouldn't be able to block it.

She was wrong.

The other man easily deflected and struck back, quickly catching Maddox in the side.

Brynnlin grimaced. That had to hurt.

Maddox seemed unfazed, and again they were back to sharing blows.

Brynnlin had to admit their speed and skill were very impressive. The sparing continued for another several minutes, until the other man got the upper hand. He lunged forward, a forceful gust erupting from the staff and knocking Maddox to the ground.

Maddox cursed and rolled to get up. His sparring partner offered a hand and pulled him to his feet. That must have signaled the end, the small crowd that gathered to observe dissipated. A few of the members threw jabs at Maddox and congratulated the other man—Declan, is what they called him.

"Lucky shot." Maddox mumbled.

Declan laughed. "Is it really luck if I continue to kick your ass?"

"He's got you there, Maddie," Verenna smirked and crossed into the circle.

Brynnlin grudgingly followed.

Maddox's head whipped towards them, he clearly hadn't seen them approach. He lifted a single brow. "Thanks for the backup, sis."

"Anytime."

Maddox's lips curved up, until he met Brynnlin's gaze. His expression closed off, and Brynnlin sighed. This was going to be fun. At least he wasn't yelling this time.

Declan didn't seem to notice the tension and laughed again, throwing an arm over Verenna. "There's my favorite healer, you've been hiding out on us."

Verenna shrugged. "Been busy."

"I'll say. Who's your friend?"

Declan's question seemed to snap Maddox out of his stupor. Maddox glared at him. "Off-limits. Just like Verenna, in case you need the reminder."

Declan put a hand to his chest. "Why can't I have friends? I'm a nice person."

"Sure you are." Maddox rolled his eyes while Verenna snickered.

"Declan, this is Brenna."

Brynnlin raised an eyebrow at the name. Maddox had told her that someone called Remi was setting her up a new identity. She hadn't realized that applied here. This was the first time she'd heard the new name. It was strange to hear.

She smiled anyway and offered a hand, "Hi."

She immediately regretted that decision when his sweaty hand engulfed hers. She let go quickly.

"So Brenna, what brings you to this neck of the woods?"

Brynnlin took a breath. Maybe Verenna was right, maybe she should just rip off the bandage.

She pointed at Maddox. "I'm hoping to speak to him."

Declan pouted. "And here I thought you guys came all the way out here for me."

Verenna patted his chest. "Maybe next time."

Maddox's eyes widened. "You want to talk?"

"Yeah, I do."

Maddox nodded. "Okay yeah, let's talk."

Verenna clapped her hands. "Great, I'll give you some space and later—"

"Actually," Declan interrupted her, "I have an idiot that might have broken his wrist, are you willing to take a look?"

"Of course," Verenna answered and left with Declan, leaving Brynnlin and Maddox alone.

"Look—"

"I'm sorry," Maddox said at the same time.

"What?"

"I'm sorry for how I reacted yesterday. I never should have yelled at you."

Brynnlin swallowed past the lump in her throat. "I'm sorry I didn't tell you."

Maddox dropped the staff and in one movement pulled her into a hug. She released a sigh of relief and hugged him back.

"I didn't ask to be born like this," she admitted softly. "I never wanted this."

"It doesn't matter what you are. With magic, without magic, you're family, and I'll be here for you no matter what. It hurt that you didn't trust me enough to tell me, but I can only imagine the pressure your parents put on you. All last night I regretted what I said and the more I thought about it, the more I understood why you kept it to yourself."

"There will forever be a target on my back if this gets out," Brynnlin whispered her biggest concern.

Maddox squeezed her closer. "It's not going to get out."

She wanted to believe him, she really did. But only time would tell.

She pulled back, her nose wrinkling. "I appreciate this moment, but you stink."

Maddox chuckled and let her go. "Unlike you, I haven't been laying in bed all day."

"Hey," she smacked him. "I think I deserve the rest after literally saving our lives yesterday."

"Yes, you did," Maddox frowned at her. "It scared the shit out of me knowing you were in that field alone. Let's not have a repeat please, for my sanity."

"Don't worry, I don't plan on facing off with another demon anytime soon."

Maddox countered. "How about never."

Brynnlin laughed. "I'll try."

A weight lifted off her shoulders as Maddox laughed with her. She hadn't realized how much yesterday had bothered her, and she was glad Verenna brought her out here.

CHAPTER 13

"One problem at a time."

THAT NIGHT at the evening meal, Brynnlin sat with a fond smile on her face as she observed the others laughing and joking around. A weight seemed to have lifted off everyone now that the demon was gone. She only wished that was the end of their worries.

Brynnlin's lips tipped further upwards as Verenna recounted a much more exaggerated version of her brother losing to Declan this afternoon. Which sent everyone into another fit of laughter, and Maddox glared at his sister, trying to defend himself.

Brynnlin took a second to embrace this moment. The lightness in the air...the way the others all teased one another...they were all a family.

For once, she felt a part of it.

She cherished this feeling. And with a new determination, she swore to herself she wasn't going to lose this.

Not again.

Things settled down some as food was brought out, and everyone dug in. Small conversation continued throughout the meal up until the last plate was cleared. A quietness settled over them as they waited for Kodak. They all knew he planned on addressing what was going to happen next.

He didn't make them wait long. "Yesterday was a hard-earned success, and the demon is no longer a threat to us or our people." Kodak released a long sigh and clasped his hands on the table. "However, we find ourselves with a rare opportunity in front of us. For years, Brynn and Selene have been cultivating a plan to track down the acolyte that attacked her home many years ago. We are in a unique position, where I fully intend to offer assistance in delivering justice once we find this individual. But this also allows us to learn more about the cult that has been destructive to our Empire for decades. Especially, if what Brynn and Selene believe is true, and that their new lead is to find a rare collector who supplies the cult's commandment."

Selene cleared her throat. "Kodak, if I may?"

"Of course," Kodak leaned back and let Selene take over.

Selene looked around the table and offered them all a small smile. "Kodak is right. Brynn and I did come across some new information and if used carefully, I truly think we'll be successful. As I'm sure you know, Draíothes are very valuable to the Creed because they possess the magic capable of performing summoning rituals." Selene paused and corrected herself. "Well not all Draíothes can do this, they have to be very powerful and have the materials necessary to perform the ritual. When I first started helping Brynn, our only goal had been to find the man that killed her parents—"

"Out of curiosity, how exactly did you plan on doing this?" Juniper interrupted and raised an eyebrow. "Atlas launched an investigation into the attack, as did we, and neither of us discovered anything of value. It was obvious that the Creed was responsible, the use of a demon was evident. The Creed may be a nuisance, unfortunately they're also quite resourceful. So I don't see how you planned to find the Draíothe they sent to that estate, let alone even identify him. Hells, it could have been a woman."

"It wasn't," Brynnlin said softly.

"What?" Juniper frowned.

"I said it wasn't—a woman," Brynnlin met Juniper's gaze across the table. "I don't need to worry about identifying him, I just need to find him."

"I see." Juniper's gaze turned sympathetic.

"You're shitting me," Maddox growled. "You saw him that night?"

Brynnlin paused. "I did."

"He got that close to you?"

Oh he had no idea. "Something like that."

Maddox ran a hand through his hair. "Do I even want to know?"

"Not tonight." Brynnlin turned back to Juniper. "As I was saying, identification won't be an issue."

She would never forget his face. She couldn't, even if she wanted to.

"I guess it won't be," Juniper said, "Selene, please continue."

"Of course," Selene took over again. "Like I said, our original goal had only been to find this guy, but we couldn't do this from the outer island—"

"Why not?" Maddox interrupted.

Selene pursed her lips, "As I explained earlier, Draíothes are very important to the Creed. They would keep them close, somewhere on the inner islands. That's where the people in control would be. They're safe there, protected."

"How do you know so much about the Creed?" Ryker questioned.

Selene's jaw clenched tight, and Brynnlin almost laughed at her friend.

Selene was losing her patience.

"Let's just say I've had a personal experience with how they do things."

Ryker's eyes narrowed. "That's vague."

"With all due respect, I don't need to explain my past to you, and it's certainly not relevant," Selene crossed her arms and glared. "So may I please continue with what's actually important?"

"Enough questions," Kodak ordered, "let her continue."

"Thank you," Selene's shoulders relaxed. "Now where was I...yes, the inner islands. Brynn had, well has, a plan to get in there, but very recently, fate was kind and dropped a little present in our laps."

Brynnlin nearly snorted at Selene's description of Penn. He certainly was no gift, but luck had been on their side to run into him.

"We were able to get a hold of a very important and powerful grimoire, or part of it at least. It's the same grimoire that you were able to identify the pucá from. And that book contains the materials necessary to perform the summoning rituals. And those items are very rare, one especially, and I'm convinced they would've needed to go to a collector to obtain it. Find the collector, and they'll lead us straight to the Creed," Selene finished with a smug smile.

Kodak nodded along with Selene's explanation. "That's why you asked me to have Zale start reaching out to our contacts about any information they had on collectors, especially the ones taking part in illegal dealings."

"Exactly." Selene grimaced. "I would have done it myself, but a lot of the information I had on them was at my store."

Maddox straightened in his chair, and his gaze shot between Brynnlin and Selene. "Is that book why your store was trashed?"

Selene looked down at the table and shrugged. "I might have borrowed it from someone who isn't keen on sharing," she admitted.

Brynnlin snickered. "That's code for she stole it."

Selene shot her a withering glare. "I told you not to call it that."

Verenna laughed. "Yeah, Brynn, it's called apportioning."

Selene face lit up, and she shared a smirk with Verenna. "I knew I liked you."

"You can argue about the definition of stealing later," Ryker crossed his arms and nodded at Zale. "What are we going to do if our contacts can't locate this collector?"

Zale seemed to think it over. "Well, I've already had quite a bit of information come in, and I'm assembling a file. Hopefully, it'll have something useful."

Ryker frowned. "You're hoping? It sounds like all of this rides on being able to find the collector. If we can't do that, we're screwed."

Zale chuckled and shook his head at Ryker. "I know you're used to action Ryker, we're not there yet. Being the General is your expertise, intelligence is mine."

"But what happens if the intelligence doesn't lead us where we need it to?"

"I can't generate information out of thin air, things like this take time," Zale's voice hardened, and his tone turned defensive.

Brynnlin's eyes swung back and forth as the two argued.

She understood Ryker's concern, but after years of dead ends, she knew to have patience.

"Let's not get ahead of ourselves," Kodak intervened. "We'll see what information we're able to generate and go from there. One problem at a time."

"He's right," Selene added with a shrug, "and while I'm confident that finding the collector is the most promising course of action, if it doesn't work, Brynn will go back to her original plan."

Brynnlin threw Selene a warning look. That information didn't need to be offered up so freely. She had a feeling certain people at this table would be difficult about it.

"What original plan?" Kodak questioned.

Brynnlin debated her answer. "Selene mentioned it earlier, the Draiothes keep to the inner islands, I'd go to the inner islands."

Kodak surprised her by chuckling. "Just like that? You'd go to the inner islands? Brynn, I hate to disappoint you, but you can't just go to the inner islands. For decades, not just myself, but other rulers have tried getting people onto those islands, it's never worked."

Brynnlin tried to not be insulted by Kodak's words. It was extremely difficult.

Did he think she was an idiot?

"I'm well aware of what it takes to get to those islands," she explained, choosing her words carefully. "This has been in the works for a while, I know what I'm doing."

Kodak's eyes gleamed, and he leaned forward. "You truly have a way to get there?"

Brynnlin hesitated. "Yes."

"How?"

Brynnlin was slow to answer him. His eagerness unnerved her.

"It's the fights, isn't it?" Ryker answered instead. "That's why you were at the club."

Well no point in lying about it.

"I was fighting long before this development, but yes," she admitted, "I have a deal with Zamir that should grant me entrance to one of the other clubs."

"That's incredible," Kodak looked at her like she was the answer to all of his problems.

"That's not quite the word I would use."

"Brynn, do you know what we could do if you used that access at the club to infiltrate their organization?"

He couldn't be serious.

She scoffed. "You want me to be your spy?"

"Yes."

Well at least he was honest about his intentions. She'd give him that.

"Absolutely not," Maddox snarled, glaring at Kodak. "What in the Hells are you thinking? We just got her out, and you want to send her back?"

"Maddox, if this was anybody else, you'd be agreeing with me. You need to set your emotions aside for a moment. Beyond capturing the Draíothe behind the attack, think of what we could accomplish with her on the inside."

Maddox slammed his fist on the table. "No, Kodak, you're the one not thinking this through. Yes, it would be great if we had someone infiltrate the Creed, but not Brynn. You're asking her to risk her life, don't you think she's been through enough already?"

"She had already planned on doing this before we were even in the picture, only now she'd have our resources at her disposal," Kodak threw back with a point look, "and last I checked—"

"I'll think about it," Brynnlin cut them off.

"You will?" Kodak's attention shifted to her, his features full of surprise.

Maddox not so much.

"Are you out of your fucking mind?" Maddox demanded. "No, you're not doing this. She's not doing this," he said to Kodak.

"I appreciate your concern, Maddox," Brynnlin tried to reassure him. "However, I'm a grown woman. And I'm not agreeing to anything, I'm willing to think about it."

Kodak was right. She'd been planning on doing it anyway before all this. There was no harm in seeing if she could find anything useful for them.

"This is ridiculous," Maddox muttered under his breath.

"Maddox, we would never ask her to do something any of us wouldn't do, if we were in the same position," Juniper stepped in. "Brynn just happens to already be involved."

Maddox rolled his eyes. "Is that supposed to make me feel better?"

"No, I would never expect you not to worry, I'm only asking you to be open-minded about the situation."

"We'll see." Maddox side-eyed Kodak, "Your wife isn't playing fair, but I'll set the matter aside for the time being. It might not even be necessary, let's wait for Zale's debrief."

"Agreed." Kodak nodded, "we'll revisit the subject another time."

Brynnlin didn't believe for a second that Maddox would let this go, but if they wanted to postpone the argument, she wouldn't disagree. And she truly wasn't agreeing to anything, not yet. She would see how things progressed before she made any commitments.

"When can we expect the information on the collectors?" she asked.

Zale thought it over. "Give me another twenty-four hours.

I'll compile the information I have and present it tomorrow evening for us to go through."

"Sounds great." Brynnlin pushed away from the table, "If that's all for tonight, I'd like to excuse myself. I'm still quite weary from yesterday's events."

"Yes, we're finished for this evening, go get some rest Brynn," Kodak offered her a kind smile.

Before she could leave, Verenna asked, "Are you feeling alright? Is something bothering you?"

"Tired is all."

Relief flashed through Verenna's eyes. "That's normal. Nothing sleep can't alleviate. If you need anything, let me know though."

"Thank you." Brynnlin squeezed Verenna's shoulder as she passed around the table. She appreciated her concern. And while she was feeling much better than when she woke up, she still wasn't fully recovered.

Yesterday had taken a toll on her. More so than she was ready to admit.

CHAPTER 14

"Nothing would have been different, you can't blame yourself."

A KNOCK SOUNDED on Brynnlin's bedroom door.

She groaned and climbed off the balcony ledge she'd been perched on, going back into her room. She left the door open, letting the cool air fill the room. The knock sounded again, softer this time. She rolled her eyes.

Impatient much.

Pulling the door open, she frowned at—

"Ryker," she tried to hide her surprise.

This was twice now he'd sought her out. He stood in the hall, one hand shoved into his pocket, the other rubbing at the back of his neck.

He also seemed surprised. "You answered."

Was she not supposed to?

"I believe that's the normal response when you knock on someone's door," she responded in a dry tone.

His lips twitched, fighting a smile. "I know, I just didn't expect you to answer."

"I can close it, if you'd like?" She started to do just that.

"Don't," his hand shot out, stopping the door, and he shook his head at her. "I didn't walk up all those stairs for nothing."

"Ah yes, to what do I owe this impromptu visit? Did Kodak still need me downstairs?"

"No," Ryker grimaced, "I was hoping we could talk?"

"About?"

"Maybe finish our earlier conversation?"

"Oh..." she struggled to keep her expression neutral, "that's not necessary." She had no desire to relive another uncomfortable conversation.

"It is though,"

"It's really not," she promised.

Ryker sighed, "Brynn, please."

His blue eyes were intent on her. Gone was the hostility from their first meeting. Her shoulders dropped. She really didn't want another apology...

Or his guilt...

Or worse, his pity...

Yet she stepped back, letting him pass.

He nodded at the balcony doors, "You really like leaving those open."

She shrugged. "I like the fresh air." She started going back outside. "We can talk out here."

Ryker followed and leaned back against the outer wall, while she got comfortable on the settee. She pulled her feet under her and sat back, waiting for him to start.

He wasn't looking at her. His attention was on the view beyond. The moon was bright above them, and thousands of stars were scattered across the sky, lighting up the night.

A quiet moment passed.

Then another.

"Did you know I knew your father?"

Brynnlin tensed.

There was no way she heard him correctly. Her focus zeroed in on him and with one look at the intensity in his gaze, she knew she had.

And no, she definitely hadn't known that.

Her mouth opened. No words came out.

She slowly shook her head.

Ryker looked back up at the sky. "He was a good man. I was actually one of his sentries that patrolled his district's border. I was with him for a while, until about a century ago when I moved back with Maddox and Kodak. Kodak offered me a position with him and I accepted." He still didn't look back at her, he continued talking into the night. "Before I left, my mother had some trouble finding work, and to this day I still don't know how your father found out about it, but he did. And of course being the man he was, he immediately set out to help. He hired her on as a cook and moved her to the estate. It was one of the best things that ever happened to us. My mom was happy and secure, and I was free to leave with Kodak. I was in your father's debt, but of course he never accepted anything."

Ryker laughed softly. But it was a sad laugh.

Brynnlin sat there speechless. Stunned that Ryker was sharing this much, and that he was connected to her father.

How had she never known that?

Then again, this was before she was even born. And she hadn't interacted that much with the staff. She vaguely recalled a few women that worked in the kitchens, but any one of them could have been his mother.

But how had Ryker even met her father?

Did he always work for him?

She bit her tongue to keep from asking questions, giving Ryker time to continue. A few more silent moments passed, before he picked up again.

"After I left, I made sure to still visit my mother often, yet I rarely stayed at the estate. Which is probably why I never crossed your path before. I knew your father had a child and that Maddox had a young cousin, but you can imagine my shock when Maddox confirmed who you were in that alley-way." He spared her a glance.

She barely refrained from snorting.

Shocked? Was that the word he was going with? Appalled would have been more suitable. Yet she kept her thoughts to herself.

Ryker shook his head. "I'm getting off track. The point was, I made sure to visit as often as I could. And I was supposed to visit her again the weekend of the attack. Maddox and I had planned to go together, but I had to cancel at the last minute. Kodak needed me to go take care of a problem in one of the outer cities. To this day it's my biggest regret." His voice dropped to a whisper, "It's the not knowing that's the worst. If I was there, would it have been different? Could I have saved her? Or would I have died right along with her and everyone else? After our encounter with that demon though, I'm sure it would have been the latter."

Brynnlin's chest clenched at his visible pain. She struggled to find the words, but she had to say something, anything to try and comfort him. She went with the truth.

"Ryker." She waited for him to meet her gaze, "You wouldn't have been able to stop it, trust me. Nothing would have been different, you can't blame yourself."

His words were forced as he clenched his jaw. "Logically, I know that. But it doesn't stop the guilt and the anger that's always there. I'm sure you know that better than anyone."

He had no idea.

Ryker pushed off the wall and moved across the balcony. He sat down across from her and held her stare.

"Look Brynn, I'm not telling you this so you feel sorry for me or as an excuse. But I needed you to know the reasoning behind why I acted the way I did. My behavior towards you has been less than ideal since we first met. We got off on the wrong foot, partly due to the misunderstanding in the alley, but also because of my own actions. When Maddox first confirmed who you were, I was angry at you. Your father was this great man, who I respected. And there was his daughter, living on the isles and hanging out with the very people responsible for his death. Hells, I thought you were actually in that gods forsaken cult. In my mind, you were betraying his memory, and I despised you for it. But I was so wrong, wrong about you, about everything." He reached for her hand and squeezed it softly. "For that, I am truly sorry. I didn't get to say it earlier, but I am. I have no idea what your life has been like, and I never should've been so quick to judge you."

He dropped her hand and ended with a grim nod, as if satisfied. He stood and stalked back towards her room, putting distance between them. Brynnlin sat there too stunned to move, before her brain caught up.

"Wait. What? Where are you going?" Her words were stammered, her mind trying to catch up.

Ryker gestured towards her room, "I was leaving."

"You can't just drop that on someone and run away."

He frowned. "I wasn't running away. I said what I needed to say."

"And what about what I need to say?" She crossed her arms and raised her eyebrows, challengingly. "You have no interest in my response, or how I feel about what you just said?"

"Gods, Brynn." He looked up at the sky as if looking for patience, before looking down at her again. "I'm under no delusions that you would forgive my behavior with a single apology. I only wanted you to know I was sorry. If I'm being

175

completely honest, I even hope that one day we can be friends."

"Ryker, then just say that," she threw her hands up, exasperated. "Don't apologize, then run off. Don't get me wrong, you definitely needed to apologize for that because you were a complete ass to me. But I appreciate the apology. And this may surprise you, but I accept it. How you acted was wrong, but after hearing that, I understand. I don't agree, though, I do understand. Besides, we're all going to need each other if we're ever going to succeed in taking down this Draíothe. We don't need petty grudges tearing us apart."

Surprise flashed through his eyes. "I must admit, you're much more forgiving than I."

"Hold on." Brynnlin held up a hand. "I said I accept your apology, not that I forgive it."

He shrugged. "Same thing."

She couldn't help but laugh. "And as for the friend thing, I'd honestly say you've surpassed that stage, jumped right over it in fact. You did practically see me naked. Not many have had that privilege."

Ryker groaned. "For the love of the gods, please never say those words in front of Maddox. I have no desire for an early and painful death."

Brynnlin laughed harder. "Relax, I would never subject an overprotective Maddox onto anyone."

Ryker let out a small chuckle. "So, you do have a merciful side to you, good to know."

"Don't get used to it," Brynnlin smiled before turning serious, "and Ryker I appreciate you sharing everything that you did. I can't imagine it was easy, and it meant a lot, so thank you."

She truly hadn't expected their conversation to go this way, and she could admit she was happy to be wrong.

Ryker surprised her yet again when he offered her a small smile, his teeth flashing. "It might not have been easy, but it was worth it. I'm glad we're able to move forward. And I know you're tired, I'll leave you to get your rest now."

Brynnlin didn't stop him this time. And she waited for the door to close before getting up. Feeling lighter than before, she prepared for bed and curled into the warm covers. Things were finally starting to look up, and with her mind at ease for once, she relaxed into an unconscious oblivion.

BRYNNLIN LURCHED UPRIGHT, reaching for her chest as each breath wheezed out of her.

Damn it.

She kicked away the covers, the weight of them too restrictive and not helping her current state. So much for sleep being peaceful. She should've known better.

Just when things started to take a turn, her darkest thoughts bombarded her as a reminder. She rubbed at her eyes and followed her breathing exercises, but they weren't helping. The unlit room was still unfamiliar to her, and an involuntary shiver shot down her spine.

Screw this.

She jumped out of bed and headed for the door, leaving the confining space behind. The hallway was dark as well, but at least moonlight filtered through the windows. She had no destination in mind. When she made it to the bottom of the stairs, she found herself walking towards the kitchen.

Now seemed like a good time for a late night snack. Food always made everything better. Before she made it to the kitchen, a light streaming from an unfamiliar hall had her turning in that direction.

Was someone else awake?

Down the hall, she found the light spilling out from a partially opened door. She knocked softly and peeked her head inside. Kodak was sitting behind a large desk, and his head snapped up at her interruption.

"You're still up? Is everyth—"

Kodak lifted a finger to his mouth, shushing her. He pointed to the other side of the room, and she saw Juniper sprawled out on the couch, sleeping.

"*Sorry.*" She mouthed.

"It's okay," Kodak answered in a whisper, "just talk quietly."

"I saw the light on and was surprised someone else might be awake." She kept her voice low.

Kodak's eyebrows bunched together, and his gaze shot to the clock hanging on the wall.

"Shit," he muttered and raked a hand through his hair. "I didn't realize how late it was."

"Is everything alright?"

"Yes," he motioned her into the room. "I lost track of time. I was looking through the information Zale had. I'm trying to help him sort through it."

"Anything promising?" She took a seat across from him and glanced at the papers scattered across the desk surface.

Kodak grimaced. "Honestly, I'm unsure. It's difficult to determine what may be useful."

"Look for the ones capable of obtaining extremely rare items," she suggested. "They're the ones that would have a better chance of finding that soil. Anyone that's dealt illegally of course, but not on a small scale, whoever we're looking for wouldn't bother with stuff like that. And don't bother with anyone supposedly associating with the Creed. That would be too obvious, and the Creed is too smart for that. They wouldn't actually work with someone who's under suspicion of getting caught. This is someone highly intelligent, who's been doing this for decades," she added.

Kodak was slow to lift his head, and he arched a brow. "You sound like you've done this before."

Brynnlin shrugged. "In my situation, you learn a lot, whether you want to or not."

Kodak folded his hands across his desk, and his frown deepened. "I can't imagine your life being easy with the way things turned out, and I was going to bring this up later, however, I suppose now works as well. I owe you an apology Brynn, for earlier. I'm sorry for putting you on the spot like that, or if I pressured you. I got ahead of myself when I realized you had an opportunity to get into their organization. I never should have asked you to go back there."

Brynnlin was taken aback at Kodak's words. He saw an opportunity, but he hadn't pressured her.

"Did Maddox get to you?" she guessed.

"He might have had more to say," Kodak admitted, "that doesn't mean he was wrong."

Brynnlin sighed and shook her head. "An apology isn't necessary. No one forces me to do anything. I said I'd think about it because there's very little I'm not willing to do to take them down. At first this was only ever about vengeance and finding my parent's killer. But there's a chance this could be so much more."

"I also hope that's the case and that this is leading to something larger, but I don't want that to be at your expense."

"Kodak, it won't be," she promised.

She'd been preparing and planning for years. And she wasn't going to back down now when they were getting closer. If they needed her to go to the islands, she would. She didn't fight her way through that place for nothing.

"We'll see what it comes to," Kodak hedged around her

words and started reaching through different folders again. He was sorting through photographs, putting them in different piles.

"What are those?"

"Sightings our informants had of different known collectors or their associates. Unfortunately, there aren't many."

Brynnlin grimaced and grabbed the closest pile to her, flipping through it. Kodak was right, there weren't many. Some of the photographs were of individuals, others of groups. They ranged from surveillance shots in cities, to pictures taken at high-scale events.

She turned through a few more and nearly dropped them all when she came across the next photograph. Her stomach turned as her focus narrowed on the mugshot.

A redheaded man stared back at her. A scar slashed across his cheek. He was clothed in a gray jumpsuit and cuffs clamped his wrists.

With a shaky hand, she lifted the picture to Kodak. "Who is this?"

Kodak squinted at the image. "He was a collector that was arrested several years ago. It was quite the scandal actually. Why?"

"I know him."

CHAPTER 15

"We might not be able to change the past, but that doesn't mean you can't have a fresh start."

"WHAT DO you mean you know him?" Kodak demanded.

Brynnlin turned the picture back towards her and studied it.

The first time she ever saw him flashed in her mind.

———

SHE RAN *into her father's office, throwing open the door, not bothering to knock.*

"Dad! Mom said you're leaving again, tell me it's not true!" She called out, a frown already forming before he answered.

Her father sat behind his desk, but jumped up at her intrusion.

"Brynnlin," he admonished. "You can't just barge in here, you know better." He scooted around his desk and intercepted her before she made it all the way into the room.

"It is true, huh? How long this time?" She pouted as he gently turned her around and ushered her towards the door.

"Not long."

"That's what you said last time, and you didn't come back for a whole week."

He squeezed her shoulders with affection. "It won't be that long again, only a few days."

"That's also what you said last time." She rolled her eyes even though he couldn't see her.

A muffled cough sounded behind them.

She spun around and ducked out of her father's grasp. A tall man stood near the bookshelf, chuckling at their exchange.

She tripped over her feet as embarrassment hit.

Her father hadn't been alone in his office.

The stranger met her wide-eyed gaze. He offered her a smile, his white teeth flashing, and his blue-green eyes stared at her intently. His bright red hair was shaggy, and a prominent scar ran down his face.

She wondered what happened. But she wouldn't dare ask. She risked a glance at her father. She was already in enough trouble, if the look he was giving her was any indication.

"Brynnlin, I'm in the middle of something, go find your mother." His voice was firm, and he raised his eyebrows waiting for her to comply.

She nodded and backtracked out of the room, not looking back.

———

THAT WAS THE FIRST EXCHANGE.

It hadn't been the last.

That man had been at their house the night before they were attacked.

She cleared her throat, trying to find the right words to tell

Kodak. "I don't know him, more I recognized him. He and my father had met on multiple occasions."

After the incident in the office, her parents had tried to hide the stranger's visits to the house. More than once, they slipped up.

"Fuck," Kodak bit out. "Why in the Hells would your father associate with that man?"

If he expected an answer from her, he wasn't going to get it. She had no idea. She hadn't known his name. Hadn't even known who he was until a minute ago.

"Brynn," Kodak frowned at her. "Did your father do business with him?"

She looked back down at the picture.

Why would her father have been meeting with a collector?

"I don't know," she admitted.

"This doesn't make any sense."

No, it didn't.

"You said he was arrested? For what? What do you know?" Brynnlin couldn't help that her voice came out demanding.

Kodak offered her a look of sympathy. "Unfortunately, I don't know as much as you probably want me to, but I'll tell you what I can. His name is Callahan Hanna. Personally, I didn't know him, however, he had been well known among the upper class in Ossory, not a noble, but still very elite. That's why it was such a shock when evidence turned up against him, and he was arrested for transporting contraband across realm lines and even to the isles. His specialty had been rare arts, and a lot of people hadn't believed the accusations at first, but the evidence was substantial. Rumor was someone in his organization turned against him, the details are unclear. He now sits in a high-security prison."

Brynnlin digested all of the information and tried to make sense of it.

What would her father have been doing with an art collector from Ossory?

She was getting more questions than answers.

"Brynn," Kodak's cautious tone had her tensing.

"What?"

Kodak cleared his throat. "I hate to even think this, but it's too much of a coincidence not to consider. We'd never been able to figure out why your parents had been targeted by the Creed. It never made sense, and their estate was definitely not a convenient target. I need to ask, is it possible your father had been—"

"Absolutely not," Brynnlin glared at him.

Kodak sighed. "I know this is hard, but could your father have been connected to the Creed? Maybe not directly," he interjected when she started to argue, "but you just confirmed an obvious tie between him and an associate. This might even explain the attack, if things went south..."

"Nothing went south. He wasn't working with them. That's not the reason they died." Her heart hammered in her chest as the words tore out of her.

"We need to consider this new development—"

"They were good people. He was good."

"I'm not saying he wasn't. People get desperate."

"That's not why that night happened," she snarled. "I know why it happened and that's not it."

Kodak's mouth dropped open. "What did you just say?"

There was no point in keeping it a secret.

"I said I know why they were targeted, at least I'm pretty sure," she admitted.

Kodak stared at her in disbelief. "Why?"

Brynnlin braced herself and blew out a rough breath. "My father was approached by Rí Atlas a few weeks before everything happened. He'd been assigned to a task force responsible for transporting the relic of Draíocht. It was moved to a new location, and my father was one of the few people who knew where. He was killed a few days after he returned home."

"Gods," the word escaped out of Kodak.

"So, no Kodak, he wasn't helping that fucking cult. My bet is that they were searching for the relic and my entire home was a casualty. And as for him knowing Callahan, I have no gods-damn idea, but you know who will know?" She tapped on the photograph. "There's our answers."

"Brynn, how do you know your father knew about the relic? Relics are sacred and dangerous, not just anyone would be trusted with that," Kodak took a moment to compose himself. "If you're right though...if anyone found out your father knew its location, he would be a target. But why would he have risked telling you about his assignment? I don't understand that. It should have been top secret."

Brynnlin shifted in her seat. "He didn't quite tell me that. I overheard it."

Kodak fought a small smile. "That makes more sense. Did you do that a lot?"

"Probably more than I should have."

"Please tell me you don't know the location of the relic."

"I don't."

Not anymore.

Kodak's shoulders relaxed. "Good. That's good."

"But Kodak, that doesn't change what I said." She hated that the words sounded desperate. "We need to get to Callahan, he'll have answers. I still don't believe my father had anything to do with the Creed, but he wasn't meeting with Callahan for nothing. And since Callahan was a collector, he'll know that world. You said he was arrested for his dealings to the isles. He could know something."

"It's worth investigating," Kodak agreed, "I'll see what I can do."

"Thank you."

"I'm not making any promises, we need to tread carefully with this."

"Of course."

"Good." Kodak glanced at the clock again, "Now, we should probably both try and get some rest. It's been a long night, and Juniper needs a real bed."

"Alright," Brynnlin pushed away from the desk, getting the hint. Kodak either really was tired, or he wanted to be alone.

Back in her room, she bundled into the bed, wrapping herself around one of the pillows. The weight of everything crushed into her, especially with what she learned filtering through her mind.

Dad, what did you get yourself into?

MADDOX HAD BEEN awake for a few hours and decided to get some work done in his office. He'd been productive and burned through some of the stacks that had been sitting on his desk. Even when they had a demon on the loose and a psychopathic cult to deal with, his normal duties as Chancellor still remained. He was reaching for another stack when Kodak strode purposely into the room.

Kodak's muscles were locked tight with tension, and dark shadows circled his eyes. Maddox doubted his friend had slept at all through the night. Juniper was going to give Kodak an earful when she saw him, if she hadn't already. He steeled himself for the news, whatever had kept Kodak up all night couldn't be good.

"You could knock you know," Maddox threw out, attempting to lighten his friend's mood.

"What?" Kodak looked up from the paper he was reading, his brow scrunched in confusion.

"The door," Maddox nodded towards the entrance, "it's polite to knock, I know your parents taught you better manners than that."

Kodak's lips upturned the slightest. "You want me to knock? In my own house? I don't think so."

"Technically, it's all of our house," Maddox rebutted.

"Is that right?" Kodak pulled up a chair and started smirking. "Does that mean you will all help me pay for this house and the staff that work here?"

Maddox laughed. "You know, now that I think about it, you're right. This is your house. You're very generous to let us live here."

That got a small chuckle from Kodak, and Maddox smiled in victory. Kodak seemed more relaxed than when he first walked in here. That relief was short-lived when Kodak immediately started frowning again at the papers in his hand.

"What's wrong now?" Maddox bit the bullet, it was best just to get it over with. "I know you're not in here over something good."

Somehow Kodak frowned even harder.

"I had an interesting conversation with Brynn last night." Kodak shook his head, "Or maybe it was this morning. Either way, it was an enlightening discussion."

Before Maddox could respond, Kodak tossed a small picture onto the desk.

"Recognize him?"

Maddox picked up the square, focusing on the man in the shot. Familiarity tickled the back of his brain, but he couldn't place the man.

"Should I know him?" Maddox set the picture down, waiting for Kodak to fill him in on whatever was going on.

"Does the name Callahan Hanna ring a bell?"

"Callahan...Callahan..." Maddox let the name play on his tongue while he racked through his memories for any association with the name. Again there was that tingle of recognition, he knew he should know the name. But—

Oh shit.

His gaze shot to the picture again.

It clicked. "He's the art collector that was arrested a few years ago. "

"Well it was more than a few years ago, nonetheless, yes," Kodak confirmed.

"Isn't he in prison? He can't be the collector we're looking for."

"Were you aware of his association with Xavier?"

"My Uncle Xavier?" Maddox scoffed. "They had no association."

Maddox frowned at his friend. Kodak was obviously suffering from sleep deprivation, or the stress of all this was finally getting to him. Kodak wasn't making any sense.

"Kodak, just spit it out already, what are you trying to get at?"

Kodak met his gaze head on. "Xavier knew Callahan, and possibly worked with him in some capacity."

"Impossible," Maddox spat out. His uncle never would have lowered himself to work with some illegal art dealer. He said as much.

"Callahan's charges extended beyond that. There was evidence he supplied contraband and weapons to the isles."

"Like I said, impossible. My uncle wouldn't have gotten anywhere near that. He was a governor for gods sake." Plus they tore into Xavier's life after the attack and never found anything to suggest something like this.

Kodak still didn't look convinced, frustrating Maddox further.

"Were you also aware Xavier had been on an assignment shortly before his death?"

Maddox studied Kodak. Where in the Hells was he going with this?

"I knew he had been away from home, I don't know the details."

"He'd been a part of the relocation of the relic, he'd been given the order by Atlas himself." Kodak dropped that bomb of information.

"What?" Maddox stuttered.

"Yes," Kodak frowned and shook his head. "It's highly likely your uncle was targeted and killed due to his involvement and knowledge of where the relic lies. However, I won't deny that it's also quite perplexing that he met with Callahan, who has an affiliation with the Creed."

"Kodak, I can guarantee Xavier didn't know Callahan. Wasn't Callahan from Ossory?" Maddox tried again. "Where are you getting this information?"

"Brynn," Kodak said, "she recognized Callahan. She revealed that he had met with her father on several occasions, including the night before the incident."

"No. There's no way," he rejected the claim.

Kodak raised his eyebrows, "Are you suggesting she lied?"

"Of course not," Maddox argued, "but maybe she's confused. That was a long time ago and she might not remember things properly, she was a child if you forgot."

"I'm not confused," a voice said sharply from the doorway.

Maddox jerked and spun towards the door to see Brynnlin

scowling at him something fierce. The rigidness of Kodak's posture revealed his own surprise at her entrance.

Neither one of them had heard her approach.

"Eavesdropping? Really, Brynnlin?" He hoped to distract her from her anger, "That's a low move."

Her eyes narrowed more as she stalked into the room and leaned against the wall crossing her arms, "I was looking for Kodak, and Juniper told me he was with you. It's also not eavesdropping if the door is wide open, and you're talking loud enough to be heard down the hall."

He cringed, she might have had a point with that.

"By all means, don't stop talking now. My presence shouldn't stop you from insulting me more," she challenged.

"I wasn't insulting you," he defended, "I was suggesting you might not have the whole picture. I can't see how your father would work with that man."

"And you think I can?" She cried out, "You think I want to believe my father had anything to do with the very people that killed him. All I know is that somehow he knew Callahan, and we can't ignore that."

"Alright fine, let's just say you are right," Maddox conceded. "He'll be easy enough to find, he's sitting in a cell."

"That's what I was coming to speak to you about," Kodak jumped back in. "Callahan could have imperative information, not just about Xavier, but also about the Creed's other suppliers."

"And? Send a request to the prison that we'd like to interrogate him as it relates to a current investigation. I shouldn't have to walk you through this," sarcasm coated his words.

Kodak rolled his eyes, "Don't you think I already did that? Sent it first thing this morning."

"Then what's the issue?" He dropped the sarcasm, turning

serious, "Explain the urgency, and we can see him by tomorrow."

"The issue is my request was denied," Kodak dropped the paper he'd been carrying on the desk and glared at it.

"What the fuck?" Maddox growled and grabbed the paper, scanning its contents. Sure enough, it was exactly as Kodak said. The request to see the prisoner was denied.

"He can't do this."

"Unfortunately, he can," Kodak leaned back in the chair with a heavy sigh. "As the prison is within his realm and is his responsibility, it's at his discretion. As you can see in his response, *The prisoner in question is too high-risk to allow access'.*"

"That's bullshit, and you know it." Maddox shook his head.

Fucking politics.

"Who denied it?" Brynnnlin asked.

"Kaceston," he spit the name like the curse it was.

"Who's that?"

"A world-class prick," Maddox mumbled under his breath.

Brynnlin's lips twitched at his response.

Kodak chuckled, "While that may be true, he's the ruler of Oícha."

"And he can deny your request just like that?" she questioned.

"He can, which puts us in a difficult situation."

"Is there any way to go around him?" Brynnlin continued to push, "I mean, he can't have the final say, right? You're a ruler, too."

"I am, however, it's his realm. I can't go do what I want, just as he wouldn't be able to here," Kodak explained.

"But we need to talk to Callahan."

"Brynn, I'm aware."

"Go to Tobin," Maddox offered. "He seems the only one

capable of leashing Kaceston, maybe he'll change Kaceston's mind."

"I'm not going to Tobin," Kodak scowled. "And no one leashes Kaceston. He and Tobin have a fragile understanding and happen to work together, that's all."

"He's not untouchable, Kodak," Maddox argued.

"I'm not starting something with Kaceston over this, we'll figure out another way."

"Are you really that afraid of him?" Maddox knew he was pushing.

Kodak shot him a withering glare. "I know when to pick my battles, and this isn't it."

"Please stop, both of you," Brynnlin intervened, "we can figure something else out."

"Like what?" Maddox snapped, "It's not like we can break in and talk to Callahan—"

Maddox stopped. A horrible but brilliant idea danced through his mind.

It was another way. And it would bypass Kaceston.

Kodak's eyes narrowed, "Whatever you're thinking, the answer is Hells no."

"We could break in," Maddox said anyway.

Kodak pushed out of his chair and loomed over the desk. "Are you out of your mind?"

"Maybe a little," Maddox admitted, "but, hear me out."

"Not a ch—"

"Kaceston would never know," Maddox spoke over him, "we could interrogate Callahan and be gone before anyone was the wiser."

"Not that I'm entertaining this, but how exactly would you break in?" Kodak challenged. "That's the most secure prison in the entire Empire. No one's ever gotten anywhere near there."

"Wesley has."

"No fucking way," Kodak sneered.

"He can get into anywhere, you know he can. I've heard he's been in and out of that prison before."

Brynnlin pushed away from the wall, her eyes bright. "There's actually someone that can get us in?"

"Not so fast," Kodak gave both of them a hard look. "Maddox, you can't seriously be considering this. Wesley is a fucking criminal, wanted in three out of the five realms. I can't be involved with this, none of us can be involved in this. And that's if he even considered taking a job from us. You know he avoids royals like the godsdamn plague."

"You won't be involved," Maddox assured him. "Look, I don't know what realm he's currently in, but I'll reach out to some people and have them set up a meeting for me alone, no mention of you at all. If you want to get to Callahan, you know this is the only way."

When Kodak didn't immediately object, Maddox knew he was considering it.

"Kodak, this will work," he urged again.

Kodak shook his head. "I can't believe I'm saying this. You can reach out. See if he'll even take the job. However, nothing moves forward without my approval."

"Done."

"Maddox, I want to go with you," Brynnlin started to say.

"No." Maddox couldn't get the word out fast enough.

"Absolutely not." Kodak echoed.

Brynnlin's eyes widened at the two of them. "What? Why not?"

Maddox only gaped at her. "Are you really asking that?"

"Brynn, this is far too dangerous, it's best to let Maddox handle this," Kodak added.

"Dangerous? Really?" Brynnlin rolled her eyes.

"Brynn, I'm already hesitant to let Maddox go along with this, I'm not sending another person."

"It's more dangerous to go alone," she argued.

"Brynn no," Kodak said with a finality. "You wanted to follow this lead, and I'm agreeing, but this is how we're doing it. Understand?"

Brynnlin's head dropped, and she mumbled an agreement.

"Good, Maddox set it up." Kodak forced a nod, but he did not look happy as he left the office.

Brynnlin started to follow him out. Maddox called her back.

"What?" She plopped into the chair Kodak just vacated.

"I have something for you," he reached into one of his desk drawers and pulled out a folder, sliding it to her.

She raised her eyebrows and gingerly opened the file, scanning through its contents.

"What is this?" Her voice was soft.

"Remi finished your new identity." He smiled as her surprised gaze shot to him. "We had to forge your background a bit, but it will hold up against any security check. As far as the world knows, Brynnlin Raigáin died eleven years ago, for your safety, let's keep it that way. But Brenna Murchadha is very much alive. When this is all over, you can build a life. We might not be able to change the past, but that doesn't mean you can't have a fresh start."

His heart cracked as she looked over the papers again, and tears filled her eyes. She blinked to stop them from falling, but one still trailed down her cheek. She gave him a wavering smile, one so genuine, he almost couldn't take it.

"Thank you."

All he could do was nod, never had two words threatened to break him. Her simple joy at something so simple was heartbreaking. No child should have had to go through what she had, and he could only pray to the gods that her future was kinder.

He cleared his throat. "Make sure to familiarize yourself with the details. We tried not to make things too complicated, but we also don't want to raise any questions."

She nodded solemnly. "I got it."

He pulled one more thing out of the drawer, hoping this would lighten the sudden weight on his chest and knowing it would make her just as happy.

"Here."

Her mouth dropped open, and her eyes lit up. She let out a little squeal as she snatched the gold cuff off his desk.

"Is this really mine?" She was so hopeful, she was already securing the bracelet on her wrist before he could answer.

He laughed at her reaction. "Yes, it's yours. It's called an orenda. About a decade ago some scholar discovered how to stabilize magic in a liquid form. Our technology has advanced tenfold since that discovery. Make sure not to crush any of those beads, or it won't work."

She nodded her head seriously, absorbing all of his directions, as he walked her through how to use the small device.

"It's already synced to everybody else's, so you're good to go," Maddox finished his explanation.

He was surprised when Brynnlin rounded the desk and threw her arms around him.

"Thank you again," she whispered, "and not just for the bracelet, for everything."

She pulled back and wiped at her eyes. She offered a soft smile, before grabbing the folder and strolling out of his office. Maddox could only watch her go. In that moment, he swore she would never know another hardship again, not if he could help it.

CHAPTER 16

"No light entered, and the smell of blood was thick."

THREE DAYS LATER, Maddox still hadn't gotten a response from Wesley. Everyone was starting to get restless, Brynnlin included. She tried to focus on the task at hand, but her mind kept wandering to what they were going to do if Wesley refused to even see them.

"Brynn. Focus. Do it again." Juniper called out, frustration lacing her words. She crossed her arms and glared. "Distraction is how you get killed."

Brynnlin heaved a deep sigh and got back into her stance. Juniper was right though, a single mistake could be the difference between life and death. And she owed Juniper. Juniper was doing her a huge favor by taking the time to train with her. The past few days she'd usually trained with Verenna and Selene, sometimes even Maddox. But everyone was otherwise busy at the moment.

Verenna got called into the nearby town to help with a medical emergency. Maddox was occupied with a backup plan to get to Callahan if Wesley fell through. Kodak was busy preparing for an upcoming summit meeting with the other rulers. Selene was working on some special project for Kodak. And Ryker and Zale were off doing whatever it is they do, she wasn't really sure.

"You need to always be ready," Juniper commanded as she circled Brynnlin.

The reminder pulled her back to the present.

They'd been at this all morning. She'd barely rolled out of bed when Juniper knocked on her door. Juniper tossed training clothes at her and told her to get dressed and meet downstairs.

From there, Juniper led her to an open field a few miles away from the palace. Trees were scattered about and rolling hills sat in the distance. The sun was shining above them and even with the cool breeze, sweat dripped down Brynnlin's back.

A bolt of lightning cracked off the ground a few feet from Brynnlin.

Heat blasted at her.

"What the Hells was that?" Brynnlin whirled and glared at Juniper.

"You aren't paying attention," Juniper reprimanded.

Brynnlin released her magic. Tendrils of shadows snaked across the ground, surrounding Juniper.

"Good," Juniper was unfazed by the threat at her feet. "Your control is improving at a fast rate. And you'd be fine if attacking, but how's your defense?"

Lightning appeared in Juniper's hand like a spear, and she was launching it at Brynnlin.

Brynnlin didn't have time to think.

Shadows shot up like a wall.

The spear struck through the barrier, and the shadows coiled tighter, barely stopping it from reaching Brynnlin's chest.

She heaved out a breath. "If I didn't know any better, I'd think you were actually trying to kill me."

The bolt disappeared, and Brynnlin let the shadows fall.

"What would you gain if I went easy on you?" Juniper raised a single brow. "The world won't."

Brynnlin took a seat on a nearby boulder sticking up in the ground, "I suppose you do have a point."

"Of course I do. And I'll admit you're doing much better than I expected. You're quite gifted."

Brynnlin chuckled. She didn't know whether to be insulted or complimented.

"What's next?" She stretched her arms out and scanned the field again.

A dark figure across the way caught her attention. A wave of anxiety slammed into her, and her muscles tensed.

No one was supposed to be out here.

She jumped up from the rock and was already moving towards Juniper. She prepared for the worst.

She narrowed her gaze, staring intently at the figure, only to realize with a closer look that it was Ryker.

She immediately relaxed.

Juniper also relaxed when she noticed him strolling towards them. When he was close enough, she asked, "Ryker, what a pleasant surprise, is everything alright?"

"Juniper, Brynn," he greeted them both. "Maddox received word from Wesley," he turned his attention to Brynnlin, "he'd like you back at the palace immediately."

Relief burst through her chest. "Wesley agreed to meet?"

"He did. Maddox needs to discuss the details with you, and it can't wait. Hence," Ryker gestured to himself, "me acting as errand boy to come fetch you."

"You would make a good errand boy, maybe Juniper and

Kodak should reconsider your position," Brynnlin snickered at her own joke.

"Perhaps you're right Brynn, I'll have to bring this up with Kodak," Juniper joined in.

"Charming, the both of you," Ryker rolled his eyes. "How about you be charming as we walk back? As I said, Maddox is waiting."

"Brynn, go ahead, I need a word with Ryker, but we'll be right behind you," Juniper said.

Ryker raised his eyebrows in question but complied.

"Of course," Brynnlin answered, walking away to give them some space.

Not even five minutes later, they caught back up with her. Her thoughts wandered to Maddox and Wesley. How much convincing would they have to do to get Wesley to agree to the job? Maybe they could—

Brynnlin's feet were tripped out from under her, and she found herself on the ground.

"What the Hells!"

Roots crawled up from the dirt, wrapping around her wrists and legs. They moved so fast, trapping her on her back before she could escape. They held her down, not allowing for any movement.

Her frantic gaze shot to Ryker and Juniper. Were they all being attacked?

Her wide-eyed gaze landed on Ryker, only to see him kneeling on the ground, one hand pressed to the earth.

This was his doing.

Juniper stood cautiously at his side. Her tight-lipped expression determined.

"Ryker, what are you doing?" Brynnlin choked out as a root came dangerously close to her neck. She wasn't in pain, only completely bound.

It was Juniper who answered. "Control, Brynn. People will fight dirty, they'll attack when you least expect it. Can you contain your shadows? Can you get out of this without exposing yourself?"

Really? A godsdamn lesson right now? That's what this was?

Before she could respond, the roots tightened around her, restricting her entire body. It was even hard to breathe.

Panic started to edge its way into her mind.

She couldn't do this.

It was too much.

She couldn't be restrained like this. She shook her head violently to clear the memories that threatened to overtake her. It was too late. Black spots danced along her vision. No longer was she staring up at the bright, blue sky, instead she was back in that dark cell. No light entered, and the smell of blood was thick.

Her blood.

She physically gagged and squeezed her eyes shut.

This wasn't real.

Not anymore.

She survived.

She repeated the mantra in her head, over and over again. She tried to picture the field they were in and force herself back there. Beyond the roaring in her ears, she was able to filter out the sound of voices around her. She latched onto them. Anything to bring her back to reality.

She opened her eyes, the rays of the sun coming back into focus. Her hands were still trapped at her sides, but she felt the tall grass and warm soil against her skin. She gripped onto the earth, anything to keep her grounded to the present.

"Maybe this was too much, too soon," Ryker murmured to Juniper.

Juniper frowned. "Give her a minute."

Brynnlin ignored them. She had to fight her panic just as much as she had to fight her instinct to let her magic explode to get her free. It would be so easy. It would barely take half a thought to unleash her abilities.

She'd be free.

It was tempting. But she managed to reign in the impulse.

In a horrible way, Juniper was right. She needed control before darkness encased this entire field and those in it.

She could do this.

She pushed past the heaviness in her chest and reached within, feeling for that power deep inside her. She pulled on a small strand, letting a shadowed tendril slither out from her palm down to the knife at her thigh.

As fast as she could, she pulled the knife to her hand, flipping it, and slicing through the root at the wrist. With a hand free, she made quick work of the rest.

The crushing weight heaved off of Brynnlin. She rolled over to her hands and knees gasping in air. She stayed in her position, just breathing, and slowing down her heart rate.

Ryker stood and took a step towards her, "Are you okay?"

She sat back on her heels and held up a hand, "I just need a second."

Something in her voice or her reaction to what happened gave her away because Juniper rushed and kneeled next to her.

"Brynn, I'm so sorry, it was supposed to be a simple exercise to test you under pressure, I didn't mean for that to freak you out." Concern flared in Juniper's eyes.

Yet when Juniper reached for her arm, she couldn't help flinching away. Deep down, she knew they didn't mean her any harm. But it had been a long time since she'd been dragged that deep into the dark hole that permanently resided within her head. Right then, she was a dangerous mixture of vulnerability and being on edge.

"I'm fine," she said, pushing up off the ground. "I just need to catch my breath," she turned on her heel and started pacing a few feet away.

Her breathing was still ragged.

In and out, she reminded herself.

She bent over, hands on her knees, and clenched her eyes shut.

'Deep breathes. In and out. Remember where you are. The past can't hurt you anymore.'

After another minute that seemed to do the trick, and she was able to get a grip on her emotional state. She rose and turned back to Juniper and Ryker, only to see curiosity and worry written all over their faces. There was no way she was going to get out of this without some type of explanation.

Slowly, she made her way back towards them.

"I..." she hesitated and looked around the field. Anything to stall and also to find inspiration for how to explain what just happened. She had to give them something.

"I'm sorry," she blew out a deep breath. "I have some issues with being restrained," she absently rubbed her wrists, "and... um...it's a bit of a trigger for me."

Technically, not a lie.

Restraint would send her into an episode.

Which she had no plans on opening up about today.

She was already fighting back memories that the flashback provoked. It took extreme effort to try and remain less traumatized than she actually was. But she would pull it off, she always did. She was excellent at suppressing her own trauma.

"Gods, Brynn, I had no idea, I never would have...with the training," Juniper sounded horrified.

"Juniper, no, I know," Brynnlin rushed to reassure her. Guilt ate at her that Juniper blamed herself. "You couldn't have known. I never would have said anything, it was just, you know with my little episode..." she waved her hand to the area on the ground. "You guys deserve an explanation. And honestly that's probably good for me, you know. If that ever happens for real, I need to be able to keep my head. It just caught me off guard, and I didn't handle it well."

Also not a lie. The exposure would be good for her, if that ever happened during a real attack and she went into an episode, she'd be screwed.

"Actually, knowing that, you handled it very well. You escaped quickly and followed orders. Your magic was very precise, slightly detectable, but only because we know what it is," Juniper commended and thankfully, didn't seem overly concerned anymore. If Brynnlin was lucky, Juniper wouldn't dwell on it, and they could move on.

Brynnlin turned to Ryker, he'd been oddly silent throughout the whole exchange. She found him already staring at her, studying her intently. She shifted her weight back and forth, uncomfortable at being the focus of his attention, while she waited for him to say something.

After a full minute she couldn't take it anymore.

"Why are you staring at me like that?" she demanded, worried that he didn't quite believe her and would push the issue.

"I'm thinking," he pursed his lips.

"About..." she gestured for him to continue.

Ryker crossed his arms and explained, "Ways that could help you overcome that fear. If anyone got you into that position, you'd be extremely vulnerable. It's a weakness that could easily be extorted."

She breathed a sigh of relief. Ryker was in full general-mode, his brain obviously working through combative strategies.

"While I think that is a great idea—" *she really did,* "—shouldn't we head back now? I think that's enough training for today, and we really do need to get back to Maddox." She started taking slow steps forward in hopes that would urge them along.

"Absolutely," Ryker said and led the way out of the field. "We've already made him wait much longer than intended and don't worry, I'll think of ways to help with your issues of being restrained. We can discuss it at a later time."

Brynnlin made a noncommittal sound and happily followed along behind him with Juniper at her side. She wasn't about to argue, she'd do just about anything to postpone that conversation.

————

BACK AT THE PALACE, they found the others huddled in Kodak's office.

Brynnlin beamed at Maddox, "You actually heard back from Wesley."

"I did," Maddox smiled back. "He's willing to meet."

"That's excellent."

"Don't get over-excited," Kodak warned. "We have much to consider."

He gestured Juniper over to him and pulled her onto his lap. Brynnlin averted her eyes as they shared a kiss.

"How did training go this morning?"

Brynnlin stiffened and prayed Juniper wouldn't mention what happened.

"It went really well," Juniper answered, "she's advancing at an impressive speed."

"Good. Very good," Kodak nodded and looked to Brynnlin. "You're going to need it if we move forward with this."

"You decided you're okay with this?"

Kodak scoffed, "Definitely not, but that's what we're here to discuss. We'll decide this as a family. I've made it clear I don't think this is a good idea. It's not worth the risk. If we do get caught, even my position won't save us. We're breaking several laws and if Kaceston gets wind of this, his response could very well be deadly."

"Kaceston did this to himself when he denied a simple request," Maddox argued. "He only did it to be difficult. And he'll never know we were even there."

"I agree with Maddox, we're dealing with something bigger than even Kaceston," Zale added.

"Really, Zale?" Kodak's lips pursed. "I'm surprised at your outlook."

"If this had just been because Brynn's father knew Callahan, I might not think the risk worth it," Zale admitted. "But he could know about the Creed's dealings, with that alone, I feel like we have to try."

"What makes you think he knows something of value?" Juniper asked with a pointed look. "And if he did, why in the gods would he talk to us?"

"He knows something, and he'll talk, trust me," Brynnlin said without hesitation.

Juniper shook her head. "You can't know that. And when he doesn't, what are you going to do? Torture the man?"

"If that's what it takes." *It wouldn't be the first time.*

Juniper's lips thinned.

"Juniper, he knows something," Ryker grimaced. "I wish that wasn't the case, but he's not sitting in a high-security prison for nothing. And from what Kodak told me, he didn't get caught, someone turned against him."

Kodak frowned, but nodded, "How about you, Selene? Verenna? You two have been pretty quiet."

Selene looked up from the couch. "I'm not sure. I feel like if he truly knew anything, the Creed would've killed him by now, but maybe he's in the one place they can't get to."

"That could very well be true," Kodak agreed, "he might not be a threat to them."

"Or they can't get to him," Brynnlin added.

"I think we should do it." Verenna's statement silenced them all.

Brynnlin definitely hadn't expected that.

Kodak didn't hide his surprise. "And you're reasoning?"

"You could be right, and he knows nothing," Verenna looked down at her clamped hands before meeting everyone's stare. "But what if he does? Are we really going to throw that opportunity away?"

"I suppose not." Kodak sighed and with a resigned look, announced the decision. "Most of you agree the risk is worth it, so that's what we'll do. Granted, Wesley still needs to agree to the job."

"Maddox, when are you meeting with him?" Brynnlin glanced at her cousin.

She raised an eyebrow when she caught him frowning.

"I'm not," he admitted. "I can't."

"What? Why?"

"Because..."

Kodak held up a hand, and Maddox trailed off.

Kodak met her questioning gaze. "Well Brynn, you see, there's been a slight change of plans. You get to meet with Wesley. It's up to you to convince him."

CHAPTER 17

"It was a risk they had to take, but it didn't mean she had to like it."

BRYNNLIN DIDN'T THINK she heard Kodak right.

"I'm sorry, what?"

Kodak shrugged. "You said you wanted to be involved. Now you are."

She did want that—but, "Why the change of heart?"

Last time she asked, the answer had been a resounding no.

"I thought you didn't want me involved with the Wesley meeting," Brynnlin crossed her arms and didn't hide the bitterness from her tone. Maddox and Kodak had made themselves very clear about their feelings on the matter.

Kodak sighed. "I didn't. I still don't. But we don't have very many options at the moment. Wesley has agreed to meet, but the circumstances which he wants to meet puts us in a precarious situation."

"How so?"

"I'm sure you are aware that the annual summit meeting is this weekend, correct?" Kodak asked instead.

Of course she knew. Kodak had been trying to prepare for it the past few days, while also dealing with everything else. It was where all the rulers and their councils met once a year.

"I'm aware." The plan had been for her to stay here with Selene, Ryker, and Verenna to continue researching.

"Yes, well, every year a different ruler takes their turn to host," Kodak explained. "And this year that honor goes to Atlas. And the sneaky bastard decided to hold the meeting the same weekend as his son's day of birth celebration. So once we finish the summit, we're all obliged to stay for the festivity."

Brynnlin shrugged. "Okay...and? Where does Wesley tie into this?"

"Apparently, Wesley somehow landed an invitation to the day of birth celebration and wants the meeting to take place there."

"I'm still not seeing the problem. Doesn't that actually make it easier?"

"Not at all," Maddox stepped in. "It's a huge event, hundreds of citizens from Atlas' realm will be in attendance. But so will every other Rí and Ríona, along with other council members. There's too many witnesses, and we can't be seen meeting Wesley. It's too much of a risk."

Ah, Brynnlin understood now. The others were too recognizable, but she wasn't.

"But it's not a risk for me to meet with him."

"Exactly. And while it goes against every fiber of my being to let you anywhere near him, this opportunity is too good to pass up."

"So what? I sneak into this party, meet the guy, then sneak out?" She considered this. "Seems easy enough."

"Not quite," Maddox said, "there's no sneaking into this party, it'll be too heavily guarded. That's why you'll be going as a guest with us."

"And how will that work? I don't have an invitation to this party."

"You won't need one. You'll be arriving with us two days before the celebration. Atlas has invited all of the realm leaders and council members to stay at his palace for the summit. It shouldn't be too elaborate, most rulers won't bring their full council, just a select few for representation. And there might be a few meals but again—"

"Maddox, stop," Brynnlin interrupted his spiel of information. Her mind was already buzzing from how many ways this wasn't going to work and where things could go wrong. It was obvious Maddox hadn't thought this through. "How exactly are you going to explain some random person showing up with Kodak? I'm not in his council, and I doubt he can just add a plus one to something like this."

"Oh, that's easy," Maddox waved away her concern and grinned. "Welcome to the council, your Kodak's newest Grand Diplomat."

She scoffed. "You're not serious, right?" There was no way he intended for her to "join" the council. "That will never work."

Maddox's grin transformed into a frown at her immediate denial of his plan. "What? Why not? It's brilliant. No one will ever question who Kodak has in his council, and it will give you a reason to attend everything."

"It won't work." Brynnlin didn't back down. She didn't care how "brilliant" Maddox thought it was. "I have zero idea on how court life works. And Grand Diplomat? I don't even know what that is." She shook her head at the sheer absurdity of this. Surely, Maddox could come up with something better.

"Brynn, I assure you, it will work," Kodak said. "A Grand Diplomat is a fancy word for emissary. It's someone who travels to other realms on my behalf. No one will expect you to know anything of value, and if people start to pry, we'll tell them we're testing it out on a trial basis because I'm tired of traveling."

"Even if that did work, and emphasis on if," she crossed her arms, "you all said you can't meet with Wesley because you're in Kodak's council. If I'm in it too, then I can't meet with him either."

"No," Maddox shook his head. "I said we would be recognized."

"And I wouldn't be? That doesn't make sense."

"Did I forget to mention this party was a masquerade theme?" Maddox smirked, as if that solved all of their problems. "People have known us for decades, some centuries, so we can't risk it. But there's no way they'll be able to pick you out in a huge crowd after only just meeting you within a few days. Let alone, pay attention to who you're talking to. It's foolproof."

She rolled her eyes. "A masquerade really? Could that be any more cliché?"

Juniper chuckled. "Atlas' son is very serious about his parties. Be thankful it's not more outrageous."

Brynnlin grimaced. "If you say so."

"So, what do you think?" Maddox asked.

What did she think?

She thought it was a disaster waiting to happen. That it was going to blow up in their faces. But she also didn't see a whole lot of other options. Not if she wanted to get to Callahan.

Brynnlin shrugged. "You know I'll do whatever is necessary. I don't know if it will work, but if you think so, then I trust you."

Maddox walked over to her and braced his hands on both her shoulders. He leaned down to look her in the eyes.

"I would never go through with something that would put you in danger. This plan is solid. And Zale will stay here, Ryker is taking his place. One of us will be at your side at all times.

You will not be left alone. You'll have some meals, mingle with pretentious people, sit through a boring meeting, and talk to someone at a party. That's it."

Maddox didn't understand. She wasn't afraid of going. She just didn't think she could possibly play the role they needed her to, which would blow the plan straight down to the Three Hells.

But she had to try. They needed Wesley.

"Okay," she blew out a breath. "But you have your work cut out for you. You have less than two days to turn me into a believable court member."

Maddox smiled confidently. "Easy."

IT HAD NOT BEEN EASY.

Brynnlin had never been so busy as they prepared for their departure. Between more training, planning, learning what she could about the other realms, and learning proper court etiquette, she was exhausted. That didn't even include the time she had to spend getting stabbed by a seamstress as Juniper rush ordered acceptable clothes for her to wear. Luckily, she only needed formal wear, Maddox had gotten her enough clothes when she first arrived.

And with all of that done, now it was finally time.

She squared her shoulders and stood in front of the mirror as Verenna finished the final touches on her hair. They would be arriving at Atlas' tonight, and he was throwing a banquet to welcome their arrival, along with the other royals.

Brynnlin didn't just have to act the part of a royal's Diplomat, she also had to look it.

She ran a shaky hand down the soft material of the dress Juniper ordered for her. The full-length, baby-blue satin dress hugged her body and was simple, yet still elegant. It was made more elaborate by the silver roses and vines intertwined throughout a layer of tulle over the skirt. And a slit traveled to her upper thigh, making it surprisingly easy to move in. Brynnlin had to admit the dress was beautiful and was easily the nicest thing she'd ever worn. Though she was a little wary about the strappy heels Verenna paired the dress with. She didn't think the extra height was necessary. Verenna disagreed.

"Stop fidgeting," Verenna complained.

"Sorry," Brynnlin mumbled back and stopped moving.

"There," Verenna stepped away with a smile after pinning the last strand of hair in place.

Verenna had curled her hair and let most of the thick mass fall down Brynnlin's back in waves, but a few pieces were expertly pinned around her face. Verenna also kept Brynnlin's makeup light, going with a more natural look.

Brynnlin eyed herself in the mirror again, admiring Verenna's work. She stared at her reflection, taking it all in.

"Wow," she finally said, "I barely recognize myself."

Verenna's smile turned soft. "You're still you, only a bit more dressed up."

"Let's just hope it works."

Verenna laughed. "It's going to work, maybe too well. Everyone's going to be too smitten with you, and won't even care where you showed up from."

Brynnlin laughed with her. "I doubt that, and we don't want attention on me, the opposite really."

"Then Juniper should have picked a different dress."

They laughed harder until a knock interrupted them.

"Brynn, are you ready?" Ryker called out.

"Yep." Brynnlin stepped out, and Verenna followed, shutting the door behind them.

Ryker gave her a quick once over and smirked as he got a good look at her. "Look at you. You clean up pretty well."

She bit her lip to hold back her smile and gave him the same appraisal. He looked handsome in an all black suit. "You don't look too bad yourself."

"That's the highest of compliments from you," he chuckled, before turning serious. "Stay with either me or Maddox at all times tonight, it'll be easier to control who you have interactions with that way."

"I know."

Ryker's reminder was unnecessary as they had gone over this at least a thousand times.

Ryker led her downstairs where they met up with Maddox in the foyer. He was ready to go in a dark navy suit that complimented him well. He looked up from his conversation with Zale and Selene at their arrival and nodded.

"You both look great."

Brynnlin forced a smile, nerves hitting her the closer they got to leaving the safety of Kodak's palace. She didn't know what to expect upon their arrival, and there was too much riding on this for it to go wrong.

Before her thoughts could completely spiral, Kodak and Juniper showed up from the opposite hall. Juniper was stunning in a strapless, burgundy gown. Her hair was expertly braided away from her face and showed off her silver crown. Kodak also looked sophisticated in a matching suit and had pulled his hair back into a bun making his features appear even sharper than usual.

Kodak nodded to all of them. "Shall we?"

When no one voiced any objections, Kodak led the way to the courtyard.

"Zale will drop us off at the front gate. Remember, I want

everyone on high alert for these next few days. I don't expect trouble, but it never hurts to be cautious."

"You look nervous." Maddox stood tall next to her and cast her a side glance.

She shot him an annoyed look, "I'm not nervous."

She had no intention of admitting the truth out loud.

She'd be an idiot to not be cautious going into this situation. She preferred calculated plans where she could either control the situation or prepare for any outcome.

In this case, she had none of the above.

There were way too many players involved and unknown variables. It was a risk they had to take, but it didn't mean she had to like it.

Maddox shrugged. "If you say so."

She narrowed her eyes. "I am saying so, don't be annoying."

"Annoying?" Maddox chuckled. "I didn't even do anything."

"I didn't even do anything," she deepened her voice, mocking him. "That's what every guy says when they obviously did something. I already told you I'm not nervous."

"You're being very defensive for someone who isn't nervous," Maddox called her out and started laughing outright as he swooped to the side to avoid the punch she threw towards his arm. "Wow. Nervous and slow. You're off your game today, Brynn," he clucked his tongue.

"I'll show you off my game," she lunged forward only to stop as Verenna stepped between them.

Verenna shook her head at their antics, "That's enough, children."

"You're one to talk," Brynnlin threw back.

"True, but I can't let you mess up all the hard work I put into your hair," Verenna teased before pulling her into a quick hug. "Be careful," Verenna whispered.

"I will," she promised and hugged her back.

"You be careful, too," Verenna looked over at Maddox.

"Always am, now don't be too much of a brat to Zale and try to keep the place in one piece," Maddox joked and tried to ruffle her hair.

Verenna ducked out of the way. "No promises," she shot back.

Maddox's lips twitched upwards, and he turned to Zale. They shared a brief one-armed hug where they slapped each other on the back

"Watch your back."

Maddox nodded. "You too."

They started talking quietly, and Brynnlin didn't bother to listen. Her attention was pulled to Selene, who without warning, threw her arms around Brynnlin and squeezed tight.

"I swear, Brynnlin, you better be careful and come back in one piece, or I will hunt you down myself."

Brynnlin squeezed her back. "I wouldn't dare risk your wrath, Selene, you know that."

"Good," Selene stepped back, "then I'll see you in a few days."

Brynnlin winked. "Don't have too much fun without me."

After everyone finished their goodbyes, they gathered in front of Zale. Brynnlin followed with only slight hesitation.

"Send for me as soon as you're ready to return," Zale gave them a final nod and opened the portal.

One by one, they each stepped forward.

Brynnlin grimaced and ignored the small stabs of pain as she passed through the vast opening.

The portal disappeared behind them.

No longer were they in Kodak's courtyard. They now stood in the middle of a large stone bridge. A roaring river flowed beneath them. Up ahead, two towers stood tall and a golden gate protected the palace behind it. Sentries stood along the gate but Brynnlin barely paid them any notice, not with what stood beyond them.

She barely held in her gasp.

The palace seemed to have been built out of the earth itself. It ascended out of the ground and towards the sky. More golden towers rose out of the structure and large balconies circled around. Greenery and vines twisted and clung to the outside of the building, blending it seamlessly into the surrounding nature.

To the right, a valley stretched out towards a forest. While on the other side sat a glistening lake where a massive waterfall rushed to the river below. Beyond the lake, snow-capped mountains rose high above them.

She hated to admit it, but the entire scene took her breath away. It was so different from Kodak's palace, which was all class and comfort, with gardens and the surrounding forest.

They were both beautiful, only in a different way. This felt like the encompassment of nature. There was a kind of wonder to it that had to be appreciated.

She probably would have kept gawking, but the gate before them groaned and inched open, revealing three men striding towards them. Kodak reached for Juniper's hand and took the lead to go meet them.

Two of the men were dressed in suits that looked tailor-made for them, while the third was in all black with knives sheathed at his hips. The leader of the trio stepped forward to address them.

Brynnlin recognized Atlas' Commanding General, Silas Turrain. He was tall, and the suit did nothing to hide his muscular build. His black hair was shaved short, and a dark tattoo climbed up his neck. His bronze eyes scanned the group, assessing each one of them.

"Rí Kodak, Ríona Juniper, welcome. Rí Atlas will be pleased

you could make it," he greeted and bowed, the other two behind him followed suit.

"General Turrain, thank you. You may rise," Kodak said firmly, but politely, and motioned them upwards.

Silas turned to Maddox and greeted him with a handshake. "Chancellor Raigáin, good to see you."

"General Turrain." Maddox nodded and clamped his hand.

Silas and Ryker shared a similar greeting.

Silas turned his attention to her, and his brow furrowed. "I don't believe we've met." His tone was only mildly curious.

She kept quiet to let Kodak answer. She was his employee after all.

"This is Brenna Murchadha, my Grand Diplomat, the newest member of my council."

She smiled demurely and held out her hand. "Pleasure."

"Likewise," Silas returned.

He released her hand and addressed Kodak again.

"Rí Atlas is already meeting other guests that arrived earlier, or he would have welcomed you himself. The staff you sent this morning with your belongings arrived without trouble, and your rooms are already prepared. Would you like to see them and have a moment to freshen up? Or would you prefer to be taken straight to the dining hall?"

"Straight to the dining hall is suitable."

Silas bowed his head. "Right this way then."

Silas led them through the gates.

Brynnlin steadied her breathing.

This was it.

No going back now.

Everyone continued to remain silent as they followed Silas into the palace.

CHAPTER 18

"Seemed like the isles and high society weren't that different."

THE ENTRANCE DOORS to the palace swung open.

A sense of apprehension pitted in Brynnlin's stomach as she entered. She joined the others on a balcony, overlooking a large throne room. Two grand staircases branched off on each side to open up into the room below them. The room was spacious, and light reflected off the marble floor making the area seem even larger. Drapes and chandeliers hung from the ceiling. And along the opposite wall, a small set of stairs led to a dais where the currently empty thrones sat tall.

"This is where the Crown Prionsa's celebration will take place, guest rooms are to the left in the west wing, and if you'll follow me, the dining hall is this way." Silas headed right and bypassed the stairs, instead leading them down a hallway. Light drifted in through the windows lining the hall, and portraits of the royal family hung on the walls.

They passed a few sentries before Silas turned down another hallway. Up ahead, grand double doors stood open.

Standing right in front of those doors, greeting the guests, was none other than Atlas Laucháin himself.

Brynnlin had seen enough pictures of the man to recognize him immediately, along with his wife and son that flanked both his sides.

Brynnlin took a quick, steadying breath.

She could do this.

Maddox fell in step next to her and gently pulled her along, following behind Kodak and Juniper.

"The first stop is greeting our host and thanking him for the hospitality," he whispered to her.

"Lovely," she deadpanned.

"Brynn, this is serious," Maddox warned a second before they reached the trio.

Atlas smiled widely at their approach.

She hadn't been sure what to expect with Atlas, but such obvious friendliness wasn't it. Then again, she was walking into this at the sides of royals.

Atlas didn't stand as tall as Kodak, but he held himself with confidence. A crown held back his dark hair, and very fine lines were the only evidence of his extensive age. In turn, his wife, Freya, was petite and almost delicate in appearance. She seemed to shy away from the attention, a much different reaction than her husband. Then there was the Prionsa. Elijah stood taller than his father, his dark hair was longer than usually suitable, and the smile he pasted on was cocky. Yet there was an unsettling gleam in his eyes that had her watching him a little more closely.

It was the way he watched people as they passed. He studied them. It was too appraising.

She would keep an eye out for him. He could easily be one someone overlooked, she wouldn't make that mistake.

"Atlas, Freya, thank you for having us," Kodak shook hands

with Atlas and nodded in respect to Freya.

Brynnlin curtsied. Maddox and Ryker bowed next to her.

Kodak then turned to the Prionsa. "Elijah, congratulations on another year and happy day of birth."

Atlas smiled fondly at his son and pounded Elijah on the back. "It's hard to believe my boy is another year older already. Did you know I'm going to have him join the council this year?"

"I did not." Kodak smiled back politely. "You must be so proud."

Brynnlin tuned out whatever small talk Kodak was making. Out of the corner of her eye, she caught Freya looking at her. The other Ríona's eyes widened for the briefest of moments before she composed herself, yet she still didn't look away.

Brynnlin fought hard to keep a serene expression and not glare back at her blatant stare. She knew her arrival was unexpected, but was the Ríona really that surprised to see an unfamiliar guest?

Kodak eventually noticed and called attention to it. "Where are my manners? Let me introduce you to Brenna, the newest member of my council."

Kodak motioned her forward, and she inclined her head. "Pleasure."

"What will you be doing for Kodak, my dear?" Atlas asked her.

Her stomach coiled at his question. She knew people would be curious. She prepared for this. "I'll be taking the role of his Grand Diplomat, he'd like to take a step back from all the traveling," she answered. She focused hard on Atlas and avoided the lingering look Elijah sent her.

"You should've done this ages ago, Kodak. Getting a Diplomat was one of my best decisions. It saved me so much trouble and kept the wife happy to have me around more," Atlas winked as if imparting some secret.

Elijah stepped forward with a smirk. "I must admit the news of Kodak retaining a new Diplomat is not unwelcome." Before she could react, he grabbed her hand and raised it to his mouth, brushing his lips across her knuckle. "I look forward to seeing you around."

Brynnlin clenched her jaw, and her serene expression hardened as she fought the instinct to yank her hand away. She had a feeling he was purposely trying to make her uncomfortable with his brazenness. If he wanted a reaction out of her, he wasn't going to get one.

"How hospitable of you," she threw back, going with diplomacy.

Elijah's smirk dropped.

"Well, we shouldn't monopolize your time, we know you have other guests to greet. We'll converse more later," Kodak stepped in with practiced grace and moved them all along.

Brynnlin's shoulders relaxed when they distanced themselves from the trio.

In the dining room, long rectangular tables stretched from one end to the other. The enormous tables were arranged in a large square to comfortably fit the guests. They were set with the finest china, and elaborate floral centerpieces were strategically placed down the middle of each table.

Brynnlin nudged Maddox in the side as they followed Kodak to their assigned seats.

"I thought you said this was small? Royals and some council members, that's what you told me. There's seats for at least sixty people in here," she mumbled under her breath.

Maddox chuckled. "That is small."

Her gaze swung up to him. "No it's not, this is a lot of people, Maddox."

"Relax, everything will be fine."

His answer didn't reassure her. Not in the slightest. But it was too late to panic. All she had to do was play a part. That was it. It would just require convincing more people than she expected.

Easy enough.

She hoped.

Kodak stopped in front of their spots, and they each took their place. She stayed on Maddox's left, Ryker moved to her left, while Kodak and Juniper sat on the other side of Maddox.

She glanced around the nearly full room. Almost everyone was already at their designated seat. She recognized most members of the respective realms from her intensive studying sessions the last few days. Only a few council members here and there escaped her recollection. She considered that a good start.

After her courteous glance, she was determined to keep a low profile. She kept her head down while people around them kept up low conversations. When people stopped talking as a new group entered through the doors, Brynnlin couldn't help but look up.

There were nine of them, five men and four women. They were all dressed in variations of gold and black. But only one had a golden crown adorning his head. His blonde hair was short, and the smile he gave the room was wide and charming.

She couldn't help doubting it's sincerity, but maybe that was just her cynical nature.

She elbowed Maddox. "Is that who I think it is?"

Maddox leaned down and confirmed what she already knew. "Tobin and some of his council."

Brynnlin straightened slightly. *Tobin Connowe, ruler of Saol.*

Zale's old realm.

No wonder everyone noticed their arrival.

The room remained oddly silent, even after the group made it to their seats, until Silas entered at the front of the room.

"Thank you everyone for taking the time to be here tonight. Rí Atlas, Ríona Freya, and Crown Prionsa Elijah, welcome you to their home and present the finest delicacies Draíocht has to offer," his voice boomed through the room as he stepped back for Atlas and his family to join the dining hall.

Atlas addressed them all with a single word. "Enjoy."

She guessed that was the cue. Staff flowed into the room and plates of food were placed in front of them. Brynnlin ate in silence, occasionally sharing a word with Maddox and Ryker. Then spent the rest of the time listening to small bits of conversation around her. After the fourth course, she was done and resorted to pushing the food around on her plate.

Hopefully, no one was watching her too closely.

She nudged Maddox's leg under the table and when he leaned down, she asked, "How long are these things anyway?"

"Long and remember after this we all go into the adjoining room to socialize."

Maddox's answer was painful to hear.

"How could I forget," she mumbled.

Maddox ducked his head to hide his smile and went back to eating.

Her gaze darted around the long tables and like the past few times, her attention landed on the pair of empty chairs.

"What's with the empty chairs?" This time she turned her question to Ryker and nodded towards the other end of the table.

She was taken back by Ryker's sudden sour expression.

"My guess would be those slots were for Kaceston, though I'm not surprised he ignored the request of his presence."

"Oh." She left it at that and stopped asking questions.

She picked up her fork and started pushing around the food again, her mind a million miles away from here. This meeting with Wesley better pay off, or she would have wasted three precious days. She needed to find a way to convince him to take the job. He was their only chance at getting into that prison. She played through different scenarios the meeting could play out and after what felt like an eternity later, the last dish was finally removed from the table. With the table cleared, another set of double doors were opened to the room next door.

Maddox stood and offered her his arm. "Ready?"

"Yeah, ready to fall asleep," she said under her breath as she hooked her arm in his.

"Always so dramatic," Maddox pulled her up, and together they filed into the other room.

Glasses, filled with only gods know what, were passed around, and gentle music played on the piano in the background. Once they were a few feet into the room, Maddox handed her off to Ryker.

"How about you guys go get some refreshments?" he suggested. "I'll circulate the room with Kodak and Juniper."

"Don't trust me to talk to people?" She raised her eyebrows. "If this is about what happened earlier with Elijah, my response could've been way worse. I was very polite, you should see—"

"Relax," Maddox gave her a patient look. "This isn't about what happened. Your earlier answer was very professional, but the little shit is used to women falling at his feet, I don't know how he'll handle your indifference. So for now, I want to keep you away from him. Also minimal interactions, remember? That won't work if you're prancing around the room."

"Okay, I'm appeased with your answer," she grinned and winked at Ryker. "Lead the way to the alcohol, while the adults go play politics."

"Best damn idea I've heard all night." Ryker swiped two flutes from a passing tray and handed one to her.

"What is this anyway?" She sniffed at the golden liquid in the glass. The bubbly substance had a sweet aroma.

"Firethorn Nectar, it's strong so pace yourself," he warned and led her towards the back of the room.

Getting to the back of the room turned out to be more difficult than anticipated. Ryker was stopped several times by people wanting to talk to him, and they were forced to make conversation. They were almost to the back when another woman stepped in front of them. Her white gown clung to her curves, leaving little to the imagination. And her sleek black hair fell in a curtain past her shoulders. But it was the jeweled crown on her head that caught Brynnlin's attention.

"General Ryker, what a nice surprise." The woman purred with a sultry voice, placing a hand on his arm.

"Ríona Isla." Ryker bowed. "How are you?"

Isla Dowling—the ruler of Ossory. And the only Ríona to rule without a Rí.

Brynnlin followed Ryker's lead and dipped into a curtsey.

Isla smiled wide. "Well I'm excellent, and you?"

"Quite well, thank you."

"It's been too long, you've been hiding out on us," Isla still didn't let go of him.

Ryker was tense at her side. Brynnlin cleared her throat softly.

Isla turned to her.

"And who is this little thing?" Isla's honeyed eyes seemed to sparkle as she looked Brynnlin over.

Brynnlin's guard was immediately up. "Brenna, your highness."

"Well Brenna, aren't you just lovely."

She smiled back, her teeth flashing. "You're too kind, your highness."

Isla raised a sculpted eyebrow, "Ryker, is she here with you tonight?"

Brynnlin bit down on her lip to stop from laughing, the Ríona was quite forward.

"Brenna is here as a member of Rí Kodak's council," Ryker's words were measured.

"Splendid news," Isla's eyes stayed on Ryker. "Why don't you let her get to know some of the guests. We have so much catching up—"

A man walked up to Isla's side, interrupting her. He leaned down to whisper in her ear. Her eyes narrowed the slightest at whatever he was telling her. After a moment Isla nodded, and the man turned his attention to them. He was classically handsome, and his reddish-brown hair was expertly styled. But it was his sapphire eyes that stood out. Brynnlin had never seen eyes that blue before.

He smiled warmly at them, and Isla jumped into introductions. "Forgive my rudeness, my dear, this is Ryker and Brenna, members of Kodak's council. I don't believe you've met them before."

The man appraised them and when his eyes landed on her, his smile appeared to grow. He held out his hand. "I always enjoy making new acquaintances," he shook Ryker's hand first and then hers. "You can call me Lonan."

Isla didn't give them time to respond.

"You'll have to excuse us," Isla pasted on a frown. "It seems my attention is needed elsewhere. We'll chat more later."

Isla and Lonan barely turned away before Ryker was pulling her in the opposite direction.

"I feel like there's some history there," she said carefully as they moved past people.

Ryker frowned at her. "Isla is very used to getting what she wants and if she doesn't get it, it turns into a challenge for her."

"I see," Brynnlin pursed her lips. "She was trying to see if I was with you."

"You're not." Ryker's answer was fast.

Brynnlin laughed. "Jeez, Ryker, don't sound so disgusted, I might get offended."

Ryker didn't laugh with her. "You don't want her to see you as competition."

"Aw, Ryker," she nudged his shoulder, "are you trying to protect me?"

"Brynn, this isn't a joke. The people here tonight, they don't follow the same rules as the rest of society. Isla may not seem like it, but she's ruthless, more than most. A simple insult could set her off. And I know you've only been around Kodak, but they're not like him. If something or someone is in their way, it doesn't last very long."

Seemed like the isles and high society weren't that different.

"I'll keep my guard up," she assured him, "thanks for looking out for me." Not that she was threatened by Isla, but she kept that to herself. Ryker was already on edge enough.

They successfully made it to the back and found a comfortable spot to observe the room.

"By the way, you're quite the popular one tonight," she remarked. Isla aside, many had stopped to talk to him.

Ryker grimaced. "I don't usually attend these events, everyone is only surprised to see me."

"How'd you get stuck babysitting me anyway?" She sipped from her glass. "Did you draw the short straw? Lose a bet?"

Ryker's brow furrowed. "I didn't get stuck with this. Why would you think that?"

"Ryker, please—"

The double doors at the entrance swung open, banging against the walls. Everybody turned, and a few people audibly gasped.

Black flames erupted from the floor, reaching to the ceiling, and a few tendrils trailed into the room like mist.

What the Hells was that?

Brynnlin braced herself, and her skin warmed. The magic in her flared to life, ready to defend her against this new threat.

Before anyone could react, the flames withered away into nothing.

Two men stood in its wake. One of them wore an obsidian crown covered in blood-red rubies.

The royal stepped up, smirking wickedly.

He stalked forward, his movements smooth and elegant. Finery aside, there was no doubt in her mind that this stranger was powerful and lethal.

She could feel it in the tension that expanded throughout the room. He was a predator, and this crowd was his prey.

He slid one of his hands into the front pocket of the charcoal suit that molded to his lean, yet muscular frame. His rich brown hair was slightly tousled, as if he just ran a hand through it, and the sharp planes of his face appeared sculpted by the gods themselves.

Despite the danger radiating from him, he was breathtaking.

She couldn't help but admire him.

"Fucking Kaceston," Ryker cursed under his breath.

And just like that, her fascination evaporated as ice washed over her. Pieces clicked together with surprising clarity.

Of course that was the ruler, Kaceston Mulryan...

After everything the others told her, she should've made the connection immediately, but she'd been too distracted...by him.

Her wide eyes shot to Ryker then back to the front doors.

Kaceston commanded the room and had everyone's attention. His steely-gray eyes scanned the crowd before him. His stare landed on her and stayed for the briefest of moments before moving on again.

"Apologies for my tardiness," Kaceston drawled out, "something came up, delaying my arrival."

His silky voice echoed through the too quiet room.

She froze.

No.

No. It couldn't be.

The blood drained from her face.

This couldn't be happening.

She knew that voice.

Had heard it the last time she had been fighting at the club.

CHAPTER 19

"Her luck could not be this bad."

BRYNNLIN GRIPPED Ryker's arm and spun around, giving her back to the front of the room.

This literally could not be happening right now.

"Brynn, what's wrong? You look like you're about to faint." Ryker's eyes flared with concern, and he ushered her closer to the wall, away from the people surrounding them.

"Kaceston," she whispered. "It's him...no...he..." she stumbled over the words as her brain refused to accept what was happening.

Her luck could not be this bad. Yet one look at the front of the room would prove otherwise.

"Hey, it's okay, he's an asshole, but he wouldn't dare hurt any of us, including you." Ryker tried to comfort her, completely misunderstanding her panic.

"Ryker, no, you don't get it." Her fingers dug into his arm. "I've spoken to him before. He was at the club the last night I fought there."

"What?" Ryker blanched. "What do you mean he was there? Are you sure?"

"Of course I'm sure," she hissed.

"What was he doing there? How'd you even end up talking to him?" Ryker growled in a low whisper.

She scowled. "How am I supposed to know what he was doing there? He was snooping in the shadows when I was talking to Leila, and when she left, I called him out on it. I didn't know who he was, he was just some stranger. I technically didn't even see him, but I remember his voice."

"Wait," Ryker's features relaxed, "there's a chance he didn't see you?"

If only she was that lucky, but as this night was proving, she doubted that was the case.

"Unlikely. I was up in the ring and then sitting openly at the bar. I wasn't trying to hide." She leaned close and said under her breath, "And let's not forget, I wasn't the only one at the club that night."

Ryker thought for a moment then shook his head. "He didn't see us. I would've known if we were being watched."

She rolled her eyes at his arrogant claim. "The place was packed that night, and how would you have known to look for him? You have no idea what he saw."

Ryker frowned, looked at the people closest to them to make sure they couldn't hear, and leaned in again. "Worst case scenario, he did see us there. We were meeting with a contact that night, we weren't doing anything wrong."

"Ryker, you know that's not true, just being on those islands would put you, Kodak, and the others all under a scrutiny we don't need right now," she said, willing him to comprehend the severity of this situation. "And what if anyone found out about my past there? Or what about Selene? She's back at the palace, and people aren't supposed to know she's there. What would people do if any of that came out?"

"Fuck. Okay, fine this could be bad." Ryker ran a frustrated hand through his hair.

That wasn't even the worst part.

"And Ryker," she waited for him to lean down again and kept her voice as low as possible. "We're worried about Kaceston placing us there that night. But you asked earlier, why was he there?"

Ryker's head whipped up, his eyes wide.

"You guys all seem pretty concerned about him, and I take it he wouldn't like us knowing he was there that night, either."

"No, I doubt he would like that at all."

Brynnlin carefully glanced around the room, trying to spot the others. "We need to find Maddox, they need to know."

Ryker nodded and stood straight, his height giving him a much better view of the room than her. "Found him."

The commotion from Kaceston's entrance seemed to be dwindling. Music started playing again, and others talked among themselves. Kaceston stood at the front, speaking to Atlas and someone else she didn't recognize. Ryker put a hand at her back and guided her through the crowd.

"We have a problem," Ryker said as soon as they reached Maddox's side and filled him in.

Maddox took the news in stride. "This is a complication, yes, but let's not panic. We can handle this. It's only a few days, we'll stay off his radar. For now, you and Brynnlin get out of here and go back to the rooms, there's a good chance he hasn't seen you yet."

"Do you think we can avoid him all weekend?" she asked.

"No, but the longer we put off that interaction the better." Maddox looked at something past her. "Now's your chance, he's occupied and away from the door."

She and Ryker agreed and took their leave. They weren't far from the door, when the man that arrived with Kaceston stopped in front of them.

Damn it.

Ryker stiffened beside her.

The man's silver-white hair was short on top and shaved on both sides. Piercings decorated his ears, and tattoos covered his hands, before disappearing into the sleeves of his suit jacket. His ocean-colored eyes were cold and contradicted the smile forming on his face.

"Well, if it isn't my favorite guard dog. Did they finally let you out of your cage?" The coldness in his eyes seeped into amusement as he tossed the insult at Ryker.

She narrowed her eyes.

"Griffin. I see you and Kaceston slithered out of your hole for the weekend," Ryker responded blandly.

Griffin's smile was quickly replaced with a scowl. "Rí Kaceston and you will address him as such. Blatant disrespect will not be tolerated."

Ryker scoffed. "Respect? I wasn't aware you even knew the meaning of that word."

"It seems I'm more familiar with it than you."

"Doubtful," Ryker said. "Now as much as I truly enjoy our little chats, we must be on our way."

"And leave without saying hello?" A voice said off to the right.

Her heart sank.

She turned her head and watched Kaceston stroll towards them, a smug look on his face. He stopped in front of them. Even in her heels, she had to look up to meet his eyes.

Kaceston tsked. "What would Kodak have to say about your manners?"

Ryker ignored the question.

"Rí Kaceston." The words were guttural as Ryker forced them out behind clenched teeth.

She knew, despite Ryker's position, outright disrespect to a ruler would be severely punished. After a tense moment, Ryker bent at the waist. She followed, dipping into a courtesy.

"Much better," Kaceston purred.

Ryker snapped up, his glare fierce.

Shit.

Ryker was many things, easy-tempered was not one of them. She hooked her arm through his again, stepping into his side. She really hoped actual physical restraint wouldn't be necessary, but she wanted to be prepared. Before, she would have been confident that Ryker wouldn't be stupid enough to attack a ruler in a crowded room.

However, he looked ready to do just that.

Why was Ryker playing into Kaceston's hand? The ruler was only baiting him to get a reaction. She saw it all the time in the ring. Truthfully, Kaceston's taunts were quite tame.

She subtly squeezed his arm.

Ryker ceased his glaring to look down at her.

Her eyes moved to the door.

They were leaving, remember?

He nodded—and seemed to compose himself. "Please, excuse us gentlemen, we're retiring. Enjoy the rest of your evening."

"Leaving so soon?" Turned out Kaceston wasn't going to let them go that easily. "And who is your lovely companion? She's not from around here."

She repressed a shiver as she became the focus of his direct and unforgiving stare. Something sinister danced behind those pools of swirling gray. But she held his gaze and refused to back down.

Call it stupid or prideful, yet she had never been one to

walk away from a challenge. Which is also probably what led her to making her next comment.

"I didn't realize you knew everyone present, along with where they are from, that's quite impressive, your highness," she said with overly sweetness.

His eyes flared, and he cocked his head to the side, studying her.

She could've smacked herself. If he hadn't recognized her already, her smart-ass mouth would connect the dots for him. Or he could just be surprised by her statement.

She was taken aback by the grin that appeared across his upturned lips.

"What can I say, I'm an impressive individual," he crooned, not taking offense to her condescending tone. "However, you might not be as unfamiliar as I originally assumed."

He was fishing.

She controlled any outward reaction and only let confusion shine through. If he wasn't completely sure about where he knew her from, maybe she could cast enough doubt.

"That's an odd thing to say," she said softly, "whatever do you mean?"

"I think you know," he took a step closer to her.

Ryker angled himself in front of her, effectively blocking Kaceston. "Brynn is a member of our council and is under Kodak's protection, you'd be wise to treat her accordingly," Ryker's warning was clear.

Brynnlin's grip on Ryker's arm intensified at his slip-up. They needed to leave.

Now.

Kaceston had managed to get under Ryker's skin, she could tell Ryker's composure was faltering.

Kaceston's eyes narrowed, and he opened his mouth to speak.

"Is everything alright?" Elijah of all people, interrupted. His gaze landed on her for an answer.

A few people around them were watching closely, so she pasted on a smile. "Of course, we were just retiring for the evening."

The last thing they needed was to draw attention.

Elijah nodded and seemed content with her answer.

He held out his arm, "If you're leaving, allow me to escort you both back to your rooms. This place can be quite confusing to new guests," he added.

Not really.

But right then she chose the lesser of two evils and took his arm. "That would be appreciated."

Elijah's returning smile was smug.

She didn't care. He was their best chance of getting out of there without any further confrontations.

She let Elijah walk her to the rooms with Ryker following a step behind.

KACESTON'S MOOD darkened as Brynn and Ryker walked away. He didn't like being disrupted, and Elijah was a fool for interfering.

"I see why you wanted me to stall their exit." Griffin stood at his side also watching the group leave. "I thought it was about Ryker, but it was who he was with." Griffin said slyly, "She's quite beautiful. The young Prionsa seems taken with her, too."

Kaceston scoffed. "Elijah wouldn't even know where to start with a woman like that. But I'm disappointed in you, Griff, you should know that I could never be affected by something so superficial. Beauty is common among our kind."

It was Griffin's turn to scoff. "Not like that, and you know it."

He only shrugged. "While her beauty can be appreciated, that's not why I sent you over to them. Things just became complicated, she was at the club the night I was following Ryker and Zale."

Which could be a very big problem. And he quite detested problems.

"I doubt she saw you."

"While I believe that, we spoke," he admitted. "I was intrigued and now I very much regret that decision. I needed to see if she recognized me."

Griffin mused, "She didn't act like it."

No, she hadn't. "That just means she's a very good actress."

She recognized him.

And he had also recognized her. He spotted her as soon as he stepped into the room. He wasn't often surprised, but when he had seen her standing in the back, he had been just that.

Her hair was lighter and gone was the brand from her neck, but there was no mistaking her. It was bold of Ryker to show up with his acolyte, a move Kaceston hadn't been expecting.

What was their play?

Was Kodak making another move already?

He needed to know what she was doing here, which was part of the reason he signaled Griffin to intervene while he had been occupied. It had been adorable that she thought she could convince him they hadn't met, but he knew the truth.

She and Ryker were trying to run out of here right after he showed up.

Coincidence? No.

She remembered him, well at least his voice, and made the connection.

Clever girl.

He had to assume she already told the others about their interaction. Which meant they would know he was on their trail. That was a complication, but he could work around that. The only thing he couldn't figure out was what to do with Brynn.

He could expose her for being a member of the Resurgence —have her imprisoned. He could just kill her outright, remove her from the table.

But she could be useful.

Kodak obviously had plans for her, or she wouldn't be here. It was very possible she had knowledge of Kodak's operation. Information he very much wanted.

Kodak had her cooperation, but what about her loyalty?

The rest of Kodak's council was out of question.

But her...

She was just an acolyte from the isles.

She would be the easiest one to break.

'Oh Brynn, you have no idea what's coming.'

He smiled in anticipation.

CHAPTER 20

"The whole dark and dangerous vibe might seem irresistible from a distance, until one found themselves alone with it."

THE NEXT MORNING Brynnlin rolled over and groaned as someone tapped on her door. It was too early for this, the sun had barely started to rise. To make it worse, she didn't get any sleep at all. Between her nightmares, Kaceston's threats, and the meeting with Wesley, it had been a night of constant tossing and turning. And now her head was killing her.

She glared at the offensive knocking as she stalked to the door and yanked it open.

"What?" she snapped at Ryker. He was already dressed in his usual attire of tactical pants and a black long sleeve.

"Well good morning to you, too, sunshine," he glanced down at her sweats and rumbled shirt. "Did you sleep at all? You look like shit."

She knew she was a mess and probably had dark circles under her eyes, but that didn't mean he had to call it out.

"Just what every girl wants to hear, you do have a way with

words, Ryker." She glared and crossed her arms over her chest. "Now what do you want? Or did you just knock on my door to comment on my morning appearance?"

"Meeting in Maddox's room, let's go," he didn't wait for her as he headed across the hall.

She huffed and followed after him, not bothering to change. In the room, the others were gathered at the seating area. Maddox and Kodak were both dressed for the day while Juniper was lounging in pants and a sweater.

"We need to talk about last night," Kodak said once she and Ryker joined them.

She went to the couch, curling into the seat next to Juniper and pulling her knees into her chest.

"Is this about Kaceston being at the club?" she asked.

"It is," Kodak sighed.

"He might not have recognized me, I think I played it off pretty well, and there's no guarantee he saw Ryker or Zale either."

"But if he did, and he happens to mention it to someone?" Kodak countered.

"If he says anything about us being there, he'd also be revealing himself," she pointed out.

Kodak shook his head, "If last night wasn't proof for you, Kaceston does not conform or care about what others think. He'd have no issue saying he was somewhere he shouldn't be. We'll have to keep a close ear to the ground while we're here." Kodak crossed the area and sunk into one of the chairs, folding his hands in front of him. "But the main reason we need to talk is to figure out why Kaceston was at that club in the first place. I don't like that it was the same night two of my men were there. I don't believe in coincidences like that. Brynn being there, too? Fine. But Kaceston? No."

Brynnlin grimaced, "A lot of shit goes down at that place.

Betting, laundering, drugs, weapons, you name it and it's probably there. It could be hard to pinpoint which vice he was there for."

"No," Maddox contradicted her, "Kaceston is too smart for that. He wouldn't risk discovery for those. And for him to show up in person, it was something important."

"You think he was meeting with someone?" Ryker questioned.

Maddox shrugged. "It makes sense."

"A cult member?"

"Who else?"

"If he was, it's not a regular occurrence," Brynnlin said, "it's unlikely he's been there before."

Kodak raised his eyebrows, "How can you be so sure?"

"You have your informant, I have my own, and I guarantee they know a lot more than yours," Brynnlin unfolded her legs and leaned forward. "If he did business there, I would've heard about it."

"You sound pretty confident."

"I am." Leila had never let her down before, and she knew what went on behind closed doors at that place.

"Could Kaceston have known about our meeting and followed Ryker and Zale?" Juniper cast wide eyes at Kodak.

"No, the only people that knew about it are in this room."

"You're forgetting your little informant," Brynnlin pointed out, "she could've sold you out."

Kodak looked shocked, as if not considering the possibility. "She wouldn't, she's always been trustworthy, and she has no reason to betray us."

"There's always a reason." She started ticking off her fingers. "Money, information, blackmail." She thought back to the black flames that announced Kaceston's entrance. "Fear. What in the Hells is Kaceston anyway?"

Juniper fidgeted beside her, and Kodak looked uncomfortable.

"He's a very powerful Oíchan," he admitted.

Brynnlin rolled her eyes. Oíchans were well feared for their abilities to manipulate the mind, but people's reaction last night had been on another level. "Yeah I got that part, he is their ruler after all, but there's something else."

"The exact extent of his magic and abilities are unknown, however, it's been discovered he's *Danann*."

Her face paled. "That's not possible."

Danann were children of the gods and goddesses. Extremely powerful and unmatched. But that was thousands of years ago. They were either long dead now or in the celestial plane.

"He's not directly," Kodak explained, "but somewhere in his family bloodline are descendants. I think Arawn is the rumored god, no one knows for sure."

"Gods," Brynnlin breathed. His power had to be unparalleled. A horrible part of her was intrigued.

What would he be capable of?

"As much as we would all love to dissect his lineage, the only way you'll learn about Kaceston's magic would be by asking him directly. Since none of us plan on doing that, how about we get back to the issue at hand?" Maddox suggested from his spot by the window.

"Of course," Kodak immediately agreed. "We've strayed from the topic. Since Kaceston's attention seems to be locked on Brynn and Ryker, I want you guys to use it. If he says anything about seeing you that night, then he's openly admitting to being there. Use that to your advantage, find out what he was doing there. Especially, if he in any way hints at knowing why Ryker was there. Clear?"

"Understood," Brynnlin agreed, and Ryker echoed the confirmation.

"Good, now go get dressed for the morning meal, the summit meeting starts afterwards," Kodak dismissed them.

Ryker walked her back to her room.

"You and I both know Kaceston will not reveal anything to us, right?" She cast him a side glance.

"I know," Ryker admitted, stopping in front of the door. "Kodak is nervous about why he was there, which I understand. But the less we're around Kaceston, the better. And I think you were right earlier, he's not convinced it was you, so we should do our best to avoid him. If that doesn't work out, then we can try and find out what he was doing there."

"Sounds fair," she said, feeling better than before.

"Now, not to be an ass, but you need to go make yourself presentable for the morning meal," he chuckled.

She flipped him off and shut the door in his face.

UNLIKE THE MEAL LAST NIGHT, the morning meal was held out on the patio. Instead of the long tables, smaller round tables were placed strategically across the cobblestone.

Brynnlin sighed in relief. There was no need to socialize, they could eat in peace.

Kodak picked a table along the edge and pulled a chair out for Juniper. The skirt of Juniper's gown gathered at her feet as she slid into the chair. Kodak sat next to her, unbuttoning his suit jacket. Brynnlin still wasn't used to seeing them dressed so sophisticated, they'd always been so casual back at Sidhe. Then again, they had to present a certain image. Maddox, Ryker, and herself included.

She had pulled her hair into a high ponytail today and had

done her best to hide the circles under her eyes. The burgundy pant suit she picked out helped add some color.

Maddox took a seat next to her, his black suit making his eyes appear more violet than blue. Ryker sat on her other side. He discarded his jacket this morning, opting to wear a vest instead. She found it quite comical how much he detested the formal wear.

As soon as they were all seated, staff started bringing trays of food to their table. She kept it light, only grabbing a small portion of eggs and a pastry.

"Not hungry?" Maddox eyed her plate.

She shrugged. With everything going on, a heavy weight had settled in her stomach, making the idea of eating unappealing. She was too anxious and knew whatever she ate wouldn't sit well.

"Are you alright?"

"Yeah, everything is just on my mind. To be honest, I'll feel better once we're back in Sidhe," she admitted.

Maddox gave her a small smile. "Me too."

They enjoyed the food and were about done when a sudden tension filled the patio. Brynnlin didn't have to turn around to know who walked in. The slight stiffening of Kodak's shoulders as he looked behind her also gave it away.

She risked a glance.

Conversation ceased as Kaceston strode through the courtyard, taking a seat at the center table with Griffin at his right. It annoyed her that he looked impeccable in a royal-blue suit, and that his tanned skin seemed to glow under the sunlight. It was an unfair world when someone like him was allowed to look like that. But there weren't enough expensive suits in the world to disguise the fact that he would devour someone at the first sign of weakness.

A wolf in sheep's clothing, that's what he was. The deadly

stillness in his movements only a glimpse at the danger that lurked beneath.

She unfortunately knew the type all too well.

People had given him a wide range, but curiosity was a killer, and she saw more than a few others eyeing him from their respective tables. Most were women.

She shook her head.

The whole dark and dangerous vibe might seem irresistible from a distance, until one found themselves alone with it.

She scoffed.

No thanks.

She cast Kaceston one more brisk glance. Only to find him already staring at her.

His lips upturned to one side, and he winked.

Her lips thinned, and she raised a single brow in challenge.

She wasn't here to play games. And his refusal was the reason she was stuck here to begin with.

He full on grinned, his teeth flashing.

She rolled her eyes and looked away, intent on ignoring him.

'That's what you should've done from the beginning.' A little voice at the back of her mind nagged.

'Well I'm doing it now.' She argued back.

"How long until the meeting starts?" she asked the group.

Kodak answered. "Not long. We can head over to the conference hall and get settled once everyone is finished eating." Kodak's lips twitched as he took in the mixture of empty plates and unfinished food. "If you guys are ready, we can go now."

He received a chorus of agreements, hers included.

Their luck for the morning held out, and they were able to leave the patio without any interruptions.

CHAPTER 21

"They all acted so high and mighty, preaching about harmony only to be secretly plotting the other's demise behind closed doors."

KACESTON WANTED TO LAUGH. He resisted the urge as Brynn followed the others out of the room.

They were so predictable.

It wasn't going to be easy getting close to her.

But where was the fun in that?

"She doesn't seem to like you very much," Griffin commented, lifting a glass to his lips.

He raised his eyebrows. "And what makes you say that?"

"I think it was somewhere between the haughty look of indifference and then leaving as soon as you sat down," Griffin chuckled.

"It wasn't right as I sat down," he corrected with a smirk.

Griffin rolled his eyes, "You're right, it was not even a few minutes afterwards. My mistake. You know, Kodak's probably told her all about what a horrible monster you are and to avoid you at all costs."

"Probably."

"You don't seem concerned?"

"I'm not." Kaceston would've been more surprised if Kodak hadn't warned her away. If Kodak was smart—which he was—he would want Brynn as far away as possible. But even with the warning, Brynn was interested, at least a little bit. He had felt her eyes on him once he walked in.

He was aware of the effect he had on women. And it looked like Brynn was no exception. Something he fully intended on using to his advantage.

Griffin stared at him expectantly. "Well, are you going to elaborate?"

"Later," he pushed away from the table. "Right now, we have a meeting to attend."

Griffin sighed heavily. "This is going to be painful."

Kaceston couldn't disagree. The last thing he wanted to do was sit in a stuffy room full of tiresome people. They all acted so high and mighty, preaching about harmony, only to be secretly plotting the other's demise behind closed doors.

It was repulsive. At least he had the decency to be forthcoming about his true motives. How unfortunate there were some things even he could not get out of, at least not without stirring the pot. This was one of them.

He started for the door, Griffin at his side. People quickly moved out of their way. A few were brave enough to offer him nods in greeting.

He smiled to himself. Fear rolled off all of them in waves. He relished in it.

They made their way down the hall and to the room dedicated for the conference. Like the night before, large tables were arranged to comfortably fit everyone. Colorful banners hung across the walls, a representation of each realm. Seats started to fill as the others filed in. Atlas stood at the door.

"Kaceston," Atlas called out as they walked up. "No big entrance today?" Atlas joked and placed a hand on his shoulder.

Kaceston eyed the hand until Atlas wisely drew it back.

"No, I'm sure my presence here alone is remarkable enough," he deadpanned.

Atlas started to chuckle.

Kaceston wanted to roll his eyes, but he refrained. It hadn't been a joke. He had no desire to sit through a boring-ass meeting, yet here he was.

A phenomenal occurrence indeed.

Kaceston was done entertaining conversation with the other royal. He didn't wait for Atlas to respond and moved into the room. He easily found Brynn sitting with the others. Her head was bent, and her face was crunched in concentration as she whispered with Maddox.

He pulled out a chair, settling himself right across from her. Her shoulders stiffened as she caught sight of him out of the corner of her eye. Another few moments passed before she and Maddox finished their whispered conversation.

Maddox looked up, a frown crossing his features.

Kaceston leveled him with a cold look.

Maddox appeared far too comfortable expressing his displeasure.

Was a reminder necessary of who the Chancellor was dealing with?

His eyes narrowed.

Maddox's jaw clenched, but he looked away.

Better.

His attention was pulled from them as the seat next to him became occupied. He turned to see a brilliant redhead giving him a warm smile.

Constance.

He let a real smile slip through. He stood and leaned over to give her a welcoming kiss on the cheek. Constance was one of the only people here he actually respected and also considered a friend. He didn't see her nearly enough as she rarely spent much time on land.

With Ossory being divided into two regions, she was kept busy "reigning" over the merrow and the rest of the undersea in the Republic of Dóchas. While Isla ruled over the land.

Constance technically wasn't a royal, but she was a ruler nonetheless. With her connection to the surrounding sea she had more power than most of the people at this table. She'd been trying for almost a century for Dóchas to be titled as an official realm, but some still stood in her way. He backed her completely, and she was slowly making headway. He didn't think it would be long before she fulfilled her goal. For now, she hadn't pushed too hard as long as she was included in meetings like this, and her people were represented.

He quite admired her patience.

His eyes shot to the thick red bracelet on her wrist that allowed the transformation to her terrain form for her to be here. All of her council were wearing a similar bracelet. If he remembered correctly, the devices only worked for several days before they had to go back. Maybe a week at the most.

"Constance, you look radiant as always, it's good to see you," he said, actually meaning the words.

"Kaceston," she greeted back, "such a charmer."

"Charming enough to convince you to run away with me, leaving your no-good husband behind?" His eyes glinted as he eyed her husband, Nathaniel, sitting on her other side.

Constance laughed lightly, her eyes sparkling. "Maybe."

Nathaniel narrowed his onyx eyes and threw a casual arm

over the back of her chair. "You know Kaceston, sometimes I find it very difficult to like you."

Kaceston chuckled. "Most do."

Nathaniel fought a grin. "However, if you keep trying to steal my wife from me, you'll leave me no choice but to kick your ass."

It wasn't the first time Nathaniel had made that threat. Nor would it be the last.

"Promises, promises," he drawled to the other man.

Nathaniel only shook his head.

Kaceston was disappointed Nathaniel ended their banter so quickly. He took great delight in messing with him. Nathaniel was very protective of his wife, which Kaceston fully approved of. Constance deserved something good in her life, and he knew his friend very much loved her husband.

Constance patted his arm, and he gazed down at her. "We quite enjoyed your entrance yesterday, you always make these tedious things more entertaining."

"I aim to please."

"I'm sure you do." Constance leaned forward, lowering her voice. "Is there trouble brewing?"

He raised his eyebrows. "Why would you think that?"

"Well trouble does seem to follow you wherever you go. However, in this instance, a certain Chancellor keeps looking over here. And he doesn't look happy. Quite unusual behavior for that group."

Kaceston glanced across the table, and sure enough Maddox was watching him with wary eyes.

"Aw, that." He leaned back in his chair. "I ate the last fruit-cake at the morning meal. It seems he's still upset."

She smacked his arm.

"Ouch," he rubbed at the spot. "So violent, how does Nathaniel put up with this?"

She rolled her eyes. "You're the worst, I was being serious."

"That's no fun."

Before she could push more, Atlas walked to the front of the room.

"With everyone here, I'd like to get started. We have a lot to discuss."

Kaceston nearly groaned.

Fantastic.

He leaned back in his chair, getting comfortable, for what would no doubt be a long, pointless meeting...and it was.

Hours later it was still continuing.

"The trade routes are no longer safe," Atlas argued, his anger directed at Constance. "I have lost men and ships while traveling to other ports."

Constance merely eyed the other ruler. "I don't see how that's my concern."

Atlas's nostrils flared. "You know more about what's going on in those waters than anyone else. You could attempt to make an effort here."

"Atlas, it is not my responsibility, nor in my interest to protect your ships," Constance waved her hand around the room. "And it seems like others don't share your issue."

"This is a problem that affects us all. And if you hadn't let those savages take over those islands, we wouldn't be in this position," Atlas snapped. "They're too comfortable and attack us as they please."

Kaceston straightened in his chair at the blatant insult, ready to intervene.

"Watch yourself, Atlas," Constance warned. "Those were never my lands to safeguard."

"She's right, Atlas," Isla commented. "Those lands were unclaimed, and it was unfortunate luck that the Creed asserted themselves there."

"The Creed," Atlas sneered. "They're a cult with weak-minded followers and should be addressed as such. And I know the only reason you," he pointed at Isla, "and Constance are so resistant is because you're still holding a grudge about the ports along the Foinse Straight."

Kaceston raised a brow. Bold of Atlas to bring up those ports so publicly. He hadn't obtained control of those in what one would consider—legally.

"Please," Constance scoffed, "I have no need for those ports you stole."

Kaceston outright smirked.

No, she didn't.

She had his. And they both made quite a profit off the arrangement.

"Enough of this. Atlas, protecting your ships and your land is your own responsibility, as the same goes for everyone else. If you are incapable, then I strongly suggest reconsidering your commandment." Tobin spoke out, and Kaceston nearly rolled his eyes at the statement.

Prestigious prick.

Though not entirely wrong.

"But the cult—"

"Is something that affects us all, yes," Tobin agreed, "however, as we discovered over the years, is more difficult to deal with than expected. We've never once come to an agreement on how to handle them and as that's still not going to happen today, I suggest we move on."

Small accordances and some trades were discussed after that.

"Did anyone have anything else they'd like to bring up before we dismiss?" Atlas asked the room.

"How about marriage?"

That had everyone sitting up.

Kaceston's gaze shot to the speaker.

Isla.

She was smiling wide, and there was a gleam in her eyes.

"What do you mean?" Atlas asked the Ríona.

"Now that Elijah is old enough for you to bring him into your council, I'm merely curious if he's going to consider taking a wife?" Isla voiced her question.

Kaceston knew where this was going. Isla had two daughters and probably wanted to pair one of them off. She was an idiot for wanting an alliance with Elijah.

Elijah spoke before his father could. "I have no intention of being pawned off through marriage. If and when I marry, it will be my decision."

Isla's disappointment was evident.

Kaceston was praising the gods. Any alliance Isla attempted to make could alter the entire dynamic of the rulers and would ultimately affect him. He had no desire to deal with that at the moment.

"Why don't you let the young Prionsa get settled into politics before trying to force a wife on him. Many of us remain unmarried, yourself included, Isla." Tobin pointed out.

Isla started to retort, but Atlas clapped his hands together. "I couldn't agree more. Now let's adjourn the meeting. We'll see everyone this evening."

BRYNNLIN SAT in front of the mirror while Juniper twisted her hair into an elaborate updo.

"You don't have to help me. You're the Ríona, shouldn't I be helping you get ready?"

Juniper smirked. "I am ready. And you looked pretty flustered with all the staff in here, so I figured I would take over."

"I appreciate that." *She did.* "But do we really have to sit through another meal? Wasn't the meeting bad enough?"

Juniper sighed. "Welcome to politics."

"It sucks, I hope you know that."

Juniper laughed. "I know, trust me." Juniper put the last pin in her hair and stepped away. "All done."

Brynnlin was impressed. Juniper managed to pin the mass of her hair on top of her head. A few pieces were left loose to frame around her face.

"Thank you." She turned to Juniper, her appreciation sincere.

"Anytime." Juniper smiled.

Juniper had left her hair down this evening and was in a blood-red dress that flared out at her waist and fell to the floor. Tonight, Brynnlin wore a deep forest-green gown with sheer long sleeves. It was unsurprisingly gorgeous. Just another testament to Juniper's great taste.

Yet she still wasn't used to the plunging v-neckline that almost reached her stomach. She kept trying to pull it up to prevent so much skin from being on display, but after being reprimanded several times by Juniper, she stopped fidgeting.

Fine. Apparently everyone got to see her cleavage tonight.

"They're waiting for us, are you ready?" Juniper asked.

"Do I have a choice?"

"No." Juniper softened the denial with a smile.

"Didn't think so." Brynnlin took a deep breath. It was only a few more hours, she could handle this. In the hall, the men stood around, ready for the evening.

"Damn, about time," Maddox remarked, pulling away from the wall.

"Unlike you, Maddox, we actually wanted to look nice this evening."

"Juniper, you couldn't tell a lie a hundred years ago, and you still can't do it now. You and I both know I look fantastic."

"Fantastically mediocre."

"Wow." Maddox clutched at his chest. "That was hurtful."

Brynnlin grinned, their banter easing some of the tension that had built from the long day.

"Enough," Kodak rolled his eyes. "Everyone looks exceptional. Especially you." Kodak pulled Juniper into his side and nibbled at her neck. Juniper melted into him. Kodak whispered something in Juniper's ear that had her cheeks flushing.

Brynnlin's eyebrows rose as she heard something about what Kodak planned to do with that dress.

"Okay, you need to save that shit for tonight," Maddox looked horrified. "I'd like to eat without wanting to throw up, if you don't mind."

Kodak leveled him with an annoyed look. "Then don't listen."

Maddox shuddered and moved down the hall. "I'll see you all over there."

"Wait for me." Brynnlin smirked at Juniper and picked up the skirt of her dress to catch up to Maddox. Ryker was right behind her, and together they weaved through the halls.

In the dining hall, they took the same seats as the night before. Kodak and Juniper showed up not much later, though late enough to be noticeable. Juniper's hair also hadn't been that messy when they left them.

Maddox opened his mouth.

"One word out of you, and I will have you doing perimeter checks for a whole godsdamn year." Kodak pulled out his chair after helping Juniper into hers. "Am I clear?"

Maddox wisely remained quiet.

"Coward," Brynnlin said under her breath as she reached for a glass of wine.

Maddox glared at her. "No, it's a strategically smart decision since I value my life."

She snickered.

They didn't have to wait long for everyone to show up and like the night before, Atlas' speech was short and to the point. As soon as he finished, he ordered the first courses to be brought out. And also like the night before, Brynnlin spent most of it listening to small conversations and pushing food around. About halfway through the third course, deep laughter pulled her attention towards the end of the table.

Kaceston.

He was with Griffin and the same redhead she saw next to him at the meeting. She had recognized Constance, and Maddox had filled her in more about her position and where she was from.

Constance and Kaceston appeared close. He looked so normal and at ease, so different from the threatening image he portrayed the previous night.

He seemed to have a sixth sense and caught her looking at him. A gleam entered those cool gray eyes, and his lips upturned into a satisfied smirk. Calculating Kaceston was back, determination settling in his features, setting off all of her warning bells.

She looked away first.

Trying to hold a stare off with him would only incite trouble. For once, she did the smart thing and kept her head down the rest of the meal.

The remaining courses passed quickly and soon all the guests filtered into the adjoining room like they did the previous night. In no time at all, drinks were flowing and couples were dancing to the raw and enchanting instrumental music. People gathered around the edges of the room, giving the couples plenty of space.

Kodak and Juniper were one of those couples. Brynnlin stood with Maddox and Ryker talking in a small group of other council members. She turned as someone lightly touched her shoulder.

"Could I persuade you to dance with me?"

She nearly groaned.

Elijah.

CHAPTER 22

"And the little voice that cautioned her to tread carefully was completely drowned out."

BRYNNLIN WANTED TO SAY NO.

Gods, did she want to say no.

But to refuse a simple dance, especially to the Crown Prionsa, whose family was hosting them, would be a blatant insult.

She could suffer through a single dance.

Maddox hearing the request, reached for her drink and gave her the slightest nod of encouragement.

"Alright." She gave Elijah her hand and let him lead her to the dance floor.

He put his other hand at her back, and they stepped into the next dance. She would never consider herself a dancer. As luck would have it, she could keep up pretty well. Her father had taught her to dance as a child, and both Maddox and Ryker had helped her refresh before this trip.

"How did you find your first summit meeting?" He asked as they spun around the room.

She thought over her answer. "Enlightening."

"Is that your polite way of saying boring?" His eyes creased and a teasing note entered his tone.

Her lips twitched of their own accord. "Not at all. It truly was very interesting."

The people were interesting.

There was a lot to be learned from observing them.

Who got along...

Who didn't...

Reasons why they would turn against each other...

All discovered by spending time in a room with them.

"Yes, I suppose it can be very interesting. Would you like to know what else I find interesting?" Elijah continued without an answer. "How someone so young found herself in such a high position of Kodak's employment. It's not often he invites in a new member, to his inner council, no less."

Brynnlin glanced up and found him staring at her. Mild curiosity crossed his features.

She didn't buy it.

He looked into her.

Why?

"I've known the Raigáin family for years."

"I see," a glint entered his eyes. "Then I suppose you're close with Chancellor Raigáin?"

It was a loaded question.

"Yes, I am," she answered, though it wasn't in the way he assumed. She had no intention of revealing the true nature of her relationship with Maddox.

His lips thinned into a hard line. It seemed like the Prionsa didn't like that answer.

Good. Maybe he'd leave her alone.

He looked at something past her, and when he met her gaze again, she didn't like the way he seemed to study her. As if he was looking for something.

"All of this dancing can be quite tiresome. How about some fresh air? We can stroll through the gardens, you must see it at night. It's quite beautiful."

Elijah stepped out of the dance and headed in that direction, as if he assumed she'd just follow along. Brynnlin stopped at the edge of the dancers, pulling her hand back.

"I'm technically working, it's best for me to remain inside," she tried to be tactful.

His smile was coy. "I insist."

She clenched her jaw.

Patience.

She warned herself.

Patience.

She didn't know what he was up to, but she was to have no part in it.

She gave him a tight-lipped smile. "I think it's time we part ways. Enjoy the rest of your evening," she said with a bite.

Elijah's eyes narrowed slightly, and he opened his mouth.

Whatever he was about to say was cut off.

"You heard her, run along now, Elijah. If I recall, it's past your bedtime." The deep voice was low, but it echoed through her head like a shout.

She stiffened and closed her eyes, praying for patience yet again.

Really? Did the gods hate her this much?

She opened her eyes and turned to see Kaceston standing behind her. His eyes zeroed in on her, and there was an intensity there that made her uneasy.

Elijah stepped towards Kaceston, his expression fierce. "I

will be Rí someday, I suggest you consider how you speak to me. My father might fear you, I do not."

Kaceston remained unfazed and barely spared Elijah a glance. "Then you lack even more intelligence than I gave you credit for. Now go." The last word was whisper soft.

Elijah took another step forward, seemed to think better of it, and turned, stalking off.

She considered testing her own luck and seeing what would happen if she made a run for it, too. She never got the chance.

Kaceston didn't waste a moment and wrapped a hand around her back, pulling her to him just as the next song started.

"Dance with me, Brynn."

It wasn't a question.

"It's Brenna."

Kaceston only smirked and pulled her closer. Even with the material of the dress, the heat of his hand seeped into her back. His head dipped, his breath brushing over her ear as he spoke.

"So many names, though I don't suppose it matters what you call yourself. Brenna, Brynn...Ciarán."

Brynnlin straightened, her muscles going tight. Her heart pounded in her chest. He couldn't be calling her that. She'd been so sure he hadn't made the connection. Panic edged its way forward.

"You seem tense." Gray orbs bore into hers. "Is something amiss?"

The question was a taunt.

She willed herself to be calm and held his stare. So what if he recognized her. She could handle this.

"Not at all." She was proud her voice came out even and almost bored.

The corner of his mouth tipped higher. "Good. Very good. You don't submit easily. I like that."

Her wariness of him completely flew out the window at his absurd comment.

He was unbelievable.

And the little voice that cautioned her to tread carefully was completely drowned out.

"And am I supposed to give a damn about what you like?" she sneered.

Kaceston's smirk dropped.

He tsked under his breath. "Careful now. We don't want that mouth of yours getting you into more trouble."

She arched a brow. "Pray tell why would I be the one in trouble here?"

"You were in trouble the moment I spotted you across the ballroom."

Brynnlins eyes narrowed. "Is that supposed to be a threat?"

"Not at all." Kaceston's hand left her back, and he trailed a finger down her cheek. "You'll know when I'm threatening you."

She stiffened at the contact and jerked her head back. She was done entertaining this. She pulled her hand free and turned away.

Kaceston was faster.

He grabbed her and spun her back into him.

"Now, now, don't be angry with me for this situation," he admonished. "Blame your precious Ryker for removing you from your little island."

And there it was.

Out in the open.

Brynnlin gave him her best belittling look that she mastered from Selene. "Is that supposed to intimidate me? If so, you're mistaken. And if I recall, you were on that island as well."

"My appearance at that trashy hole they consider a club is

completely irrelevant. And even if it was, I'm going to let you in on a little secret," his voice dropped to a whisper. "The others can't touch me. But you? You, Cairán, are not untouchable. Not even close. Which begs the question, what to do with you? I could expose you, have you imprisoned. I could just kill you. No one would stop me. But I feel like that would be such a waste. Not when you have so much potential. So I would highly recommend listening closely, you don't want me as your enemy."

Brynnlin couldn't believe what she was hearing. He was actually threatening her. Right here, in the middle of the dance floor.

She hated threats. And unlike everyone else, Kaceston didn't scare her.

"What was your goal with that spiel?" She was truly curious. "To frighten me? To taunt me? Force me into submission and do your bidding? You see there's a reason I don't bother with threats—they're nothing but empty words. And as you so eloquently put it, I believe it's my turn to let you in on a little secret." Brynnlin stepped into his space, giving him a frigid smile, "It's you that doesn't want me as your enemy."

He didn't have a clue what she was capable of. And if he thought he could take her out, he was in for a rude awakening.

Kaceston stared at her a moment, studied her.

The tension built.

An amused gleam entered his eyes, and he chuckled, the dark, twisted sound sending goosebumps across her skin.

That was not the reaction she expected. Maybe anger at her disrespect, but not for him to be entertained. And he was definitely entertained. His eyes lit up, and his face split into a wolfish grin.

This was almost worse.

"Oh you are fun," he crooned. "How unfortunate we find

ourselves in these circumstances. In any other situation, I would quite enjoy you."

Brynnlin was stunned silent for a moment before irritation rippled through her like a tidal wave.

This was all a godsdamn game to him.

She wasn't going to play.

"Whatever you were hoping to gain with this little stunt, you can consider it a wasted effort," she hissed and gave him a slow, patronizing once-over. "And if you ever attempt to 'enjoy' me," she spat the word. "I will take great pleasure in castrating your favorite appendage."

She ripped her hand away, but his grip tightened preventing her retreat.

His gaze slid down her, returning her earlier scrutiny, his smile widening. "Such violent fantasies. Good to know."

Her jaw slammed shut as she bit back her rising anger. She needed to control herself. No matter how infuriating he proved to be. The music came to an end, and she stepped back, taking her hand with her.

"We're done here."

Kaceston let her go with ease and winked. Without a second thought, she spun on her heel and started walking away.

"We're just getting started," his whispered warning followed after her.

Brynnlin's steps were measured as she put distance between them. She forced herself to take a deep breath.

Was this how Ryker felt the other night? If so, she understood now. Kaceston had a knack for getting under someone's skin.

She clenched her jaw, their conversation playing through her mind again. This whole situation wasn't good. Whether they wanted to be, or not, it seemed they were on Kaceston's radar.

Her especially.

And it was very clear that he wanted something.

He could make threats about imprisoning her or killing her for coming from the isles, but if he was serious he would've tried already.

No, he was after something else. There was something bigger behind this. She wasn't looking forward to finding out what it was.

KACESTON'S SMILE was slow to spread across his face as he watched Brynn walk away from him.

Her body was tense at his whispered promise. She thought she could hold her own against him.

It was adorable.

She had wanted to end the game so quickly. But this was only the beginning.

He liked that she didn't concede.

That would've been too easy.

She also didn't fear him. Fire had raged in those pale green eyes as she stood against him. Something very few dared to do.

That had been unexpected...

Though not unwelcome...

It would only make it that much more enjoyable once she surrendered to him. And when this was all over, she would.

His second, Griffin, joined him at his side.

"I think you're losing your touch, old friend."

Kaceston chuckled, not at all insulted. "This one's going to be a challenge."

Oh how he looked forward to it.

Griffin's smirk dropped, a frown creasing his features. "Is all of this trouble even worth it? Do you really think she knows anything of value?"

He considered this. "I do. They wouldn't bring her here otherwise."

"Do you actually think that? Or are you just excited with a new toy to play with?" Griffin shook his head. "Don't forget she's with Kodak. And don't forget why we're doing this."

Kaceston arched a brow, and the look he shot at Griffin told him to tread carefully.

"Never question my commitment to what we're doing, understand, Griff?" The warning was clear.

"I saw the way you looked at her," Griffin argued, "is this going to be a problem?"

Kaceston repressed the urge to retaliate at Griffin's display of disrespect. Griffin was one of three people in his life he allowed insolence from. But even that had its limits.

"I will explain this once. I may be intrigued, but you damn well know that would never affect my judgment. Kodak and the others will be punished for what they did. Brynn included. However, I want to know what plan Kodak has up his sleeve first."

"I think you're wasting time. Punish them all now and that will teach them never to fuck with us again."

He couldn't help but smirk at the idea. It did have a certain appeal. "So bloodthirsty today, Griff. But we need to have patience, rest assured they will get what's coming to them."

"Good."

With that settled, he turned, scanning the room and those around them. He saw Brynn with Maddox. He wasn't surprised, the others rarely left her alone.

He wanted to know why. Did they distrust her that much?

Yet that train of thought paused as someone headed their way.

His lips turned up.

The dark-haired woman had her topaz eyes locked on them.

This was sure to be interesting.

Only he wasn't her target.

"Incoming," he hummed to Griffin.

Griffin turned to look, and his whole body stiffened as he saw who walked towards them.

"Fuck." The word was barely audible, but Kaceston heard it nonetheless.

He forced himself to contain his laughter.

"Be nice, I'm tired of hearing her mother bitch to me every time you hurt her little Bana-phrionnsa's feelings."

"That's rich coming from you. The guy who doesn't give a shit about anybody's feelings and does whatever he wants."

Kaceston adjusted his jacket, already planning his escape. "Rule a realm, and you'll have that same privilege."

Griffin eyed him. "Any chance you're stepping down?"

"Not in a million years." He slapped Griffin on the shoulder just as the pretty brunette joined them.

"Narissa," he purred with glee. "How lovely to see you."

"Your highness," Narissa executed a perfect courtesy, but her smokey eyes were focused on his second. "Griffin."

Griffin clasped his hands behind his back and inclined his head. "Bana-phrionnsa."

Narissa was Isla's youngest daughter. And while he didn't particularly like Isla, he also didn't want unnecessary issues. And Griffin's constant refusal of the Bana-phrionnsa's advances was starting to become noticeable to the other royal. Which then became Kaceston's problem, it was highly irritating.

He was almost to the point of telling Isla to fuck off and control her daughter, but he found Griffin's uncomfortableness with the whole thing damn entertaining.

So he wouldn't intervene. Not yet.

"Are you enjoying yourself?" Kaceston asked.

"Very much," Narissa smiled. She fluttered her eyelashes at Griffin. "Are you?"

"For now."

"You know what would make this night even more enjoyable, Griff? A dance with Narissa," Kaceston offered up the suggestion, oh so helpfully.

Griffin's head swung to Kaceston, his eyes blazing.

"I'd be honored." Her eyes lit up and she latched onto Griffin's arm.

Kaceston cringed as her nails dug into his friend's arm. But he still didn't feel guilty. Griffin shouldn't have given him a hard time after his dance with Brynn. His eyes gleamed while Griffin glared daggers back at him.

Payback was a bitch, old friend.

He watched Narissa drag Griffin into a dance and finally allowed himself to laugh.

"That was mean."

He looked down to see Constance at his side. He hadn't heard her approach.

"Nothing he didn't deserve."

Constance laughed. "Do I even want to know?"

"Probably not."

Kaceston glanced to her other side. "Where's your shadow? He never lets you out of his sight."

Constance's grin was smug. "Like he would ever take his eyes off me. But I believe he is still talking to Isla and her council. I had to excuse myself before I died of boredom."

He nodded. "Understandable."

"So here I am. And you're going to escort me to the dance floor." She said, holding out her hand.

His brow rose. "I am?"

"Yes." Something he couldn't recognize danced behind her smile. "There's something you'll be interested in hearing."

"Then I guess we're dancing." Ever the gentleman, he took her hand.

His gut told him he wasn't going to like whatever she had to tell him.

CHAPTER 23

"You are a gift to this world, and we'll set you free."

BRYNNLIN LUCKED out when she spotted Maddox and Ryker standing alone by the refreshments table. She beelined it towards them and when she was close enough she hooked her arm through Maddox's.

"Whatever favor you want, it's yours, if you get me out of here."

Maddox glanced down at her. "That's a dangerous bargain to make, cousin. Was one dance really that bad?"

She scowled at him. "It was two, and I know you're aware of that fact."

"What did Kaceston want?" Ryker crossed his arms and leaned against the table.

To kill her.

Imprison her.

Intimidate her.

Take one's pick.

She scoffed and kept that part to herself. "I didn't stick around long enough to find out. But he wants something, and I doubt that was the last of him."

"Ignore him," Ryker suggested. "Keep your distance, it's the best we can do this weekend."

Yes, because Kaceston would be such an easy man to ignore. Again, she kept that to herself.

"And if that doesn't work?" she pushed.

Ryker stiffened, "It will. We'll make sure he doesn't get to you. He caught us off guard by approaching you, and we couldn't intervene without making a scene. We won't make that mistake again."

Somehow that wasn't a comforting thought. She nodded anyway.

"Come on, I'll take you back to the room," Ryker offered his arm.

She accepted, bid Maddox goodnight, and together they made their exit. She was quiet as they walked the halls. The conversation with Kaceston disturbed her more than she wanted to admit. Everything about him screamed trouble. She didn't like that his interest seemed vested in them.

She needed to keep her guard up. Anything less would be a fatal error.

"Tomorrow's the big party," Ryker stopped at her door, and his words pulled her from her thoughts. "One more night, then we're done. Try and relax and get some rest."

"Thanks."

That was easier said than done.

BRYNNLIN WAS TRAPPED. *Her arms and legs bound. She yanked against the chains. The rattle echoed throughout the cell, but they wouldn't budge. She was weak from blood loss, the excruciating pain numbing as death threatened her.*

This couldn't be happening.

Not again.

"No," she screamed. "No. No. No."

She'd gotten out.

She couldn't be back here.

Her head whipped around, straining to see, but it was too dark. She was too weak for even her shadows to help her.

Hissing and whispered words of anger could be heard from outside the cell.

No, they couldn't be coming back already. She wouldn't survive a second time.

Her cell door creaked open, scraping against the floor.

This was it.

She braced herself for the pain that she knew would come next.

Footsteps sounded, getting closer. She squinted and could barely make out a figure moving towards her. The figure stopped just outside of the open door.

"This is very unexpected, Brynnlin."

The words penetrated through the fog of pain like a knife.

Her entire body stiffened. The hair on her arms rose and an involuntary shiver raced down her spine.

The man clicked his tongue and stepped into the cell, looking down at her. He flipped his hood back, revealing light brown hair, or at least she thought it was brown—it was hard to tell—that was cut short making his face visible.

Straight nose, narrow cheeks, chestnut colored eyes.

Such average features.

Yet the worst ones were always the least suspecting.

It didn't matter how long it had been, she would never forget that face.

The Draíothe stood above her.

Her first nightmare.

The one responsible for most of her pain.

It shouldn't be possible. He didn't belong here.

He shook his head, dragging her out of her thoughts.

She yanked against the chains again, holding her to the floor. The shock of seeing him quickly fading as anger took its place.

She was going to kill him.

There was no doubt.

This man took everything from her and for the first time in eleven years, he was in front of her and within her reach.

"Oh, Brynnlin," he said her name again, completely unfazed by her thrashing. "This is dark and twisted and that's coming from me."

She pulled harder even as her wrists screamed in pain. "I'll kill you. I'll fucking kill you," she seethed.

He continued as if he didn't even hear her. "When I was informed that you were back and alive, I couldn't believe it. I was convinced you were dead. I had to see for myself if it was really true. And here you are."

He looked down at her again, an awed expression crossing his features.

"Hey asshole, did you hear me?" Her voice was hoarse from her screams, but that didn't stop her. "You better pray to the gods, I never get out of these because when I get my hands on you, it will be the last breath you take. I will rip your godsdamn heart right out of your chest."

He finally met her stare. "Enough of the theatrics, your threats are vulgar and unseemly."

Unseemly? Did she look like she gave a shit?

She opened her mouth—he kept talking.

"Look at what they did to you." She couldn't understand as a pained look entered his eyes. "Such vile creatures. How old were you when this first happened?"

Yeah, like she was going to answer.

She still had no idea what was happening.

She jerked as some invisible force pushed against her mind. With the memory of this night at the forefront, it wasn't hard for him to dig through for details.

"Fourteen," he croaked, "I can't look at you like this."

The room spun and in a flash of light, she found herself sitting in a small, green meadow, wispy smoke curling around her. The sun shone above. The cell was gone. The whispers were gone. Most importantly the chains were gone. She winced at the brightness and cradled her wrists to rub out the pain. The grass was soft beneath her, and she stood on wobbly legs. Her bloody clothes were replaced with a long flowing, white nightgown.

"Isn't that better?"

She swung around, coming face to face with the monster that ruined her life.

"You never should've let me out."

She pulled at her power, ready to release a decades worth of rage at him.

Only it wasn't there.

It was like she had the sigil again and was completely cut off from that part inside her. It ached, but she pushed it aside. She didn't need her abilities for this. With barely contained fury she flew at him.

He was right in front of her, she lunged forward, swinging her fist.

Her hand went through him, hitting nothing but air.

She stumbled past him.

Spinning back, she saw him casually standing there with his hands in his pocket.

"Was that really necessary?"

She clenched her eyes shut before slowly reopening them. "You're not here."

That realization hit hard. To be so close only for this to not be real.

He walked in a small circle. "This is your dream. Your mind. I'm only a visitor."

Of course it was.

She should've made that connection as soon as she found herself back in that cell. Too many emotions swirled inside her, and she had to keep it together. She wondered how it was possible for him to invade her dream. But she didn't bother voicing her question, he was a powerful Draíothe there was probably a lot he could do.

"What's with the meadow?" *She settled instead, while trying to get her thoughts in order.*

"I told you, I couldn't see you like that. I had no idea you had such terrible memories. Most would never survive that kind of torture, how did you?" *He gave her a curious look.*

She laughed harshly. She was so not talking about that. "Aw, are your feelings hurt? You're not the only monster in my life. I must say though, they had me for years and came a Hells of a lot closer to killing me than you did. But now you're what? Back to finish the job?" *she taunted.*

The speed at which his head jerked back was almost comical.

"What? Why would you think I'm here to kill you?"

She couldn't believe he actually asked her that question. Rage burned inside her, but she had to control it. She had to be smart. There was no hurting him here. But maybe, just maybe, she could get something, any kind of hint that would lead her to him once she woke up.

"Oh I don't know." *She tapped her chin with her finger as if in thought.* "Maybe because you murdered my family, our staff, and would've killed me too, if I hadn't escaped?"

"Oh, Brynnlin." *He shook his head at her.* "There's so much you don't know."

"Well then why don't you enlighten me?"

"All in good time."

"Typical answer." She forced herself to keep calm, and she started examining her nails as if she didn't have a care in the world. "However, I feel I'm at a disadvantage. You seem to know so much about me, and I don't even know your name." She looked up and stared him down, waiting for an answer she knew he wouldn't give.

He smiled.

Actually fucking smiled.

She hated it.

Hated him with every fiber of her being.

"I've had many names, none of them of much significance."

She gave him her own venomous smile. "Figures. Insignificant names for an insignificant man."

His smile dropped. "If you hope to anger me with insults, I must warn you I'm not nearly insecure enough to be susceptible to that tactic."

She shrugged. "I guess it doesn't matter what you call yourself. I guess none of this really matters in all actuality. I know why you're here, and it's a waste of time."

He stepped towards her, his brow rising. "Why would you think this is a waste of my time?"

"I don't know where the relic is," she said the words almost gleefully. "You thought you could use me to tell you what my father couldn't, but you can't."

He laughed.

The sound echoed through the clearing.

"You truly don't know anything, do you? But that's not your fault," he was quick to comfort. "None of this is your fault. You've been kept in the dark for too long. But I'll do you a kindness and let you in on a little secret. We secured that relic years ago, rest assured that's not why I'm here."

Brynnlin's world spun, the ground swaying as she found herself on her knees.

They already had the relic.

Then why?

"Why?" she snapped. "Why are you here?"

He was in front of her in a heartbeat. "All in good time the truth will be revealed. But don't let those so-called friends fool you. You are a gift to this world, and we'll set you free. I'll come for you soon."

In a snap he was gone.

The meadow contorted, caving in.

Darkness claimed her.

———————

BRYNNLIN JERKED UPRIGHT, her hands automatically reaching for the knife she kept under her pillow. Her breathing was labored and sweat dripped down her back. Her gaze swung around the room looking for threats. The flickering of the candles she lit the previous night cast shadows that danced along the walls, reminding her where she was.

The palace. The summit. This was real.

She was awake.

The Draíothe wasn't here.

It was just a nightmare.

She pushed the covers off and crossed her legs in front of her to sit up. She rubbed her eyes, swiping the tears from her cheeks, and set the knife down to cradle her head in her hands.

"Son of a bitch."

She didn't even know how to process what just happened. The nightmare still clung to her, and his voice echoed through her head.

'I'll come for you soon.'

That bastard had sounded determined. Though there was

no fear with that knowledge. Let him come for her. It would save her the trouble of tracking him down.

But why?

Why bother?

If he was telling the truth, they had the relic. A sickening thought on its own. But they wouldn't need her.

He had said she was a gift. A gift for what?

And that she would be free? She was already free from the isles. It sounded like he was talking about Maddox and the others.

But why?

It didn't make any sense.

She took a deep breath, filling her lungs, and slowly exhaled.

She needed to think, to consider every angle, and dissect every word he said in that dream. It was unlikely she would get another opportunity like this, she had to handle this right.

But she couldn't do that here.

She glanced at the clock on the wall. It was barely past four in the morning. It was too early to get up, but no way was she going to try and sleep again.

Not after that.

She needed fresh air. The idea of staying cooped up in this room for a second longer sounded nauseating.

What she really needed was a good long run. With that idea in her head there was no getting it out. It's not like anyone would be awake right now anyway. She would be back before anyone would even notice. And with a clear head, she could come up with a plan and talk to the others once they were up.

Decision made, she pushed herself up and off the bed. She pulled on a pair of pants and tossed her sweat-soaked shirt aside, exchanging it for a long sleeve. She piled her hair up and tiptoed into the hall. The last thing she wanted to do was alert the others to her being awake. She didn't have the energy to deal with the concern and the questions she knew would come. The halls were quiet and dark, the only light coming from the moon shining through the windows. Even the sun was still sleeping.

A sentry stood up ahead and eyed her with suspicion as she got closer.

"Morning miss, you're up already?"

"Early riser," she murmured and kept her head angled down. The last thing she needed was him seeing her puffy face. "Is there anywhere good to run around here?"

He considered her question. "There's a good trail outside the wall. It runs through the valley and into part of the forest before circling back around. Just don't stray from the trail, we wouldn't want a guest getting lost," he warned.

She nodded her thanks as he let her pass. She had to explain herself to several more sentries before she made it outside. The brisk air was refreshing against her overheated skin. She slowed down as she strolled through the manicured lawn. Breathing in the morning air seemed to calm her over-loaded senses. The stars above her added to the peacefulness.

After a moment, she found the path that led her to a gate that would let her outside the property. A sentry stood stationed there, and after a quick explanation, he seemed unconcerned with her presence. Past the wall were open fields, and the edge of the forest was a dark backdrop in the distance. A well-worn trail led in that direction, and she assumed that was the one the sentry mentioned. She started with an easy jog while her thoughts boomeranged through her head.

There was no denying the Draíothe was coming for her. He'd said so himself.

But why?

If he attacked their estate with the hopes of getting to her father and the relic, it obviously failed. Yet they still managed to find the relic—granted, if he'd been telling the truth. But what would he gain from lying? To throw her off? She didn't know where it was. It would be a wasted effort anyways.

Again, why bother with her?

That was the part that didn't make sense.

He'd also said someone told him she was alive. There was someone that managed to recognize her and make the connection to her past. That person was clearly working with the Draíothe and most likely the Creed.

And that person had to be here.

A person she crossed paths with.

Her heart hammered at that deduction.

She could admit she wasn't completely surprised that the Creed had managed to infiltrate this high in the empire. It would explain how they've lasted as long as they have. But there were so many people here. It would be near impossible to single them out. If it even was a single person.

She immediately wanted to jump to Kaceston. He'd been at the island, it made the most sense. Yet something about that didn't sit quite right. He threatened to both imprison her and kill her. He'd wanted to scare her into cooperation for gods know what.

But the Draíothe had been surprised she was alive. Had seemed happy even. He didn't want her dead. Not at all.

He wanted to free her.

Whatever that meant.

A gift to be freed? A gift to be freed? A gift to be freed?

She continued to repeat the mantra in her head in hopes that something would click.

Why would he use the term gift?

She was a gift to the world? She'd been an only child to her parents. A gift to them? But that wouldn't be to the world.

Her magic was certainly no gift...

Brynnlin stumbled over her feet, coming to a stop in the middle of the trail.

There was no way that was what he was referring to.

It wasn't possible.

As far as the world was aware, she didn't have magic.

And her magic was absolutely no gift. It was an anomaly against nature itself. The Creed stood against magic.

Though they had no qualms when they used it to their advantage.

She stood there trying to make sense of it. There was no way they knew about her. For gods sake, Maddox hadn't even known about it until recently.

But if they did? If it ever got out? Is that what he meant by freeing her?

Her magic had always been concealed, did he think to free her from that secret? It shouldn't be possible, yet she couldn't deny it could fit.

Was that what this was about?

She shook her head. What she needed to do was talk to the others. She couldn't figure this out alone. She came out here to clear her thoughts and all she was getting was more questions.

She started running again, pushing herself harder, increasing her speed. The ground was rough under her feet, and she put all her focus into not tripping. She was a few miles away from the palace and well into the thick trees of the forest before she slowed back down to a jog.

It was darker here. The dense branches blocked most of the moonlight. The trail was still clear to see, but she eased into a walk, carefully taking in her surroundings.

Something was off.

The forest was eerily quiet around her. When she had first

entered she could hear rustling and other small signs of life. Now there was nothing.

The hair on the back of her neck rose as she approached a bend in the trail. She crept forward while simultaneously reaching for the knife at her thigh. She grasped at air.

Startled, she came to an abrupt halt and looked down at her sheath. Her empty sheath.

Where was her knife? Why wasn't it there?

Panicked, she tried to mentally retrace her steps to when she had it last. It was under her pillow, she had it when she woke up from the dream th—

Shit.

She left it on the bed. She had been in too much of a hurry to get out of her room to remember to grab it.

Gods, how could she have been so stupid?

Pushing back her irritation with herself, she loosened out her arms, and wiggled her fingers, pulling her shadows forward from the powerful well within her. They answered with plea-sure as the familiar tingle rushed through her veins. She continued forward again, keeping to the trees to stay out of direct view.

As she reached the corner, she smelt it before she saw it. Rotting and decaying flesh assaulted her nose. She gagged, and her stomach immediately revolted. She covered her nose and tried to only breathe through her mouth, not that it helped. The smell was so potent, she could practically taste it. She prepared herself for whatever carnage she was about to see as she inched closer and peeked up the trail.

There was nothing.

No dead bodies were piled ahead, and there wasn't anything to explain that awful smell. Everything looked normal. With extreme unease, she stood straighter, and her steps were more purposeful. She still stuck to the tree line, not fully ready to drop her guard. She advanced a few more feet, her eyes scanning the area.

A figure appeared in the middle of the trail.

She froze, and her pulse jumped. The air around her dropped in temperature, and she involuntarily shivered. She hugged herself to the nearest tree as she observed the thing before her.

What was that?

It seemed to float just above the ground and easily stood seven feet tall. A hooded cloak hid its shape and most of its appearance. The smell was stronger now, coming from whatever that thing was.

She held her breath and waited.

It moved in a small circle.

Stopped.

And turned in her direction.

It zeroed in on her as if sensing her.

Fuck.

Before she could blink, it was right in front of her.

She didn't even have time to jump.

Bony claws reached out and lifted her by her neck, slamming her up against the tree. Bark bit into her skin, and her head throbbed. An ear piercing scream ripped out of her, and she squirmed trying to break free.

Struggling accomplished nothing and her magic flared. Shadows burst from her and shot outwards, wrapping themselves around the creature before her. They went for the neck, curling themselves tight. She had every intention of suffocating it.

It didn't release her.

She willed the shadows to squeeze harder, pushing with everything she had while her own lungs screamed in pain.

Why wasn't it working?

She strained to look up under its hood. She stopped cold. The blood drained from her face, and ice filled her veins in horror. Soulless, black depths filled the eye sockets of the otherwise faceless creature. Silvery, white skin wrapped around its head and disappeared into the rest of the cloak.

There would be no choking this thing.

BECAUSE IT DIDN'T BREATHE.

Unlike her, whose vision was starting to blur by the lack of oxygen. Thinking fast, she gripped the claws at her neck, and shadows seeped from her palms into it. They went straight for the chest. Pronged shadows tore through it, searching for its hearts.

This had to be a demon.

It couldn't be anything else.

Precious seconds passed.

She fought harder even as her muscles protested.

Where were its hearts?

A pulsing beat fluttered against her shadow as she reached its spine.

Thank the gods.

The shadow coiled around the heart it found.

But where were the other two?

Black spots danced in her vision, and her lungs were ready to burst.

Screw it.

The shadow stabbed through it. The thing released a pained sound and dropped her to the ground. She greedily gulped in oxygen and tried to scoot away from the demon looming over her. It hovered above and sprang forward. It caught her shirt, dragging her forward.

Shit. Not again.

The front edge of a sword plunged through the middle of its head.

The sword stopped mere inches from her face.

Thick, black blood sprayed over her.

The creature disintegrated into dust.

Oh gods, that was disgusting.

She nearly gagged again.

With a shaky hand, she used the bottom of her shirt to wipe the goop from her face and looked up. Kaceston stood above her, holding the handle of the short sword.

CHAPTER 24

"Afraid one good deed will tarnish your wicked reputation?"

BRYNNLIN STARED up at Kaceston with wide eyes. Words deserted her as she looked to the small pile of ash on the ground then back up to him.

Kaceston's chest heaved.

"What in the Three-fucking-Hells are you doing out here?" The words were forced through his clenched jaw.

She couldn't form an answer. Fear still clung to her after the near run-in with death.

What kind of demon monstrosity was that?

Kaceston shook his head and sheathed his sword. He stomped towards her and gripped her under the arm, yanking her up.

"Do you have a fucking death wish?"

She choked on her words, quickly swallowing the thank you that had been on the tip of her tongue. She pulled her arm away and leveled him with a glare.

"Not that I know of," she responded blandly.

His jaw ticked, but in a blink any emotion disappeared from his face, and his lethally calm mask was back.

"Could've fooled me, wandering around in the middle of the night suggests otherwise."

Her legs were still shaky, but she willed herself to stand tall. "Last I checked it was morning. And I was running, not wandering," she clarified snidely.

His eyes glinted. "Actually it looked like you were choking, until I saved your ass. Very heroically, I might add."

She crossed her arms over her chest to ward off the sudden chill. She would never let him see how truly rattled she was by the truth in his statement.

He had saved her.

"Do you want a parade?"

He smirked. "If that's how you'd like to convey your appreciation, I wouldn't object."

Before she could respond, leaves crunched behind her, and she whipped around. Surprise hit her as Griffin skidded to a stop a few feet away from them. His gaze swung to her before shooting to Kaceston.

"I heard a scream, but I was a good distance away."

"The situation is under control," Kaceston answered.

Griffin eyed her again and seemed to take in her appearance. "You killed the sluagh?"

Kaceston stiffened slightly. "Yes," he said tersely.

Brynnlin's entire body froze.

A sluagh.

She recognized the name from Selene's book.

That's what attacked her?

She couldn't have heard him right.

"Did you say sluagh? As in the soul-eating demon? That sluagh?" She couldn't help that her voice had turned slightly high-pitched. Those were not some low-level demons. "What in the fuck is that doing here?"

EARLIER THAT MORNING...

Kaceston waited impatiently outside Griffin's door. He leaned against the wall, his frustration growing. He was about to pound on the door again, when it swung open.

Griffin stepped out, pulling a shirt over his head.

"Finally," he huffed.

Griffin rolled his eyes, but his gaze widened as he took in the knives strapped across Kaceston's chest.

"Expecting trouble?"

"Not expecting, there is trouble." He didn't wait for Griffin and started down the hall like a man on a mission.

And in a way, he was.

"What do you mean? What's happening?" Griffin hurried after him.

Kaceston didn't slow. "That tip Constance gave me last night might actually be true. Someone claimed they spotted a demon outside the gates."

To give Griffin credit, he barely missed a step at that revelation.

"That's not possible. Wouldn't you have sensed it?"

"I should have, yes," Kaceston grumbled. "Yet I'm not taking any chances." He hadn't believed Constance when she told him what she heard. It wasn't common knowledge, but he had a certain expertise when it came to demons. His other form, as he liked to call it, could sense them for miles. It made him very adept at tracking them and even better at killing them.

He would have known if one was near. So her spouting about someone seeing one near the grounds was outrageous.

But the itch to look into the claim pestered until he finally gave in.

He spent most of the night searching for any truth to the statement. And much to his dismay, it had been more difficult to ferret out the information than he'd ever admit. Something of that regard should have been easy to discover. Yet he had to go through several levels of sentries and use multiple forms of...persuasion...before he found one that actually knew something.

Constance had been right. A demon had been spotted, but no one had believed the drunken sentry who claimed to see it. He didn't know if he did either, but he was going to check. If it was true, he needed to have some words with Atlas. A conversation that would not be fun for the other royal. Atlas should've informed him immediately of the issue, and he could've handled it without all of this godsdamn fuss. And how Constance even found out about this in the first place, he desperately wanted to know, but knew she wouldn't share.

"What's the game plan?" Griffin asked.

"Find the demon if it's there and make sure it doesn't fucking kill anyone."

And that was how he found himself climbing past trees and bushes where there were indeed signs of a demon. From what he could tell, it might even be a sluagh.

Fucking great.

This was the last thing he needed out here.

He relayed the information to Griffin. "Watch your back and go for the kill."

Sluaghs were no joke. He wasn't risking its survival.

"Got it."

They followed different paths when a scream echoed through the night.

PRESENT...

Brynn's already pale face went a shade paler under the blood covering her skin. Her freckles were stark across her cheeks, and red marks crisscrossed around her throat.

Kaceston wondered if she was about to pass out as she realized what it was she had been up close and personal with. Honestly, he could admit he was impressed she was still alive. Most didn't walk away from an encounter like that. Though he knew his intervention was the reason for that.

He saved her life.

As he saw it, she now owed him. What a fortunate turn of events. It made this whole little ordeal extremely worthwhile.

He couldn't wait to cash in on her debt.

Yet it seemed that was going to have to wait a moment.

Brynn's voice had risen as she demanded to know about the sluagh and what it was doing here.

"What an excellent question indeed," he drawled, stepping into her space. "I was wondering the same thing."

Her green eyes narrowed at him.

"Are you implying something?"

He shrugged. "Merely connecting the dots. An acolyte from the isles, out here all alone, with a demon on the loose no less. And not just any demon, no, a sluagh, which you seem to know quite a bit about." He arched a brow. "It's all a little peculiar, wouldn't you say?"

She didn't like his question if her glower was anything to go by.

"Yes, what an excellent deduction," she snapped, "a demon that tried to kill me was my doing."

His lips thinned, and he took her in again.

Mother of Danu, she really was a mess.

It was unlikely she was responsible for the demon. From his understanding, a demon couldn't—or wouldn't—attack its summoner. Secondly, there was no evidence of a ritual being performed here. He couldn't sense any other magic around, other than that belonging to a demon.

"No, you didn't summon it, did you."

"What an astute conclusion," Brynn crossed her arms and rolled her eyes. "Your intelligence is truly astounding, your highness."

Gods, she really did have a mouth on her, didn't she? He shouldn't find it as nearly entertaining as he did.

"Yes, my intelligence is one of my best qualities," he smirked and mirrored her, crossing his own arms. "Which is why I know you're not the one that summoned it, but I guarantee you know who did."

"What?" Surprise flashed across her face.

Interesting.

"Tell me who's responsible."

"I have no godsdamn idea."

His patience was thinning. "I won't ask again. Tell me, and I'll assure you aren't sentenced to the same punishment."

"I came out here for a run, not to be strangled." She shook her head at him, and her expression was unreadable. "Trust me, if I find out who did this, they won't have to worry about your punishment. I'll kill them myself."

She stomped past him, giving him a wide berth.

He couldn't help but chuckle.

"Cairán."

She whirled, leveling him with an icy glare. "Don't call me that."

He pointed towards the trail, opposite of her. "Palace is that way."

Her features fell into a defeated frown.

For once he took pity on her.

He nodded to Griffin. "Let's get her back."

He didn't know if he necessarily believed her. But she was pretty shaken. No one was that good of an actress. Not even her.

Griffin inclined his head and led the way towards the path. Kaceston held out his arm in a gesture for Brynn to follow. She hesitated for a moment as if debating her options, but trailed after Griffin. He almost kneeled over in shock. Mother above she actually listened—and didn't throw a fit.

"Pop the champagne, she does have sense," he snickered under his breath as he took up the rear of their little line.

Brynn flipped him off.

He smiled.

They walked on in silence. The sun was still down but small sounds of life started to erupt around them with the danger now gone.

"If I ask you something about the sluagh, will you answer it?" Brynn's voice was so soft, he was sure he imagined it.

Until she looked up expectantly.

It was the first time she'd ever initiated a conversation with him.

"Maybe," he allowed.

"I tried piercing it through the chest, it didn't work," she hesitated. "Why did it die when you went for the head?"

"Oh," Kaceston was not expecting that. He debated giving her that information. It was harmless enough to answer. "I imagine you were going for its hearts, yes?"

He glanced down to see her nod.

He continued, "Not all demons have the same anatomy. The stronger they are, the more difficult it is to find their weakness. A sluagh in particular has one located by its spine and two in its cranial cavity."

She nodded again and seemed to absorb the information.

"If you get to ask a question, I feel it's only fair for me to do the same," he drawled out seeing if she'd bite.

She eyed him warily but didn't object.

"Why were you out here running?"

Brynn stiffened, and he didn't think she would answer.

"I needed to think," she admitted, taking him by surprise. "I do that best when I can run."

"Why'd you need to think?" he pushed.

"That's two questions."

"Nothing is stopping you from asking a second."

"Okay, fine. Why were you out here?" she challenged.

"Oh Brynn, if you think I had anything to do with this, you are looking in the wrong direction. I was out here to hunt a demon." He winked. "Quite successfully as you saw."

She pursed her lips and sped up.

No comeback?

That was a first.

Kaceston moved forward and walked in step beside her. He observed her out of the corner of his eye. This quiet and serious side of her was intriguing, so different from the snappy and sarcastic girl he'd witnessed previously. He also didn't miss the way her gaze darted around constantly looking for threats, or the way her fingers kept grazing at an empty sheath.

Again interesting.

They reached the forest's edge and there was only a short distance until they reached the gates. He needed to clear something up before they made it back. He gripped her wrist, pulling her to a stop. She immediately jerked free.

"Do not manhandle me," she warned.

"Or what?"

She wasn't one to be giving orders around here.

Her mouth quirked to one side, and a glint entered her eyes. "Do it again and find out."

His lips twitched despite the situation. Damn she was refreshing—and so entertaining.

"As much as I would love to see where that goes, unfortunately we're of limited time. We need to get you back to your safe little room, but first," his voice turned serious, deadly, "we're going to come to an understanding."

She crossed her arms and cocked her head, "Now why would I agree to that?"

"Because," he started, his tone deceptively soft, "as I see it, you now owe me a favor. I could've just let that sluagh kill you, but I didn't. Now let's discuss repayment."

She still didn't give in, only asked, "You didn't save me out of the kindness of your heart?"

"Not at all."

"Well aren't you the gentleman," Brynn mocked before she turned wary. "What's the favor?"

"There's going to come a time, where I need something from you, and you're going to oblige."

"No. That's too vague."

"This isn't a negotiation." She wasn't going to deny him. Not when this opportunity presented itself. "And to put your pretty little mind at ease, you can relax, it's nothing illegal."

Brynn frowned. "It doesn't sound like you're giving me a choice here."

"Good, you're catching on. No, I'm not."

Brynn eyed him with annoyance. "Then are we done here?"

He fought a victorious smile. There was no need for him to rub it in. "One more thing. Don't discuss what happened out here. Not with anyone."

Her nose scrunched up, revealing her confusion. "Why don't you want people to know about this morning? Afraid one good deed will tarnish your wicked reputation?"

She had no idea. "Something like that."

"That sounds like two favors to me."

"Only one. Consider the second matter a gesture of your good faith."

Brynn was slow to answer. "Fine."

"Fantastic," he let a predatory grin shine through. A glimpse at what she would be dealing with if she disobeyed.

She remained unfazed and mirrored one right back.

"Can we get moving, or do you two still need to finish your pissing contest?" Griffin broke in.

"Griffin, when one is dealing with a being of a more primitive nature, dominance has to be established," she said, a taunting look crossing her face.

She was trying to bait him.

Cute.

"Sweetheart, it's adorable that you believe there's any dominance to be established at all." Kaceston spun forward and started walking with Griffin. He wasn't going to entertain her ridiculous notion. He had only been curious to see how long she would have held his stare.

Apparently, it would've been very long.

An annoyed huff sounded behind him, but footsteps soon followed.

He looked over his shoulder and winked.

Brynn barred her teeth.

He almost laughed.

In no time, they were back within the walls of the palace. A few sentries took notice of them, but at his glare they quickly looked away. The rest of the palace was still sleeping except for a few staff members rushing about—all of whom were too busy to pay them any attention.

They made it to the west wing without incident.

At Brynn's door, Kaceston stopped her from going inside.

"Remember, you don't say anything. Not about the deal. Not about the sluagh."

She rolled her eyes but nodded her head. He didn't trust that for a second. When she tried to pass him, he blocked her path and gripped her chin, forcing her to look up.

"I want your word."

A lesser man would've cowered at the daggers in her eyes.

"You must have a memory problem, I already agreed, didn't I?" Her words were mocking.

"Just covering all the bases," he applied just enough force for her to feel the pressure and leaned in close enough for their breaths to mix. "Now go clean yourself up, you reek of death, it's quite repulsive."

"Maybe I'll bottle it into a perfume and wear it daily if it keeps you away," she responded with sickening sweetness.

"Careful, Brynn," he caressed the column of her throat with his thumb, "if you keep insulting me, I'll start to think you like my company."

"What a travesty it would be if that statement were true."

Brynn shoved against his chest, gaining space between them, and ducked her head, twisting out of his hold.

"Was that really necessary?" Kaceston questioned.

A distinct pressure pushed against him.

He stilled, glancing down.

And blinked.

And blinked again, just to be sure.

He was not in fact imagining it.

Brynn was holding a knife precariously close to his groin.

A knife he recognized.

As it was his.

He hadn't even felt her swipe it from its sheath. He slowly looked back at her and raised an eyebrow.

She only smirked. "I did tell you not to manhandle me."

His power pulsed underneath his skin, demanding an outlet at the threat before him. And Brynn was indeed proving herself to be a threat.

He let out a slow chuckle.

"You seem quite partial to my dick." His lips upturned into a devious smile. "Subconscious desire is it?"

She inched it closer. "Want to find out?"

His smile dropped.

Even he had his limits. He could kill her for the stunt she was pulling. But he'd let it pass. Just this once. A quick glance at Griffin told him Griffin thought he'd lost his damn mind.

Maybe he had.

"Alright, Brynn, message received. But don't ever pull the shit you just did again, you won't like the consequences."

Brynn stared at him a moment longer before stepping back, taking the knife with her.

He held out his hand. "Don't force me to take it back."

"I rather like it," Brynn admired the knife in her hand, running a finger along the blade.

It was sleek. Easy to maneuver. One of his finest.

"Mhmm," he agreed. He liked it, too.

She inched around him, easing closer to her door, and shot him a winning smile.

"I think I'll keep it," she said, slipping through the door, and shutting it in his face.

The lock clicked into place.

Kaceston couldn't help but laugh. Brynn refused to act in the way he expected. It was such a welcome change.

Gods, when was the last time he had this much fun?

He turned on his heel walking away, letting her have her little victory.

"Excuse me, what the fuck was that?" Griffin growled at his side.

"What?"

"For starters, she attacked you, that's grounds for imprisonment."

Kaceston scoffed. "She was proving a point, nothing more. I'm not concerned."

Though she wasn't one to be underestimated. If given the chance, she would fight dirty. Not surprising, but good to know.

Griffin didn't look convinced. "You've killed people for less."

He shrugged. "I don't want her dead."

"Yeah? Is that why you saved her from the sluagh?" Griffin argued.

Kaceston stopped in the hall, turning to Griffin. "Must I explain everything? You are missing the bigger picture. I need her alive if I'm going to use her against Kodak, and I can't do that if she's getting murdered by a godsdamn sluagh. She's my one chance in getting information on Kodak. So can you stop fucking questioning me for one minute?"

Griffin rolled his eyes, easing up. "That's asking a lot."

Kaceston gave Griffin a shit-eating grin. "You're right. A whole minute is well beyond your level of restraint."

Griffin shot him a glare. "Gods, are you always such a fucking prick?"

Kaceston raised his eyebrows. "I think you know the answer to that."

CHAPTER 25

"Death was coming, and he didn't doubt that she would gladly deliver it."

BRYNNLIN LEANED against the closed door, glaring at the empty room.

Gods.

He was so insufferable. And arrogant. Egotistical. Demanding. An asshole.

Some of her momentum faded as she thought of more adjectives to describe the royal that was going to drive her completely mad. Two more popped up.

Powerful. Lethal.

She shouldn't have pushed Kaceston like she did. She let her temper get the better of her. She crossed a line. She had only wanted to wipe that smug-ass look off his face and destroy that authoritative gleam in his eyes.

But it had been a risk.

She was lucky he didn't retaliate. He would've had every right.

While she wasn't afraid of him, it could've gotten messy very quickly. She stared down at the dagger she kept. Another line she shouldn't have crossed. Though she couldn't say she regretted it. The onyx blade was curved. Deadly. Ideal for inflicting maximum damage, and the handle fit perfectly in her palm. It was a beautiful weapon with a mastery design.

No, she didn't regret it at all.

Kaceston would learn she wasn't someone he could bend and break to his will. And if he tried, there would be consequences.

She pushed off the door, stalking into the room. A few pieces of hair fell forward, and she pushed them back, her fingers tangling with the blood-stained mess.

Her stomach turned.

The events of the attack hit her all at once, and suddenly she couldn't get out of her clothes fast enough. She ripped off the offending piece of cloth that was her shirt and was already shrugging out of her pants on the way to the bathroom. She needed to clean herself up and remove the evidence of this morning. She closed herself in the bathroom and risked a glance at the mirror.

Brynnlin cringed.

Her hair was more down than up, and the dried-up blood made pieces look more brown than silvery-blonde. At least the marks on her neck hadn't pierced her skin and were already fading.

She turned the shower on and jumped in. The water took a few seconds to warm, but she didn't care. She grabbed the soap and scrubbed until her skin was raw. She wasn't satisfied until the water flowing down the drain was back to clear.

She stood there, letting the water pour down on her as she watched the water circling around her feet. There was no denying or hiding from the truth in front of her. The Draíothe was coming for her. There was a good chance he was already here.

She hadn't been completely honest with Kaceston when he demanded to know who summoned the demon. She was pretty sure she knew exactly who was responsible. She just hadn't expected him so soon. But she doubted it was a coincidence that he showed up in her dream, and less than an hour later a demon was loose on the premises. She had been an idiot for leaving the safety of the palace, but she truly hadn't expected him to move so quickly.

She needed to tell Maddox—all the others.

She wasn't alone in this anymore. And to think Kaceston expected her to keep the events of this morning to herself. It was laughable. He obviously didn't think her very loyal.

His insistence to keep everything under the radar made her wonder if he was more involved than she originally thought. But if so, he easily could've let her die. He also seemed pretty concerned about the demon. There were too many anomalies.

She also didn't trust this "favor" of his.

He was a fool if he thought he could use her. Others had tried before him, and all had failed. He would be no different.

Shutting off the water, she dried and dressed in record time. She didn't bother with her hair and braided the still wet strands. Then she made a point to secure the new blade into the sheath on her outer thigh. She wasn't going to forget a weapon again. Another once over in the mirror confirmed that she was at least presentable now.

Good enough.

She rushed out of her room and was across the hall, knocking softly on Maddox's door.

Time was not on their side.

She frowned when after a moment he didn't answer. She

pressed her ear to the door. No sound could be heard from the other side.

She knocked again.

She didn't think it was that early, but considering how long it was taking Maddox to answer had her re-evaluating.

She knocked a third time, her fist practically banging off of the wood. Shuffling finally sounded on the other side.

It was the door to her left that swung open, and Brynnlin jumped.

"Brynn? What the fuck?" Ryker's voice was rough from sleep.

She turned to him ready to apologize for waking him. She stopped, the words drying up. Ryker stood shirtless and a pair of silk pants hung precariously low on his hips. She shouldn't be surprised by the smooth expanse of skin. She'd seen him during training, but this was still more than she'd ever planned on witnessing up close. She'd have to be blind to not appreciate the image he created in front of her.

"Damn, Ryker, you should leave your clothes off more often."

She swore his cheeks darkened, and she bit her lip to stop herself from laughing. Who knew he was so easily flustered.

Ryker crossed his arms over his chest, but if it was an attempt at modesty, he failed. He frowned at her before glancing down, "I was sleeping, be happy I'm even in pants, and you're not getting more of an eyeful right now."

She gave him a saucy smile. "I wouldn't complain."

He rolled his eyes. "Good to know. Now if you're done ogling me, would you like to explain why you're trying to break down Maddox's door?"

She chewed on her lip, debating her response.

She didn't need one.

The door to Maddox's room was hastily pulled open.

302

"Brynnlin, what's wrong?"

She spun to Maddox and thanked the gods her cousin was fully clothed. Even if it was in a tank top and sweats. Unlike with Ryker, she had no interest in seeing what he had to offer the world.

Maddox's hair was messy from sleep, and a panicked look filled his eyes. Guilt ate at her for putting that look there, but this couldn't wait.

"We need to talk."

He'd barely taken a step back, and that was all the invitation she needed to slip into his room. He started to close the door, but Ryker was there in an instant, filling out the door frame.

"What's going on?" Ryker demanded.

She knew the others would be told, either by her or Maddox, but she needed to talk with Maddox first. She needed the comfort of family, not an interrogation.

"I need to speak to Maddox. Alone."

Ryker didn't budge.

Maddox gave him a level look. "You heard her. Out."

"Something happened," Ryker argued.

"Rest assured, you will be told about it." She added with a hard stare, "Afterwards."

"I thought we were getting past this, you can trust me." Ryker almost seemed hurt.

She hugged her arms to her stomach. "This isn't about trust, this is me needing my cousin."

Maddox inched closer to her and pulled her towards him, rubbing a comforting hand across her shoulder blades.

"What's going on?" he asked softly.

"Brynn," Ryker moved into the room and bent down to look her in the eyes. "Maddox doesn't need to be the only family you have here. We have each other's backs, no questions asked."

She gave him a dubious look. "Are you even capable of listening and not jumping in to interrupt, or drilling me with questions?"

"Yes."

"No." Maddox said at the same time, his eyes narrowing in warning at Ryker. "That is beyond his capabilities."

"No, it's not," Ryker threw back. "Let me be here, I'll be nothing but supportive."

"Fine. Whatever." Brynnlin gave in. She was done wasting time with this.

Ryker nodded and eased the door closed behind him. He followed her towards the couch but took a seat in the chair across from her. Maddox moved around the room, flipping on the lights before drifting to his dresser.

"Here." He pulled a shirt out of a drawer and threw it at Ryker.

Ryker caught it before it hit him in the face. He shrugged it on. "Thanks."

Maddox didn't respond, only made his way back to the sitting area and sat next to her.

She blew out a breath, not quite sure how to start. Maddox stayed quiet, giving her time while she gathered her thoughts.

"Fuck, here it goes, the Draíothe is coming. I saw him. Sort of." She blurted out in a rush. "I was having a nightmare and somehow he showed up in my dream, but then he was controlling it and when he disappeared, I woke up."

The stiffening of Maddox's shoulders was the only outward sign of any reaction, otherwise he seemed oddly calm.

Ryker was unusually silent.

She didn't bother glancing at him, only kept her eyes on Maddox.

"Okay," Maddox said slowly, as if processing. "Can you walk me through exactly what happened, everything he said?"

She nodded and pushed past the lump in her throat. Step by step, word for word, she told him what happened.

"He's coming for me," her voice was a whisper, "I don't know why."

"No." The ferocity in the one word had her flinching, and Maddox immediately softened his tone. "He will not get to you. Not again."

Ryker abruptly stood, and she eyed him warily. He stalked behind the chair, pacing back and forth. "He has to know what you are, it's the only thing that makes sense."

She couldn't help but scoff. "I don't even know what I am."

"Then he knows about your magic at least," he argued. "Why else would he go through the trouble if they already have the relic?"

"But how would they know?"

Ryker stopped pacing and stood with his arms crossed. "I know you don't want to think this, but if your father was working with Callahan and in turn the Creed in some way, they might have known about your magic."

Deep in her heart, Brynnlin couldn't believe that. Her parents had worked so hard to keep it a secret. But she also couldn't be blind. She couldn't deny that it might be a possibility just because she didn't want to believe it, not after everything that's come to light.

It pained her to even think it, but her father had known Callahan. She'd seen it herself. And over the years she learned there was a lot they didn't tell her.

"What would they want with my magic?" The soft question escaped. She hadn't meant to say it aloud. She didn't need the answer, she knew it was nothing good.

"It doesn't matter," Maddox snarled. "They're not getting it. They're not getting you."

She needed to tell them the worst part.

"I think he's already here."

The room itself seemed to freeze over.

"Why would you think that?" Maddox's voice was far too calm.

Brynnlin bit down on her lip. "A demon was loose on the grounds this morning," she admitted. "So I don't know for sure, but I think he may have used it to get to the palace."

"What the fuck, Brynnlin?"

She winced at the anger radiating off him.

Maddox clenched his eyes shut. "How do you know there was a demon loose?"

"Does it matter?"

"Yes."

She debated lying. "I saw it, Maddox, that's how I know. But it's dead now."

She refused to give more details than that, or about Kaceston's involvement. She didn't trust her cousin's reaction.

"We need to leave," Ryker cut in. "Now. It's not safe here."

"You're right," Maddox immediately agreed. "We have no idea what he's planning. At least back home, we have control. If that bastard is stupid enough to come for her, we can stop him there."

"Wait." Brynnlin's mind spun as she tried to catch up with them. "We can't leave. Not yet."

Maddox shot her an incredulous look. "Why would we stay?"

"I have to meet with Wesley tonight. It's the only reason I came here." She kept talking when they looked like they would interrupt. "I still want to see Callahan and find out why he was working with my father. And he could still have information on other collectors, we can't throw that away."

"Brynnlin, we'll find another way."

She was already shaking her head. Wesley barely agreed to

meet with them as is. They weren't going to get a second chance. "The meeting is tonight. We can make it until then."

"Absolutely fucking not," Maddox glared at her. "You think that Draíothe is here, and you want to wait to leave for some meeting with Wesley—where he might not even agree to our plan?"

"Yes, Maddox I do," Brynnlin refused to back down. They didn't come this far for nothing. "We are close, closer than I've ever been. And I also don't think the Draíothe will make his move tonight. He showed his face in a godsdamn dream. Do you think he'll face me in person so soon, let alone at something so public?"

"You're being reckless. What if he does make a move tonight?"

In a sick twist of fate she thought him showing up might actually be easier than trying to track him down.

The curve of her lip promised nothing but violence. "Then this might all finally end."

MADDOX LOOKED AT BRYNNLIN, seeing a whole new side of her.

He was surprised to hear the words coming from her lips. Surprised to see that kind of coldness in her. The sinful smile was eager, and there was no hesitancy. Death was coming, and he didn't doubt that she would gladly deliver it.

She had said before that she would kill the person responsible.

This was just the first time he believed her.

She wasn't the little girl from his memories. He had to stop picturing her as such. Before him was a woman shaped by years of hardships, ready to do whatever it took.

He hated that for her.

And she might be willing to risk everything. He was not.

"Get Kodak in here." He jerked his head towards the door, and Ryker was already nodding and turning to leave.

"You think Kodak will agree with you?" Brynnlin asked from her spot curled on the couch.

"I do."

"He won't."

He raised a single brow. "And why is that?"

"Kodak has an image to uphold. If we leave, he'd be disrespecting Atlas and raising suspicion."

Maddox frowned, calculating the situation. And damned if she wasn't right.

His silence urged her to continue. "I know you have a single outlook on this, but Kodak can't afford to think that way."

"Then we'll just take you home."

Brynnlin shot him a withering glare. "I'm not leaving. And you would abandon Kodak?"

His lips thinned.

Of course he wouldn't.

"Thought so," Brynnlin said, knowing he wouldn't.

Silence surrounded them, and Maddox watched Brynnlin carefully. She might seem okay, but he knew that was just a ruse. There was no way she wasn't rattled, at least a little. Shadows seemed to circle around her as she stared at the closed door. He wondered if she even noticed.

"It's going to be alright." He felt the need to reassure her.

Her gaze shot to him. "I know."

"Whatever happens—"

The door burst open, Kodak stomping in, Juniper and Ryker behind him.

"We can't catch a break can we," Kodak grumbled, going to the couch, pulling Juniper down with him.

"Ryker filled you in?" Maddox asked.

"He gave me a brief run down and made sure I was aware of both of your feelings on the matter."

Maddox didn't like the sound of that. "Do you disagree with leaving?"

"This new development makes things messy, however, we can't leave."

"You can't be serious."

"Why do I have to explain this to you?" Kodak frowned. "You know better. I cannot insult the hosting royal family by leaving without explanation. And we're taking a risk by meeting with Wesley, I think Brynn should see it through."

"He's coming for her," Maddox argued.

"Yes, Brynn is a target," Kodak arched a brow, "and you want to take away her decision on how this matter is handled?"

Maddox pushed off the couch. "This is unbelievable. She's not thinking straight."

Brynnlin surprised them all when she chuckled. "I assure you, my thinking is quite clear. Maddox, I believe you're more distraught than I."

"I'm sorry, Maddox, we'll all be on guard, but we can't leave until after the party." Kodak's decision was final.

"I can't argue with you, but I can at least add a stipulation," Maddox pointed at Brynnlin. "You are not left alone at all. You will be with one of us at all times. Agreed?"

Brynnlin's features softened. "I can agree to that."

"We should warn Zale, too," Ryker said. "He'll want to know that the Draíothe made contact. We don't know what his next move is, and they should be on guard."

Maddox was already nodding. "I had planned on notifying Zale, I was waiting until it wasn't so early."

Ryker looked at the time. "He should be awake, if not we can try Vee, she's an early riser."

Maddox sat down in one of the chairs and activated his

orenda band. It lit up, and he swiped through the symbols in front of him until he landed on Zale's contact. After selecting the call operation, he waited for it to connect. It took a few minutes before Zale's hologram appeared. Zale's image took a moment to focus, and when it did, Maddox frowned at him.

"You took your sweet time answering."

Zale glared. "You are aware of the time, yes?"

"Yes, we're aware, Zale, but this is important," Kodak took over the conversation.

"Of course, Kodak," Zale immediately turned serious. "Has something happened?"

Kodak explained about the Draíothe reaching out through Brynnlin's dream.

"Do I need to come get you?"

"Not yet. We don't know what his next move will be. We're still planning on leaving first thing in the morning, but fill in Verenna and Selene about this new situation. I want everyone to be extra precautious. When we return, we can delve into an ulterior plan."

"I'll double the perimeter rotations and increase the number of sentries at each post. If he comes here, we'll be ready," Zale promised.

"Good."

Zale and Ryker ended up discussing a few more defensive strategies before Kodak was satisfied.

"Stay safe," Maddox told him when Kodak nodded to end the call.

"You too."

Zale's image disappeared.

"Now all we have to do is get through tonight," Maddox grimaced, and Ryker shared a similar look. At least he wasn't alone in his reluctance to attend tonight's celebration.

CHAPTER 26

"Do not ever threaten me."

THE KNOCKING on the door was entirely unwelcome, and Kaceston growled as he removed himself from the couch.

"Are you expecting someone?" Griffin asked from his reclining position on the settee.

Kaceston only raised his eyebrows, and Griffin chuckled while swirling the contents of his glass.

"I'll take that as a no."

"Smart deduction."

He opened the door and tensed. His original feeling on the unsolicited intrusion completely on the mark.

"Tobin," he said tersely, "to what do I owe the pleasure?"

Tobin grinned and clasped his hands behind his back. "Kaceston. May I come in?"

Tobin stepped forward, but Kaceston didn't move.

"Give me a moment. I'm debating."

He and Tobin had a very tenuous understanding of leaving each other the fuck alone, except when it was absolutely necessary for them to associate. Which meant he should not be standing here right now.

Tobin's friendly demeanor dropped. "It's important, and I don't want this overheard."

"Then maybe you should keep it to yourself."

Tobin didn't leave. "Trust me, you'd like to hear what I have to say."

"Doubtful." But he stepped back, allowing Tobin entrance.

Tobin eyed Griffin. "We should speak privately."

"This is privately." Griffin was included in all of his business, and Tobin knew that.

He was caught off guard when Tobin smirked.

"Well then I'll get to it. I heard something quite disturbing."

"And what might that be?" Kaceston contained his yawn, already bored with the conversation.

"That a demon is loose within the palace perimeter." Tobin let the words hang between them.

Kaceston didn't move. Didn't react.

He blinked slowly. "And where did you hear such an embellishment?

"Is it true?" Tobin countered.

"Shouldn't you be asking Atlas."

"I'm asking you."

Kaceston arched a brow. "Watch your tone, Tobin. Don't forget who you're speaking to."

Tobin dipped his head the slightest. "Is there any truth to the statement?"

Kaceston merely shrugged. "Atlas has not notified me or requested my assistance. Though I did hear whispers of the possibility," he admitted. "I looked into the matter this morning and did not find any trace that there was actually a demon."

"Wonderful. I'd hate to think of the damages such a situation could warrant." Tobin gave them his court smile, but Kaceston had always seen straight through his bullshit. "And I'll speak to Atlas myself. Demon or not, we should have been notified to properly handle the situation."

Kaceston downed the contents of his glass. "You do that."

"And Kaceston?"

He nearly groaned. "Gods, you're still talking?"

Tobin didn't look at all offended. "The last delivery of yours was unusable due to the damage you inflicted. If I discover there's some truth to this account, remember our agreement and take care with its capture."

The emphasis on the final word was not lost on him.

Kaceston gave his own half-grin that was full of warning. "Tobin, don't ever think to give me orders, and you are more than welcome to go after these things yourself."

Tobin's smile dropped.

Kaceston's grew. "That's what I thought. However, since there is no trace of a demon, I feel no need to further this conversation."

He opened the door and gestured to it.

Tobin inclined his head, but paused at the threshold, "I'm glad this was resolved so easily. I'd hate for our dealings to come to an end, if you couldn't follow through. Take care, Kaceston."

"Oh I will," he assured.

When the door was firmly closed, he spun to Griffin, "Someone talked."

"Well you know it wasn't Constance."

No, she wouldn't do that, he trusted her.

Griffin stood and paced, "How about where Constance heard it? Could word have spread?"

"Unlikely." He made sure all talk of the demon was quickly forgotten. There were a lot of things he was willing to do, handing over a sluagh to Tobin wasn't one of them. And after this morning, there was no proof of the thing anyway. "But we can't forget who else knew."

Griffin couldn't hide his reluctance. "You think Brynn opened her mouth?"

His lips thinned. "For her sake, I really hope she didn't."

His retaliation would not be pleasant.

BRYNNLIN GLARED at Maddox from across the room.

"You can't keep ignoring me."

Maddox didn't look up from the book he was reading.

"I can when you keep repeating the same question."

Brynnlin rolled her eyes and stomped over to him, grabbing the book from his hands.

He sighed and lifted his head. "I was enjoying that."

"And I enjoy fresh air."

Maddox hadn't been exaggerating when he demanded she not be left alone. What she hadn't expected was for him to take it to a whole different level and not let her leave her room.

"Brynn, we've been over this."

"I can't stay cooped up in here anymore, I'm going crazy. Nothing will happen if we go downstairs for a little."

"We're not risking it. Just wait for the party, then you can leave the room, and we can go home."

Brynnlin groaned and flopped onto the couch across from him. "What about food, Maddox? It's nearly time for the afternoon meal, and I'm starving. Are you going to deny me that, too?"

"When did you become so dramatic?" Maddox pushed off his chair, heading for the door. "I will ask Ryker to go down and bring you back some food. Will that appease you?"

"No." What she really wanted was to leave this room. "But I'll take it."

"You'll have less than five minutes to yourself, enjoy it," he said and closed the door behind him.

Brynnlin basked in the now empty room. It wasn't that much of a hardship to have Maddox following her every step. She just hated being locked in here like some prisoner.

For protection or not, it was sure to drive her insane. She stared at the walls and attempted to enjoy the small stint of silence and waited for Maddox's return.

Five minutes slowly worked its way into ten.

Did it really take Maddox that long to talk to Ryker about food?

A prickle of unease settled in her stomach.

Did something happen that they weren't telling her?

She'd give it a few more minutes. If he wasn't back, she was going over there.

Not even fifteen minutes later, there was knocking on her door. Her shoulders sagged in relief, and the tension drained away.

Maddox was back.

Though he was going to get an earful for making her get up, it's not like she locked the door.

"Why with the knocking," she swung the door open, "just come in—"

Kaceston stood on the other side.

He arched a brow.

"Is that an invitation?"

"Not in the slightest." She hissed and looked past him, eyeing the empty hall. "What are you doing here?"

The last thing she needed was his presence igniting questions.

Didn't she have enough on her plate without adding Kaceston to the mix?

When he didn't answer her, her gaze shot to him. She was taken aback by the hard set of his features, gone was the signature smirk and mirth she'd been used to seeing. He leaned against the frame and crossed his arms, essentially blocking the doorway.

Her eyes narrowed the slightest at the gesture.

"You don't look happy to see me."

How observant.

"Yes, well I did think I would have a reprieve from you for at least a few hours, especially after the events of this morning," she drawled out, still hoping Maddox continued to stay occupied.

"Such gratitude towards someone who saved your life."

"You sure enjoy bringing that up."

"I feel the reminder is necessary."

"It's not."

"Noted," he responded dryly. "But did you really think you could get away with what you did? Did you think I wouldn't find out?"

"What are you talking about?" Brynnlin's brow furrowed, and her mind came up blank as she tried to keep up with him.

Kaceston's jaw clenched tighter.

"Brynn, I suggest not fucking with me right now. I'm not in the mood."

"Fucking you is the last thing on my mind," a smirk played on her lips, "but I have no idea what you're talking about."

Kaceston pushed off the doorframe and stepped closer, towering over her.

"I was very clear this morning. Was it really that difficult for you to keep quiet?" He sighed, closing his eyes for the briefest of moments. "Apparently, it was. And you might find this hard to believe, but I really didn't want it to come to this."

Keep quiet?

Did he think she told someone?

She didn't even admit to Maddox the full truth of this morning.

"I didn't tell anyone about the sluagh." She refused to step back and glared up at him.

"Don't bother denying it. I know all about your little conversation with Tobin." He hissed, his frustration shining through.

His words caught her off guard.

"Tobin? The Ruler of Saol?" She let out a harsh laugh. "I've never even spoken to that man. So sorry to disappoint, but whatever you think I did, I can assure you I'm not involved."

"And I'm supposed to believe you?" His tone was purposely condescending.

She shrugged, completely unfazed. "I don't really care."

"I'm done debating this," he sneered, "you are the only other person—"

"Get the Hells away from her," Maddox's voice boomed behind Kaceston, and she jumped. She never heard him come out of the other room.

Looking past Kaceston's shoulder, Maddox was storming towards them.

"Whatever fucked up game you're trying play, Brynnlin will have no part in it," Maddox snarled, and Kaceston turned around.

The two men faced off in front of her.

Not good.

Kaceston stared down at Maddox and blinked slowly.

Assessingly.

Then ignored him.

He turned his stare to her. "Brynnlin? Now that's a pretty name," he purred.

Her name rolled off his lips, and she clenched her jaw tight.
Damn it, Maddox.

She refused to respond to the barb, but her eyes widened as Maddox took a step closer to Kaceston, apparently taking offense.

"Maddox, stop." Her tone was harsh.

He needed to get control of himself.

"No, he's done tormenting you."

"Tormenting?" Kaceston chuckled. "You give me too much credit."

Maddox scoffed, "That's all you're capable of, now leave her alone."

"Why would I do that?"

Maddox's shoulders stiffened, and she knew he was very close to completely losing it. Maddox surprised her though when his next words came out calm, a little too calm.

"Because you're not going to like what happens if you don't."

As the words left Maddox's mouth, the air turned still, and a coldness seemed to wrap around them.

"Do not ever threaten me." A lethalness had entered Kaceston's tone that even had her warning bells going off. This wasn't the playfulness he used with her when she pushed him.

He was deadly serious.

This needed to stop now.

Before it went too far.

As if sensing the brooding trouble, Kodak stepped out into the hall. He took a moment and gauged the situation before finally saying, "Do we have an issue out here?"

"It would be in everyone's best interest if you get control of your boy, Kodak. Teach him some manners, too." Kaceston's voice had lost some of its edge, but the command was still there.

"Maddox," Kodak jerked his head to the side, a clear indication to step away.

Maddox opened his mouth, probably to argue.

Kodak silenced him with a long stare.

A satisfied look crossed Kaceston's face.

"I think I'll take my leave." While straightening his jacket, he winked at her. "We'll finish this later, Brynnlin," he dragged out her name, testing it.

She bit back her retort. He was leaving, she didn't need to escalate this.

Maddox shot him a withering glare but stayed in his spot. And miraculously kept quiet.

Kaceston passed by Kodak, who stopped him with a hand to his chest.

"You might think you're untouchable, but you're not. I called Maddox off because you're not his problem, you're mine. And if you continue to harass one of my people, we will have an issue. Am I clear?" Kodak warned.

There was something in the way Kaceston regarded Kodak that had her straightening. The look in his eyes was too calculating, too vindictive.

Yet his voice dripped with sarcasm. "Oh golden boy Kodak, getting his hands dirty. And here I thought you only paid people to do your work for you."

Instead of reacting, Kodak kept his cold demeanor. "Really, Kaceston? Baiting? You can do better than that."

Kaceston picked up Kodak's hand, removing it from his chest, and patted Kodak on the shoulder.

"Be grateful that's all I'm doing right now." As usual, Kaceston had the last word as he strutted away.

When he was out of ear shot, she turned on Maddox. "You have to know how idiotic that just was to go off on him like that."

Maddox still looked pissed, but his shoulders dropped. "When I saw him at your door I couldn't take it anymore. He keeps focusing on you. I don't give a shit who he is, you've been through enough and don't need some psychotic asshole obsessed with you."

"Maddox," she said his name clearly and waited until he made eye contact with her. "I appreciate where you're coming from, I really do. But this is all a game to Kaceston, and you reacting like that will only entice him more. I can handle him."

"You think you can, but you can't," Maddox snapped. "You don't get it, he's dangerous."

"So am I." Her voice hardened in challenge, daring him to contradict her.

Maddox was the one that didn't get it. He didn't understand what she was fully capable of. Didn't know the depth of the power that pulsed within her. She was the dangerous one. And if Kaceston ever went too far he would learn that, too.

"Both of you need to stop, now." Kodak interrupted, "Kaceston is excellent at getting under people's skin, don't take it out on each other."

She'd forgotten he was still there, but gave a small nod of acknowledgement.

"We have one more night here, that's it. We have enough going on right now, and we don't need to add a war with Kaceston on top of that. If he becomes an issue, you leave it to me. I am his equal and can act accordingly, you two are not. Am I clear?" Kodak stared hard at both of them until they nodded in agreement.

"Good." He blew out a breath. "Now, Brynn, why don't you go and hang out with Juniper? You two can get ready for the party together, she would love your company. Maddox, a word?"

He may have phrased it as a question, but they both knew the order for what it was.

She didn't need to be told again and with a final look at both of them, she went across the hall to Kodak and Juniper's room. Going through the door, she heard Kodak berate Maddox for losing his cool. Part of her felt guilty since Maddox only acted that way in her defense, but she wasn't going back out there. What Maddox did was stupid, and Kodak was right to get involved.

They didn't need to start trouble.

Not with only several hours left.

CHAPTER 27

"Gods, he hated being wrong."

BRYNNLIN KNEW Juniper was only trying to distract her from last night, but even this was extreme. It did not take hours to get ready for a single party.

She tried to refuse.

Juniper had been insistent.

That was how she ended up being unnecessarily pampered the rest of the afternoon. And now she sat in front of the vanity while some girl, she'd said her name was Nila, curled her hair.

Nila kept gushing about the party and how excited she was to be there, even though she'd be working. Brynnlin was surprised the girl could talk so much about one event. She tried to share her enthusiasm, but she knew she wasn't pulling it off.

Luckily, Nila didn't comment on it.

After curling her hair, Nila braided and pinned it to the side so that the long curls trailed over her shoulder. Nila even did her makeup, using much more than Brynnlin ever bothered with. When she was done, Brynnlin's eyes stood out even more against the smokey eyeshadow. Brynnlin drew the line when Nila offered to assist her with the dress.

"Thank you, Nila, that will be all," Juniper politely excused her.

Juniper, already ready for the evening, laid out the other dress bag on the bed. Brynnlin unzipped the bag and stared at the gown before her.

"Really?" She cast a sly glance at Juniper.

Somehow each dress Juniper selected for her seemed to lack even more material than the previous one.

Juniper pasted on an innocent smile. "You'll look great."

Brynnlin rolled her eyes and grabbed the dress, going to the bathroom.

She carefully stepped into the dress and by some miracle didn't tear the delicate material. The lace corset clung to every dip and curve, and off-the-shoulder lace sleeves cuffed at her wrists. The midnight-black skirt fell to the floor. Two slits ran up both sides, but there was enough material that she felt mostly confident no one would see something they weren't supposed to. The final touch was the black lace mask. She tied it in place, and the material hid the upper half of her face.

She considered the look.

If there were really that many people in attendance tonight, there was a good chance she'd blend into the crowd.

This might work.

She released a deep breath. Now all she had to do was convince Wesley to take the job.

No pressure.

She exited the bathroom, and Juniper gushed at her.

"Gods, you look even more amazing than I expected."

Brynnlin offered a small smile. "I like the color."

Juniper's smile grew, "It does suit you."

Brynnlin laughed.

That it did.

"The others are waiting, let's go," Juniper ushered her out to the hall.

Maddox stepped towards her, offering his arm.

He must have noticed some hesitancy on her part because when she accepted, he leaned in close. "We don't have to go tonight, say the word, and we'll leave right now."

The words were for her ears only as the others started walking.

She gave the slightest shake of her head. "No, we're not stopping now."

Maddox didn't move. "Are you sure?"

She appreciated his concern, but it was unnecessary. She gave him a small smile. "I'm sure."

He didn't respond, only led her forward. Together they all moved down the hall, Kodak and Juniper leading the way to the party. They stopped at the balcony edge, taking a moment to overlook the throne room.

Brynnlin raised her eyebrows as she took in the transformed room before them. Fire chandeliers floated through the air, casting the whole room in dusky shadows. Silks hung from the ceiling, and aerialists expertly performed above while other entertainers worked their way through the crowd. Seductive music drifted past them, and a sea of people were already filling up the space below. They were adorned in colorful garments and masks of all designs. And more guests filtered through the open double doors and down the staircase.

"Wow," Brynnlin mumbled. "You weren't kidding about them going all out."

"The Prionsa does enjoy his parties," Maddox responded.

She couldn't disagree as she spotted who had to be Elijah sprawled across a couch near the thrones. Staff with trays of drinks surrounded him along with scantily clad women swaying to the music.

"I can tell."

"Let's get this over with," Ryker approached her other side. "We have two hours until you're supposed to meet with Wesley."

She nodded that she heard him, and they descended into the celebration.

THEY MINGLED THROUGH THE CROWD, stopping for small conversations, until they found a group of other council members and settled with them near the back of the room. Things remained quiet, and Brynnlin made an effort to stay under the radar.

It was going quite successfully. That was until someone made their approach. A stir rippled through the small group at the arrival. Brynnlin couldn't hide her surprise at the royal who joined them.

"Tobin," Kodak greeted the other ruler, "how are you this evening?"

Brynnlin dipped into a courtesy, others followed suit, bowing in respect.

Tobin cast them all a winning smile. "Kodak, good to see you."

"How is Saol treating you?"

"Keeps me busy, as always. And Sidhe?"

Kodak shrugged. "It practically rules itself."

Tobin chuckled.

"Are you here alone? I don't see the rest of your party?"

"No," Tobin waved a hand towards the people dancing.

"They found other forms of entertainment. However, I must admit I did come over here with a purpose."

"Oh. What might that be?"

"To persuade your lovely new Diplomat to have a drink with me."

The words hung in the air, and all focus shifted to her.

Brynnlin tried not to gape. Surely, she hadn't heard that correctly.

Tobin stared at her, waiting for an answer.

Gods, did she even have a choice?

"You don't need my permission, Brenna is free to do as she wishes." Kodak said the words lightheartedly, but she could hear the slight strain in his tone.

Looked like she wasn't the only one that didn't like this turn of events.

Tobin held out his arm in escort. She didn't see any other choice than to accept. With a forced smile, she took his arm. "That would be lovely."

Tobin led her across the way towards the bar.

"Are you enjoying yourself this evening?"

"Yes, I am, your highness," she said in a calm, gentle voice, doing her best to appear unaffected and demure. "Yourself?"

Tobin smiled wider, flashing his perfect white teeth. "There's no need for titles. Call me Tobin."

Brynnlin fell silent, surprised yet again.

It was one thing for Kodak to disregard titles, but for Tobin to give her permission for familiarity was incomprehensible.

Their statuses were miles apart. For gods sake, she wasn't even a real council member.

Meeting his gaze she realized he was waiting for a response.

"I couldn't possibly—"

"I insist, Brenna."

He could insist all he wanted, it didn't mean she would oblige.

Instead she asked, "If I may be so bold, why did you seek me out?"

Tobin laughed richly. "Why wouldn't I? It's not everyday a new council member is introduced. I've been meaning to get an opportunity to speak to you."

"Really?" She didn't even attempt to hide her skepticism.

They reached the bar, and she waited while Tobin ordered drinks.

"Absolutely. Your arrival caused quite a stir. But I was especially surprised to notice you captured Kaceston's interest as well." Tobin looked past her before returning a small smirk. "If his glare is anything to go by, I don't think he likes sharing your attention."

Brynnlin fought hard to stop from snorting and didn't bother turning around. She didn't want to see if Kaceston was in fact here and actually looking at them.

"I hate to correct you, but you have misread the situation. Rí Kaceston and I had a difference of opinion earlier, and let's just say he doesn't like being contradicted."

Tobin hid his smile as he lifted his drink to his lips. "That sounds like Kaceston. But if you haven't noticed already, Kaceston isn't as good as he thinks he is." Tobin gave her a pointed look. "Which is another reason I wished to speak to you."

She raised her eyebrows in question.

"Kaceston has obviously been slacking in his responsibilities as evidenced by this morning. I was deeply concerned when I heard about the incident, and I wanted to make sure you were alright. And to let you know this is being handled with the utmost care."

She didn't think she was breathing after Tobin's little speech, and the tension thickened around them.

So that was why Kaceston was pissed. He hadn't wanted Tobin to know.

And he thought she was the one that told him.

Great.

She swallowed carefully. "This morning? Why wouldn't I be fine?"

Tobin looked disappointed. "There's no need to cover for him. One of my men reported what happened."

"Well as you can see, I'm perfectly fine, thank you for your concern."

She figured brushing this off was the best course of action. Tobin obviously knew what happened, but he didn't need the details from her. It was also best for her to get away from this conversation. Not even six hours ago, she had told Kaceston she'd never spoken to Tobin. Now here she was, sharing a drink with him at the bar. That did not look good, whether or not she'd been telling the truth.

Something told her Kaceston wasn't lying about retaliating. She might not fear him, but that didn't mean she had to be stupid about it.

She needed to go. And like a life-raft in a storm, she spotted Ryker speaking to someone several feet away. She didn't know when he made his way over here, but she wasn't going to question it. And even better, she made eye contact with him.

She turned her sweetest smile to Tobin. "Thank you so much for the drink and company, but you must excuse me, duty calls."

She gestured behind him, and when he turned, they both saw Ryker motioning her over.

Gods, bless him for catching on.

"Well then I mustn't keep you," Tobin stepped back to let her pass.

Brynnlin didn't waste time. She and Ryker had come a long

way from that alleyway, that he was now her saving grace, getting her out of unwarranted situations.

KACESTON WATCHED Brynnlin beeline towards Ryker, even with the mask, relief was clear on her face.

That was an unusual look for her. Then again, he was used to annoyance or irritation when she was in his company. But even when she left him, it was with some sarcastic comment or insult, not relief.

What the Hells did Tobin say to her?

He turned his attention back to the man at the bar. Tobin was watching Brynnlin too, a calculating gleam in his eyes that had Kaceston clenching his fists.

He didn't want her anywhere near that asshole.

He almost laughed, the irony was not lost on him, that Maddox had just said as much about himself.

Then again, why did he care? He knew she had broken their deal, what more proof did he need? And why in the gods was he hesitating?

He shook it off. He was done with this arbitrary reaction. She screwed him over, she would pay. It was that easy.

Just as he was about to move forward, Griffin appeared out of thin air at his side.

Kaceston hissed out a breath. "Fucking gods, I hate when you do that."

"I know." Griffin smirked and adjusted his suit jacket while glancing around to make sure no one saw his little reappearance. Considering Kaceston had been watching from the shadows against the wall, Griffin was in the clear.

"Were you able to get close enough?"

Griffin frowned and cast him a dirty look. "Of course I could. What kind of question is that?"

"A valid one, considering you still haven't told me what you heard."

"Well there's good news and some bad news," Griffin held up his two hands as if weighing the options, "which do you want first?"

"Griff, get to it."

"Alright, alright," Griffin dropped his hands. "Good news is your girl wasn't the one that spilled to Tobin."

Huh. That was unexpected. So Brynnlin hadn't been lying earlier.

But he rolled his eyes at Griffin's words. "She's not my anything." Especially not while she was with Kodak. "Though that is good to hear."

He was pleasantly surprised to know her word might actually be worth something. But that also meant he had been wrong in accusing her.

Gods, he hated being wrong.

And if their last conversation was anything to go off of, he had some serious ground to make up. If he didn't, any chance of turning her against Kodak would be shot straight to the Three Hells.

He was anything if not determined.

She of course wouldn't make it easy.

But where was the fun in that?

Focusing back on the current conversation, his gaze narrowed at Griffin, "Then who told Tobin?"

Griffin cringed, and Kaceston braced himself, this wasn't going to be good.

"And this is where the bad news comes in. Tobin said one of his men told him."

"Well he's lying," Kaceston stated the obvious. "There was

no one else out on that trail, I would've known. And the halls were empty when I got you this morning."

"Unless they weren't actually empty," Griffin hedged. "I think Tobin brought Pierce with him."

Kaceston let out a string of colorful curses before taking a deep breath and rationalizing. "We can't know that."

"It's the only thing that makes sense."

Unfortunately, it did make sense. It made a lot of sense.

"Fuck," he muttered.

Pierce was a glorified member of Tobin's council, but all he really did was spy for Tobin. And considering he was a light elemental like Griffin, he excelled at it.

He was also an annoying little shit.

When Pierce hadn't been seen with Tobin, Kaceston thought they lucked out, and he was back in Saol.

Apparently, not.

"I want to leave at first light, watch your back until then. The sluagh is handled, and they can't prove otherwise, but who knows what else they'll try to pull."

Griffin's brow furrowed. "Why not leave now?"

Kaceston grinned. "The night is still young, and we're at a party, are we not?"

"You hate these things," Griffin crossed his arms and eyed him with question.

"True enough," he allowed, and his gaze wandered over to Brynnlin. As usual she was surrounded by the others.

For protection?

Or a prison?

"I need to rectify a previous transgression."

CHAPTER 28

"You haven't even begun to see violent."

IT WAS TIME.

Ryker pulled her close and whispered in her ear, "Keep your head down while we go out the back door."

They had done a good job blending into the crowd. The people around them didn't even glance their way as they exited out the double doors, leading to a large balcony. The balcony overlooked the gardens and was otherwise empty, with the exception of a couple talking amongst themselves by the ledge.

Ryker nodded towards a few pillars along the other side. "Wait over there, if he doesn't show in another fifteen minutes, call it quits, and we'll get out of here. I'll be just inside the door, come find me when you're done."

"Got it, now get out of here, you don't want to be seen in this, remember?" Brynnlin shooed him back towards the door.

Ryker hesitated, but reluctantly slipped back inside. Brynnlin glided towards the edge of the balcony and leaned against the railing, taking a moment to admire the night sky above her.

Gods, it really was beautiful here.

"Shouldn't you be inside enjoying the party?"

She didn't startle at the deep voice coming from behind her. She had suspected Wesley was already out here waiting for her, it was why she wanted Ryker back inside.

"Is this the part where I say some pre-rehearsed line about parties not being my thing, so you know you're meeting with the right person?" She glanced to the side as the man approached the railing next to her.

She couldn't see much of him. It was dark, and he stayed out of the light shining from inside, instead sticking to the shadows. She could tell his unruly hair was dark, but a golden, full-faced mask covered his features, except for the small opening around his mouth and chin.

A mouth that tipped upwards at her response.

"Usually, yes. One can never be too careful."

"A bit cliche don't you think?"

She figured if she had any chance of getting Wesley to accept, he not only had to be interested in the job, but also in working with her. To do that, she had to be different from his usual clients. Questioning his methods might not be the best way to go about that, but her smart-ass mouth had gotten her this far in life. Why not let it keep going?

He seemed amused as he chuckled. "It might be cliched, but it is very effective."

"Well then, who am I to question effectiveness."

"Who are you indeed?" He purred.

She stiffened at the loaded question.

"I have been very curious to know the woman who has Maddox risking his reputation all to set up a meeting with little ole me?" Wesley leaned against the railing facing her, as if he actually expected an answer.

He wasn't going to get one.

She gave him a half smile. "I'm only an interested third party, nothing more."

"You see, I find that very hard to believe." He waved his finger at her. "In case you didn't know, Maddox doesn't play on this side of the law. So I was very intrigued to find out about his request to see me. And that only amplified when I learned he set up the meeting on someone else's behalf. Your behalf."

She leaned forward and kept her voice low. "Let's just say Maddox owed me a favor, and he had people who could get in touch with you, I didn't have said people. It's very simple."

It's a good thing she had prepared for this earlier. No one could know her connection to Maddox, or why he was so involved with this.

Instead of backing off, Wesley smiled wider. "The plot thickens. Our dear Chancellor owed you a big enough favor that he dared to reach out to me?"

She rolled her eyes. "You can't actually expect me to discuss my previous dealings, you of all people should know better. My business is mine alone. Now let's talk about the job, or stop wasting my time. I don't have all night."

She held her breath and waited. Wesley was too interested in Maddox, and they needed to move on.

Wesley finally sighed. "Fine."

"Good. Because I need to get into Sorrow's Gaol."

The infamous prison of Oícha.

Wesley started laughing, and her confidence plummeted.

"Is that so?"

"Rumor is you've gotten in and out...more than once."

Wesley smirked. "Not a rumor. Now why would you have an

interest in Spike Island? You know why they call it that right? The executed prisoners—"

"I don't need a history lesson, I'm well aware of its reputation."

Wesley stepped closer to her, his voice dropping, "Then you know what you're asking for is a one way ticket to the Three Hells."

"Yet here you stand."

"I'm an exception."

"I have someone that can get us out," she pushed, "that's not the issue, I need to get in."

Wesley paused, studying her. "Are you trying to break someone out?"

"No."

"Then?"

The question hung between them.

She debated how much to tell him. She needed him to agree. "I need to talk to one of the prisoners, he has imperative information to me."

"Why not request an inquisition? Kodak certainly holds the position to do so."

If only.

"Out of the question."

"I see," Wesley pursed his lips. "Who's the target?"

Brynnlin shook her head. "Unnecessary until you agree."

She wasn't stupid enough to trust their entire plan to him.

"I'll need to know what area of the prison this individual is being held in."

"And if," Brynnlin emphasized the word, "you agree then that information will be passed onto you when the time is right."

"I'm usually the one that makes demands here."

"You're not the only one that has to protect themselves."

Wesley was silent for a long moment. "It'll be dangerous. Risky. But I'm intrigued, and I've never been one to turn down a challenge."

"Does this mean you accept the job?" She forced her question to come out natural and bored-like. She couldn't let him see how much she had riding on this.

"I guess it does. Congratulations."

"That's excellent to hear. And in case it's not obvious, this is extremely time sensitive." Brynnlin slipped him a folded piece of paper that had ways to get in touch with her. "Will that be an issue?"

"Not at all, but it's going to cost you." Wesley slipped the paper into the inside of his jacket. "And I want seventy-five percent up front."

She scoffed. He was dreaming.

"No. You'll get fifty up front and the rest after the job is completed." She stared him down. "And that isn't negotiable, I know how this works, and that's a fair offer."

Wesley crossed his arms and eyed her. "Alright, I'll accept those terms, but only because I like you. Expect instructions on where and when I want the first payment. I'll be in touch."

Wesley didn't wait for her response. He spun on his heel and slunk back into the shadows. She watched him crack open the door back to the throne room before disappearing into the crowd. It wasn't until he was out of sight that she released the breath she'd been holding.

She did it.

Wesley agreed.

She was one step closer to finding the truth.

With the stress of the meeting off her shoulders, she headed back to the party with a renewed sense of energy. Inside she expected to see Ryker waiting for her, instead she found the doorway empty.

Damn it.

Where the Hells did he go?

Easing back into the crowd, she shuffled past people trying to find a familiar face. It wasn't until she was at the edge of the dance floor that she spotted the dark head she'd been searching for.

There was Ryker, spinning around the room with Isla. When he caught her gaze she swore he tried to give her an apologetic look.

She waved it off and returned a reassuring nod. She was fine and was content to wait for him. That was until she felt a heat at her back. She didn't need to turn around.

Kaceston's woodsy scent enveloped her.

"Hello, little thief."

She stiffened, but still didn't turn around. She wasn't going to grace the barb with a response.

"Would you prefer Brynnlin?"

"For the last time, it's Brenna," she ground her teeth together. "Brynnlin, Brynn for short, is a secondary name permitted only to those close to me. Of which you are not."

Kaceston chuckled. "I wouldn't be too sure about that. I did save your life and in return you threatened my dick with my very own knife. I think that makes us pretty close."

She released a heavy sigh, making sure it was loud enough for him to hear. "Just tell me why you're here so we can get this over with."

"We never finished our earlier conversation."

She whirled. "For the last time, I didn't tell Tobin, and I'm not—"

"I know." Kaceston's words stopped her cold.

"What?"

Kaceston's lips twitched upwards. "If you'd stop throwing a fit and listen—"

"Oh listen? Like you did earlier?" she shot back at him.

The slightest grimace flashed across his features before disappearing. "I might have been too quick in so easily condemning you."

Her jaw might have actually dropped.

Holy gods.

Was Kaceston apologizing? If so, it needed a lot of work.

"Is that supposed to be an apology?" She wasn't letting him off the hook that easily.

His smile dropped. "Don't be absurd. However, it's the closest thing you'll ever get."

She narrowed her own eyes, yet still asked, "What convinced you to see reason?"

He sighed heavily. "Does it matter?"

"Yes."

"Too bad."

Brynnlin opened her mouth to retort when the room around them erupted into chaos. One minute, she'd been watching Ryker on the dance floor. Another minute, she'd been arguing with Kaceston.

In the next, a blast exploded through the throne room.

The room rocked, and the walls shuddered.

Glass sprayed everywhere as the windows shattered.

Brynnlin was thrown to the ground, the jarring impact resonating through her. The cold stone pressed into her, and she tried to lift her head.

Spinning.

The room was spinning.

She blinked, trying to focus through the dust and rubble. People might have been screaming, she couldn't tell past the ringing in her ears. Bodies pushed and shoved, knocking her around, as the crowd scrambled to escape.

Her head whipped around, looking for a familiar face in the cluster of people.

Maddox.

The others—she needed to find the others.

Rough hands grabbed her by the shoulders, yanking her upwards. She fell into a hard chest, her legs struggling to keep her upright. Fingers snapped in front of her, and Kaceston's face appeared inches from her.

A trail of blood dripped down his cheek.

"Brynnlin. I need you to keep it together. We have to go."

'Maddox.' She tried to say. 'I need to find Maddox.'

"You can find him afterwards."

He grabbed her hand, tugging her along, fighting against the crowd. His size alone created a barrier, protecting her from the onslaught of people rushing towards the doors.

A door they weren't heading towards. She stopped, tugging against his hold. They were going the wrong way.

Kaceston shot her a glare and snarled, "I'm trying to get you out of here."

She stopped fighting and followed. She chalked it up to being in shock for why she was trusting him.

People continued to scream, and dust still floated through the air. Some people were sprawled across the ground, and they weren't getting back up.

Brynnlin clenched her eyes shut and looked away. She didn't take her eyes off Kaceston's back after that. He somehow managed to get them towards the back of the room.

Brynnlin froze.

The two thrones that had been there were in shambles.

Crumbled and broken.

But it was the blazing symbol of the Creed, aflame on the wall, that had her stomach plummeting.

They actually attacked a palace.

Brynnlin watched Kaceston's shoulders stiffen as he saw it, too. After a long moment, he continued on, pulling her to the balcony doors she had just come through not long before.

The doors laid in shattered pieces. Kaceston kicked some debris aside and stepped out into the night. She followed behind him.

"I doubt the balcony is stable, but we can get down to the gardens from here." He strode towards the ledge.

"Are you insane?" she hissed.

He leveled her with an annoyed look. "Feel free to stay here, or go back inside." He crawled over the side and dropped down out of sight.

Brynnlin rushed forward, her heart dropping. She peered over the ledge ready to see him sprawled on the ground. Instead, she watched him land on the grass below in a crouched position.

An exhale of relief escaped her.

She eyed the distance. It was only about fifteen feet down, not nearly as bad as she first thought. She'd grudgingly admit he'd been right. It would be much easier to get out and go around then fight through the sea of people. She kicked off her heels, hiked up the skirt of the dress, and crawled over the ledge. She gripped the bottom rail and lowered herself down, letting her feet hang down. If she could minimize the distance of the fall, the impact would lessen.

"Please, take your time," Kaceston called from below her.

"Shut up."

Fuck it.

She let go.

Air whipped past her as she dropped down.

She waited for the impact.

Strong hands gripped her waist, slowing her descent. Her feet touched the grass as Kaceston lowered her.

"Thanks," she muttered, stepping out of his hold.

She turned to see him watching her closely.

"Are you alright?" he asked.

"I'm fine."

"Good."

In a move so fast, she barely processed it, Kaceston's hand was around her throat, and she was pushed up against the column of the balcony. Her breath rushed out of her at the impact. A trickle of pain shot down her spine as her back hit the solid surface. Kaceston's features were contorted in rage, and she swore his eyes flashed black.

"Then you're fully capable of explaining what the fuck is going on."

The hand at her throat tightened, dangerously. The shock of what was happening quickly faded as she processed his words.

"What the Hells is wrong with you?" she growled, and her own hand pulled at his to release the pressure.

The power within her awakened at the threat, and her body burned, ready to release its wrath at her command. She held onto it with the thinnest amount of control. Juniper had warned her against losing control and exploding. It was times like these she had to keep her head. It didn't matter that Kaceston just attacked, he was a royal, and she couldn't kill him.

Yet.

She might have a change of heart at his next words. Consequences be damned.

Kaceston seemed unaware of her internal battle, his entire focus on his own fury. He might sound in control, but his eyes told another story.

"We both saw that symbol and know who's behind this. Were you a part of it? Is that why Kodak brought you here? To help stage this attack?" Kaceston's voice was barely above a whisper and that alarmed her more than any yelling ever could.

She pried his fingers away from her windpipe, and her tone was icy. "Let me go, now." She was not a patient person. If he continued down this path, she'd be forced to act accordingly. "We have nothing to do with any of this. You are wrong—"

"Do not lie to me," he hissed. "The only thing I want coming from you is answers."

Before she could register his meaning, she doubled over as pain sliced through her head. Kaceston let go of her, and she fell to her knees as the pain intensified. Her hands reached up, grabbing at her temples—anything to release the building pressure.

What the Hells was happening to her?

Kaceston bent down and gripped her chin, forcing her to look up at him. His features were blurry as her eyes watered.

"It hurts, doesn't it? I can make it all go away, you just need to tell me what I want to know." He offered it as if he was doing her a favor.

If she wasn't in so much agony, she would've laughed in his face. Instead she could barely think as pain clouded every working brain cell. The more she tried to focus, the more it hurt, the stabbing pain unrelenting. But if she was anything, it was stubborn, and whatever this prick was doing to her wouldn't break her.

"What the fuck are you doing to me?" She squeezed out in little huffs of breath.

He clucked his tongue. "I'm the one that gets to ask questions here. I saw you on that island. I know Kodak sent his men there, too. Just tell me how you're working with the Creed."

"We're not." That was all she would say on the matter when he wouldn't listen anyway. "Now do me a favor and go join Arawn in his Three Hells."

"You are only making this harder for yourself." A healthy mix of anger and annoyance flashed in his eyes. "I don't have all night, and there is no line I won't cross." Kaceston slammed his fist against the brick next to her head.

She wasn't surprised by his accusation. She should tread carefully. But there was no changing his mind. And she was done with this bullshit pain.

With Kaceston kneeling in front of her, she lunged forward, latching onto his wrist. Her body protested, and her head spun, but physical contact was all she needed. Tendrils of shadow seeped from her palm into him, attacking back with a vengeance.

Kaceston's back arched. He released a low groan, and the assault against her mind immediately dissipated. She practically sighed in relief as the pounding ceased and the pressure abandoned. She struggled to her feet, using the column as support.

She glared at Kaceston and readied herself for his retaliation. She understood his anger and why he thought they were involved. From the beginning, he accused her of being an acolyte. Yet he still attacked her, and she wasn't exactly the forgiving type.

Kaceston stood before her, his jaw clenched tight.

"You shouldn't have done that."

"Likewise," she snarled back.

Smoke started to circle around their feet, and she eyed it warily. She had no idea the full extent of Kaceston's magic, and she wasn't going to be caught off guard. She glanced up at him again. Her stomach tightened when she saw him watching the smoke, too. His eyes were narrowed as he followed the wispy haze.

An uneasy feeling settled in her stomach.

"This isn't your doing, is it?" She risked asking.

His eyes flared. "It's not yours?"

"No," she whispered.

She studied the smoke again and watched it curl around her feet. Her heart hammered as she stared at the purple hue. She'd seen it before.

In a certain meadow...

It couldn't be? Yet...

The loose demon.

The attack.

There was no questioning it.

He was here.

Her attention snagged on a shadowed movement further behind Kaceston. Someone was coming...

No.

Not just someone. An eerie calm settled over her.

"Are you going to hide out in the dark all night?" She yelled.

Kaceston followed her gaze, a frown edging across his features.

A silent moment passed.

Then a cynical laugh echoed around them. A dark figure moved forward.

Kaceston's frown deepened, and he actually took a step towards her, angling himself in front of her.

Stepping out of the shadows, the Draíothe stood before them. He lifted the hood of his cloak back, revealing himself.

It had been over ten years. Yet he appeared the same.

He had always been a monster in her head.

But...here...now...

He was nothing but a man.

He smiled at them. "I told you I would come for you. How courteous of you to be waiting for me."

He was really here—right in front of her, after all these years. This was her chance.

"I didn't expect you so soon."

"Yes, well I didn't want to risk losing you again."

"So instead, you risk your life?" She smirked, very much enjoying this. "I didn't realize you were so eager to meet your death, but I'm happy to comply." She wasn't letting him leave here alive.

The Draíothe shook his head, a look of disapproval crossing his face. "Didn't we conclude your violent behavior was unnecessary?"

"You haven't even begun to see violent." She stood tall, shaking off the remnants of Kaceston's pain. The Draíothe had her full attention.

"This doesn't have to be messy."

It was Brynnlin's turn to shake her head. "Oh it's far too late for that."

The Draíothe eyed Kaceston. "You wouldn't want to risk your friend getting hurt."

"He's not my friend."

The Draíothe lifted a brow. "No? Either way, he can't stop me."

"That's quite the assumption," Kaceston chuckled softly.

"I know who you are, Rí Kaceston, and I can assure you this will hold no interest to you." The Draíothe spread his hands in a way to appear non-threatening. "We have no quarrel with you. Leave now. I'm only here for the girl."

Brynnlin's gaze shot to Kaceston when he still didn't move.

"You see that doesn't quite work for me," Kaceston said, lazily, "she stays here."

The Draíothe's lips thinned, and his hands dropped. "Unfortunately for you, I wasn't asking."

The smoke at Brynnlin's feet thickened and started to swirl upwards from her legs and encasing her.

Brynnlin cursed, trying to get away from it.

It was too late.

The garden in front of her spun out of focus. Her stomach turned as darkness surrounded her, and the garden vanished all together.

CHAPTER 29

"Not my best night."

BRYNNLIN STUMBLED forward as they landed in a room. Her gaze shot around, and relief consumed her as she recognized the bedroom she'd been occupying the last few days.

Thank the gods. They were still at Atlas' palace. She still had a chance.

She glared at the Draíothe standing a few feet in front of her.

"Now, don't give me that look," he admonished. "I couldn't have Rí Kaceston interfering."

"I agree," Brynnlin spat and lunged forward.

Shadows were already curling around her fingertips. She was done waiting. Kaceston's absence would only make it that much easier for her.

An arm wrapped around her waist, jerking her backwards. Pain slammed into her neck as a needle pierced her skin.

Brynnlin's mouth dropped open, and a gasp escaped her.

Panic edged its way forward as the Draíothe in front of her dissolved, and she spun to see him standing behind her.

Oh gods.

How could she have fallen for such a simple illusion?

"What did you do?" She hissed, her eyes widening.

She grabbed at her neck. She could already feel herself weakening. Her movements were heavy, and she took a step towards him only for her leg to collapse under her. A cold rush was seeping through her body. Darkness threatened to consume her mind. Through sheer force she fought it, and her breathing turned labored as her body struggled.

She reached desperately for her magic.

Only it wasn't there.

Like when she had the sigil, that door was firmly shut, locking her out from that part inside her.

What the Hells did he inject her with?

She lifted her head and sneered at the man above her.

"Really? You had to drug me?"

"We don't want you getting hurt, and we can't have you using that magic of yours," he smiled down at her. "Don't fight it. It'll be like taking a nap, I promise. And once he gets here, we can leave. Don't fret."

Brynnlin clenched her eyes shut, and her mind raced. Someone was coming. She didn't have much time.

She couldn't let it happen like this.

Not after all this time.

Opening her eyes again, she gritted her teeth. She pulled her leg closer. Her movements were sluggish, but not impossible. Crouching low, she pulled at everything she had and launched herself at him. He wasn't prepared for a physical attack. Together they crashed into a chair, breaking it, before rolling to the floor. She ended up on top of him—as hard as she could, she landed a sickening punch to his face.

And then another.

Blood sprayed everywhere, and she delighted in it.

He might need his magic.

She did not need hers.

She pulled her fist back for another blow when an enchantment erupted from him. She shielded her face as the floorboards flew towards her. With her distracted, he flipped their positions. Using his momentum, he grabbed the side of her head and bashed it against the floor.

The impact echoed through her skull.

With her head reeling, she tried to remember how to breathe. His thighs dug into her ribs, and his weight crushed her chest. Above her, blood dripped down his face, and cold eyes glowered at her.

"Must you be so troublesome?"

She glared at the man who had haunted her nightmares for so long.

He thought this was trouble? She was just getting started.

Out of the corner of her eye, she spotted the broken remnants of the chair. Her fingers inched towards the splintered wood. When she felt the rough edges, she curled it in her fist.

"Yes, I must," she hissed a second before plunging the makeshift stake into his side.

He groaned in pain, and blood spilled from the wound. She managed to shove him off of her, and he stumbled back.

He wheezed and coughed, his features twisting into murderous rage. "How dare—"

Her hands wrapped around his throat, cutting him off. If she had to end this with her bare hands, then so be it. She even relished the idea of watching the life drain from his eyes. She squeezed tightly and savored in the constrictions of his chest as he fought for air. His face reddened, and a flash of panic entered his eyes as his body processed the lack of oxygen. His crimson-soaked hands scratched at her own, but her determination was unrelenting.

She wasn't letting go.

"Don't be troublesome," she said darkly.

His eyes fluttered, and a sick sense of pleasure washed over her.

That was until the room itself shuddered.

A wave of magic slammed into her, threatening to crush her under its impact. She clawed at his neck, clutched at his clothes, anything to keep her hold. But the force of it was too strong, throwing her backwards. She was flung through the air and crashed into the mirror, glass raining down around her as she hit the floor.

She clenched her jaw, ignoring the pain that radiated over her. She pushed herself to a sitting position—only to freeze. The Draíothe was standing at his full height again, and that damned smoke curled around him.

His face was red, and he was holding a hand to his side right over the wound. His lips curved into a hateful sneer, and his eyes flashed with fury.

But that wasn't what had her stopping in her tracks.

The shattered pieces of mirror floated in the air and were aimed directly at her. All of them zeroed in, and she was their target. Dozens of knife-like shards were ready to pierce through her with a single command.

"Do not move." The Draíothe spat at her, and the pieces inched closer to her as if in warning. He used them to hold her in place as he tried to close the gash. "You're lucky he needs you. Or I'd save us all the trouble and dispose of you right now."

She burrowed that slice of information for later. Right now

she needed to keep him talking and get out of this. The glass pieces were too close for her to even try and escape.

"What happened to being happy to find me?" She reminded him with a cruel smile.

"That was before you stabbed me."

He drove one of the shards deep into her side before she could stop it.

A fiery pain licked through her, and her skin burned. A groan escaped her lips, and her hand immediately cradled her ribs as blood flowed down. It was an exact reflection of what she did to him.

"You son of a bitch," she snarled through clenched teeth.

The Draíothe only glared back. "You did this to yourself. This could've been easy on you, but now—"

"Brynnlin! Open up!" Maddox's voice bellowed from the other side of the door.

She felt the blood drain from her face.

No.

Not Maddox.

The Draíothe might not kill her, but that meant nothing where others were concerned. She'd seen first hand what he did to people who got in his way. Her shout of warning was drowned out as Maddox blasted through the door, splintering it in half.

The Draíothe cursed violently, and his head shot to the door. A second later, a thick cloud enveloped around him.

Shit.

Brynnlin crawled to her knees, but it was too late.

He disappeared, leaving nothing but empty space in his wake. The pool of his blood staining the floor was the only sign he'd ever been there.

"Brynnlin!" Maddox barged in, Kodak, Ryker, and Juniper

right behind him. His face turned ashen as he saw her on the floor and took in the state of the room.

He rushed to her side, dropping to his knees. "Don't move, let me see it."

His hands reached to pull out the glass embedded in her side, but she waved them away.

"I'm fine, it's only a flesh wound."

"Now's not the time—"

She didn't let him finish and pulled out the offending, improvised weapon, throwing it aside. She hissed as more blood spilled out of her.

That wasn't good.

"Gods, Brynn," Maddox admonished and pressed his hands to the wound.

"For fucks sake," she glared at him, and ground her teeth at the pressure.

Juniper dropped to her other side. "You need a healer." Juniper turned her head to Kodak.

"I'm already summoning Zale." Kodak assured her.

"You're going to be okay," Maddox said.

She didn't know if he was trying to comfort her or himself.

Ryker tore off his jacket, tossing it to Maddox. Maddox rolled up the material and added more pressure to the wound. She grimaced at the onslaught of pain.

"How did you know to find me?" she choked out, attempting to distract herself.

Juniper knelt next to her and reached out, brushing away loose hair from her face. "After the explosion went off, and we didn't see you, Maddox immediately tracked your orenda band. At first it looked like you were outside, but then you showed up in the room."

Brynnlin exhaled a long breath. "He—"

A portal opened up in the middle of the room cutting her off.

Zale rushed through, his eyes panicked. "Are you all okay? Oh shit..."

"Not my best night," she muttered, and Maddox glared at her.

"Let's get her back." Maddox shifted, scooping her off the floor into his arms.

Brynnlin's head spun with the movement. Her eyes fluttered while her stomach turned. She was either going to throw up or pass out. She tried to issue a warning, yet no words came out. Between the drug still flowing through her system and the loss of blood, her energy was waning.

She tried again, but the effort was exhausting.

Tired.

She was so tired.

Fighting this was too much.

She let her eyes close, and her head fell back.

Darkness followed.

KACESTON LUNGED FORWARD. Brynnlin's muffled curse floated towards him, and her eyes flashed with uncertainty as smoke swelled around her. An unwelcome tightness formed in his chest, and Brynnlin disappeared before him.

Only wisps of smoke were left behind.

He whirled, his entire focus on the unknown man that joined them.

"What the Hells did you do with her?" He snarled.

He had no idea what the fuck was going on anymore. He thought he had. With this turn of events, however, it seemed the situation was more complex than he expected. When he saw that symbol on the wall, he'd been convinced Brynnlin and her crew were behind it. She was a damned acolyte after all.

Yet with this Draíothe showing up and seeing Brynnlin's reaction to him, Kaceston was questioning everything.

This man had come for her.

Why?

And the one person who could give him answers was now nowhere to be seen.

The Draíothe before him pursed his lips, a deep frown crossing his features. "My deepest apologies, Rí Kaceston. Your involvement was unforeseen, and I can't have you interfering."

A wave of magic slammed into Kaceston, knocking him back. He shook it off with ease and rolled his shoulders back.

So that's how this was going to go.

Power swelled at his fingertips as he eyed his opponent.

He raised a brow. "You're going to have to do a lot better than that."

The Draíothe shrugged. "Another time. Take care, your highness."

More smoke swirled along the ground and, like Brynnlin, the Draíothe disappeared.

"Fucking bastard," Kaceston rushed forward only for the ground around him to flood with more of that damned smoke.

It circled his feet, climbing higher like a vortex surrounding him. He pushed through it. But as soon as he came into contact with it, the smoke stopped swirling, freezing into ice at his touch. The rest of the smokey vortex froze over, ice spreading around him, caging him in, faster than he could blink. More ice flooded up from the ground, filling the small space. It locked him in place.

Oh this was just getting better and better.

"You've got to be fucking kidding."

Kaceston released his flames. He let the heat flow through

his body and swallow the coldness attempting to consume him. The flames raged around him, melting down the ice. The ice barrier thinned, and puddles of water rested at his feet. Yet the walls still stood tall.

Fucking Three Hells.

He called upon more flames. The blaze crackled around him, torching through the frozen cell. Ever so slowly the walls thawed out, shrinking down.

Precious minutes passed.

The Draíothe better hope he was long gone by the time Kaceston got out. This was now personal.

"Kaceston."

He heard Griffin's voice call out as he shattered through the last of the blockade.

His second ran towards him. "I saw you leave out the back, but I had to fight through everybody to get out. Why are you frozen up like a godsdamn iceberg?"

Kaceston glowered.

Griffin threw up his hands, fighting a smirk. "Did little Brynn get the best of you? I saw her with you."

"One more word, Griffin," Kaceston said slowly, "and I will not hesitate to remove your tongue."

Griffin relented. "Seriously, what the Hells happened?"

"Another individual is involved. A Draíothe I highly suspect is behind tonight's bombing."

Griffin's eyes widened. "I saw the symbol. So the Creed sent one of their Draíothes?"

Kaceston shook his head. "There's something else going on. He was here for Brynnlin."

"That doesn't make sense. Doesn't she work for them?"

"That was my impression."

"Then why—"

"I don't know, Griff," he snapped, "I was trying to get answers when he took her."

"Took?"

"Gods damn it, must I repeat everything? Yes, he took her. As in unwillingly if you need the vocabulary lesson."

Kaceston recalled the look on Brynnlin's face when the Draíothe showed up. There was a deep hatred that she couldn't hide. She knew him, and from their exchange there was history. And not a good one.

She'd threatened to kill him.

There was so much more going on here.

And now she was gone, but... "The others?" he demanded. "Did you happen to see Kodak and the others still inside?"

Griffin's head swung towards him, "Everyone was rushing to get out, but Maddox caught my attention. He was pushing against the crowd to get to the back, like I was. I think he might've seen Brynn go with you. But then he turned and rushed towards the hall to the rooms, not the exit like everyone else."

"They might still be there, we'll try the room. Mask our arrival."

Smoke curled around them both. Griffin cursed and coughed, but it was too late, flames already encircled them.

When they reappeared, they were standing in the hall, steps away from Brynnlin's suite. The door was smashed to pieces, and voices filtered towards them. Kaceston moved forward with caution and gestured for Griffin to keep close. He was confident no one would see them through Griffin's manipulation, but he wasn't going to risk detection. He looked into the room, every muscle freezing at the sight before him.

The room was trashed.

Splintered floorboards and broken glass scattered the floor. A broken chair laid off to the side. Blood spilled across the floor. Kodak and his people were gathered around a portal, and a limp Brynnlin was cradled in Maddox's arms.

He willed himself to stay still. To not react.

What the Hells had happened here?

"Maddox, be careful with her," Juniper's cry filled the room.

"I can't help her being unconscious, Juniper," Maddox snapped back. "She needs Vee."

"What happened here? Why didn't you call me sooner?"

Kaceston recognized Zale's voice. He'd actually been surprised when he hadn't seen the other man this weekend. Kodak must have left him home for a reason.

"The Draíothe happened, what else would it be?" Maddox growled.

"We should have left the second he threatened her," Ryker hissed and gestured to Brynnlin. "Look at what he did to her."

Kodak glared at Ryker. "None of us expected him to go after her so quickly, or like he did. Let's just get back, and we'll handle the matter."

Maddox pushed past them, going to the portal. "Argue about this later, I'm getting her to Vee."

The others followed Maddox, and the portal vanished, leaving the room empty.

Kaceston stood there, the silence surrounding him deafening.

Brynnlin had been attacked. The evidence of that fact was on full display—by a Creed's Draíothe no less. Which only further contradicted everything he thought before tonight.

Why would he have attacked her?

Were they not on the same side?

"You were right," Griffin muttered, "there's more to this."

Yes, there was.

How unfortunate this became complicated.

"I'm aware."

"If this Draíothe is in the Creed, why go after her?" Griffin echoed his thoughts.

"That's what we need to find out."

He went to leave the room, there was nothing for them here.

"Kaceston," Griffin hesitated. "Is it possible we were wrong?"

"Wrong?"

"About Kodak." Griffin shook his head. "He had always been a neutral party, it never made sense that he would go after us."

Kaceston's lips thinned, "The evidence of the attack against us is hard to ignore. And let's not forget that I followed two of his men to a meeting on the isles in cult territory. They also brought back an acolyte, who they brought to a summit meeting, where a bomb went off."

Griffin's shoulders dropped. "It just doesn't make sense. None of this."

"On that I can agree. Which is why I need answers, and I'm not going to get them here."

If he had any luck, he might have some information waiting for him back at home. He didn't give Griffin a chance to respond. Within seconds his flames withered around them, and they were standing in his throne room.

His shoulders relaxed.

It was good to be home.

CHAPTER 30

"He was never one to suffer from a savior's complex, but even he had his limits."

KACESTON'S FLAMES WITHERED AWAY, revealing himself and Griffin. The few people bustling through the hall all stopped and bowed at his arrival.

"Welcome home, your highness," one of them stepped forward. He bowed low, but lifted a brow. "Did you encounter trouble? We weren't expecting your return until tomorrow."

Kaceston rolled his eyes and gestured downward at his ruined suit.

Such a disappointment.

He had rather liked this one.

"I think you can conclude we ran into some issues, Fin," he addressed the other man. "Now have you seen Theana?"

"Not recently, sir."

"Send for her and Dax immediately. The matter is urgent."

"Right away, sir." Fin bowed again. With a snap of his fingers, two others followed him out of the hall.

Kaceston knew Fin would find them quickly and strolled up to his throne. He ran his finger along the smooth, carved stone as he graciously took his seat. Griffin took up the position at his side.

As he suspected, he didn't have to wait long before Theana and Dax entered the room. Their steps were hurried as they both rushed in. Dax came to a halt, stopping for a deep bow. Theana stayed upright. Her dark hair hung in waves, and her eyes bore into him. A mask of concern crossed her features.

"You're back early. Are you alright, brother?"

"I'm fine, Thea." Affection laced his tone as he regarded his younger sister. "I see you were able to keep the place standing in my absence."

Her features relaxed, taking on a smirk. "The tantrum you would've had if you came back to a home in disarray was very unappealing. So yes, I managed just fine." She turned that mischievous smile to Griffin, "Was he a complete menace while away?"

Griffin coughed into his hand. "Only slightly, Bana-phrionnsa."

Theana's smirk dropped into a disapproving frown at the old nickname. Kaceston always found it comical how much she hated being called that, which of course only made Griffin more inclined to use it.

"Why are you back early?" she asked. "Something must have happened for you to have Fin fetch us."

"There was an incident at the Prionsa's celebration, an attack by the Creed no less."

He let them absorb the information.

"That's bold, even for them," Theana surmised. "They'd have to be highly motivated to risk something like that."

"I believe they had interest in a certain individual at the party, which is why I called you both here." He turned his attention to Dax. The man had worked for him for centuries and excelled at digging up information. "Two weeks ago I sent you to find out about a female acolyte fighting at that club, what did our informants come up with? I want everything."

Dax cleared his throat and clasped his hands behind his back. "Unfortunately, nothing good."

When he hesitated to continue, Kaceston arched a brow. Dax was never one to hold back.

"And?" He pushed, annoyance lacing his tone. He didn't appreciate having to ask twice.

"Very well," Dax straightened, as if bracing himself. "Based on your description and the name Ciarán, we were able to deduce the identity of the fighter in question. Around the club, many referred to her as "The Kid", only a few seemed to know her as "B". She's very good, brings in a lot of money, no other known names, and no address. Apparently no one fucks with her because she's under the protection of a Draíothe, Selene Aspen."

Kaceston frowned. That wasn't much. "This Draíothe? Is that how she's tied to the Creed? What about her work as an acolyte?"

Dax shook his head. "According to word on the street, Selene Aspen does not work with the Creed. She's up to something, but no one would talk. She owns a bookstore there, but it was trashed out a few weeks ago. She hasn't been seen since."

Interesting.

That would've been around the time he'd been at the island himself.

Yet a Draíothe on the isles that was not in line with the Creed? He didn't think so.

"Back to the girl, there has to be something. She had the acolyte brand, and she has to be involved. What about her past? Did you find out anything on that end?"

She didn't just materialize on those islands. Someone had to know something. Dax grimaced, catching Kaceston by surprise again. This was unusual behavior for him.

"The girl has been fighting at the club for the last nine years, when the owner, Zamir, bought her."

Kaceston stilled. He lifted his head to stare into Dax. "Bought?"

Dax shifted his weight. "Yes, sir. I had one of my men break into the club to confirm after I learned this. We looked into his records and found the sale. He bought her at the age of fifteen from the Olc Ring."

"Son of a bitch," Kaceston's words were forced. He ran a hand through his hair as he quickly did that math. That only put her at twenty-four now. He suspected she was young, but fuck, she had only reached maturity four years ago. She'd barely been more than a girl at the age she'd started fighting.

"What do you know about the Olc Ring? Is that another club?"

He didn't care what Brynnlin's agenda was. He wanted to know who was responsible.

"It's a shitty club on the outermost island. But the club is a front for what they really do. It's a trafficking ring, Kaceston," Dax blew out a rough breath. "That's why I said it was bad. The girl was trafficked and has been fighting since, that's all we got."

Kaceston's muscles locked tight, his mind racing to comprehend. He was aware things on those islands were unsavory.

But this...

This was unthinkable.

For a child to be sold. Trafficked.

He thought of Theana being forced into that, and his blood ran cold. He was never one to suffer from a savior's complex, but even he had his limits. That club would soon be nonexistent, and those responsible would be dealt with.

He'd make sure of it.

An icy calm settled over him at the thought.

Yes, they would be dealt with alright.

"I want you to get me everything I would need to destroy that club and everyone in it," his tone was soft and menacing. "I don't care how long it takes. Do I make myself clear?"

"With pleasure," Dax's eyes gleamed with a dangerous edge at this new assignment. "However, there's one more thing you should be aware of regarding the girl."

Kaceston braced himself. "And what's that?"

"She's been missing. Ever since you sent me to look into her, she hasn't been seen at the club."

Kaceston waved away his concern. "She's not missing, she's not at the club because she's been here on the mainland."

Dax's features turned grim. "Well her boss seems unaware of her whereabouts. He is not happy about the girl's absence. He's losing money with her not around to fight and has a price out on her. Apparently, he wants her back. Badly."

Kaceston straightened at that little piece of information.

That low-life scum dared to put a price on Brynnlin's return?

He knew why she hadn't been fighting, she'd been here in Éire.

Why? He still wasn't sure.

But no one was forcing her anywhere. That shit wasn't going to happen. She had information he needed, and no one was going to get in his way.

"At the moment, I have a vested interest in her. I want that taken care of and teach that bastard some manners while you're at it."

He heard Griffin chuckle softly, but his second was smart enough not to comment.

"It will be handled." Dax responded loyally.

Dax appreciated violence, and it was one of the many qualities Kaceston liked about the man.

"Good," Kaceston said, not nearly appeased, but this would do for now. "And finally, a few days ago I called and told you to look into Brenna Murchadha, what do you have?"

Dax's silence stretched on, and Kaceston resisted the urge to snap. He did not relish repeating himself.

"My men on the ground found nothing," Dax admitted. "Absolutely nothing. I think you might need Owen to look into her."

Kaceston wasn't surprised at Dax's admission. After what he just learned, it was very likely Brenna wasn't her real name. Which meant Owen truly was necessary.

"Where is he?" Kaceston asked Theana.

She scoffed, "Where do you think?"

"The tower?"

A nod in confirmation.

"Alright," he pushed off his throne. "Griff, get Thea caught up on everything while I speak to Owen."

He didn't wait for Griffin to agree and started towards the tower. Dax fell into step beside him.

"I'll accompany you."

They walked in comfortable silence. When he reached the door at the top of the tower, he didn't bother knocking. Inside he found Owen, his head bent over, and his focus entirely on the multiple crystal screens surrounding him. Liquid tubes ran interconnected through the setup, lighting up the room with a golden hue.

"Little brother." Kaceston greeted.

Owen's head whipped up, his dirty blonde hair in disarray and long enough to sweep across his features.

Owen grinned. "I knew when you arrived home. My sensors picked up a spike of energy when you crossed into the palace."

Owen's excitement was clearly visible.

Kaceston was impressed. His flames had always been able to bypass most barriers and systems. It seemed like Owen's new sensors could detect pyroportation. How handy.

"It seemed your little project was successful then."

"Did you ever doubt it would be?" Owen turned smug.

Kaceston hid his grin. "Not for a second."

Owen seemed to realize Kaceston wasn't alone when Dax chuckled.

Owen flushed, and he stammered slightly. "Hello, Dax."

Dax's lips twitched. "Owen."

A few awkward moments of silence passed, and Kaceston couldn't take it anymore. "I have a project for you."

"What kind of project?" Owen asked, his lips upturning in anticipation.

"The kind where you find everything you can about this person and dig into every aspect of their life," Kaceston answered. This should be easy for Owen.

"All I need is a name."

"Brenna 'Brynnlin' Murchadha."

A BURNING PAIN flared through Brynnlin. Her eyes flew open, and she lurched upwards. A groan escaped her lips when the burning intensified and a throbbing ache flared through her side.

"You idiot." A hand pushed her back down.

She didn't fight it as she recognized Selene's voice. She blinked a few more times, and the bedroom around her came into focus.

"You're going to rip your stitches," Selene muttered, her

voice harsh, "and trust me when I say you don't want Verenna coming back in here."

Brynnlin twisted her head to see Selene bent over her, cleaning her wound. Brynnlin grimaced when the cold antiseptic brushed against her skin.

"How long have I been out?" she managed to ask.

Selene's eyes flickered upwards, a frown crossing her features. "Several hours at least, but we did give you something to keep you out longer so Verenna could stitch you up."

"Was it that deep?" Brynnlin's brow furrowed. She didn't think it had been that bad. "Verenna wasn't able to seal it?"

"The internal damage was quite severe and required her immediate attention," Selene explained. "And unfortunately for you, there was a training accident hours before you arrived, and Verenna had just finished mending all of them."

"Is she okay?" Brynnlin demanded.

"She's fine." Selene continued cleaning the wound. "She's pretty drained though and needed to rest. She did what she could, but stitches will have to suffice for now. She's also not pleased with you showing up on the doorstep unconscious twice now in less than a month." Selene side-eyed her. "I'll admit I'm also not happy about these circumstances."

"That makes three of us," Brynnlin muttered under her breath.

"This isn't a joke, Brynnlin," Selene stopped and glared. "A bomb went off, and the Draíothe had you alone. He could've killed you," Selene's voice cracked. "You're lucky to be here right now with only some stitches."

"He wouldn't have killed me, he and whoever he's working with want me alive."

"That doesn't make it any better."

"I don't need a lecture right now, Selene," Brynnlin's voice rose, her frustration getting the better of her. "I was this close," she held up two fingers, centimeters apart, "to ending all of this. My hands were literally around his throat. All of this could have been over. But that bastard got away. I failed."

Selene's eyes softened. "Brynn..."

Brynnlin pushed herself up, wincing as she repositioned to sit against the headboard. "Look, I don't want comforting words, and I don't want a lecture. I just want to know what the next move is. He's obviously here, and he's not done, so what are we going to do about it?"

Selene stood, perching on the side of the bed, and studied her. "You might not want a lecture, but you're going to get one. It was stupid and reckless to stay at the palace when you knew he was coming for you—"

"That's not—"

Selene held up a hand. "And while I might be furious at you for putting yourself at risk, I'm not going to let you sit here thinking you're a failure. You survived a kidnapping attempt. You managed to fight off a very powerful Draíothe. And you didn't walk away from that encounter empty handed."

Brynnlin refrained from scoffing. She knew Selene meant well, but she wasn't being modest when she said she didn't want to be consoled. She was frustrated, hurting, and pissed the Draíothe drugged her then ran like a coward. She didn't need sympathy. She wanted action. She wanted to know what their next move was. She wanted—

Her mental tirade stopped as the last of Selene's words registered.

"What do you mean I didn't come back empty handed?"

Selene raised a delicate brow and reached towards the nightstand. She reached for a circular object and handed it over. Brynnlin took the object without question, and it weighed heavily in her hand. Brynnlin stared down at the gold piece taking up most of her hand. Unrecognizable symbols covered the surface.

"I have no idea how you managed to get this," Selene said with a small laugh. "I'm not sure I want the details, but shit Brynn, you sure know how to make an impact, I mean..."

Brynnlin tuned out the rest of what Selene was saying. Her mind raced as she tried to figure out what she was holding.

She lifted her eyes to Selene. "I don't know what this is."

"Really?" Surprise flicked across Selene's features. "You were the one clutching it like a lifeline."

Brynnlin tried to remember coming across anything like this, but her memories were a blur. The object in her hand rippled with power, and she flinched, nearly dropping the thing.

Selene chuckled. "You really don't know, do you?"

Brynnlin shook her head. Selene took it back, her fingers running along its edge.

"It's very powerful, very rare, and very dangerous," Selene said softly, meeting her gaze. "It's a summoning amulet, Brynn. It's what my kind use to summon and control demons."

Silence raged between them.

Brynnlin's heart hammered in her chest as everything in her rejected what Selene was saying.

"No." *There's no way.*

Selene had to be wrong. Because if she wasn't...

Brynnlin was too afraid to hope.

"Yes, Brynn. I wouldn't mistake this. You must have managed to get a hold of it when you fought. And in the struggle he didn't notice," Selene shared her theory. "If he had noticed, he never would have left without it."

"What do we do with it? We can't risk him getting it back."

"I know. After I realized what you brought back, I told Kodak we needed to destroy it. Luckily, he agreed. I can't do it.

Unfortunately, I don't know how, but I think I know someone who can."

"What are we waiting for?"

Selene's lips twitched. "We're moving as fast as we can. Maddox pulled in Remi to help find my contact's current address, and we'll take it to him."

"Good. That's good," Brynnlin mumbled, her thoughts already three steps ahead.

With the amulet gone...demons were out of the picture.

She was slow to smile. "We took away his greatest weapon against us."

Selene's eyes gleamed. "This changes everything."

CHAPTER 31

"Was someone else pulling the strings in all of this?"

KACESTON SAT in his office enjoying a much needed drink. He rubbed at his eyes, fighting the weariness. It had been nearly two days since he last slept. After arriving home in the early hours of this morning, he hadn't had a moment rest.

This Kodak and Brynnlin mess was driving him absolutely mad. He still wasn't any closer to having answers. And his patience was thinning. He might need to come up with an alternative. That idea was gaining traction when his door burst open.

He glared at the intruder, but eased up when Owen entered. "Yes?"

"You wanted me to let you know when I found something on Murchadha."

A shot of adrenaline raced through him. But he frowned when Owen hesitated.

"I did a lot and I mean a lot of digging..."

Kaceston waited, but Owen didn't seem inclined to continue. "And?" he pushed.

Owen met his gaze.

"Brenna Murchadha doesn't exist."

Kaceston's head dropped back, and he released a heavy sigh. He'd been expecting this. That didn't stop the disappointment. "What do you have?"

Owen pulled up a file on the small screen he was carrying and started reading from it. "Whoever created this was good. Brenna Murchadha, born twenty four-years ago to Vivian and William Murchadha, both of whom are deceased with no record of any other living family. Schooling was documented as being privately tutored and no evidence that she ever attended university."

"A background that you can't verify."

"Exactly," Owen agreed, "it was too clean. Upfront everything looks good. She has the right documents, the right accounts, but there's nothing personal about her whatsoever. No record of politics which would lead to a high-level position. It didn't check out, which is why I kept digging."

Kaceston braced himself. "You found something?"

"Oh I found something. I looked into the coding...all of her accounts and documentation were dated a few weeks ago." Owen met his stare. "Like I said, whoever gave her this background was good, very good. And they hid their tracks, but they couldn't hide the timestamps."

Owen looked a little too smug at that while Kaceston processed.

A fake identity was set up a few weeks ago which would've been the same time she left the club and probably came here. That wasn't a coincidence. She had powerful people backing her. She had Kodak backing her.

But why?

Kodak had to be involved. She had to be involved.

But then why did another acolyte—a Draíothe no less— attack her?

Nothing was adding up. He needed to think.

"You did good, Owen, I don't need anything else at the moment," Kaceston dismissed him.

"But," Owen's face dropped, "you didn't even let me get to the good part."

Kaceston's head shot back up. "What more is there?"

Owen's eyes were bright as he pulled up the chair across from Kaceston. "You told me this girl, Brenna, had a secondary name, Brynnlin, right? But she doesn't. There was no secondary name documented in Brenna's record. I thought maybe you got the name wrong, especially after Brenna was obviously a fake. Well no records for a Brynnlin Murchadha existed either."

"Get to it, Owen."

"Right. I'm going. In case you're unaware, there aren't that many Brynnlin's in the world." A slow grin slipped across Owen's features. "So imagine my surprise when I came across a record for a Miss Brynnlin Raigáin."

For a brief moment Kaceston felt time stop.

"Raigáin? As in Maddox Raigáin?"

"The one and the same. After that, it was only too easy to dig into their past. Brynnlin Raigáin was Maddox Raigáin's younger cousin, born to Xavier and Alannah Raigáin. Her father was a governor for Atlas."

How very interesting.

At least it was, until he latched onto Owen's phrasing. "Was? Is he not a governor anymore?"

Owen's smile dropped, and he flipped the screen towards Kaceston. An article filled the screen. The headline 'GOVERNOR MURDERED' was splayed across the top.

"Eleven years ago, one of Atlas' governors and the family

was killed by a Creed attack. From what I read, it was brutal, everyone was left for dead, even the staff."

Kaceston cursed. He vaguely remembered the time it had happened. It had been a huge deal among high society.

Owen pulled the screen back, swiping to a new page, and flipping it around again. Kaceston found himself staring at a picture of a couple with a young girl between them. Pale blonde hair hung past the girl's shoulder, and her green eyes were bright as she smiled for the picture.

His mind tried to catch up as he stared at the familiar features. She was obviously much younger, but he couldn't ignore the resemblance of this girl to the Brynnlin he met.

It couldn't be? Could it?

"The governor and his wife were found dead," Owen said softly, "but their daughter was never accounted for. When she didn't turn up, she was presumed dead. And if she did happen to survive, she's been missing for eleven years."

Ever so slowly, like missing pieces to a puzzle, things started to click into place. And the picture the past was painting...

Kaceston shook his head.

It sure as Hells wasn't a pretty one.

There was no doubt in his mind that Brenna/Brynnlin was Maddox's missing cousin, Brynnlin. And thanks to Dax, he knew exactly where she spent those missing eleven years.

Which only added more holes to the story. He found it very difficult to believe the Brynnlin he met would help a group that murdered her family and forced her to fight in a cage like an animal. In the short time he'd been around her, she hadn't taken shit from him or anyone else, and she seemed pretty loyal. He couldn't picture her betraying her family's memory.

Unless her hand had been forced.

He considered this.

Was someone else pulling the strings in all of this?

Griffin hadn't been wrong when he admitted it was strange when they discovered the evidence against Kodak. Kaceston had thought the same thing, but he also couldn't ignore what was in front of him. Kodak's men going to the island could be explained away if they were going there for Brynnlin. But there was no explaining away what he found when his territory had been attacked. Gods, he was getting tired of this guessing game.

Fuck this.

He was never one to sit around and wait.

Kaceston shoved away the desk.

Owen startled at the abrupt movement. "Where are you going?"

"To get some answers."

MADDOX FOUND Selene out in the back garden. Her back remained to him, and leaves danced around her to a tune only she could hear. She seemed unaware of his presence. He approached with caution and pulled out a chair at the small table. At the sound of the metal scraping, her gaze whipped to him, the leaves dropping to the ground.

"I didn't mean to startle you."

"You didn't."

Her gaze stayed wary as he took a seat.

"I was surprised you weren't with Brynn," he admitted.

"She's sleeping."

"I see. And how are you holding up?"

She arched a brow. "Out of everyone here, I'm the last person you should be asking that question to. Why wouldn't I be fine?"

His lips twitched. She was an evasive little thing. "I didn't ask if you were fine. I asked how you were holding up. You're in a new land and around new people for weeks on end. The pressure of everything has to be building, it is for me, and your friend was just hurt. It was a perfectly reasonable question."

Throughout the weeks, he noticed Selene had become better acquaintanced with them. She was friendly enough and always took part in conversations. But there was still a noticeable distance that she kept between herself and the others.

"I would never expect you to trust us, but in case it's in question, you are safe here," he took a chance, trying to reassure her.

She gave him a small shake of her head. "Safe is a relative term and unrealistic at the moment, just look at what happened to Brynn."

A sad expression crossed her features before hardening.

"But that's not my concern at the moment," she continued before he could speak.

"What is?"

Her loud sigh filled the air. "That bastard needs to pay for what he's done. I want him to hurt. And sitting here, waiting around, it's driving me crazy."

"Well that I can help with."

"And how's that?"

Maddox rose from the table. "Remi not only found your contact's address, but got a message to him, and he's agreed to meet. I was coming to find you."

Selene jumped up from the table, glaring, "Why did you not lead with that?"

"Truthfully, I was trying to make sure you were up to it, I was a little concerned when I found you out here alone."

"I'm perfectly fine," she snapped and muttered, "I can't believe you would waste time like that."

He frowned. "Apologies for wanting to make sure I wasn't about to go see a stranger with someone currently unstable."

"You're lucky this is so important, or I'd make you pay for that insult."

He held up his hands and gestured for her to lead. "Zale is ready for us."

She stormed past him. "Be sure to keep up."

Minutes, later Zale and the portal disappeared, leaving Maddox and Selene in front of a large farmhouse.

"This is it," Maddox eyed the nice house and empty space around it.

"Let's hope he can help," Selene was already starting for the door.

CHAPTER 32

*"Just because someone becomes capable, doesn't mean you should
diminish what they were forced to endure."*

FLAMES DISSIPATED, and Kaceston straightened his suit as he
strode towards the palace gates of Sidhe. Griffin and Dax
flanked each of his sides. This was going to be settled once and
for all. Armed sentries rushed forward at their approach. Kaceston
regarded them and the high volume of sentries stationed
along the watchtowers with an arched brow.

Were they expecting trouble?

The sentries froze as they closed in. Kaceston was slow to
smirk. Even without his crown or any other royal trademarks,
they recognized him.

Their reaction did not disappoint. Faces paled, fear radiated
in the air, one even took a step back as if distance would
save him.

One of the guards braved a step forward with a bowed head.
"Rí Kaceston, we were not aware you would be arriving."

"Kodak didn't pencil me into his schedule? I'm hurt," Kaceston mocked with a hand to his chest. "Nonetheless, inform Kodak I'm here for an audience."

The one who'd taken the lead on this interaction nodded, and with a jerk of his head another sentry separated from the group. He rushed towards the nearest tower, no doubt relaying Kaceston's message. Less than five minutes later, the gates were sliding open, and Kaceston and his men were ushered through. They stopped in the courtyard, and Kodak's men stepped back, but Kaceston noticed they didn't leave.

Someone was being cautious.

"Quite the welcome party," Dax muttered.

Kaceston allowed himself to chuckle.

The palace doors burst open, and Kodak strode towards them. His features were tense, as were Juniper's as she kept up at his side. Zale and Ryker trailed behind them.

The whole gang was here.

Though with a quick glance—not quite the whole gang. A certain Chancellor and a snarky 'Diplomat' were noticeably absent.

Interesting.

"Kaceston, this is quite the surprise," Kodak's words were measured. Wary. "To what do I owe this unexpected visit?"

Kaceston was slow to answer and made a point of looking around. "You have a substantial amount of sentries on watch. Expecting trouble?"

Kodak's eyes narrowed. "After the attack at Atlas', one can never be too careful. However, I find it very difficult to believe this unorthodox arrival of yours was to inquire about the number of men I have on patrol."

"No, in truth I couldn't care less," Kaceston drawled, quite enjoying how uncomfortable they all seemed. "I'm here because it's high time we have an overdue conversation."

A scoff filled the air, and Kaceston's gaze swung towards the source.

Ryker was shaking his head and dared to address him. "You think you can just show up here and make demands?"

Griffin was stepping forward, his tone deadly soft. "You're just itching for a lesson on respect aren't you?"

"Enough," Kaceston growled, silencing them both. He wasn't in the mood for this. His cold stare focused on Kodak again. "Are you going to invite us in or not?"

"And if I'm not?" Kodak challenged.

"Then I would highly suggest reconsidering." Kaceston tampered down his annoyance and offered, "This might surprise you, but this is of interest to us both."

Kodak crossed his arms and was silent for a long moment. Juniper whispered something in his ear, and after another tense moment, Kodak nodded.

"Alright, Kaceston, let's talk." Kodak's voice dropped low—lethal even. "But if you even think to cause an ounce of trouble, I will not hesitate to retaliate."

With that warning, Kodak led the trio into his home.

Kaceston pushed down his surprise as they bypassed the throne room, instead going down a long hall. Dax caught his eye and raised an eyebrow. Kaceston shook his head, and they continued to follow in silence.

Another turn. Another hall.

Kodak stopped in front of a door and led them into a large office. Kodak took a seat behind the desk and gestured to the chair across from him. Kaceston sat with ease and leaned back, his eyes wandering around, taking in the room. He'd never been in Kodak's office before.

Never had reason to be.

Kodak rested his hands on the desk, waiting for Kaceston. His brow rose in a silent prompt.

"I do appreciate your willingness to speak to me on such a short notice," Kaceston started with diplomacy. "I wish to resolve this matter with as little trouble as possible."

Kodak sat tight, tension radiating off of him. The others around the room weren't much better.

"And what exactly needs to be resolved?"

Kaceston weighed his answer. If he was going to get anywhere with them, he needed to lay some cards on the table. "A few months ago, one of my districts was attacked. A temple to be exact and a small surrounding town. There were many casualties."

Kodak's head jerked back, and his eyes widened before he could mask his reaction.

Kaceston studied him closely. His surprise seemed genuine.

"We never heard about such an attack," Kodak's hard gaze shot to Zale.

Zale shifted and gave a small shake of his head.

Kaceston fought a chuckle. "Don't be too hard on your Minister of Intelligence. I went through a lot of trouble to make sure that information was not accessible."

"If you went through all that trouble, why divulge it now?"

Kaceston took another long moment to answer. The gamble he was taking was not foolproof and could easily back-fire. Yet he was never one to second guess his decision. "It was not difficult to uncover that the Creed was behind the attack..."

Kodak shook his head, stopping Kaceston's next words.

Kodak's features softened the slightest. "They are getting way out of hand. I'm sorry to hear about the lost lives, there's been far too much loss of late."

Kaceston inclined his head, an acknowledgment of Kodak's condolences.

"Those responsible will be properly dealt with, but that's

not why I'm here. We, of course, launched an investigation, and it was unexpected to find evidence of another party involved."

Silence reverberated through the room at the admission.

Kaceston let the words hang between them, waiting to hear their response.

Kodak's features remained unmoving.

His demeanor was calm.

Unsuspecting.

"Another party was involved with the attack on your realm?"

Kaceston answered with a nod. "It appears so, yes."

"I see," Kodak was slow to react and rolled his shoulders back, eyes narrowing. "And you believe it to be us?"

A gasp echoed through the room. *Juniper.*

"What the fuck?" *Ryker.*

Kaceston smirked. He should've expected this from Kodak, he was never one to dance around a subject.

"I never said that," Kaceston drawled.

"Do not insult my intelligence, Kaceston," Kodak growled. "You don't show up here and say something like that—"

"Get out," Juniper lurched forward, rounding the desk. "Get the fuck out of my home."

Kaceston's head jerked back at the hostility flowing off Juniper. He hadn't been prepared for her outburst.

If looks could kill, he'd be making his way to the Hells right now.

"Juniper," Kodak grabbed her hand, stopping her advance. He pulled her to his side, running a hand up and down her back. Amusement flashed across his features. "While I completely agree Kaceston deserves whatever you were about to do, let's hold onto that for a minute." Kodak turned to him, all amusement evaporating. "I should kick your ass out right now, Kaceston, but I know you're not a complete idiot. If you thought we acted against you, you would retaliate, not show up like this. So I'm only going to ask this once, what the fuck is going on?"

Kaceston crossed one leg over the other and relaxed into the chair. He'd been correct in his assumption, there was more to this. This was not the reaction of a guilty party. There were no excuses, threats, or apologies. Only a demand for an explanation.

"There was evidence against you. Damning enough evidence that I couldn't, nor wouldn't, ignore."

"What evidence?"

"I'll get there, bear with me for a moment. I think it's imperative for me to share what led to this," Kaceston offered a rare moment of complete honesty.

"This is bullshit," Ryker barked, coming over to the desk with crossed arms. "And his "evidence" is bullshit. He probably doesn't have anything, this is all about his agenda with Brynn."

Kaceston raised an eyebrow, staring Ryker down.

"My agenda with Brynn?" The question was a challenge.

"Do you think she keeps things from us?" Ryker didn't back down. "We're well aware of the accusations you threw at her for being an acolyte, that's the only reason you would think to associate us with the Creed."

"That's quite the theory, Ryker. Did you come up with that all on your own?"

Ryker's jaw snapped tight, but he maintained his composure, "You can be a condescending asshole all you like, that doesn't mean I'm wrong."

Kaceston rolled his eyes. "My ability to be an asshole has nothing to do with how wrong you are. I was suspicious of you well before Brynnlin showed up. She wasn't even on my radar until you," he emphasized the word, "met with her at the club. Your little trip to the isles, bringing back an "acolyte", and showcasing that "acolyte" as a council member, only furthered my suspicions. But rest assured, Maddox's cousin has nothing to fear from me at the moment."

The rate of which they all stilled was almost comical.

He allowed himself to grin. "Oh I'm sorry, is that still a secret?"

Kodak released a long sigh. "Things never can be easy with you, Kaceston, can they?" Kodak didn't wait for a response. "How do you know?"

"Whoever set up her identity was good, mine is just better."

A resigned acceptance flared in Kodak's eyes. "What's it going to cost me for you to keep that information to yourself?"

The seriousness in Kodak's tone had Kaceston straightening. "How about an explanation? Why'd you wait until now to bring her off that island? I'm assuming you sent Ryker and Zale to go get her, yes? And why all the trouble to hide who she is?"

Kodak's lips twitched, catching him off guard. "You're right about a lot, Kaceston, but not everything. And since you're being so forthcoming, I'll do the same. Ryker and Zale weren't there to meet with Brynn, we didn't even know she was there."

"What?" The word was out of his mouth before he could stop it. "Why the Hells were you there if it wasn't for her?"

It was Kodak's turn to take a long moment to answer. "A demon was loose within our realm, it was dangerous and was causing a lot of damage. We were trying to track down the Draíothe who summoned it, so they could find it."

Kaceston's shoulders slumped, and he ran a hand through his hair, not caring that he appeared rattled. All of this was taking a turn out of his control. A loose demon was not to be taken lightly. "What happened?"

"The matter is handled, the demon is dead, and Brynn is back home where she belongs. Satisfied?"

Not even a little.

They hadn't gone to the club for her like he thought.

It was about a godsdamn demon.

A surge of anger took him by surprise. He was leaning forward before he even realized he was moving. "I'm going to need you to walk me through this one more time. You didn't know she was on the island at the club? It was just a fucking coincidence?"

"Why the fuck does it matter to you?" Ryker arched a brow.

"It should matter to you," Kaceston threw back. "Are you not the closest thing she has to a family? She was missing for eleven years, and when you finally find her it was by godsdamn chance? What were you doing for eleven years?"

He should really stop. This wasn't his business. But their words were infuriating.

Did they not care?

If that had been his cousin, family member, or even a close fucking friend, he never would've given up on them. Brynnlin deserved better than that.

"With all due respect, Kaceston, this is not your concern, and you are not in a place to question us on this matter," Kodak's tone was full of warning. "Brynn is one of our own, and we protect our own. End of discussion."

Kaceston shook his head. "That's what you call protecting?"

"What the Hells is your problem?" Juniper snapped at him and glared. "You've known her all of two minutes, and you think to lecture us. What happened to Brynn and her parents was a tragedy, but she's a big girl. She can handle herself, more so than anyone I know."

A scoff sounded behind him, and Dax's gruff voice filled the room. "Just because someone becomes capable, doesn't mean you should diminish what they were forced to endure."

Juniper's brow furrowed.

Understanding hit Kaceston like a freight train. He threw up a hand to prevent Dax from saying more.

Gods, they didn't know.

They had no idea what happened to Brynnlin. If they did, they would never be this callous. She never told them. And he wasn't about to enlighten them.

"If she's so capable, why the fake identity?" Kaceston dropped the matter, turning their attention. "Would this have anything to do with the Draíothe that showed up at the party?"

"Do I even want to know how you're aware of that?" Kodak's frustration started to shine through.

"I happened to be outside with Brynnlin when he showed up. I was able to piece together they weren't exactly friends." Kaceston shrugged and offered more. "Be happy I was around, that interaction was the tipping point of my questioning your involvement. Brynnlin's background was the other solidifying factor."

"So because Brynn was attacked by a Draíothe and you found out she's Maddox's cousin, we're now innocent of whatever you think we did?" Kodak rolled his eyes. "That's not how you work, Kaceston."

"No, it's not, but it wasn't adding up. And I don't like when things don't add up. So, why is a Draíothe that's working for the Creed after Brynnlin?"

"Why would I tell you that?"

Kasecton narrowed his eyes at the insulting question. "Did I not come here to resolve this? Have I not been very honest and open with information? The least you can do is offer the same."

"This isn't about sharing information, Kaceston, this is about Brynn's safety. You want to know why her identity is a secret? He's why. He and whoever he's working for."

Kaceston frowned. "Why are they after her?"

"We believe it has something to do with the attack on her family. That Draíothe is the same that killed her parents."

"Fuck," Kaceston breathed. No wonder Brynnlin had been

ready to kill him. Was the Draíothe back to finish her off? "What do they want with her?"

"Excellent question."

"You don't know?"

Kodak glared. "We're working on it."

"Gods," Kaceston massaged his temples. "This is all a shit show."

"Thank you for that enlightening piece of information, feel free to leave at any time," Juniper bit out.

Despite the situation, Kaceston chuckled. She was fun.

"Kaceston," Kodak's tone was full of resignation, "I won't deny that I appreciate you opening up to us, but it's high time you share that evidence against us. We've answered your questions, and I need to know why you thought we were involved."

"Alright," Kaceston agreed. "I find it hard to believe you're involved after all of this, unless someone forced your hand, or you're being framed."

"The evidence, Kaceston."

"In the district that was attacked, the town's security and the temple's barrier system had been hacked and dismantled. That's how the team infiltrated the area so easily."

"What does that have to do with us?" Ryker's question was wary.

"We traced the source of the hack. It came from here."

"Here?" Kodak jerked back. "From my realm?"

"From your palace."

CHAPTER 33

"Do not make me regret my decision."

"That's not possible." Kodak's denial was instinctive, a wave of emotions crossed his face. Shock. Anger. Fear. Denial.

"I wouldn't lie about this," Kaceston reasoned.

"Then you're wrong."

"I'm not wrong," Kaceston didn't want to rile him up, but Owen wasn't wrong.

Kodak took a deep breath and studied him.

Kaceston didn't break his stare.

"There has to be an explanation for this."

Kaceston held up his hands. "That's what I'm here to find out."

"Get Remi in here now," Kodak barked at Ryker. "He's the best one to look into this."

"On it," Ryker was already striding out of the room.

Kodak turned to Zale next and lowered his voice, "Get Brynn down here too, she deserves to know what's going on."

Zale nodded, and he too stepped out.

Kaceston stayed silent and observed. He said what he needed to. He could wait to see what they found. And it was best to let Kodak handle his situation. The fact that Kodak was immediately looking into this was a promising sign.

Zale returned to the room, his expression grim. "Kodak, if there's any truth to this at all, we've had a breach," Zale's words were low, but not low enough.

"I'm aware," Kodak ground out.

"Something like this could be extremely damaging," Zale's gaze slid to Kaceston and his men. "We should take precautions."

Kaceston tensed. He would not be excluded.

"I understand the concern and under normal circumstances would agree. But we wouldn't even know about this had Kaceston not brought it to our attention, and I have nothing to hide. From what Kaceston told us, he has a right to know who was responsible for the attack on his realm."

Kaceston relaxed at Kodak's words. He inclined his head to the other ruler. A silent thanks.

"Do not get used to this," Kodak warned. "This is an unusual circumstance."

Kaceston bit back a smirk, he wouldn't antagonize Kodak. Not when he was getting what he wanted.

"What's an unusual circumstance?" A crisp voice cut into the room.

Kaceston turned to see Brynnlin enter the large office. Her eyes scanned the room, and when they landed on him and his men, they narrowed into slits.

"Kodak, I see you still have an infestation problem."

"Brynn—"

Kaceston's chuckle interrupted Kodak's admonishment.

"Hello to you, too, Brynnlin. How kind of you to grace us with your lovely presence."

Brynnlin's lips upturned in a viscous smile, and he waited with anticipation for her response. She didn't disappoint.

"How unfortunate for us you decided to do the same."

Kaceston's smile stretched. "Don't be like that, I know you missed me."

"Like one misses a rash," she said sweetly.

"How reassuring to see the events of the other night haven't dampened your ability to insult me. You are recovered, yes?"

She seemed recovered. One wouldn't even be able to tell he last saw her unconscious. Her hair was pulled back away from her face, her sharp features on display. Dark training leathers encased her delicate curves. She looked dangerous. Enticing.

He shouldn't allow himself to have such thoughts. But he couldn't deny that she intrigued him. He'd address his poor judgment at a later time.

Brynnlin's lips flattened, out and when she moved, it didn't escape his notice that she was favoring her left side. "I've recovered, no thanks to you."

Kaceston's own smirk dropped.

He deserved that one.

"It seems a misunderstanding might've occurred."

"A misunderstanding?" Brynnlin raised a brow in challenge. "Or just lack of intelligence?"

Kaceston shot her a warning look. "Careful, I will only tolerate so many of your insults."

"Enough of this," Kodak's voice was sharp. "Brynn, I didn't call you down here to exchange barbs with Kaceston."

Like a switch, her demeanor turned serious.

"Has something happened?"

She listened in silence as Kodak gave her the rundown of their earlier conversation. She remained emotionless, not reacting once as Kodak gave her the details. Even when Kodak revealed her uncovered past she was impassive.

It was quite impressive.

It wasn't until Kodak mentioned the breach that she stiffened.

"Your security has been compromised?" The whispered question was hoarse.

Kodak's features tightened. "We're not sure, but we can't ignore the possibility."

Kodak had barely finished speaking when the office door burst open.

An out of breath Ryker stormed into the room.

"I can't find Remi."

———

A LONG SILENCE penetrated the room at Ryker's declaration.

Brynnlin was sure she hadn't heard him correctly, as were the others.

Kodak recovered first. "What do you mean you can't find him?"

"He's not in his room, he's not answering, and I have people searching the grounds for him but nothing yet."

"Let's not get ahead of ourselves," Juniper intervened. "Are you sure he hasn't just stepped out?"

Ryker was already shaking his head. "I had everyone at the gate and perimeter towers check in with me, they don't recall him leaving."

"Okay that doesn't mean anything," Juniper pursed her lips. "This is a large property, and he was just with us not even an hour ago."

"But why wouldn't he answer?" Ryker pressed. "He never doesn't answer."

"Gods, do you think something happened to him?" Zale's frown turned fierce as he considered that possibility.

Kodak raised a hand, silencing everyone. "I'm aware everyone is rather on edge right now. But there is a reasonable explanation for this, let's not waste time jumping to conclusions."

Brynnlin was quiet as she considered the ramifications of this new development. Kodak was right, there could be a number of reasonable explanations.

But what about the unreasonable ones?

Gods, if something did happen—

"How well do you know this guy?" Kaceston asked.

Her eyes flew over to him only to see him staring expectantly at Kodak. The implication wasn't lost on her or anyone else.

"Very well," Kodak ground out.

"And you trust him?"

"Absolutely." There was no hesitation with the answer.

She understood Kaceston's immediate suspicions, but she'd seen firsthand all the trouble Remi had gone through for them. Kaceston was looking in the wrong direction.

"I think you've thrown around enough accusations for one evening. I think it's best you let us handle this," Juniper snapped, her eyes flaring with displeasure.

Brynnlin's eyes widened. She'd never seen Juniper so worked up before.

What had happened before she joined them?

Kaceston's lips thinned. "I meant no disrespect."

"Is that so?" Juniper scoffed. "You come to our home, question the integrity of our people, and—"

A soft beeping filled the room, silencing Juniper.

"It's Declan," Ryker announced to no one in particular before answering the call. "Yes, Declan?"

A quiet moment passed over the line when a throat cleared.

"Um sorry, Ryker, it's me, not Declan."

"Remi?" Ryker's surprise mirrored Brynnlin's own, along with the others in the room.

"Yes—"

"Where in the Hells are you?" Ryker interrupted. "And why are you calling me from Declan's orenda?"

"I'm out at the training center, their communications went out. I was getting it back up when Erin burst in and started yelling that everyone was looking for me."

Brynnlin could feel the tension leaving the room as everyone relaxed at Remi's explanation.

"We need you back here now, there's an emergency. Which you would know if you'd answered my calls," Ryker's voice was harsh.

"Oh shit, I'm real sorry," Remi's words were rushed. "My band is in the room, I had to—never mind, it doesn't matter—I'll be right there."

"Good." The call ended, and Ryker shook his head.

"I told all of you there was no reason to get worked up," Kodak relaxed back into his chair. "Remi will be here soon and can look into this matter."

"Speaking of the matter at hand," Kaceston's low voice filled the room. "I'd like to offer my assistance."

Kodak's brow shot upwards. "You want to help?"

"Well not myself in particular," Kaceston explained slowly. "I'm offering for an individual in my court to be of service."

Brynnlin studied him, unease creeping forward.

Why in the Hells would he help them?

"That's a generous offer, Kaceston, however, unnecessary." Kodak was quick to decline.

Kaceston's lips pursed, and his shoulders tensed. "I understand your hesitancy, but I do see it as necessary."

"Do you think we are incapable?" Kodak's voice hardened, and fire danced in his lethal gaze.

"Not at all." Kaceston appeared unfazed by Kodak's anger. "But if your system was compromised, this Remi, didn't notice, and I have someone who without a doubt can help find the breach."

"One, we don't know for certain if there's been a breach and two, Remi didn't know to look for one." Ryker stepped in, defending Remi.

Kaceston rolled his eyes. "It's highly likely you had a breach, and you should always be checking your system."

Ryker glowered, and Kodak shot him a warning look.

"I understand where you're coming from, Kaceston, but I can't let one of your men have access to my entire realm. The answer is still no. Remi can handle this."

"And if he can't?" Kaceston challenged.

"He can." Kodak retorted.

"In case you forgot, I have a vested interest in this, too," Kaceston snarled. "I could have easily handled this my own way from the start, instead I came to you out of respect. Do not make me regret my decision."

Kodak leaned forward, arms crossed. "Is that supposed to be a threat?"

"It's a reminder."

"Enough. Both of you." Brynnlin snapped.

Heads whipped towards her, surprise lacing their features.

"Brynn..." Kodak warned.

"No," she cut him off. "I'm sick of this back and forth political bullshit. We have a bigger problem on our hands and don't have time for this."

Kodak's frown turned fierce but she continued, trying to reason. "Kodak, it would be stupid to turn down Rí Kaceston's offer. He's right, Remi didn't know there was a breach. If someone can find it faster, you should take advantage of that."

Kodak stood. "You overstep."

Brynnlin stopped, her frown matching his. She was over-stepping, but she wasn't wrong.

"Brynn," Ryker stepped towards her, his hand grazing her arm. "Kodak knows you mean well, but a lot is at play here. Don't be naive to Rí Kaceston, he can't be trusted."

She jerked away from Ryker, glaring at him. "Do not accuse me of being naive when none of you are capable of setting aside your precious pride. And I'm not saying to trust him with the key to the realm. I'm saying to work with him for a common goal."

Ryker opened his mouth, but she continued, "Let's not forget he attacked me. Yet I'm willing to look past that because he is not the problem right now." Her voice started to rise, "He is not the current threat to our safety, and I'm getting damn tired of having to remind all of you that time is not on our side."

Silence followed her outburst.

"Very well said, Brynnlin," Kaceston drawled, his eyes gleaming. "I'm so delighted you agree with me and see it from my point of view."

She whipped towards him. "I'm not doing this for you," she said, her tone icy. "And it would be extremely idiotic of Kodak to allow another ruler uninhibited access to information, and you would never agree to that as well."

Kaceston's eyes narrowed. "What is it you're then suggesting?"

She crossed her arms, unflinching under his gaze. "The only way to protect us would be to make sure whoever you were going to have help has limited access. They would only have access to the central palace system, since you said you traced the breach here. Everything else Remi can easily restrict access to."

"Brynn, I appreciate what you're trying to do," Kodak cut in, his features softening. "But how can you be sure Kaceston's individual won't access anything else if they're as good as Kaceston claims?"

Brynnlin didn't break her stare with Kaceston. "I'm sure he wouldn't even think to do that, as any act against us is grounds for war."

Kaceston's lips twitched. "Rest assured that's not on my agenda." He faced Kodak. "You have my word, we would not compromise anyone or anything within your realm, if given access."

The room was quiet for a long minute after Kaceston's declaration. Kodak looked to Juniper who gave the slightest of nods.

Kodak's shoulders dropped, resignation radiating off of him.

"Alright, Kaceston, you have an agreement."

CHAPTER 34

"I will not let pride, yours, mine, or anybody else's get in the way of the safety of my realm."

"This is bullshit." Remi continued to rant, his anger fully directed at Kodak.

Remi returned to the office shortly after Kaceston's departure. Kaceston went to retrieve whoever he wanted to help them. Kodak had filled Remi in on the situation, and to say he wasn't taking it well would be an understatement.

"Remi, this is very serious—"

"You don't think I know that?" Remi burst out. "You trust me to handle this stuff, yet not only are you saying I missed a breach, but that some outsider is going to do my job?"

"Remi, take it down a notch." Zale warned from his place behind Kodak.

Remi tensed, his glare shooting to the other man. "Easy for you to say, Zale, you're not being replaced."

"Gods damn it, Remi," Kodak growled. "You're not being replaced, Kaceston has only offered assistance—"

Remi scoffed. "Oh yes, assistance from the very man who accused you. How do you know this isn't some ploy of his to plant something incriminating?"

"Watch yourself." The warning came from Griffin, who stepped forward from the corner of the room. Kaceston had left Griffin and Dax here, claiming he'd be right back. They'd stayed quiet until that moment.

Brynnlin mirrored his step, cutting him off.

"Stay out of this and let them sort it out," her voice was low.

He glared at her. She refused to budge.

A moment passed and he nodded, relenting. She released a sigh. The last thing they needed was more testosterone adding to this mess.

"Remi, I have always valued you," Kodak stood, leaning over his desk, forcing Remi to look up at him. "But I will not allow insubordination. What Kaceston did today was a bold move, and he trusted us to do the right thing. He already had reason to believe we attacked him, he doesn't need to plant anything. Do I trust him? Hells, no. But I do trust he wants to find who's responsible for this, as do I. I will not let pride, yours, mine, or anybody else's get in the way of the safety of my realm. Am I clear?"

Remi took a long minute to answer. "Yes, you've made yourself clear."

"Good," Kodak took his seat again. "And I want you to find this breach faster than whoever Kaceston brings in."

Remi didn't look amused at Kodak's words. He only nodded and slumped into one of the chairs, anger still radiating off of him.

"When does this so-called prodigy show up?" The question barely left Remi's mouth when dark flames circled in the doorway.

Brynnlin tensed, still not used to Kaceston's unusual form of travel. She forced herself to relax when the flames dissipated.

Kaceston stood there with a boy at his side.

Her eyes widened at the duo. It was indeed a boy he'd brought back. Dirty blonde hair hung loose to his shoulders, and silver-blue eyes were filled with uncertainty as he took in the room. His features were young, and he hadn't quite filled out his lanky form.

Gods, he couldn't be any older than his teen years.

What in the Hells was Kaceston doing?

Kaceston took in the quiet room with an arched brow. "This is Owen," he put a hand on the boy's shoulder. "He'll help you find your breach."

"A kid?" Remi jumped up from his chair, roaring, "He brought a fucking kid?"

Owen jerked back, and Kaceston moved in front of him, a deadly coldness crossing his features. "Are we going to have a problem here?"

Remi shrunk at Kaceston's wrath. "No, your highness."

Kaceston didn't spare Remi a glance. "I wasn't speaking to you," he seethed, his gaze fully locked on Kodak.

Kodak shook his head, and his eyebrows rising in challenge. "What game are you playing at, Kaceston? Why'd you bring a kid here?"

Before Kaceston could speak, an affronted Owen stepped forward, looking pissed. "I'm here because you need my help. I'm not the one whose system got hacked."

Kodak's head jerked back at Owen's statement, and Brynnlin swore she caught Kaceston's lips twitch in response. Even she had to bite down on her lip to contain her chuckle.

Owen was bold.

She'd give him that.

He also wasn't wrong.

"Owen is the best," Kaceston crossed his arms, daring anyone to argue. "So are we ready to get started or not?"

Kodak shook his head, "I swear to the gods, Kaceston, you better not be screwing us over." He gestured to Remi, "Remi can take Owen to the central system."

"Excellent," Kaceston moved towards the door. "My men and I will accompany them."

"Is that really necessary?"

Kaceston halted. "Owen will not be left alone here."

Kodak only rolled his eyes. "Fine." He jerked his head towards Zale. "Go escort them. Juniper and I need to address a security matter, and we'll be right down."

"Kodak," Zale hesitated, "I'm on standby to hear back from Maddox and..." he paused, "...and I need to be ready when he calls."

"Shit, you're right."

"I'll take them," Ryker offered.

Kodak smirked, "I appreciate your offer, but I think the goal is to prevent a war, not start one."

Ryker glowered, and Brynnlin couldn't help but snicker. Ryker alone with those three, even for a short time period, would be inviting trouble on a golden platter.

Kodak's gaze shot to her. "Brynn, you go."

"What?" Her humor evaporated, and she frowned. "Why me?"

His brow rose in challenge. "Wasn't this your idea to begin with? Us working together?"

She couldn't deny it.

"That's what I thought. Now go keep them in check, we'll join you in a few minutes."

"Yes, Brynnlin, do come keep us in check," Kaceston purred, his eyes lighting with mirth.

She gestured to the door with a sneer. "After you, your highness."

OVER AN HOUR LATER, Remi and Owen were still determinedly typing on their respective screens. The room containing the central system and Remi's work station wasn't very large. Brynnlin and Kaceston rested against the wall while Kodak, Juniper, and Ryker spoke to sentries out in the hall. Griffin and Dax also stood silently outside the door. The last hour had been spent in mostly silence with the occasional interruption from Kaceston. He either checked in with Owen, or tried to probe her with invasive questions—all of which she decidedly ignored.

"I must say, Brynnlin, the silent treatment is quite the childish approach, and extraordinarily boring," Kaceston tried again.

Brynnlin rolled her eyes skyward. He really didn't give up. "I'm not here to be your source of entertainment."

"Yes, that's abundantly clear. You'd be astronomically failing if that were the case."

Her teeth clashed together as she bit back an insulting retort. He was a royal, she reminded herself. An esteemed ruler for which it was illegal to assault.

No matter how irritating he proved to be.

"I have nothing to say to you," she ground out, "so let me introduce you to this foreign concept known as silence. We can practice it while they work."

"Now why would I do that," Kaceston drawled out, "when we have so much to talk about."

"There's nothing to talk about."

"Oh I must disagree. We can start with why that Draíothe is

trying to kill you? I was caught in the crosshairs of that little tiff."

She didn't bother to correct his assumption. "What a great question, you should ask him yourself."

Kaceston's chuckle was slow. "Okay, if you don't want to answer that, then how about your friend Selene Aspen? I'd love to learn more about how that came to be."

She shot him a withering glare. "Congratulations, you dug into my past and now feel entitled to everything there is to know about me. Hate to disappoint, but you're wasting your breath."

His smirk only grew. "That topic off limits, too?" He didn't wait for an answer. "How about your dear cousin? I haven't seen the Chancellor around lately, where is he off at?"

"You must think you're so smart and have us all figured out." It was her turn to smirk. "But you truly have no idea what's going on, and I have zero intention of enlightening you."

His eyes flashed with an emotion she couldn't decipher. She didn't care. She'd finally hit a nerve, and it was nice to put him on the defensive instead.

"You know, Brynnlin," she hated how he dragged out her name, how it flowed off his tongue like a song, "did you ever think that I might actually be able to help? If your problems have to do with the Creed, we all have a vested interest in this."

A scoff burst out of her before she could stop it.

He arched a brow.

"You might not be actively against us now, but you've made your stance quite clear."

"How so?" He sounded genuinely curious.

"You're really going to stand there and act like you didn't threaten to either imprison me or kill me a few days ago?"

He had the nerve to shrug. "Things were different a few days ago."

She shook her head, her irritation only growing. "Nothing was different, not for us. And if that isn't bad enough, how about the fact you denied Kodak's request out of spite? Or did you deny it because you thought he attacked you?"

His eyes flared. "I am under no obligation to explain anything, but I can see the accusations and conclusions exploding in that pretty little head of yours. Rest assured, I had a legitimate reason to turn down Kodak."

"You really think I'm dumb enough to believe that?" She spat back.

"I have no reason to lie. And while it gave me immense pleasure to deny Kodak, and I did assume he was up to something, I would've said no to anyone. It's too much of a risk to allow access to inmates for a simple interrogation."

"Risk?"

A brow shot up. "Do you not know about Sorrow's Gaol?"

"I'm well aware of its reputation."

"So the answer's no." A smirk played across Kaceston's lips. He leaned down, his breath ghosting against her ear. "That's where we lock up all of the monsters too dangerous to play with the rest of us. And trust me, we don't want them getting out of their cages."

Brynnlin angled her head, meeting his stare. "And yet you're not there," she challenged, refusing to budge even with the little space between them.

Kaceston let out a low chuckle.

"Never doubt, Brynnlin, I'm so much worse."

She didn't doubt that.

Not for a second.

She knew he was dangerous, and his powers were probably incomparable, neither of those things seemed to stop her from engaging with him.

She knew better, yet she couldn't seem to stop herself.

A blaring alarm blasted through the room, breaking them apart. Brynnlin jumped back with a curse. She swung towards Remi and Owen, her ears ringing from the high-pitched volume of the still blaring alarm. Remi jumped to his feet, typing furiously. His livid gaze fell on Owen.

"What did you do?" he seethed.

To her surprise, Owen glared right back.

Remi ignored him, going back to the numbers and symbols flying across the screen. "I knew you couldn't be trusted and would try to pull something."

Shuffling sounded at the door, and Kodak pushed forward. "What the Hells is going on?"

Remi spun to Kodak. "Owen tried to access our outgoing communications. Those were secured for a reason, the gods only know what he would've tried to steal."

Remi's explanation halted as Kaceston stepped towards him.

"Are you accusing Owen of something?" The Hells could've frozen over with the iciness of his tone.

Some of Remi's bluster faltered, but he managed to stay standing and held Kaceston's glare. "He broke the agreement."

"I'm more than happy to explain my actions," Owen jumped in before Kaceston could respond.

"Well then I'm all ears," Kodak crossed his arms, studying the boy with intent.

"You're all going to wait a moment," Kaceston interrupted Kodak, turning to Owen, a demand for an explanation clear in his gaze.

"The matter will be resolved," Owen shrugged, appearing unconcerned.

Brynnlin's eyes narrowed as she studied the boy. Owen was unusually calm for this situation, and while he didn't say much, he and Kaceston continued their stare off. The slight tensing of

Kaceston's shoulders caught her attention, and she straightened off the wall.

"Would you like to share with the rest of us?" Brynnlin swore something unspoken passed between them again before Kaceston turned to her.

She flinched back at the ferocity in his eyes, but in a flash it was gone. Expressionless features stared back at her, and she doubted whether she had seen it in the first place.

"It's best for Kodak to determine the severity of the situation." Kaceston addressed the other ruler. "I need a word out in the hall."

It wasn't a request.

Brynnlin's frown was immediate.

Since when was Kaceston one to defer to another?

Kodak's eyes narrowed as well, but he agreed. "Very well."

Kaceston nodded on an exhale and stepped to the door. "Griffin, go to Owen."

No sooner than Kaceston and Kodak stepped past the door frame into the hall...

All Hells broke loose.

CHAPTER 35

"He would try to kill her or worse. She had no doubt."

A METAL DOOR SLAMMED SHUT. Several bolts locked into place, encaging Brynnlin in the small room with Remi and Owen. Remi was up and out of his chair. His eyes flashed an eerie yellow, and his fingers extended into deadly talons. He lunged at Owen, pinning him to the desk.

"Remi!" Brynnlin shrieked, her eyes not believing what was right in front of her.

Remi attacked Owen. Remi was Ossarian.

How did she not know he was Ossarian?

Why was he after Owen?

"What did you see? How did you find it?" Remi snarled down at Owen, their faces inches apart.

"I don't know what you're talking about. I didn't see anything." The color leached from Owen's face, and his eyes widened as Remi breathed down on him.

"Remi, you need to get off him," Brynnlin moved forward.

Before she reached the duo, Remi spun, dragging Owen with him.

"Stay the fuck back, Brynnlin."

Remi used Owen as a shield, and his talons pressed into Owen's neck. Small drops of red painted his skin.

She froze, her gaze shooting to Owen.

He had to be terrified.

Loud banging echoed off the door, and she was sure she could make out Kaceston yelling.

"And you," Remi hissed in Owen's ear, "I know you're lying. I can practically taste the stench oozing off you."

Owen's shocked features morphed into a mask of indifference, eerily resembling Kaceston. "And you think using me is going to save you? You're not getting out of this."

"Oh I think I am. And you're going to make sure of it."

The words barely escaped Remi's mouth when dark flames erupted from the floor. Kaceston stepped out of them, unrestrained rage seeping off of him as he took in the scene before him.

"I highly suggest you release Owen if you want any hope of a quick death."

Brynnlin thought she had seen Kaceston angry before and had heard his lethal threats. Those were nothing compared to the promised death now filtering through the room.

Remi had the idiocy to stand his ground. He pulled Owen closer, refusing to budge.

"That's not how this is going to go."

"We're not negotiating."

"You came in here with this kid and forced me into this position." Remi's voice started to rise, "It wasn't supposed to happen like this."

"You thought you would just get away with this?" Owen scoffed.

"I was getting away with it," Remi snarled.

"You're a traitor to your realm," Owen shouted.

Brynnlin staggered at Owen's words. Everything clicked into place with precise clarity.

Remi was the breach.

"You bastard," the words tore out of her as she realized how deeply he betrayed Kodak and everyone else here.

"Like you're any better," Remi spat at her. "You might have the others fooled, but I know how badly the Creed wants you. There's no way you didn't get your hands dirty for them on those islands."

She flinched at the accusation.

At the same time, Kaceston let out a guttural growl and inched forward a step.

"Watch it," Remi swung his attention back to Kaceston. His talons dug deeper into Owen, inciting a wince as blood seeped down his neck.

Her hand shot out, pulling Kaceston back a step. Her mind raced for a way to get Owen away from Remi. The room was small, leaving little space to maneuver. One wrong move and Remi could rip open Owen's jugular without a second thought.

She eyed Kaceston, anger and frustration rolled off of him. Whatever he was capable of, he either couldn't do it from a distance, or it was too risky with Owen's position.

She considered the possibilities of her own magic. Could she get to Remi without him hurting Owen?

He would see her move...

But if he couldn't see her coming...

Was she fast enough? Was she willing to risk exposure? It was one thing for her family, but with Kaceston here?

He would try to kill her or worse. She had no doubt.

She looked at Owen. The pit in her stomach grew the

longer she watched him. He was just a kid. He came here to help. He didn't deserve this.

Was her secret possibly worth his life?

She knew the answer even as every survival instinct she had fought against her.

She moved before she could stop herself. Consequences be damned.

————————————

KACESTON RAGED as he watched Remi continue to hold Owen hostage. This was all his fault. He never should have brought Owen here. And gods damn it, he couldn't even do anything. With Owen that close to Remi, he couldn't risk getting within touching distance. But Remi couldn't hold Owen forever. As soon as there was an opening, Remi was a dead man.

Out of the corner of his eye, he caught the slightest shift in Brynnlin's stance, and his eyes narrowed. She better not try anything stupid. If she put Owen in danger—

The entire room fell as black as night before he even finished his thought.

"Fuck," he snarled as an endless void of darkness swallowed everything around him, rendering his eyesight useless.

A grunt and a clash sounded somewhere in front of him.

"Owen." Kaceston surged forward, colliding with a solid form.

"I'm okay," Owen's voice shook.

Relief nearly buried Kaceston, and his arms circled Owen, attempting to shield him from any more threats.

Another crash vibrated through the room. A moment later, light bathed the area as if it had never disappeared to begin with.

In its wake, Brynnlin held Remi against the wall, his feet

dangling as her hand circled his throat. One arm rested uselessly at his side, unmoving. The other was pinned to the wall as Brynnlin drove a dagger straight through the middle of his hand.

A dagger he distinctly recognized.

"You fucked up," Brynnlin's voice was cold—colder than he'd ever heard.

Remi didn't respond. Couldn't.

Any breath he took was fighting for air.

Kaceston shook his head, taking in the scene again. Seconds had passed in that darkness, only seconds.

Just what exactly was she capable of?

In that moment, he didn't care about the answer. All that mattered was that she had gotten Remi away from Owen. He would figure out the rest later. He pulled Owen to his feet, checking for himself that he was alright. After verifying Owen's injuries weren't too serious, Kaceston took his first calming breath.

He staggered, nearly falling to his knees.

His gaze swung back to Brynnlin, who still effortlessly held Remi to the wall.

His senses sharpened, eyes narrowing as he stared at the woman in front of him.

He inhaled again, taking in the demon magic circling the room.

CHAPTER 36

"It would be a dangerous game to enter into, and none of the outcomes would end in her favor."

CHAOS.

That's all Brynnlin could think as everything passed in a blur. After Owen had gotten the door back open, the small room had been filled to the brim with people. Kodak struggled to believe, but with the truth right in front of him, it was hard to ignore. Remi had been taken away, Ryker going with him and a group of sentries to lock him in a cell. Ryker would stay with Remi while the others waited to see how deeply he compromised them.

Owen had agreed to stay and decipher the messages, much to Kaceston's chagrin. Kaceston remained brooding in the corner, arms crossed, and his eyes rarely leaving Owen.

"You should get that looked at." Juniper settled next to her against the wall, gesturing to her arm.

Brynnlin glanced down at the ripped sleeve of her shirt and at the gash from Remi's talon.

"I want to know what Owen finds."

"And I'll call you as soon as he does. Go change and have Verenna close that up for you," Juniper nudged her to the door.

"Okay." She agreed with some reluctance.

As soon as she pushed off the wall, Kaceston straightened, his narrowed gaze swinging to her.

She ignored him.

He'd been giving her strange looks ever since the Remi incident. She knew he was biding his time until he could confront her. She hoped to postpone that for as long as possible.

Stepping out into the hall, Dax and Griffin cast her curious looks.

Not her.

Past her.

"Go stay with Owen, he doesn't leave your sight," Kaceston's gruff voice carried over her.

Her shoulders fell.

So this was happening now.

She continued down the corridor, Kaceston following silently. She went all the way up to her room, not even attempting to block Kaceston from entering.

Kaceston shut the door behind him, and Brynnlin spun. Lifting her hands, shadows unrolled from her palms and sprang at him. She'd seen firsthand how he reacted when he thought she was behind something. She had no intention of letting him make the first move after what he witnessed downstairs.

She didn't make mistakes twice.

Tendrils of shadows curled around his wrists and ankles locking him against the door.

Kaceston raised an eyebrow. "Is this really necessary?"

The slightest pull of resistance tugged at her shadows. She

reinforced her dark magic, leaving him unmoving. She wasn't hurting him.

Yet.

But he wasn't getting anywhere near her.

"If you think I'm going to go quietly or without a fight, you have another thing coming."

Genuine confusion flashed across his features before understanding settled.

"Brynnlin, I didn't come up here to hurt you."

She didn't relax. She didn't believe him.

Kaceston chuckled when she refused to budge.

"Brynnlin, I'm not even fighting back against your magic right now, consider that my gesture of good will. Let me out, and we can talk."

"Talk now."

His eyes narrowed. "You're powerful. I admit. But do not let that fool you. I've been fighting demons long before you were even alive, so whatever magic of theirs you possess, it is no match to me. Release me now."

The command vibrated through the room, but it might as well have fallen on deaf ears.

Brynnlin rocked back as if physically struck.

Her mind refused to accept Kaceston's words while her stomach turned at the possibility.

"What did you just say?" The words were barely a whisper.

Kaceston's brow furrowed, and his head cocked to the side as he studied her intently. A dangerous gleam swam in his eyes, darkening those swirls of gray. A taunt of a smirk played across his lips.

"Now which part of what I just said, would get that kind of reaction out of you?"

Her jaw slammed shut.

He'd caught her off guard. She revealed too much. If he sensed her hesitation, he would latch onto any show of weakness. Instead she glared and tightened her hold, forcing him to wince.

"You like to play games, Kaceston," she hissed and lifted him higher up the wall. More shadows swirled around him. She couldn't have him forgetting who had the upper hand here. "But this isn't a fucking game. I don't care who you are or what your title is. If you want any hope of walking out of here, you're going to explain what you expected to accomplish when you followed me into this room."

Instead of looking concerned, his smirk only grew. "You're quite hostile when you're vulnerable."

"I don't know if it's boldness or idiocy that you continue to ignore your delicate position. But I'll give you one more chance to answer my question before this gets messy."

"One more chance, huh? I guess I better make it worth it then," he drawled out, testing her.

Her stomach pitted in frustration. He would never concede, not to her. But he wasn't leaving her much of a choice. She never wanted this, but if it came down to a threat to her life, she would do what she had to do.

She shook her head. "I really didn't want it to be like this."

Something unfamiliar flashed in his eyes. "Before you attempt to do whatever you're planning. Let me see if I have this right..."

She waited a breath, and a victorious grin split his lips.

"You looked like you were about to be sick at my earlier statement. But you wouldn't be surprised at my experience with demons, you'd have to expect that. My age also wouldn't shock you. You have to be aware that I've been around much longer than you. Which leaves us with two..."

He continued, "You either were taken aback at the fact that you're no match for me, which I would expect from most, but I don't think that's the case here. Not once have you ever feared me, though you should, and you push me at every chance you have. Which brings us to one. You panicked at what I said about your magic. Why?"

Every part of her locked tight, she refused to give him the satisfaction of reacting.

"Is this your attempt to stall? Grasping at thin air and trying to come up with something? Come on, Kaceston, you're better than that."

"You weren't aware of the source of your magic, were you?"

She scoffed. "What a pathetic attempt to mess with my head. Who in their right mind wouldn't know their own magic?"

"Apparently you."

She slammed him against the wall, earning a groan. "I'd be real careful about insulting me right now. I know my magic, and I'm not a fucking demon."

There was a lot she didn't know. But she did know that.

"I didn't say you were."

"You said—"

"I said you possess demon magic, Ciarán, that's a very different thing."

She rolled her eyes and ignored the nickname he seemed so fond to bring up. "How stupid do you think I am? Something like that isn't possible."

Kaceston attempted a shrug, "I wouldn't have thought so either, yet here you are."

"Stop lying," she snarled, baring her teeth. Her patience was nonexistent. "Whatever game you're trying to play, I'm not falling for it."

Burning pain exploded through every nerve, nearly

blinding her. She whimpered as she crumbled to the floor. She curled in on herself, a failed attempt to shield herself from the fire coursing through her.

Kaceston dropped down, rubbing at his wrists. He eyed her curiously.

"Interesting, are you aware that your shadows are an extension of yourself?"

He didn't look like he expected an answer. He strode towards her and kneeled down next to her. She couldn't even lift her head, and she was helpless to prevent the tears leaking down her cheeks as her body responded to whatever magic was behind this.

Kaceston lifted a hand and cupped her head. Brynnlin flinched, but the touch was surprisingly gentle. He threaded his fingers through her hair, and in an instant the pain disappeared. Her muscles fell limp as her body relaxed at the release.

"I'm sorry," Kaceston's voice was gruff. "I didn't mean for it to hit you that hard. I wasn't lying when I said I didn't come up here to hurt you."

"You're a fucking asshole," Brynnlin grunted, trying to ignore the lingering pain and pushed herself to a sitting position.

"I know," Kaceston leaned back on his heels, his hand trailing through her hair as he pulled it back. "But you didn't want to listen, and I was tired of being up against that damn wall."

"You think that stunt you just pulled is going to make me more inclined to listen?"

"I think you're an intelligent woman that can recognize that if I wanted to hurt you, I would have already. So how about we table the violence for a moment and have a simple discussion?"

Brynnlin couldn't deny that he had done some damage. She

was hurting from that small amount of magic. She also wasn't stupid and knew that he had been holding back—a lot. A fact that was terrifying on its own.

"Fine." She forced herself to stand, refusing to look any weaker in front of him. She propped herself against the edge of the bed and crossed her arms. "Talk."

Kaceston stood with ease and surprised her when he pulled a chair over. He was slow to sit and stretched his legs out in front of him, looking far too comfortable considering the circumstances.

"The ease at which you disarmed your friend downstairs was alarming. Given the source of your magic, it could even border on unnatural. Originally, I had every intention of demanding answers from you about how you obtained this... extensive power. However, I fear I'm going to be disappointed. You didn't even know you possessed demon magic."

"How do you even know that?" Brynnlin finally snapped. "You keep saying that, yet I'm just supposed to believe you?"

"I have no reason to lie to you."

"I hardly find that reassuring."

"If you think I can magically prove it to you, you're mistaken," Kaceston let out a low chuckle. "How about I let you in on a little secret, though? Very few are capable of detecting the demon race, I'm one of those few. It's how I know you aren't a demon, but your magic definitely is."

Brynnlin was quiet for a long moment. She searched for any sign that he was lying to her, but she had no way to tell.

She could keep denying what he said...

Or she could consider the possibility that he was telling the truth.

She didn't know which was worse.

While the possibility of that truth was sickening, she couldn't ignore the questions it answered. For years, she had searched for any explanation to no avail, and now she might know why.

"Let's say, just for a moment, I did believe you. Do you have any idea how something like that would be possible?" Her question was soft, wary.

"Some speculation, maybe, but not a definitive answer."

"What speculation?" Brynnlin would take any ideas she could.

"You were attacked by a demon as a child, yes?"

She was already shaking her head.

"You weren't?"

"No, I was," she corrected, "but that had nothing to do with it. I was born like this."

Kaceston's head jerked back in the slightest of movements. "You were?" He leaned forward in the chair, resting his arms on his knees and continued without an answer, "And your parents?"

She knew where he was going with this, and he was wrong again.

"Normal."

She was taken aback at his immediate frown.

"Normal is an arbitrary construct designed by a distorted society to feel better about averageness. It is unremarkable and boring, of which you are neither. So I must insist you do not use that term with such longing."

A small warmth filled her chest, and Brynnlin couldn't stop the tiny smile that spread across her lips. "Careful Kaceston, that almost sounded like a compliment."

His intense stare met her own, he raised a single brow. "Oh Ciarán, if you believe that to be a compliment, you need to get out more. But I'm happy to demonstrate a real compliment, just say the word."

The sudden heat in his eyes had warmth spreading through

her for an entirely different reason. One she decidedly ignored. Lust was not a new concept to her, and any warm-blooded woman would be affected by Kaceston. But to act on it or take his light flirting seriously would be the height of stupidity. It would be a dangerous game to enter into, and none of the outcomes would end in her favor.

"Maybe another time."

He smirked and shrugged, not at all concerned at her decline. "Now going back to your parents—"

"I told you they were..." she trailed off at the narrowing of his eyes. "They weren't like me," she amended.

"That you are aware of," Kaceston countered. "You were young when they died, they might have kept it from you. If one of your parents had been of the demon race, I can see why they would keep it from a child."

"You can't be serious right now, neither of my parents were a demon." She laughed at the absurdity of the idea.

"Just because we've never heard of it, doesn't mean it isn't possible for one of our own to procreate with the demon race."

Gods, he was actually being serious.

"Kaceston, come on."

"What, Brynnlin?" His gaze turned challenging. "You're going to deny it's even a possibility? Maybe it wasn't your parents, but further up your lineage, and your magic is an evolved outcome from generations of matings?"

She wanted to argue. Wanted to tell him how ridiculous his theory was. Something stopped her. A thread of doubt, a mixture of hope, both ignited at the prospect of a possible explanation to something she thought didn't have an answer.

He took her silence as agreement. "I'll have Owen look into it and see what he can find."

He pushed up from the chair, as if that now concluded their

conversation. In two steps, Brynnlin was in front of him, blocking his exit.

"Why?" she demanded, and the close proximity forced him to look down at her.

"You're going to have to be more specific with your questioning. Why am I getting up? Why am I so intelligent? Charming? Irresistible?"

"Why are you offering to help me?" she interrupted his list of so-called qualities. "You don't do things out of kindness."

"Brynnlin, I'm not some monster. Does everything I do have to have an ulterior motive?"

"Yes." She was well versed with how the world worked. Favors didn't come without strings.

"Call it a shared interest."

She still didn't move.

Kaceston released a long sigh, but his features turned solemn. "If you don't know your own magic you're dangerous, not only to yourself, but to others as well."

Brynnlin lifted her eyebrows. "I find it hard to believe you're now concerned for my well-being."

"How about everyone else's?"

"I'm flattered you see me as such a threat."

"That wasn't a compliment. The world doesn't take kindly to things it thinks is a threat. Trust me." His voice turned grave. "You can't be in the dark about where you got your power, not when it's this extensive." She opened her mouth, but he cut her off. "Don't bother lying. I can feel it, Brynnlin, even right now, just standing here. Now that I know what to look for, there's no hiding it. And if others find out and you don't know exactly what you are, that ignorance will be a weapon they use against you."

Brynnlin's mind reeled as she absorbed Kaceston's words.

He said if.

"You're trying to protect me." The words were blurted out, and her gaze flew to his.

Surprise washed across both their features.

Hers at the realization.

His at the accusation.

"Now who's being absurd." He rolled his eyes and stepped past her.

Her hand shot out, grabbing his arm, stopping him yet again. His eyes drifted down and lingered on where she was grabbing him.

"You don't like being manhandled as you so called it, but it's acceptable for you to do so? A tad hypocritical, don't you agree?"

"If I recall, you didn't listen very well either," she responded sweetly. "But I deserve an answer for why you're trying to protect me."

"Deserve?"

"Would like one. Please." She added.

"You're exasperating, you do know that, right?"

"Yes, very much so."

He still didn't answer her.

"Kaceston, please, this is my life we're talking about."

"Downstairs," he said, reluctantly. "You saved Owen down-stairs, and he means a great deal to me. Consider this me returning the favor."

Her mind went back to what happened earlier. She considered Kaceston's protectiveness of the boy. She pictured the rage he displayed at Remi, and the way she looked at Owen and saw pieces of Kaceston.

"Is he your son?" she asked softly.

Kaceston's head whipped towards her, his eyes wide. "What?"

"Owen's your son, right?"

She jerked back when Kaceston's laughter bubbled out of him. She stared blankly as the alluring sound surrounded her.

"Owen is my brother," Kaceston admitted with a sly smile.

"Oh." Brynnlin chewed on her lip.

"I'm trusting you to keep that piece of information to yourself. His life doesn't need to be at risk because of his relation to me."

"Is it?" She knew better than to prod, yet couldn't seem to stop herself. "Is his life in danger if people knew his relation to you?"

"As I'm sure you've concluded for yourself, I'm not a good person, Brynnlin. Never claimed to be. And I don't lose any sleep over it. But I've made my share of enemies over the years, most well-deserved, but still enemies. And Owen shouldn't be affected by my life choices, don't you agree?"

She saw past the question. Kaceston wasn't really asking. Even without the lingering threat, she would never expose Owen like that.

"Owen's relation to you is safe with me."

Without thought she reached down and squeezed his hand, trying to reassure him with more than words of her sincerity. Owen would not be in danger because of her.

Kaceston's eyes flared at the contact, but he didn't pull immediately away. He looked down at their hands, and his gaze dragged back up to her own.

Another moment passed.

She was about to take her hand back when Kaceston's fingers wrapped around her own.

"Your secret is safe as well."

Brynnlin's head dropped down in a wave of relief. "Thank you."

Kaceston merely nodded and released her hand going for the door again.

"I want to get back to Owen."

The words were barely out of his mouth when her band buzzed against her skin. Her gaze shot down.

"It's Juniper," she announced, accepting the call.

Before she could speak, Juniper was already talking.

"Owen deciphered the messages."

CHAPTER 37

"Oh don't worry, violence is perfectly rational."

RYKER WATCHED the prisoner in the cell. Remi hadn't put up a fight as they dragged him down here. He hadn't even said a word when they chained him to the chair.

Absolutely nothing.

It was enraging. That rage grew by the second the longer Remi sat there with his emotionless expression.

There was no remorse. No apologies for his betrayal. Nothing.

"You're lucky Brynn was the one in that room," Ryker finally broke the silence with a deadly calm voice. "Had it been myself, I would've spared us a cell and killed you right then and there."

Remi spared him a glance, a frown pulling down on his lips. "After all these years together, you're so quick to think the worst of me."

Ryker leaned against the cell, glaring. "You're making it pretty fucking easy. You attacked that kid, that's not the action of an innocent man."

"Did you see me attack that kid?" Remi raised a brow. "Did anyone? No," he spat. "You're all taking the word of outsiders over one of your own. It was only too easy for them to set me up, and all of you fell for it like fools. Kaceston is trying to weaken us, and you're letting him."

Ryker could only shake his head in disgust. "Those are pathetic words from a desperate man. And you seem to be forgetting a very important factor in your little spiel. Brynn's not an outsider."

"She's more of an outsider than anyone," Remi burst out before laughing maniacally. "Gods, all it takes is a pretty face, and you roll over. What is it you think she did on those islands? Why do you think the Creed wants her so badly? Did you even know that she possesses magic? There's a darkness in her, Ryker, that will destroy everything and everyone, and you're blind to it," Remi finished on a yell, his breaths coming out in uneven gasps.

A long moment passed between them.

"You know what, Remi, I was blind."

Remi leaned forward as much as the restraints allowed. "You see it now, don't you?" His voice dropped in volume.

"Yes, I see it now, so very clearly." Ryker pushed off the bars, turning his back to Remi. One of the other sentries could stand guard. He was done.

"Where the Hells are you going?" Remi shouted to Ryker's retreating form.

Ryker cast a glance over his shoulder. "I'm not wasting a second longer listening to your bullshit." Just for the satisfaction he added, "And I'd advise against talking poorly about Brynn in front of Kodak, he and Juniper have grown quite fond of her."

An incoherent growl filled the room as Remi fought the chains. Metal scraped against the floor.

"He didn't see her in that room, she's a monster."

Ryker's muscles locked tight. His entire body went rigid. Images of Brynnlin flashed through his mind...

Her standing alone between them and a demon. The scars across her flesh. Her bloodied in Maddox's arms after nearly being kidnapped and still managing to steal the summoning amulet. Everything she'd done had been for her family.

Remi dared to call her a monster?

He spun back to the cell, slow precision marking each of his movements.

"Brynn is not a monster, but I'll be happy to show you a real monster if you call her that again."

"Her magic—"

"Has saved us and probably countless others," Ryker snarled. "Be happy she didn't use it to rip you to shreds. It would have been child's play for her to do so, and I certainly would have if I was in her shoes."

Remi's face paled a shade, and Ryker thought he finally got the picture until he opened his mouth again.

"You knew?" Remi struggled to get the question out. "This whole time you knew that darkness existed within her?"

Ryker let out a humorless laugh. "Yeah Remi, we knew, you were the one that didn't know."

Remi's glare turned murderous. "There's no saving you. You all deserve what's coming to you. Every last one of you."

Ryker's blood turned cold at the ominous threat. "What the Hells did you do?"

Remi's returning grin was sinister. "It's too late."

Ryker slammed his hand against the steel bars. The room rattled.

"What the fuck did you do?"

"Maddox and that whore, Selene ,are already done for—"

Ryker was sprinting for the door.

"—You and the others are next."

Remi's laughter followed him up the stairs.

———————————

MESSAGES DATING BACK years were spread across the screens in front of them. Brynnlin watched with despair as Owen continued to retrieve more and added them to the growing accumulation of betrayal. Muttered curses filled the room each time a new folder was opened.

"How in the Hells did we miss all of this?" Kodak glared at the full screen.

Juniper inched her way to Kodak's side and ran a hand up and down his back in a soothing motion. Kodak relaxed into the gesture and shook his head.

"If it's any consolation, he hid it well," Owen said from the chair. He didn't bother to turn around, continuing to swivel between the screens. "We're lucky he didn't erase it all, but this was probably his safety net for if they ever turned on him."

"What can you tell so far from the messages?" Kaceston pulled up a chair next to his brother.

"He's been in contact with multiple sources throughout the years. A lot of mentions of possible relic locations, weaknesses in the districts, who to intercept information from—"

"I want to know his most recent communications," Kodak interrupted. "Who was it to, and what was it pertaining?"

Owen merely nodded at the command.

Brynnlin's stomach plummeted at the implication. Any knowledge Remi could have passed on could be detrimental, especially with their recent movements.

Owen typed frequently, and symbols rushed across the screen before more correspondences popped up.

"It looks like there's been a lot of back and forth between

him and someone going by Oberon. That name mean anything to you?" Owen asked.

"No."

More typing.

"Every message keeps referencing..." Owen stopped, he looked to Kaceston before turning around. Uncertainty filled his gaze.

"References what?" Kodak pushed.

Owen cleared his throat, his eyes landed on her. "You."

A silent minute passed between everyone in the room.

"Me?" Brynnlin asked slowly, even though she heard him the first time. She moved to stand behind his chair. "What exactly about me?"

Owen's throat bobbed, but he pulled up some messages.

And he hadn't been wrong.

They were about her.

From when she got here from the isles. Information on her new identity. Their plan to lure the demon. Even her intention to go to the summit meeting.

Her body shook as she continued to read.

'You're sure she will be attending the summit?'

'Yes, they are bringing her along.'

'This intel better not be mistaken, or there will be consequences. We will send an old friend to intercept her.'

Remi had led the Creed right to her.

Grabbing the nearest thing off the desk, a porcelain decor of some beast, she turned, hurling it at the wall.

"That son of a bitch," she snarled, her chest heaving.

The figure shattered, and broken pieces scattered across the floor. The satisfaction of breaking something did nothing to calm her. What she really needed was to break who was responsible.

She started for the door.

"Brynn, wait," Juniper rushed to stand in front of her, putting her hands up in a calming gesture. "I know you're mad, we all are. But let's think this through for a moment, you can't go kill him."

"I won't kill him." She'd only break every non-vital part of him.

"I certainly would," Kaceston murmured loud enough for everyone to hear. "Personally, I think you should let her have some time alone with him. I'll even supervise, if a witness is necessary."

"You are not helping." Juniper shot him a withering glare.

Kaceston gestured to Owen with raised brows, "I actually think we're helping quite a lot."

"That's not what I meant, and you know it—"

"Juniper, move," Brynnlin stared down the Ríona before her. She didn't want to force her way past someone she considered a friend, but she would.

"This is getting far out of hand," Zale muttered and pushed off the wall, stalking forward. "Everyone needs to maintain control of themselves." A pointed look directed to her.

Her eyes narrowed in return. "And yet you don't seem concerned enough."

"I can be concerned while still staying rational."

"Oh don't worry, violence is perfectly rational."

The door to the small room crashed open, preventing Zale's retort.

A heaving Ryker leaned against the frame.

"Maddox and Selene," Ryker rushed, "have they checked in?"

A knot cemented itself in her chest at the pure panic in his voice.

Why was he asking about Maddox and Selene?

"Ryker, what's going on?" Her heart started racing without

even hearing his answer. She'd never seen Ryker frightened. Ever. "Ryker?" Her voice trembled. He still hadn't answered her.

"Call Maddox, now," Ryker ignored her, his complete attention on Zale. "Find out if he and Selene are still with her contact and get them the fuck back here."

Zale was already moving and nodding without question.

"Ryker," Kodak growled. "Explain."

"They're in trouble," Ryker's wide eyes finally looked to Kodak. "Remi did something. I don't know what," Ryker said before Kodak could ask.

"Fuck," Kodak breathed. A second later he was turning to Owen. "Owen—"

"Already on it," Owen's hands flew across the screens.

"No answer," Zale announced. "And the tracking on his orenda band is disabled."

Brynnlin's world felt like it was collapsing. It took everything in her to stay focused. They couldn't be in trouble. They were fine. If they weren't—

Stop.

She couldn't think like that. Whatever was going on with Maddox and Selene, she needed to be ready. She would be useless to them if she spiraled.

Every second that passed seemed like hours.

"Oh shit," Owen's whisper had the entire room tensing.

"What is it?" Brynnlin snapped when he remained silent.

"There are messages from this morning, they were hidden deeper than the others..." Owen trailed off. "Were your friends meeting someone?"

"Yes, one of Selene's old contacts. They needed his help with something."

Owen's sympathetic gaze fell on her. "Remi set them up, they walked right into a trap."

Brynnlin fell to her knees, a sob caught in her chest.

CHAPTER 38

"He could only hope the others were smart enough to stop her."

DARKNESS.

All Maddox could see was darkness. In a panic he reached for his face only for his limbs to remain unmoving. Everything felt weighed down, and his mind struggled to comprehend.

Was he dead?

How did he die?

His memories were fuzzy and pain shot through his head as he tried to remember.

Why couldn't he remember?

He pushed past the pain. He had to remember. Slowly, missing pieces floated forward. He had gone to talk to Selene.

They were meeting someone? *Yes!*

Her contact. The amulet.

Everything started to click into place. Zale had brought him and Selene to meet the contact. He had dropped them off at some farmhouse. Selene had approached the door, some man,

Neill, had answered. She recognized him and greeted him as an old friend.

He'd let them in...

But then what?

Things began getting fuzzy again.

He remembered entering the house...

Then...

His head started to pound.

Fuck.

Remember.

He had to remember. Their lives depended on it.

He froze at that intrusive thought.

His gut was screaming that something was wrong. He would be an idiot to ignore it. If he just pushed harder...

The pain intensified.

Darkness swallowed him again.

THE NEXT TIME Maddox came to, the pain in his head dissipated. With extreme effort, he forced his eyelids open. He blinked, attempting to take in his surroundings. The room was blurry at first, but after a moment a sparse living room came into view.

"Good. You're awake."

Maddox jerked back as the man Selene had greeted kneeled before him. He shook his head, trying to make sense of what was happening.

This man was her friend. *Why was he doing this?*

"Neill?" His voice sounded hoarse to his own ears. "She's your friend. What's going on?"

Neill looked down at himself and threw his head back,

laughing. "Oh Maddox, my dearest apologies, you must be so confused."

With a snap of his fingers, Neill's skin flaked away, leaving another man in his wake.

"You." Maddox lurched forward, rage overtaking as he recognized the Draíothe from Brynnlin's room. He didn't make it far. His limbs jerked back, and his gaze shot down to find himself tied to a chair.

That bastard.

Thick rope bound his wrists to the armrests and his legs to the frame of the chair. He struggled to rip free only for the rope to tighten around him, digging deeper into his skin.

"Now, now. I wouldn't do that if I were you, less you want to lose a limb." The other man smirked and stood to his full height.

"You're a dead man," Maddox hissed.

A fond smile crossed the other Draíothe's face. "You're so much like Brynnlin—"

"Don't say her fucking name."

A glare overtook the man's face. "So similar, yet also so much weaker."

He pulled a syringe out of his pocket, and Maddox stiffened.

"You know I gave this to Brynnlin once, I should've known she wouldn't go down that easily. But you..." The man smirked, "You and Selene were out like a light."

Selene.

Maddox's stomach plummeted.

Where was Selene? His gaze swung around—

Relief slammed into him when he saw her next to him. She was tied down, her head slumped over, still unconscious. But there was the slight rise and fall of her chest.

She was still alive.

Maddox turned his attention back to the threat in the room. He could get them out of this.

Reaching for his magic—

Ice filled his veins.

Heart pounding, he reached deeper. There was nothing there. His magic was gone.

How was that even possible?

Something must have shown on his face, as the other man started cackling.

"Your expression is priceless. I bet you just tried to use your magic, didn't you?" He waved around the syringe. "Those research institutes in Saol come up with some of the most creative things. Don't worry the inhibitor isn't permanent." The Draíothe offered a coy smile. "But I can't promise you'll still be alive when it wears off."

Adrenaline crashed through Maddox, along with a small dose of fear. He had to find a way out of this, or they truly would end up dead.

"What do you want?" He hoped to buy some time, and any information might be of use.

"Well," the Draíothe clicked his tongue, "at the moment, nothing." He stalked back to the chair and slammed the syringe down on Maddox's leg.

"Fuck." Maddox jerked at the stab of pain and at the coldness coursing through him.

Not again.

"Don't worry, no more lights out. I lowered the dose." The Draíothe smirked. "I just didn't want you getting any stupid ideas."

"You bastard," Maddox seethed.

The Draíothe's smirk dropped, and he shook his head. "Name calling is quite unnecessary. Maybe I should have knocked you out again. I'd much rather talk to Selene anyways,

I owe her a thank you." He pulled out another object from his pocket. Maddox's stomach twisted as he saw the amulet. "After all, she was such a sweetheart to bring my amulet back to me, and you were just a bonus to accompany her. So how about you sit there like a good hostage and the rest will handle itself."

Hostage.

Maddox closed his eyes and attempted to force the panic down. It didn't take a genius to realize he was going to use them to lure Brynnlin out. And knowing her, it would work. He could only hope the others were smart enough to stop her.

Opening his eyes again, he buried his emotions. "It won't work. Brynn is somewhere safe. You can't get to her."

The Draíothe merely lifted a brow. "You and I both know that's not true. She will come to me. She'd never leave her cousin and dearest friend to suffer at my hand."

Maddox wanted to curse. Wanted to throw something. Beat something. Someone.

But he didn't want to show the bastard he was right.

"Don't look so dejected, you're fortunate to have someone in your life that cares so much. And when this is all said and done, Brynnlin will be in much better hands with us."

"Like Hells she will," a feminine voice snarled.

Maddox whipped his head to the side to see Selene rip through the ropes. She stood on shaky legs and a burst of power erupted from her, sending the other Draíothe crashing through the wall into another room.

Selene rushed to his side. A second later, the ropes were gone. He was free.

"Run." Was all she said as she pulled him along.

He stumbled to keep up as she sprinted to the door. She yanked at the handle. It didn't budge.

"Fuck," she hissed, pulling harder on the unmoving door.

Rough laughter echoed behind them.

"You didn't think it would be that easy, did you, Selene?" The other Draíothe sauntered back into the room, dusting debris off his shirt.

"It was worth a shot, who knew you were so prepared, Valerian?"

The other man halted, his gaze narrowed to slits. "Where did you learn that name?"

Maddox side-eyed Selene to see her smirking. "Maybe next time, don't inscribe your amulet."

Valerian's features twisted before turning expressionless. He merely shrugged instead.

"A name is required for its use, I guess it doesn't matter if you have knowledge of it. You won't be alive much longer anyway."

Valerian pulled the amulet out and laid it on the floor. With a whispered word it started to glow. Other symbols appeared along the ground lighting up the room in a red hue.

"Shit." Maddox grunted as Selene slammed into him, taking them both to the floor. She huddled them into the corner, a ward warping around the two of them as sparks rained down from the ceiling.

Valerian shot them a sinister grin. "Now the real fun begins."

CHAPTER 39

"Fuck the plan."

HELPLESSNESS WAS something Brynnlin had long ago determined she would never feel again. Yet that's exactly what threatened to drown her after Owen's revelation.

The others argued in the room.

She could only stand there in silence.

How could she let this happen?

She should've seen it coming.

She knew that Draíothe wouldn't give up. And now he had Maddox and Selene. She wouldn't forgive herself if something happened to them, and she wasn't going to let it.

A new determination sparked.

Fuck feeling helpless.

Fuck waiting.

She wasn't a kid anymore who couldn't do anything. If the Draíothe wanted her attention, he had it. And once and for all, he was going to learn the consequences of touching her family.

"Zale."

The room quieted, and attention turned to her at that harsh single word.

Zale lifted a brow and eyed her warily. "Yes?"

"You said you took them to a farmhouse in Draíocht?"

"I did."

"Take me there."

Zale stuttered. "I'm sorry, what?"

Brynnlin fought down her irritation. "Take me there. Now."

"Brynn, we don't even know if they're still there," Zale attempted to reason.

"Then it's a great place to start."

"Brynn, I don't think you understand," Kodak stepped forward, his gaze full of sympathy. "I know you're worried about Maddox and Selene, but if they were set up, we need to be smart about this. If you show up, you could be walking right into a trap."

They were the ones that didn't understand.

"I'm counting on it."

"You're what?" Kodak's sympathy morphed into disbelief.

"The Draíothe would only go after them to get to me. It's me he wants, and that's exactly what he'll get."

"Brynn, you can't possibly think to trade yourself over," Juniper shook her head, worry and disappointment flowed off her. "That's reckless and stupid."

"With all due respect, I'm not asking for permission. And I'm not trading anything. He dies today. This ends now."

Brynnlin could see the others thought her insane. She didn't care. She wouldn't leave Maddox and Selene to suffer.

"Brynn, you really should think this through, come up with a plan—"

"Fuck the plan," she snapped. "Planning hasn't gotten us anywhere. It's time to act."

"I'm not agreeing to anything, but what are you thinking?" Zale relented.

"Just take me to the farmhouse, they're probably not there anymore, but let me see what I can find."

"I can't allow that," Kodak interrupted, a frown pulling at his lips. "It's too dangerous."

"Kodak—"

"Now is not the time to act rashly. The Draíothe probably has the amulet back, and we all know he won't hesitate to use it. Say we do go there, and we walk right into an ambush. Or Hells, he could even be on his way here already. I know you don't want to hear this, but we need to appropriately prepare for any outcome."

Zale eased forward, "If Brynn can just go and see—"

"No." Kodak's frown hardened into a glare. "I won't consider this a second further. That is probably exactly what the Draíothe wants. Say Brynn goes there, and then he attacks her again. But this time we don't get her back. Then what? We are going to come up with a plan that won't get anyone else hurt."

Zale frowned. "Kodak—"

"Enough." With a single look from his ruler, Zale stopped.

"Shouldn't it be my choice?" Brynnlin argued.

"Not when you aren't thinking straight."

Ryker of all people, nodded along. "Kodak is right."

Brynnlin's furious glare flew to Ryker. He ignored her.

"Maddox would never want any of us to risk each other. What we need to do is prepare. The Draíothe wants Brynn, he'll come for her. We need to be ready for him to show up, and we'll have the best advantage on our own grounds."

"And what happens to Maddox and Selene in the meantime, huh?" she snarled. "What about them?"

"She's right," Zale pushed forward. "We can't leave them, and honestly, Ryker, I'm surprised you think that way."

"Zale, of course I want to go get them right now, but we can't ignore everything and willingly walk into a trap."

"Then don't." Brynnlin shook her head, tired of arguing. "No one else has to be at risk. You guys stay here, prepare the sentries for an attack on the palace in case he does show up. Zale will only bring me to the farmhouse. If he's still there, I'm the one person he won't kill."

Ryker finally looked at her and glared. "That's not—"

"This is not a debate," Kodak snapped, his attention solely on her. "We will do this the right way. We are not losing another person today. Am I clear?"

Brynnlin bit back a string of words that no doubt would've landed her in a cell. He was wasting precious time. Time Maddox and Selene might not have. Inside she raged as she held Kodak's unforgiving stare.

"Crystal." She forced the word out.

"Good." Kodak turned away, directing the others, and she decidedly tuned them out.

Kodak might be used to barking out orders, but she wasn't one to give in to commands. Deep down she knew he was only trying to do what was best. But his actions were putting Maddox and Selene at risk. And she had no intention of standing by to watch.

"Let's take this upstairs." Kodak's voice filtered back in, and she watched them head for the door. "Ryker, go prepare the sentries. Zale, gather a small group that can go scouting, I want them on standby when we're ready to move. We'll reconvene in the briefing room. Kaceston, we need—"

Kaceston had been uncharacteristically quiet during the exchange, but raised a brow and waved off Kodak's words. "You have an urgent matter at hand, that is clear. Yet I must insist Owen be able to continue his work. I'd like to see if he can find any trace of those who raided our land. And you don't need to babysit us. Rest assured, we'll be out of here as soon as he has what we need."

Kodak frowned, but after a moment nodded in agreement. "This is quite unusual, but given the fact Owen has done us a great service today, I'll allow him to continue. A group of sentries will stay here to assist. I'll also send Declan here, he's not like Owen, but he knows his way around the systems."

"Very well."

With Kaceston's agreement, Kodak left the room, the others followed behind.

Zale stopped at the exit and cast her a pleading look when she didn't move. "Don't be difficult, Brynn, come help us. I know you're upset, but we do things together for a reason."

"Every second we waste is a second Maddox or Selene might not have."

"You'll be no help to them fighting Kodak on this. Let's go make a plan to get them back alive."

"Fine." The single word lacked emotion. "Head on without me. I need a moment before subjecting myself to standing around a table."

With a small nod of his head, Zale left.

Kaceston's low chuckle filled the room a minute later, and her head whipped towards him.

"What?"

"Nothing, it's surprising is all." Those steely gray eyes studied her with intensity.

"What is?" she snapped, not in the mood for games.

"They really don't know you all that well, do they?"

She pursed her lips, refusing to acknowledge the question with an answer.

Kaceston held his hands up, "Hate to break it to you, but even I know you have no intention of sitting here and waiting."

"Perfect," she smiled sweetly. "Since you seem to know me so well, that will make this so much easier. Will you take me there?"

Kaceston nearly choked.

Recovering quickly, he raised a brow. "I know I misheard you. Would you care to repeat that request?"

She braced herself, taking a deep breath. Shoving down the sarcasm, she let him see the seriousness in her eyes. "It will take me hours to get to them on my own, with you, minutes. Will you please take me to the farmhouse?"

"Brynnlin," Kaceston frowned. "This is Kodak's business. It's not for me to get involved."

"Don't give me that bullshit. You play by your own rules. I've seen it."

Kaceston lifted a brow at the accusation. "While I may choose to do as I please, I rarely ignore another ruler's authority."

"Say I did take you," he continued before she could argue, "what if they're right, and you walk into a trap? There could be a group of armed men waiting for you. Or even demons. What will you do then? A plan isn't always a bad thing—"

"I don't give a shit what's there," she snarled. "Ten men. One hundred. Demons. If Maddox and Selene are there, I will destroy anyone or anything standing between me and them. You and the others might think you know what I'm capable of, but you truly have no idea. I will unleash darkness on this entire gods forsaken world if I have to."

"That's quite the threat."

Brynnlin heaved out a sigh, frustration weighing down on her. "Mock me all you want, but Kaceston please, they're my family."

Indecision danced in his eyes. "Brynn—"

He was going to say no.

She couldn't let that happen. Maddox and Selene needed her.

"Whatever you want."

His eyes flared.

She wasn't going to let him deny her.

A slow smirk took over his features. "I considered your other favor settled after saving Owen, are you truly that eager to be in my debt again?"

"If you do this for me, you can name any price. It's yours."

"That's a very dangerous bargain to make." There was a challenge in his eyes.

She met his stare, unwavering. She meant every word. And for Maddox and Selene...she would do anything. Give anything.

Kaceston shook his head, chuckling again. "You really don't have a single self-preserving bone in your body."

She bristled at the insult. "Excuse me—"

"I'll do it."

Brynnlin nearly collapsed. "You will?"

Kaceston's smile was slow and full of dangerous promise. "Yes, just remember you signed up for this."

Brynnlin swallowed sharply, but nodded. Whatever this cost her, she would pay it.

Kaceston turned to Dax and pointed to Owen. "Dax, don't leave his side. And if anything even starts to go down here, you guys get home, understand?"

"Understood." Dax moved to take his place at Owen's side.

Kaceston stepped into her space, staring down at her. "Are you sure about this?"

No. "Yes."

"Good." Kaceston gestured Griffin over to them. "Griffin,

obscure our arrival." Kaceston's hand shot out, grabbing her waist, and yanking her into him. "No going back now."

Dark flames erupted from the floor.

Moments later, they stared down at the farmhouse.

CHAPTER 40

"I'm not going to dignify that with an answer."

Brynnlin forced in a deep breath. Kaceston did exactly as she asked. Whatever he wanted in return, she would oblige. She was never one to break her word.

"I can take it from here." She kept her voice quiet and studied the scene in front of her.

The farmhouse stood still. Too still.

No armed men stood ready for her. No demons lurked around.

Shit.

Maybe they weren't here.

She eased into a crouch, scanning the perimeter again. She hadn't missed anything. There truly was no one around.

Kaceston bent to her level. "At the moment, there are no demons in the area. You lucked out."

Did she?

At least if demons had been here, Maddox and Selene would have been, too.

Standing tall, she started down the small hill. A hand shot out, pulling her to a rough stop. She glared at the hand then up to its owner.

Kaceston frowned down at her. "It pains me that I have to ask, but what in the Hells do you think you're doing? There might not be demons about, that doesn't mean you're in the clear to strut down to that house."

Brynnlin jerked out of his hold, her glare turned scalding. "I'm not an idiot, but I need to see what's inside. And as I said earlier, I'll take it from here."

Kaceston leaned into her space. "Careful, Brynnlin, I'm not some pet you can order about as you please."

"You're right. Pets listen."

The little space between them disappeared. Her gaze flew to his. Gray swirled with black.

"Keep pushing, Ciarán, see where that gets you." Warm breath brushed across her skin.

She refused to retreat even an inch. She wanted to push him. See how far he would go—

"There's movement in the house."

Her attention ripped away from the ruler hovering over her.

"What did you see?" she demanded from Griffin.

Griffin continued to stare at the house. "Something passed by the window. Too quick for me to make it out, but there is definitely someone or something inside."

Now she really needed to see inside. "Griffin, if we get up to the window, can you continue to conceal us?"

"I'm not going to dignify that with an answer."

The question had clearly insulted him.

"Sorry," she muttered, and she was—sort of. "Let's just try to get closer. If that's alright with his highness," she tossed the barb at Kaceston, already moving.

The corner of his mouth twitched. "I'll allow it."

She bit her tongue to silence her unsavory retort.

With extreme caution the trio made their way around the base of the house, creeping up to the window. Brynnlin leaned to peer through the glass. Kaceston placed a hand on her shoulder

"Let me look first."

"Why?"

"You might not be prepared for what could be in that room."

Swallowing sharply, she nodded. Kaceston moved around her and glanced into the window. His body tensed, and Brynnlin swore her heart dropped with that movement.

"Good news, Maddox and your friend are here and are alive at the moment."

The relief that slammed into Brynnlin nearly took her to the ground.

"The bad news?" she asked, crawling next to him to look inside herself.

"That doesn't appear very promising."

Looking inside, Maddox and Selene huddled against the corner, a ward clear as day surrounded them.

The rest of the room raged in chaos.

A deep red was cast across the walls, and glowing symbols rotated at a blurring speed around the floor. Lights flickered. Broken furniture littered the space. Standing in the middle of it all was the Draíothe.

His hood was pulled back, his head lifted to the ceiling, and the marking on his brow was on full display. His arms were raised outwards, orbs of magic already settling in his palms. Hovering in front of him, the amulet blazed.

Brynnlin's stomach heaved, nausea threatening its way forward. She lurched away from the window, already running for the door. She shouted at the two behind her, hoping they were smart enough to keep up.

"He's trying to summon a demon."

BRYNNLIN DRAGGED in a deep breath and dove into her well of magic. Further and further she dug deeper, pulling that endless power to the surface. And let the darkness take her.

She blasted straight through the front door, splintering it into pieces. Shadows unfurled into the house, flooding every inch. She sauntered through the broken wood.

"It seems I missed the invitation to the party." Her voice came out calm. Collected. So at odds with her pounding heart.

The Draíothe's eyes flew open, and he wasn't quick enough to hide his surprise.

Good. Maybe she wasn't too late.

The fizzling of the ward dissolving had her head whipping around.

"Brynn, you can't be here, Valerian set this up as a trap for you!" The pain in Selene's voice and her panic as she rushed forward made Brynnlin's heart ache.

"I would never leave you," Brynnlin whispered as Selene crashed into her.

"Get out. We all need to get out." Selene's fear was clear as she urged and pulled Brynnlin towards the now destroyed door.

Brynnlin stood her ground and hoped Selene could see the apology in her eyes. This all happened because of her. But she wouldn't let it go on any longer.

"You and Maddox get out of here. I promise this ends now."

With those solidifying words, Brynnlin braced herself to

face Valerian. Her stomach tightened when she found him staring at her, a sickening grin spread across his features.

"I must admit you made it quicker than expected, but you're just in time."

Her stomach plummeted as his sinister laughter filled the room.

The earth itself seemed to shudder. She tried to rush forward. If she could make it—

Blinding magic erupted from the gateway, and the ground beneath them opened. Brynnlin recoiled, stars dancing across her vision. The house itself pulsed with energy and walls exploded around them.

CHAPTER 41

"Ever so slowly, it rose."

KACESTON WAS AIRBORNE.

He'd barely had any time to react after Brynnlin rushed away from the window. She was going to get herself killed. And like a fool, something in him refused to leave her here.

Letting out a string of curses, he had followed, making it to the doorway when the blast of the house had slammed into him. He hurdled through the air, the ground whizzing past him. He braced for the impact as his body crashed into the hard ground.

"Burning fucking Hells." He rolled, forcing in a deep breath, pain radiating through him. He cursed every god and goddess he could think of as he crawled to a sitting position.

A half groan, half growl sounded next to him.

His gaze swung, finding Griffin pushing himself to his knees.

"What the fuck was that?" Griffin ground out, glaring at the leftover debris of the once standing house. Smoke still surrounded the wreckage, obscuring the view.

"Nothing good," Kaceston managed to get out.

The stench of a demon invaded his senses.

So that summoning had been successful.

And from what he could tell, it was a powerful one.

Fantastic.

Movement in front of him caught his attention. A feminine figure stood on wobbly legs. Sunlight glinted off auburn hair.

Disappointment tugged at his chest.

Selene's head whipped around. He watched with a raised brow as she took two shakey steps towards the destruction. Gods, she was just as reckless as Brynnlin.

In a flash, he was in front of her, blocking her path. He didn't think Brynnlin would appreciate her friend getting devoured by a demon.

"Unless you're well versed with fighting demons, I'd advise against your current course of action."

Sharp hazel eyes stared up at him. "Who in the Hells are you?"

"Rí Kaceston?" Maddox's voice sounded to the left.

Kaceston glanced at the Chancellor, noticing him for the first time. He tried not to grimace. Kodak's second had seen better days.

Maddox's brow furrowed. "What are you doing here?"

"Your cousin can be very persuasive."

Maddox's confusion morphed into a fierce frown. "Where is Brynnlin?"

"Good question," Kaceston muttered, wondering the same. They'd all relatively landed in the same area. She should be around here somewhere. He scanned the area, an unfamiliar tightness growing in his chest the longer he didn't see her. Thick smoke still curled in the air.

"Clear away this damned smoke," he ordered at Maddox, fully aware of what the Chancellor was capable of.

Maddox shifted his weight, a look of discomfort crossing his features. "I can't at the moment."

"What do you mean you can't?"

"I—"

"Move." Selene pushed past Kaceston. With a whispered word, magic whipped through the air, funneling up the smoke, and it disappeared without a trace.

Kaceston immediately found Brynnlin.

His relief was short-lived.

She faced off with Valerian. The Draíothe obviously had plans for her, a protective barrier clearly surrounded them. It separated the duo from what lay beyond.

But when those deadly shadows started circling at her feet and coiled ready to strike, Kaceston nearly smirked. That bastard had no idea what he was dealing with.

"Brynn," Selene cried out the second she spotted her. She tried to rush forward. Kaceston stopped her again.

"Let go—"

"She can handle herself, we have a different problem on our hands."

Selene stopped, following his gaze. Her breathing hitched as she caught sight of what held his attention.

About fifty yards away, the demon kneeled, a lethal barricade between them and Brynnlin. Mangled skin wrapped around bulging muscles. Its head lifted, voidless eyes taking in its new surroundings. Ever so slowly, it rose. It stood tall, unnervingly tall, on two legs.

"Selene, what is that?" Maddox's whisper brushed against the wind.

Selene was slow to shake her head. "I don't know."

"Kaceston?" Griffin asked next, a slight hitch in his tone.

This was sure to be interesting.

"I have no idea."

THE HOUSE HADN'T STOOD a chance against the gateway into the Hells. Brynnlin had felt the heat coming at her. Had prepared herself for the impact.

It never came.

Time had seemed to slow.

Bands of magic had caressed against her skin, warping around her...shielding her.

One second, she was at the front of the house. The next, she was behind the wreckage, safely away from the destruction.

Valerian stood before her. The air rippled with energy as a barrier closed around them. He looked down on her as one would an errant child.

"That was quite close. Try to be more careful in the future, those gateways can be nasty business."

Brynnlin's heart sank.

He had opened the gateway. She'd been too late.

Her attention swung between him, the now present demon, and her friends across the way. They seemed well enough at the moment.

For now.

Her gaze shot back to the demon. A shiver raced down her spine the longer she stared at it. Whatever this was, it was dangerous. She didn't need Selene's book to tell her that.

"What have you done?" Her snarl snapped through the air like a whip at Valerian.

He wore a victorious smile. "That's my assurance this goes as planned." He lifted a single eyebrow. "So how about you put those away, less you really want to see your friends get hurt."

She didn't move. Her eyes narrowed to slits, and she continued to let the shadows roam. They weaved through the small area, testing the shield he placed around them. It was flimsy, but mobile, and held strong.

Valerian's lips turned down in a frown. "Don't test me on this." He lifted the amulet. "One word from me, and they die."

Brynnlin's chest constricted at his words. But she refused to do as he said. He would not have the upper hand here.

"That's where you're wrong. They are the only thing keeping you alive at this moment. You even think to hurt them, and I'll rip your fucking head right off your body." The ice in her voice could have frozen over all Three Hells.

"You don't threaten me," Valerian hissed, fury taking over his features. "And it's time you learn your place."

"Kill them," he ordered into the amulet.

"No!" Brynnlin screamed. Shadows erupted. Pouring out of her like a wave, they crashed down, encasing them in darkness.

CHAPTER 42

"You're not getting out of this."

KACESTON STOOD PRECARIOUSLY STILL. The demon hadn't moved to attack yet. The others stood tense at his side, all waiting to see what would happen. He hesitated to make the first move. He wanted to end this quickly, but without knowing what type of demon they faced, he wasn't quite sure what he was dealing with.

A guttural scream echoed through the small valley.

The demon charged towards them, moving at an unnatural speed. Kaceston didn't waste a second longer. Black flames erupted from the ground swallowing the demon.

He let them rage higher and higher. He wasn't taking any chances.

"You can call on the flames of the Hells?"

His attention slid to Selene, her face horror stricken.

He didn't bother to answer. He was surprised she recognized them for what they were, most didn't. He also wasn't surprised by the fear now lining her features. The flames of the

Three Hells were lethal to their kind. Unfortunately, not as lethal to most demons, but they sure as shit slowed them down.

"I'm not your biggest concern at the moment."

He fueled more power into the flames. The demon still hadn't emerged.

Good.

The flames flickered higher.

Higher.

And disappeared.

The demon stood there. Torched ground surrounded it. It remained unscathed.

Kaceston's blood ran cold. *What the Hells just happened?*

"Why'd you stop the flames?" Griffin accused.

"I didn't."

Deadly silence passed between them.

The demon started forward again.

A glowing orb gathered in the sky and slammed downwards, smashing the demon to the ground. The earth rattled and caved in at the force. Before the demon could recover, Selene pressed a hand to the dirt. Jagged spikes shot through the terrain, impaling the demon upwards. The wounds were large, and dark blood seeped down.

A tense second passed.

And another.

The demon stirred, struggling to remove its body from its skewered position.

"You missed its hearts."

"Really? I couldn't tell," Selene snarled, glaring daggers at him.

"It's regenerating," Griffin announced, as they all watched it close an open wound.

"Fucking Hells, what is this thing?" Maddox asked no one in particular.

The demon was back on its feet, still several yards away. Its body shuddered, and glowing orbs of magic formed in its hands. It launched them forward.

Selene was quick to deflect them, a fierce frown crossing her face. "Something's wrong."

"What?"

"Those attacks felt like mine."

No sooner had the words left her mouth, jagged spikes erupted from the ground, striking around them. Kaceston's flames surrounded him and the others. In a blink, they were standing on the other side of the valley.

"How is that possible?" Maddox's face paled as the growl left his lips.

The others all looked pretty shaken, too.

There was only one creature in all of the Hells that could absorb an attack like that.

Kaceston heaved out a rough breath, a small dose of fear rushing through him. "It's a mimic."

And he gave it the biggest tool against them.

The demon tested the black flames, letting them circle around it. They charred the surrounding earth. The demon then sent the flames racing towards them.

BRYNNLIN'S SCREAM echoed through the small space, and shadows tore towards Valerian.

They would not die.

Not today.

Valerian's pupils dilated at the rage coming at him. She didn't try to temper it. She let it build. Let it consume.

Valerian threw a small barrier up between them, a pathetic attempt to keep her away.

"It seems you've embraced your magic," Valerian commented, and she smiled at the hint of fear.

"You have no idea." Her voice was animalistic.

Shadows shredded through his shield like butter.

His face paled.

Conjuring a ball of magic, several blasted at her. Her shadows shattered them. He took a retreating step back.

Smoke started to circle at his feet, and Brynnlin snarled. "You're not getting out of this."

Shadows cascaded onto him. Latching onto each of his limbs, she dragged him to her and forced him to his knees.

"Call off the demon."

"No. You're going to watch them die."

His threats only fueled her rage.

"They're not the ones dying today."

"You won't kill me," he spat. "You'll never know the truth if you kill me."

"Do you know how long I've waited for this moment?" She kneeled down so their faces were level. "For years, I've dreamed of this. Thought of all the ways you would die at my hands. And here you are." Her smile was deranged. Absolutely vicious. "I wish I had more time. I would torture you for days for the pain you caused me, but I'm not willing to risk it. So this will have to suffice."

"You can't! You won't—"

"I'll see you in the Three Hells," she promised.

Coiled shadows ripped his arms from his body. Blood gushed to the ground.

Brynnlin summoned a shadowed blade and drove it through his neck. The darkness sang with pleasure as the light left his eyes. The sword disappeared, and his head rolled off, more blood pooling at her feet. For good measure, a shadowed hand tore into his chest, yanking his heart right out of its cavity. Satisfaction rang through her as she crushed it to pieces.

The body slumped to the floor.

The weight of its fall was like a weight being lifted off her. She felt like she could breathe for the first time in years.

After all this time, it was finally done.

Her parents' killer was no longer free.

A broken sob pulled at her chest.

But this wasn't over. Not even close.

The shield around her dissolved, melting away. She rushed for the amulet resting in a pool of blood. Her wild gaze shot to the others. Even with its master gone, the demon still fought on. She knew no one else could command the amulet, but maybe they didn't need to.

She raced towards Selene.

CHAPTER 43

"Please be ok."

"I DON'T KNOW how much longer I can hold this," Selene's voice was strained and sweat dripped down her brow.

Kaceston didn't know if it was from the heat or exhaustion. Somehow Selene's ward was still standing strong even as fire raged against it. He cursed himself for allowing this to happen.

"Griff, I need you to create a distraction," Kaceston said, his mind racing through a plan. "Pull it's attention and conceal yourself and the others. Then get to a safe distance away."

"What about you?"

"Once I'm close to it, I can kill it."

"But the flames—"

"Won't kill me."

"Kaceston—"

"Do it. Now."

Griffin was solemn, but nodded his agreement. Pressing a hand to the ward, beams of light zipped downwards, bathing the entire area in a blinding flash.

The flames ceased.

It was a small opening. It was all he needed.

In less than a second, Kaceston was behind the demon. Grabbing the creature by the neck, he lifted, and slammed it backwards into the ground.

Heat surrounded them as the demon tried to attack with his flames.

Kaceston released a feral grin.

BRYNNLIN NEARLY CRASHED to her knees as she watched black as night flames erupt towards the others. Too familiar flames.

She didn't have time to question how it was possible. She needed to move. Faster.

Summoning shadows—

A blinding light crashed down and she stumbled, shielding her eyes. Looking back, the others were gone, and Kaceston appeared behind the demon.

No. He couldn't.

Fire enveloped the duo.

"Kaceston!" she screamed, pain ripping through her chest.

She ran harder. She wasn't too late. She wasn't.

An invisible force slammed into her, knocking her to the ground. Her chest heaved as she gasped for breath. Griffin appeared above her, his features apologetic.

"What the Hells?"

"You'll only get hurt if you intervene."

"Kaceston needs—"

"Kaceston can survive his own flames, you will not."

A wave of relief crashed into her. He was okay. For now.

The ground rumbled, and they both spun. The flames were gone again. The demon managed to break free and punched

Kaceston in the chest, sending him backwards. The demon pulled daggers out from its head and chest, tossing them aside.

"I'm not letting him fight that thing alone." She shoved the amulet into Griffin's chest. "Get that to Selene, see if she can destroy it."

She pushed past Griffin. He didn't stop her.

"You can't use your magic to attack, it'll use it against you," he shouted the warning.

As unnerving as that was, she didn't let it deter her.

She ran to Kaceston.

Another wave of magic slammed into him, knocking him back. He shook it off, fire raging in his eyes. The demon summoned another orb, larger than before, launching it forward. A wall of shadows shot upwards, splintering through the attack as she made it to his side.

"That one would've hurt," she smirked, taking in his shocked expression.

"What are you doing?" He growled.

She rolled her eyes at his warm welcome. "What does it look like I'm doing?"

"Like you're being reckless, again. Go stay with the—"

"Don't even think to finish that sentence."

"You can't use your shadows to attack, we'll all be fucked if you do."

She waved away his concern. "I know. Griffin told me. No magic attacks. Got it."

"This isn't a game."

She whipped her head around, glaring. "Does it look like I'm laughing?"

The demon threw another orb at them. Brynnlin deflected.

"How do we kill it?"

"Working on it," Kaceston grumbled. "I'm hesitant myself to use any of my other magic, which leaves a physical strike."

"Where are its hearts?"

"Working on that, too. It can move them throughout its body at will."

Moving targets. This shit just got better and better. "Lovely."

The demon stalked towards them and fire raced forward. Brynnlin braced herself as the flames met another wall. She grimaced at the onslaught of heat.

A moment later, they withered away.

The demon turned its back on them, its movement a blur.

Her body tensed. It was running?

Why?

Realization hit. "It's going for the others."

"Why?"

Brynnlin was running. Again. "I gave Griffin the amulet."

"Shit." Footsteps sounded behind her.

She didn't see the others, which meant they were still concealed, and the demon couldn't see them either. But it could obviously sense the amulet.

The demon moved at an intense speed across the small valley, heading for the treeline. Brynnlin forced her feet to move faster, not closing the distance fast enough. Taking a chance, shadows raked across the ground and launched her forward. She crashed into the demon, and together they rolled to the ground. With a surprising burst of strength, it tossed her aside. Her back smacked into a hard surface.

Magic rained down on her. In an instant, Maddox was at her side.

Gods, that hurt.

It threw her into the ward.

"Are you okay?"

"Fine."

The demon took a step towards them, tilted its head, and

charged to the side. It went straight for Selene, who was blasting magic at the amulet.

Maddox moved, blocking its attack. Griffin was at Selene's side in an instant, using the small opening Maddox provided to conceal them again.

The demon snarled, striking out at Maddox. They shared a string of quick blows. The demon spun, its heel landing on Maddox's chest, sending him into the dirt. Maddox rolled, clutching at his chest, a whimpered groan leaving his lips. The demon stalked towards him.

Brynnlin hurled herself forward. A dagger clutched in her hand. She was on the creature in seconds, digging the dagger deep, and dragging it down its back. Dark blood spilled to the ground. A savage growl ripped from its lips, and it spun, clawing at her. She dropped low, spinning on a knee, and driving the blade upwards through its abdomen.

It was already healing.

She sliced again. Aiming higher—

A golden orb rammed into her, knocking her back. Her body curled in at the stabbing pain now dancing across her skin.

Too close.

She'd been too close. She hadn't even seen it summon the attack.

Pulling in a lungful of air, her chest constricted—

The ground at her feet crackled, ebony fire rising around her.

Brynnlin shrunk away from the heat, her shadows coiling around her. A body slammed into her, arms wrapping around her, and the flames disappeared before she could react.

The demon now stood several feet away.

Her gaze shot up to find Kaceston staring down at her. His

jaw clenched tight, and those normally gray orbs were completely onyx.

Words escaped her.

"Forget what I said earlier about your magic." The words were harsh. His chest shuddered against her, and his breathing was ragged. "If I get you an opening, can you take out all three hearts at once?"

"I..." Her head spun. "Maybe."

"Yes or no?" he snapped.

"Yes."

She hoped. No. She had to.

A terse nod. "You'll have seconds at the most."

He was already moving. At a speed her eyes could barely follow, Kaceston was upon the demon. His right arm swung at the demon, a scaled claw and deadly talons extended from where his hand had been.

She didn't have time to think of how it was possible.

Talons shredded through the demon's flesh, tearing its head right off its body. Blood escaped in mass even as its skin tried to piece itself back together.

This was the opening Kaceston had given her.

She couldn't waste it.

Shadows ripped through the air. Sharp as a blade, they tore into its body. Digging into the demon, her shadows probed for any signs of its hearts.

Faster.

She needed to be faster.

She needed to find—

The lightest of pulses touched against her.

There.

And there. And there.

With a savage snarl, she crushed through the hearts.

The demon's body slumped to the ground.

At the same time, the sound of glass shattering echoed through the air. A wave of magic erupted through the valley. The body that had started to disintegrate to ash, disappeared without a trace.

The amulet was gone.

She didn't need to see it to know Selene had destroyed it.

Brynnlin caged in her magic. Her chest heaved, air struggling to make its way in.

It was over.

She turned, searching out the others.

Maddox laid on the ground.

"Maddox," Brynnlin sprinted over, sliding to his side and pulling him up. "Please be okay. Please."

"I'm okay," Maddox coughed, blood spilling from his lips, and he yanked her against him. "Thank the gods you are, too."

His chest heaved, and he coughed up more blood.

"Oh gods." She tried to elevate his head, turning him to the side. "You're going to be okay." She tore at his shirt to see a horrific bruise already forming and spreading across his skin.

Fuck there was internal bleeding.

She tried to position him upright when Griffin appeared next to her. She didn't even flinch, too focused on Maddox. Selene was there, too, kneeling to help.

Griffin grabbed her hands, stopping her. "Does Kodak have a healer?"

"Yes, Verenna."

"Good," without another word Griffin was lifting Maddox up. Kaceston was at her side next, helping her up, and pulling her to his side. "I'll get us back."

She gripped his arm, "Thank you."

Those two little words would never truly convey her appreciation for what he'd done for her.

But it was all she could offer at the moment.

CHAPTER 44

"The time for living in the past was over."

MADDOX WOULD BE OKAY.

Between Verenna and Selene, they had stopped the bleeding and had patched the lung that had been pierced. His ribs were also reset and were already healing. Brynnlin continued to thank the gods for that small miracle.

After the scare with Maddox, everyone had then turned their anger on her for acting against Valerian alone. They were smart enough to leave Kaceston out of it and thanked him instead for his help.

She hadn't gotten the same treatment. She sat back, letting them lecture. She recognized they were upset because they cared. Although, Kodak did threaten to throw in a cell overnight for disobeying direct orders. She did not find that as endearing.

Instead she promised not to do it again.

She really hoped she could keep it.

466

The cold breeze fluttered against her hair. She tipped her head back, enjoying the night air and the quietness on her balcony. She needed a moment alone to come to terms with everything that had happened.

Luckily everyone seemed to understand and were giving her space.

Well, almost everyone.

Brynnlin didn't flinch at the dark flames that conjured along the stones as Kaceston appeared.

His gaze roamed over her, and he offered a wolfish grin. "Hiding up in your room, are we?"

"Not hiding. I just needed a moment."

"Fair enough. I'm sure it's not everyday you rip a man apart. Don't worry, it gets easier."

Her lips pressed into a line, suppressing a smirk. "I like to think of it as a fragmented execution."

Kaceston threw his head back and laughed. "I like that one. Glad to see you're not falling apart on me."

She lifted a brow. "Is that why you're here? To check up on me?"

Kaceston shrugged, his gaze turning warm. "It's not out of the realm of possibility."

"Well, thank you." Brynnlin turned to face him, her back leaning against the ledge. She wasn't one to feel self conscious, but with a sudden nervousness, she looked down at her hands in front of her. "And thank you for your help today," the words were soft against the night. She was well aware things would have gone much differently had Kaceston not been there.

Kaceston prowled forward, his feet stepping into her field of vision. His hand lifted to her chin, forcing her to look upwards.

"I didn't quite hear you," he murmured, smirking wickedly. "Could you repeat that for me?"

She rolled her eyes. "Don't be an ass."

His chest rumbled as he chuckled. "Always with the insults. You're starting to wound me."

"I think you can handle it," she started to pull out of his hold, liking the heat of his skin against hers far too much.

He didn't let her get very far. His fingers trailed up her cheek to brush a strand of hair behind her ear. Her heart rate spiked at the sparks now dancing along her skin at his simple touch. Kaceston's eyes gleamed, sensing her reaction.

But a moment later, his smirk dropped. "Owen found a lead on the group that attacked my temple, we need to follow up on it."

"You're leaving?" She couldn't explain why her chest ached at that.

"Will you miss me?"

"No."

His smile turned tender. "I won't miss you either."

She bit down on her lip to stop her own smile.

"Don't worry, I already promised I'd bring Owen back soon. He'll assist more after our own matters are settled."

"That was awfully generous of you."

"What can I say? I'm a generous individual." He leaned his head down, his lips brushing the corner of her lips. Then her cheek. Her breathing hitched at that unexpected contact. Unconsciously, she tilted her head back, giving him better access.

His lips trailed up the side of her jaw, stopping at her ear, sending shivers through her. "Try not to get into too much trouble while I'm away."

Her heart pounded in her chest, but she managed a breathy, "No promises."

"See you soon, Ciarán." Kaceston stepped back and winked, disappearing into flames.

Brynnlin collapsed against the ledge, her body on fire from the briefest of touches. Gods, he was the worst.

She smiled nonetheless. She didn't know how soon she would be seeing him, but she would be in Oícha soon. And it wasn't for Kaceston. They had a prison to break into. She laughed to herself.

Who knew she would look forward to breaking into his realm this much?

Things really were looking up.

As she stared out at the night sky and at the city lights along the horizon, a calmness enveloped her. For the first time since she could remember, she was at peace. They still had a long way to go. She was aware the Creed was still out there, and that whoever hired Valerian wouldn't give up on her.

But for now...

For tonight...

She could rest easy. Her parents could finally rest in peace, knowing they'd been avenged. That lost, little girl who only knew pain could finally let go. And Brynnlin could finally start to move forward.

The time for living in the past was over.

It was a beautiful feeling.

"There you are."

Brynnlin startled at Verenna's voice. She spun to see her cousin standing in the doorway, a smile lighting her face. "We've been waiting for you, the evening meal is ready."

Brynnlin returned the smile. "Sorry, lost in thought."

"Everything okay?"

"Better than okay." She meant every word.

"Well then, come on, everyone is waiting." Verenna pulled her along, and Brynnlin followed easily.

Down at the table, laughter filled the room. Brynnlin cherished it.

She looked at each person surrounding her. There was the family that had been returned to her, the one she gained, and the others that no doubt would become family as well.

A war was coming their way, and this right here was everything she was ready to fight for. She had everything to lose, but she was done losing.

EPILOGUE

HE SAT AT HIS DESK, combing over some files when a soft knock sounded on the door.

"Enter."

He looked up as the door pushed open, and one of his informants stood at the threshold. He masked his surprise at her arrival. He hadn't been expecting her until later in the week.

Silently she entered the office, clicking the door shut behind her. Her brow was furrowed, and her muscles were tense as she stopped in front of him, hands clasped at her back.

"We have a situation."

He figured as much, she wouldn't be here otherwise. With an impatient wave of his hand, he gestured for her to continue. He narrowed his eyes as he watched her chest rise in a steadying breath.

"Valerian is dead."

The words took a moment to register. And when they did, he forced himself not to succumb to his frustration. Composure was key.

He clenched his jaw and rolled his neck. "You're certain?"

"I saw it, sir."

And his frustration was back, he glared at her. "And you didn't think to intervene?"

She straightened her shoulders and met his stare. "With all due respect, sir, Valerian went in with a half-assed plan. He was unprepared. The girl had the aid of the ruler of Oícha. I'm not equipped to deal with that. Not alone."

He eyed her carefully. That was a fair assessment. And Valerian had always been somewhat unpredictable. Useful, but undisciplined. The loss of him would hurt, but they would manage. He didn't fault her for her decision.

"What happened?" He wanted details.

She didn't disappoint.

When she finished her account of the events that occurred, he couldn't help the small grin that inched across his face. He leaned back in his chair, his mind racing through all the possibilities this could mean. Valerian was a fool. He never stood a chance. Not against her. The girl was brilliant.

"She's even more powerful than I could have hoped," the words were barely a whisper.

All of that time...

All of that studying...

The sacrifices and pain he endured...

It had all been worth it.

The shadowed experiment had been a success.

And she wasn't even using the full potential of her magic. With the right training, under the right mentor, she'd be...unstoppable.

"How do you want us to proceed?" His informant pulled his attention back to the present. "Without Valerian, retrieving the girl might prove difficult."

"Valerian is of little consequence, leave the girl to me." If he played his cards right, he was confident he could convince her to come willingly. "As for proceeding, go after the last of the relics. They will more than make up for the loss of Valerian and anyone else along the way. I want to ensure we have the power behind us to guarantee our victory."

The ancient relics were powerhouses of magic. They could nourish the land. They could also destroy it. No one would think to go against him while he beheld those.

The smile she shot him, the first one she had offered since entering his office, was cunning, and her eyes gleamed with anticipation.

"Yes, sir. I'll inform the others." With a slight bow of her head, she left him alone again.

It was getting closer. The time he spent waiting, making sure all of his pieces were perfectly in place, had been well worth it. Soon he'd be done hiding behind the scenes. And when he made his reveal, no one would dare stand in his way, especially not with Brynnlin at his side.

ACKNOWLEDGMENTS

This book has been years in the making, and to finally be able to share it with the world is surreal. I am extraordinarily fortunate to have such an amazing group of people that supported and encouraged me throughout this entire process. This book wouldn't exist without them.

To my wonderful husband—I couldn't have asked for a better partner in life, even if one was written. You are my very own book-boyfriend brought to life. Through all the long nights, the countless re-writes, and the endless list of ideas; you were there for them all and always pushed me to keep going. I love you.

To Mom—the amount of gratitude I have would take a whole book on its own and that probably still wouldn't be enough. You were my very first reader; draft after draft, every chapter, and every edit, you read it all. You were invested in this story just as much as I was, and not once did you ever doubt that it would make it to this point. Thank you for always believing in me.

To my grandparents—you two were my second set of readers and always supported my book. After never reading a fantasy book before, you guys finished mine in two days. You have no idea how much that meant to me. Grandma, your library inspired my love for reading and thank you for always sharing your Julie Garwood books. Grandpa, I will always cherish all those stories you told us as kids, and I can only hope I'm half the story-teller you are.

To my sister—you were the first person that knew about Brynnlin's story before any words touched a page. As an avid reader, with a book collection larger than my own, I knew you would love the idea just as much as I did. You were always there to bounce ideas off of and encouraged me to keep writing. I am so excited for my own book to join your bookshelves.

To my brother—to be honest I never expected you to read this book, the fact that you did means the world to me. Your critique and ideas were so unexpected, yet so valued. Choreographing the fight scenes in the living-room was one of my highlights of writing this book.

A special thank you to Rachel—when I was younger, you introduced me to *Twilight* and the first book in the *Gallagher Girls Series*; that day changed my life (even though I didn't know it at the time). You introduced me into a new genre of books that kick-started a new love for reading. And now after spending majority of my life devouring books, I've written my own.

And finally, a very big thank you to all of the readers that made it here. You took a chance on an unknown book from an unknown author, and for that, I am grateful. Thank you.

Brynnlin's story will
continue in book
two of the
Empire of Éire Series